Outstand⋯
GROW⋯

"Can't praise Paul Tremblay's ⋯ ⋯ ⋯ ne-
teen creepy classics that will t ⋯ ⋯ ⋯y chair into an
uneasy chair. One of the best collections of the twenty-first century."

—Stephen King

"In these nineteen stories, Tremblay doesn't just hold a mirror up to
reality, but livestreams it, projecting the whole spectrum of our modern anxieties so vividly it feels as if we're watching in real time. . . .
You can't help feeling that he is a writer whose reach will continue to
grow and grow and grow." —*The New York Times Book Review*

"Paul Tremblay has mastered creepy, interstitial spaces with his own
brand of supernatural-adjacent horror. This collection proves again
that in any form, at any length, Tremblay is a must-read."

—Chuck Wendig, *New York Times* bestselling
author of *Wanderers* and *Invasive*

"It is a terrible thing to read a Paul Tremblay story. . . . Terrible because
you know, going in, that it's probably going to mess you up. That his
stories and his words have this way of getting under your skin. Of
crawling inside you like bugs and just . . . living there. They become
indistinguishable from memory. . . . It's terrible to read these stories,
but you do it anyway. . . . They're fun because they're dangerous. Because, word by word and title by title, I can feel the damage accruing.
The scars." —NPR

"[*Growing Things*] brilliantly takes ordinary situations—an author
reading, an AP history class, a family vacation—and seamlessly
sprinkles in a sense of unease that quickly builds to a sense of pure
horror. . . . These are stories that live in the increasing popular space
between literary fiction and horror, where speculative terrors and
very real universal truths collide." —*Booklist* (starred review)

"Both wildly entertaining and deeply unsettling, Paul Tremblay's writing has a way of sneaking under your skin and messing with your head. On the surface, *Growing Things* is a collection of bite-sized, disturbing, and brilliantly observed stories, each one a tour de force of originality and verve, but it's far more than that. Some are interconnected in surprising ways; some will make you question everything you thought you knew about the craft of writing and the horror genre. And like the unstoppable undergrowth in the titular story, all are infused with an atmosphere of creeping dread. Superb. Can't rate it highly enough."

—Sarah Lotz, author of *The Three* and *The White Road*

"These frighteningly imaginative slices of horror are often far more chilling than their relatively mundane inspirations. . . . From high fantasy to monsters to (literally) Hellboy, [*Growing Things* has] something for everyone who digs things that go bump in the night."

—*Kirkus Reviews*

"Tremblay's unsettling prose, filled with poetic metaphors, sets an ominous tone, and readers will be sucked in from page one."

—*Library Journal*

"These aren't just stories—they're spirits that linger, shadows that haunt, terrors that follow you even after you've closed the book. . . . *Growing Things* is a collection of Paul Tremblay's most searing and powerful work yet."

—Christina Henry, author of *Alice* and *The Girl in Red*

"Those hoping for the perfect balance of terror and psychological insight that makes for the most frightening reading should flock to *Growing Things*." —*Los Angeles Times*

"A skilled purveyor of the uncanny who always seeks meaning amidst the fear, Paul Tremblay is one of the key writers who have made modern horror exciting again."   —Adam Nevill, author of *The Ritual*

"On display is Tremblay's gift for inventive storytelling techniques, most notably his bold use of metafictional narrative conceits such as invented emails, blog entries, articles, and other detritus of the digital world. A great introduction to Tremblay's oeuvre."   —*Toronto Star*

"*Growing Things* exists in a strange liminal state: in certain places, it links up with Tremblay's larger bibliography and gives a fine sense of his recurring themes and images. But it's also a showcase for his range as an author and a place for him to experiment with things that might not click on the scale of a longer work. There's plenty to applaud here, but even more to send readers shivering—a fine blend of technique and terror."   —Tor.com

"Taken as a whole, the book confirms Tremblay's atmospheric mastery, his ability to capture a growing sense of Not Right, the moment when dream goes nightmare."   —*Boston Globe*

"Intensely gripping. . . . Tremblay weaves these dark and often macabre narratives quite deftly, cradling the reader between reality and the implausible."   —TheNerdDaily.com

"A short story collection from a favorite author is just the best possible thing in the world; *Growing Things* is among the best of them."   —*Cemetery Dance*

GROWING THINGS

AND OTHER STORIES

ALSO BY PAUL TREMBLAY

The Cabin at the End of the World

Disappearance at Devil's Rock

A Head Full of Ghosts

Swallowing a Donkey's Eye

In the Mean Time

No Sleep Till Wonderland

The Little Sleep

GROWING
THINGS

AND OTHER STORIES

PAUL
TREMBLAY

WM

WILLIAM MORROW

An Imprint of HarperCollinsPublishers

Grateful acknowledgment is made to The St. Pierre Snake Invasion for permission to reprint an excerpt from "Sex Dungeons & Dragons," words and music by The St. Pierre Snake Invasion © 2015.

P.S.™ is a trademark of HarperCollins Publishers.

Page 337 constitutes an extension of this copyright page.

This is a work of fiction. Names, characters, places, and incidents are products of the author's imagination or are used fictitiously and are not to be construed as real. Any resemblance to actual events, locales, organizations, or persons, living or dead, is entirely coincidental.

GROWING THINGS AND OTHER STORIES. Copyright © 2019 by Paul Tremblay. All rights reserved. Printed in the United States of America. No part of this book may be used or reproduced in any manner whatsoever without written permission except in the case of brief quotations embodied in critical articles and reviews. For information, address HarperCollins Publishers, 195 Broadway, New York, NY 10007.

HarperCollins books may be purchased for educational, business, or sales promotional use. For information, please email the Special Markets Department at SPsales@harpercollins.com.

A hardcover edition of this book was published in 2019 by William Morrow, an imprint of HarperCollins Publishers.

FIRST WILLIAM MORROW PAPERBACK EDITION PUBLISHED 2020.

Designed by Leah Carlson-Stanisic

Title page photograph by ipag collection/Shutterstock, Inc.; Contents image by Chansom Pantip

Front cover seal from The New York Times. ©2019 The New York Times Company. All rights reserved. Used under license.

The Library of Congress has catalogued a previous edition as follows:

Names: Tremblay, Paul, author.
Title: Growing things and other stories / Paul Tremblay.
Description: First edition. | New York, NY : William Morrow, [2019]
Identifiers: LCCN 2018051852| ISBN 9780062679130 (hardcover) | ISBN 9780062906687 (trade paperback) | ISBN 9780062934185 (audio) | ISBN 9780062679147 (Ebook)
Subjects: LCSH: Horror tales, American—21st century. | Short stories, American—21st century.
Classification: LCC PS3620.R445 A6 2019 | DDC 813/.6—dc23
LC record available at https://lccn.loc.gov/2018051852

ISBN 978-0-06-290668-7 (pbk.)

23 24 25 26 27 LBC 9 8 7 6 5

For the (not so) little ones

CONTENTS

Tears water our growth.

—*William Shakespeare*

What terrified me will terrify others . . .

—*Mary Shelley*

Daddy's gonna show me the monsters.
Mummy's gonna show me the creeps.

—*The St. Pierre Snake Invasion,*
"Sex Dungeons & Dragons"

GROWING THINGS

1.

Their father stayed in his bedroom, door locked, for almost two full days. Now he paces in the mudroom, and he pauses only to pick at the splintering doorjamb with a black fingernail. Muttering to himself, he shares his secrets with the weather-beaten door.

Their father has always been distant and serious to the point of being sullen, but they do love him for reasons more than his being their sole lifeline. Recently, he stopped eating and gave his share of the rations to his daughters, Marjorie and Merry. However, the lack of food has made him squirrelly, a word their mother—who ran away more than four years ago—used liberally when describing their father. Spooked by his current erratic behavior, and feeling guilty, as if they were the cause of his suffering, the daughters agreed to keep quiet and keep away, huddled in a living room corner, sitting in a nest of blankets and pillows, playing cards between the couch and the silent TV with its dust-covered screen. Yesterday, Merry drew a happy face in the dust, but Marjorie quickly erased it, turning her palm black. There is no running water with which to wash her hands.

Marjorie is fourteen years old but only a shade taller than her eight-year-old sister. She says, "Story time." Marjorie has repeatedly told Merry that their mother used to tell stories, and that some of her stories were funny while others were sad or scary. Those stories, the ones Merry doesn't remember hearing, were about everyone and everything.

Merry says, "I don't want to listen to a story right now." She wants to watch her father. Merry imagines him with a bushy tail and a twitchy face full of acorns. Seeing him act squirrelly reinforces one of the few memories she has of her mother.

"It's a short one, I promise." Marjorie is dressed in the same cutoff shorts and football shirt she's been wearing for a week. Her brown hair is black with grease, and her fair skin is a map of freckles and acne. Marjorie has the book in her lap. *All Around the World.*

"All right," Merry says, but she won't really listen. She'll continue to watch her father, who digs through the winter closet, throwing out jackets, itchy sweaters, and snow pants. As far as she knows, it is still summer.

The vibrant colors of Marjorie's book cover are muted in the darkened living room. Candles on the fireplace mantel flicker and dutifully melt away. Still, it is enough light for the sisters. They are used to it. Marjorie closes her eyes and opens the book randomly. She flips to a page with a cartoon New York City. The buildings are brick red and sea blue, and they crowd the page, elbowing and wrestling each other for the precious space. Merry has already colored the streets green with a crayon worn down to a nub smaller than the tip of her thumb.

They are so used to trying not to disturb their father, Marjorie whispers: "New York City is the biggest city in the world, right? When it started growing there, it meant it could grow anywhere. It took over Central Park. The stuff came shooting up, crowding out the grass and trees, the flower beds. The stuff grew a foot an hour, just like everywhere else."

Yesterday's story was about all the farms in the Midwest, and how the corn, wheat, and soy crops were overrun. They couldn't stop the growing things and that was why there wasn't any more food. Merry had heard her tell that one before.

Marjorie continues, "The stuff poked through the cement paths, soaked up Central Park's ponds and fountains, and started filling the streets next." Marjorie talks like the preacher used to, back when Mom would force them all to make the trip down the mountain, into town and to the church. Merry is a confusing combination of sad and mad that she remembers details of that old, wrinkly preacher, particularly his odd smell of baby powder mixed with something earthy, yet she has almost no memory of her mother.

Marjorie says, "They couldn't stop it in the city. When they cut it down, it grew back faster. People didn't know how or why it grew. There's no soil under the streets, you know, in the sewers, but it still grew. The shoots and tubers broke through windows and buildings, and some people climbed the growing things to steal food, money, and televisions, but it quickly got too crowded for people, for everything, and the giant buildings crumbled and fell. It grew fast there, faster than anywhere else, and there was nothing anyone could do."

Merry, half listening, takes the green crayon nub out of her pajama pocket. She changes her pajamas every morning, unlike her sister, who doesn't change her clothes at all. She draws green lines on the hardwood floor, wanting their father to come over and catch her, and yell at her. Maybe it'll stop him from putting on all the winter clothes, stop him from being squirrelly.

Their father waddles into the living room, breathing heavily, used air falling out of his mouth, his face suddenly hard, old, and gray, and covered in sweat. He says, "We're running low. I have to go out to look for food and water." He doesn't hug or kiss his daughters but pats their heads. Merry drops the crayon nub at his feet, and it rolls away. He turns and they know he means to leave without any promise of returning. He stops at the door, cups his mittened and gloved hands around his mouth, and shouts toward his direct left, into the kitchen, as if he hadn't left his two daughters on their pile of blankets in the living room.

"Don't answer the door for anyone! Don't answer it! Knocking means the world is over!" He opens the door, but only enough for his body to squeeze out. The daughters see nothing of the world outside but a flash of bright sunlight. A breeze bullies into their home, along with a buzz-saw sound of wavering leaves.

2.

Merry sits, legs crossed, a foot away from the front door. Marjorie is back in the blanket nest, sleeping. Merry draws green lines on the front door. The lines are long and thick, and she draws small leaves on the ends. She's never seen the growing things, but it's what she imagines.

The shades are pulled low, drooping over the sills like limp sails, and the curtains are drawn tight. They stopped looking outside after their father begged them not to, and they won't look out the windows now that he's not here. When it first started happening, when their father came home with the pickup truck full of food and other supplies, he stammered through complex and contradictory answers to his daughters' many questions. His knotty hands moved more than his lips, removing and replacing his soot-stained baseball cap. Merry mainly remembers that he said something about the growing things being like a combination of bamboo and kudzu. Merry tugged on his flannel shirtsleeve and asked what bamboo and kudzu were. Their father smiled but also looked away quickly, like he'd said something he shouldn't have.

Outside the wind gusts and whistles around the creaky old cabin. The mudroom and living room windows are dark rectangles outlined in a yellow light, and their glass rattles in the frames. Merry stares at the wooden door listening for a sound she's never heard before: a knock on her front door. She sits and listens until she can't stand it any longer. She runs upstairs to her bedroom, picks out a pair of new pajamas, changes again in the dark, and carefully folds the dirty set and places it back in her bureau. Merry then returns to the nest and wakes her older sister.

"Is he coming back? Is he running away, too?"

Marjorie comes to and rises slowly. She lifts the book from her lap and hugs it to her chest. Her fingers crinkle the edges of the pages and worry the cardboard corners of the cover. Despite the acne, she looks younger than her fourteen.

Marjorie shakes her head, answering a different question, one that wasn't spoken, and says, "Story time."

Merry used to enjoy the stories before they were always about the growing things. Now she wishes that Marjorie would stop with the stories, wishes that Marjorie could just be her big sister and quit trying to be like their mother.

"No more stories. Please. Just answer my questions."

Marjorie says, "Story first."

Merry balls her hands into fists and fights back tears. She's as angry now as she was when Marjorie told all the kids at the playground in town that Merry liked to catch spiders and rip off each leg with tweezers, and that she kept a jar of their fat legless bodies in her bureau.

"I don't want to hear a story!"

"I don't care. Story first."

Marjorie always gets her way, even now, even as she continues to withdraw and fade. She leaves the nest only to go to the bathroom, and she walks like an older woman, the joints and muscles in her legs stiff with disuse.

Merry asks, "You promise to answer my questions if I listen to a story?"

All Marjorie says is "Story first. Story first."

Merry isn't sure if this is a yes or a maybe.

Marjorie tells of the areas around the big cities, places called the suburbs. How the stuff ruined everyone's pretty lawns and amateur gardens, then started taking root in the cracks of sidewalks and driveways. People poured and sprayed millions of gallons of weed killer, Liquid-Plumr, lye, and bleach. None of it worked on the stuff, and all the chemicals leached into the groundwater, which flowed into drinking-water reservoirs, poisoning it all.

Like most of Marjorie's stories, Merry doesn't understand everything, like what groundwater is. But she still understands the story. It makes a screaming noise inside her head, and it is all that she can do to keep it from coming out.

She says, "I listened to your story, now you have to answer my question, okay?" Merry takes the book away from Marjorie, who surprisingly does not resist.

"I'm tired." Marjorie licks her dry and cracked lips.

"You promised. When is he coming back?"

"I don't know, Merry. I really don't." With the blankets curled and twisted around her legs and arms, it's as if she's been pulled apart and her pieces sprinkled about their nest.

Merry wants to shrink and crawl inside one of her sister's pockets. She asks in her smallest voice, "Was this how it happened last time?"

"What last time? What are you talking about?"

"When Mommy ran away? Was this how it happened when she ran away?"

"No. She wasn't happy, so she left. He's going to get food and water."

"Is he happy? He didn't look happy when he left."

"He's happy. He's fine. He isn't leaving us."

"He's coming back, though, right?"

"Yes. He'll come back."

"Do you promise?"

"I promise."

"Good."

Merry believes in her big sister, the one who once punched a third grader named Elizabeth in the nose for putting a daddy longlegs down the back of Merry's shirt.

Merry leaves the nest and resumes her post, sitting cross-legged in the mudroom, in the shadow of the front door. The wind continues to increase in velocity. The house stretches, settles, and groans, the sounds eager for their chance to fill the void. Then, on the other side of the front door, brushing against the wood, there's a light rapping, a knocking, but if it is a knocking, it's being done by doll-sized hands with doll-sized fingertips small enough to find the cracks in the door that nobody can see, small enough to get inside the door and come through on the other side. The inside.

Merry stays seated, but twists and yells, "Marjorie! I think someone is knocking on the door!" Merry covers her mouth, horrified that whoever is knocking must've heard her. Even in her terror, she realizes the gentle sounds are so slight, small, quiet, that maybe she's making up the knocking, making up her very own story.

Marjorie says, "I don't hear anything."

"Someone is knocking lightly. I can hear them." Merry presses her ear against the wood, closes her eyes, and tries to finish this knocking story. Single knocks become a flurry issued by thousands of miniature doll hands, those faceless toys, maybe they crawled all the way here from New York City, and they scramble and climb over each other for a chance to knock the door down. Merry wraps her arms around her chest, terrified that the door will collapse on top of her. The knocking builds to a crescendo, then ebbs along with the dying wind.

Merry rests her forehead on the door and says, "It stopped."

Marjorie says, "No one's there. Don't open the door."

3.

Marjorie hasn't eaten anything in days. They are down to a handful of beef jerky and a half-box of Cheerios. In the basement, there are only two one-gallon bottles of water left, and they rest in a corner on the staircase landing. Flashlight in hand, Merry sits on the damp wood of the landing, plastic water jugs pressing against her thigh. It's cooler down here, but her feet sweat inside her rubber rain boots. The boots are protection in case she decides to walk toward the far wall and hunt for jars of pickles or preserves her father may have stashed.

Merry has been sitting with her flashlight pointed at the earthen floor for more than two hours. When she first came down here, the tips of the growing things were subtle protrusions; hints of green and brown peeking through the sun-starved dirt. Now the tallest spearlike stalks stretch for more than a foot above the ground. The leafy ends of the plants would tickle her knees were she to take the trip across the basement. She wonders if the leaves would feel rough against her skin. She wonders if the leaves are somehow poisonous, despite never having heard her sister describe them that way.

Earlier that morning, Merry decided she had to do something other than stare at the front door and listen for the knocking. She put herself to work and rearranged the candles around the fireplace mantel, and she lit new ones, although, according to her father, she wasn't old enough to use matches. She singed the tips of her thumb and pointer finger watching that first blue flame curl up the matchstick. After the candles, she prepared a change of clothes for Marjorie and left the small bundle, folded tightly, on the couch. She picked out a green dress Marjorie never wore but Merry not-so-secretly coveted. Then she swept the living room and kitchen floors. The scratch of the broom's straws on the hardwood made her uneasy.

Marjorie slept most of the day, waking only to tell a quick story of the growing things cracking mountains open like eggs, drowning the canyons and valleys in green and brown and drinking up all the ponds, lakes, and rivers.

Merry runs the beam of her flashlight over the stone-and-mortar foundation walls but sees no cracks and scoffs at the most recent tale of the growing things. Marjorie's stories had always mixed truth with exaggeration. For example, it was true that Merry used to hunt and kill spiders, and it was true all those twitchy legs were why she killed them. Simply watching a spider crawling impossibly on the walls or ceiling and seeing all that choreographed movement set off earthquake-sized tremors somewhere deep in her brain. But she was never so cruel as to pull off their legs with tweezers, and she certainly never collected their button-sized bodies. Merry never understood why Marjorie would say those horrible, made-up things about her.

Still, Merry initially believed Marjorie's growing things stories, believed the growing things were even worse than what Marjorie portrayed, which is what frightened Merry the most. Now, however, seeing the sprouts and stalks living in the basement makes it all seem so much less scary. Yes, they are real, but they are not city-dissolving, mountain-destroying monsters.

Merry thinks of an experiment, a test, and shuts off the flashlight. She hears only her own breathing, a pounding bass drum, so big and loud it fills her head, and in the absolute dark, her head is everything. Recognizing her body as the source of all that terrible noise is too much and she starts to panic, but she calms herself down by imagining the sounds of the tubular wooden stalks growing, stretching, reaching out and upward. She turns the flashlight on again, surveys the earthen basement floor, and she's certain there has been more growth and new sprouts emerging from the soil. The sharp and elongated tips of the tallest stalks sport clusters of shockingly green leaves the size of playing cards, the ends of which are also tapered and pointed. The stalks grow in tidy, orderly rows, although the rows grow more crowded and the formations more complex as the minutes pass.

Merry repeats turning off the flashlight, sitting alone in the dark, breathing, listening, and then with the light back on, she laughs and quietly claps a free hand against her leg in recognition of the growing things' progress.

Merry indulges in a fantasy where her father returns home unharmed, arms loaded with supplies, a large happily-ever-after smile on his sallow face, and he's not squirrelly anymore.

The daydream ends abruptly. In a matter of days her father has become unknowable, unreachable; a single tree in a vast forest, or a story she once heard but has long forgotten. Was this how it happened with Marjorie and their mother? Her sister was around the same age as Merry is now when their mother ran away. To Merry, their mother is a concept, not a person. Will the same dissociation happen with their father if he doesn't come back? Merry fears that memories of him, even the small ones, will recede too far to ever be reached again. Already, she greedily clutches stored scenes of the weekly errands she ran with her father this past spring and summer while Marjorie was at a friend's house, how at each stop he walked his hand across the truck's bench seat and gave her knee a monkey bite, that is unless she slapped his dry, rough hand away first, and then the rides home, how he let both daughters unbuckle their belts for the windy drive home up the mountain, Merry sandwiched in the middle, so they could seesaw-slide on the bench seat along with the turns. Did he only tolerate their wild laughter and mock screams as they slid into each other and him, hiding a simmering disapproval, or did he join the game, leaning left and right along with the truck, adding to the chorus of his daughters' screams? She already doesn't remember. Merry cannot verbalize this, but the idea of a world where people disappear like days on a calendar is what truly terrifies her, and she wants nothing more than for herself and her loved ones to remain rooted to a particular spot and to never move again.

Merry considers asking Marjorie all these questions about her parents and more, but she's worried about her sister. Marjorie is getting squirrelly. Marjorie didn't even open the book for this morning's story. And when Merry left the living room to go to the basement, Marjorie was sleeping again, her eyelids as purple as plums. What if Marjorie runs away, too, and leaves her all alone?

Merry puts the flashlight down on the landing, leaving it on and centering its yellow beam in an attempt to illuminate as much of the basement floor as possible. She lifts a one-gallon water bottle and peels away the plastic ring around the cap, then steps off the landing and walks toward the middle of the floor, unable to see anything below her ankles, which is as low as the focused beam of light hits. Under her feet, the disturbed and clotted earth feels lumpy and even hard in places, a message in Braille she cannot decipher. She hopes she is not stepping on any of the new shoots.

She pries off the cap, jarring the balance of the bottle in her arms, spilling water onto her hand and her pajama shorts. Her forearms tremble with the bulky jug set in the crooks of her pointy elbows. Water continues to spill out and gathers on the leaves. She knows they can't spare much, so she pours out only a little, then a little more, hoping the water reaches the roots.

Merry puts the cap on the bottle and walks back to the landing. She'll take the water upstairs, pour two cups, and give one to her sister, force her to drink. Then she'll curl up in the nest with Marjorie and sleep, thinking about her plants in the basement. She will do all that and more, but only after she sits on the landing, shuts off the flashlight, listens in the dark to the song of the growing things, and listens some more, and then, eventually, turns the flashlight back on.

4.

She did not blow out the candles before collapsing and falling asleep on their nest of blankets. All but three candles have burnt out or melted away. Wax stalactites hang from the fireplace mantel. Merry wakes on her left side and is nose to nose with her sister. Having gone many days without being able to bathe or wash, Marjorie's acne has intensified, ravaging her face. Whiteheads and hard, painful-looking red bumps mottle her skin, creating the appearance of fissures, as if her grease-slicked face is a mask on the verge of breaking up and falling away. Merry wonders if the same will happen to her.

Marjorie opens her eyes; her pupils and deep brown irises are almost indistinguishable from each other. She says, "The growing things will continue to grow until there aren't any more stories." Her voice is scratchy, obsolete, packed away somewhere inside her chest like a holiday sweater, a gift from some forgotten relative.

Merry says, "Please don't say that. There will be more stories and you have to tell them." She reaches out to hug her sister, but Marjorie buries her face in a blanket and tightens into a ball.

Merry asks, "How are you feeling today, Marjorie? Did you drink your water?" On the end table between them and the couch is the answer to her question: the glass of water she poured last night is full. "What are you doing, Marjorie? You have to drink something!" A sudden all-consuming anger wells up in Merry and she alternates between hitting her sister and tearing the layers of blankets and sheets away from the nest. It comes apart easily. She throws *All Around the World* over her head. It thuds somewhere behind her. Marjorie doesn't move and remains curled in her ball, even after Merry dumps the water on her head.

Merry kneels beside her prone sister and covers her face in her hands, hiding what she's done from herself. Eventually she musters the courage to look again, and she says, "Tell me a story about our father, Marjorie. About him coming back. Please?"

"There are no more stories."

Merry pats Marjorie's damp shoulder and says, "No. It's okay. I'm sorry. I'll clean this up, Marjorie. I can fix this." She'll gather their nest blankets and sheets, and she'll dry her sister and force her to change out of the wet clothes and into the green dress, then they'll really talk about what to do, where they should go if their father isn't coming back.

Merry stands and turns around. The nest blankets Merry threw into the middle of the living room have become three knee-high tents, each sporting sharp, abrupt poles raising the cloth above the floor. The poles don't waver and appear to be supremely sturdy, as if they would stand and continue standing regardless of whether the world fell apart around them.

Merry puts her fingers in her mouth. Everything in the living room is quiet. She whispers Marjorie's name at the tents, as if that is their name. She bends down slowly, grabs the plush corners of the blankets, and pulls them away quickly, the flourish to a magician's act. Three stalks and their tubular wooden trunks have penetrated the living room floor, along with smaller tips of other stalks beginning to poke through. The hardwood floor is the melted wax of the candles. The hardwood floor is the poor blighted skin of Marjorie's face. Warped and cracked, curling and bubbling up, the floor is a landscape Merry no longer recognizes.

She believes with a child's unwavering certainty that this is all her fault because she watered the growing things in the basement. Merry tries to pull Marjorie up off the floor but can't. She says, "We can't stay down here. You have to go upstairs. To our room. Go upstairs, Marjorie! I'll get the rest of the water." She wants to confess to having poured almost half the one-gallon jug on the growing things, but instead she says, "We'll need the water upstairs, Marjorie. We'll be very, very thirsty."

Merry maps out a set of precise steps. The newly malformed floorboards squawk and complain under her careful feet. Green leaves and shoots on the tips of the exposed stalks whisper against her skin as she makes her too-slow progress across the living room. She imagines going so slow that the stalks continue to grow beneath her, pick her up like an unwanted hitchhiker and carry her through the ceiling, the second-floor bedrooms, and then the roof of the house, and into the clouds, then farther, past the moon and the sun, to wherever it is they're going.

Merry pauses at the edge of the living room and kitchen, near the mudroom, and there is someone rapping on the front door again. The knocking is light, breezy, but insistent, frantic. She's not supposed to open the door, and despite her absolute terror, she wants to, almost needs to open the door, to see who or what is on the other side. Instead, Merry turns and yells back to Marjorie, who hasn't moved from her spot. Merry urges her to wake, to go upstairs where they'll be safe. There are shoots and stalk tips breaking through the floor in the area of the nest now.

Merry runs into the kitchen, and while there are the beginnings of stalk tips in the linoleum, the damage doesn't appear as severe as it is in the living room. She takes the flashlight off the counter and opens the door to the basement stairwell. She expects a lush, impenetrable forest in the doorway, but the stairs are still there and very much passable; her own path into the basement, to her garden, is preserved. She ducks under one thick wooden stalk that acts as a beam, outlining the length of ceiling, and she descends to the landing, where the bottles of water remain intact.

Once on the landing, which is pushed up like a tongue trying to catch a raindrop or a snowflake, Merry adjusts her balance and gropes for the water bottles. She tries picking up both, but she's only strong enough to take the one full bottle and hold the flashlight at the same time. She contemplates making a second trip, but she doesn't want to go back down here. The half-full second bottle will have to be a sacrifice.

Before going up the stairs, she points her flashlight into the heart of the basement, starting at the floor, which is green with countless new shoots. She aims the flashlight up and counts twelve stalks making contact with the ceiling, then traces their lengths downward. The tallest stalks have large clumps of dirt randomly stuck and impaled upon their wooden shafts. There are six clumps; she counts them three times. One clump is as big as a soccer ball but is more oval shaped. Four of the other dirt clods are elongated, skinny, curled, and hang from the stalks like odd overripened and blackened vegetables. Three stalks in the middle of the basement share and hold up the largest of the dirt formations; rectangular and almost the size of Merry herself, it's pressed against the ceiling.

Merry rests the flashlight beam on this last and largest dirt clod. Something else is hanging from it, almost dripping or leaking out of the packed dirt. After staring for as long as she can stare, and as her house breaks into pieces above her, Merry realizes what she is looking at is a swatch of cloth, perhaps the hem of dress. She can almost make out its color. Green, maybe.

Although the previous night was more about the rush of her discovery of the growing things, and of her flashlight game, looking at the basement now and seeing what she sees, specifically the cloth, Merry remembers walking the basement floor in her rubber boots, walking on what she couldn't see, the unexpectedly hard and lumpy soil, and she now knows she was walking upon the bones of the one who disappeared, of the runaway.

Merry shuts off the flashlight and throws it into the basement. Leaves rustle and there's a soft thud. She climbs the stairs in the dark, thinking of all the bones beneath her feet. Merry is furious with herself for not recognizing those bones last night, but how could she be blamed? She never really knew her mother.

Merry runs up the basement steps into the kitchen and stumbles over and past the continued growth. The knocking on the front door is no longer subtle, no more a mysterious collection of dolls' hands. The sound of the knocking is itself a force. It's a pounding by a singular and determined fist, as big as her shrinking old world, maybe as big as the growing new one. The door rattles in the frame, and Merry screams out with each pounding.

She shuffles away from the mudroom and into the living room. Marjorie is still there but is up and out of the nest. She's knelt between the stalks that have erupted through the floor. She pinches the shoots and leaves between her fingers, plucks them away, and puts them in her mouth.

The pounding on the front door intensifies. Her father said if there was a knocking on the door, then the world was over. A voice now accompanies the unrelenting hammering on the door. "Let me in!" The voice is as ragged and splintered as the living room floor.

Merry shouts, "We need to go upstairs, Marjorie! Now now now!"

More pounding. More screaming. "Let me in!"

Merry imagines the growing things gathered outside her door, weaved into a fist as big as their house. The leaves shake in unison and in rhythm, their collected rustling forming their one true voice.

Merry imagines her father outside the door. The one she never knew, eyes wide, white froth and foam around his mouth, spitting his demand to be allowed entry into his home, the place he built, the place he forged out of rock, wood, and dirt—all dead things. His three-word command is what heralds the end of everything. She imagines her father breaking the door down, seeing his oldest daughter eating the leaves that won't stop growing, and seeing what his youngest daughter knows is written on her face as plain as any storybook.

Marjorie doesn't look at her sister as she gorges on the leaves and shoots. Then Marjorie stops eating abruptly, her head tilts back, her eyelids flutter, and she falls to the floor.

Merry drops the water jug, covers her ears, and goes to Marjorie, even if Marjorie was wrong about there being no more stories.

Merry tells Marjorie another story. Merry will get her up and take her upstairs to their bedroom. She'll let Marjorie choose what she wants to wear instead of trying to force the green dress on her. They'll always ignore the pounding on the door, and when they're safe and when everything is okay, Merry will ask Marjorie two questions: What if it isn't him outside the door? What if it is?

SWIM WANTS TO KNOW IF
IT'S AS BAD AS SWIM THINKS

What I remember from that day is the road. It went on forever and went nowhere. The trees on the sides of the road were towers reaching up into the sky, keeping us boxed in, keeping us from choosing another direction. The trees had orange leaves when we started and green ones when it was over. The dotted lines in the middle of the road were white the whole time. I followed those, carefully, like our lives depended on them. I believed they did.

We made the TV news. We made a bunch of papers. I keep one of the clippings folded in my back pocket. The last line is underlined.

"The officer said the police don't know why the mother headed south."

I need a smoke break bad. My fingertips itch thinking about it. It's an early-afternoon Monday shift and I'm working the twelve-items-or-less register, which sucks because it means I don't get a bagger to help me out. Not that today's baggers are worth a whole heck of a lot. I don't want Darlene working my line.

We've never met or anything, but Julie's youth soccer coach, I know who he is. Brian Jenkins, a townie like me, five years older but looks five years younger, a tall and skinny schoolteacher type even if he only clerks for the town DPW, wearing those hipster glasses he doesn't need and khakis, never jeans. Always easy with the small talk with everyone in town but me. Brian isn't paying attention to what he's doing, lost in his own head like anyone else, and he gets in my line with his Gatorade, cereal, Nutter Butters, toothpaste, and basketful of other shit he can't live without. Has a bag of oranges, too. He'll cut them into wedges like those soccer coaches are supposed to. I'm not supposed to go to her games, so I don't. From across the street I'll walk by the fields sometimes and try to pick out Julie, but it's hard when I don't even know what color shirt her team wears. When Brian sees it's me dragging that bag of oranges over the scanner, me wondering which orange Julie will eat, sees it's me asking if he has a Big Y rewards card, and I ask it smiling and snapping my gum, daring him to say something, anything, he can barely look me in the eye. Run out of things to say in my line, right, coach?

I get recognized all the time, and my being seen without being seen is something I'm used to, but not used to, you know? I never signed up to be their bogeywoman. Yeah, I made a mistake, but that doesn't mean they're better than me, that I'm supposed to be judged by them all the time. It isn't fair. Back when I could afford to see court-appointed Dr. Kelleher he'd tell me I'd need to break out of the negative-thoughts cycles I get stuck in. He was a quack who spent most of our sessions trying to look down my shirt, but I think he was right about breaking out of patterns. So when I start thinking like this I hum an old John Lennon tune to myself, the same one my mother used to walk around the house to, singing along. She'd drop me in front of the TV to do what she called her exercises. She'd put on her Walkman headphones that just about covered up her whole head, the music would be so loud she couldn't hear me crying or yelling for her, that's what she told me anyway, sorry honey, Momma can't hear you right now, and she'd walk laps around the first floor of the house, she'd walk forever, bobbing her head and singing the same part of that Lennon tune over and over. So I find myself singing it now, too. The song helps to ease me out of it, whatever it is, sometimes. Sometimes it doesn't.

I'm humming the song right now. The notes hurt my teeth and god-dammit, I want my cigarette break. It'd take the edge off my fading buzz. I scratch my arms, both at once, so maybe it looks like I'm hug-ging myself to keep warm. It is cold in here, but I'm not cold.

Monday normally isn't too busy, but there's a nor'easter blowing, so the stay-at-home moms in their SUVs and all the blue-hairs are in, buzzing around the milk, juice, bread, cereal, cigarettes. Only three other lines open and they're all backed up, so Tony the manager runs around, the sky is falling, and he runs his fingers through his nasty greasy comb-over, sending people to my line. Storm's not supposed to be bad, but everyone's talking to each other, gesturing wildly, check-ing their phones. I don't listen to them because I don't care what they have to say. I keep humming my Lennon tune to myself and I keep scratching my arms, making red lines.

Darlene's fluttering around registers now, asking the other cashiers questions, eyes and mouth going wide, and she puts a hand to her chest like a bad actor. She's checking her own phone. I don't know how she can see it or knows how to use it. Everyone but me has one. Like Dr. Kelleher, I can't fit a smartphone in my lifestyle anymore, financially speaking.

Tony sends Darlene down to me. Great. Not being mean or noth-ing, but she slows everything down. I end up having to bag almost everything for her anyway because she can't see out of one eye and her hands shake and she doesn't really have a gentle setting. Bagging isn't where she should be, and none of the shoppers, even the ones who pretend to be friendly to her, want her pawing their groceries, especially when her nose is running, which is all the time. Basically they don't want to deal with her at all. It's so obvi-ous when you have Darlene and then no one goes in your line even when the other lines are backed up into the aisles, and it sucks because I have to talk to her, and she'll ask me questions the whole time about boyfriends and having kids. I don't quite have it in me to tell her to leave me alone, to tell her to shut the fuck up with her kid questions. I guess she's the only one in town who doesn't know who I am.

The woman in the baggy gray sweatshirt and yoga pants stops her whispering with the woman behind her in my line now that I'm in earshot. I feel a stupid flash of guilt for no reason. I haven't even done anything to anyone here yet, you know, and I hate them and I hate myself for feeling that way, like yeah of course it's because of me and not a stupid little snowstorm that everyone is freaking out about in the Big Y. The woman says nothing to me, then takes over the bagging of her own stuff. She just about elbows Darlene out of the way, who for once doesn't seem all that crazy about bagging groceries.

I can't resist saying something now. "In a hurry? Leaving town?" I say the "leaving town" part almost breathlessly. Like it's the dirty secret everyone knows.

"Oh. Yes. No. I'm sorry. I'm so sorry," she says to Darlene but keeps on bagging her own groceries. Her hands shake. I know how that feels. I run the woman's credit card and have a go at memorizing the sixteen numbers without being obvious about it. You know, just for fun.

Darlene doesn't mind getting elbowed out of the way any. She's staring at her phone, gasping and grunting like it hurts to look at. Humming my song isn't working. Seeing Julie's coach messed me up good.

Tony's still directing traffic into the lines, which is totally useless. We're all backed up and the customers are grumbling, looking around for more open lines. It's as good a time as any for me to yell back to Tony that I have to take a break.

He opens his mouth to argue, to say no, you can't now, but the look I give him shuts him down. He knows he can't say no to me. He shuffles through the crowd to behind my register and takes my line. "Be quick," he says.

"Maybe." I grab my coat. It's thinner than an excuse.

Then he says something under his breath, something about not knowing what's going on here, not that I'm listening anymore.

Darlene with all her fidgeting, customers rushing around the aisles, cramming into the lines, just about sprinting out of the store, hits me all at once, and for a second it's like all the times I've blacked out, then woken up with that feeling of oh shit, I wasn't me again, and the me who wasn't me did something, something wrong, but I don't know what. Like that one time in my newspaper clipping when, just like the cops, I didn't know why the crazy wasn't-me chick was going south with my daughter either.

I say to Darlene, "Can I see what you're watching, darling?" and I try to grab her phone. No go. Darlene has a death grip on the thing, and she taps my hand three times. Same OCD tap routine she goes through with the customers. Sometimes she'll tap the box of Cheerios before stuffing it into a bag, paper or plastic, or she'll tap the credit card if I leave it out next to the swipe pad instead of putting it back in the customer's hand.

She says, "It's a news video. Something terrible is happening. Something weird came out of the ocean." Then she whispers, "Looks like giant monsters!"

"Well, I gotta see that, don't you think? Show me. Don't worry, I won't grab again. You hold the phone for me and I'll watch."

I try and get close to Darlene but she's always flailing around like a wind chime in a storm. The video plays on the phone but she obsessively moves the little screen away from me and when I try to hold her still she clucks and starts in with tapping me again so I can't see much. What little I see looks like footage from one of the cable networks. A news ticker crawls along the bottom of the screen. Can't make out the words. I think I see what looks like giant waves crashing into shoreline homes, and then a dark shape, smudge, shadow, something above it all, and maybe it has arms that reach and grab, and Darlene squeals out, "Oh my god, there it is!" and starts pacing a tight circle around nothing.

"Hey, I don't think that's the real news, hon. It's fake. Pretend, yeah? I bet it's a trailer for a new movie. Isn't there a monster movie coming out soon, right? Next summer. There's always a big monster movie coming out in the summer."

"No. No no no. It's the news. It's happening. Everyone's talking about it. Aren't you talking about it, too?"

Tony shouts over to me, "What are you doing?"

That's enough to chase me out. I wave bye-bye with my cigarette pack, the one with a little hit of yaba tucked inside. I say, "Don't wait up," loud enough for myself, and I walk through the sliding doors and outside. I'm supposed to have four more hours on my shift. It'll be dark then. Who needs it. I'm still humming.

The snow is falling already, slushing up the parking lot. I dry-swallow the yaba that I wrapped in a small strip of toilet paper, I imagine it crashing into my stomach like an asteroid. Then I light up a cig. Breathe fire. I close my eyes because I want to, and when I open them I'm afraid I'll see Julie's coach waiting for me in the snowy lot. I'm afraid he'll tell me to stay away from the soccer fields. I'm afraid he and the whole town know I'm not supposed to get within two hundred yards of Julie's house when I do it all the time. I'm not afraid of Darlene's monsters. Not yet, anyway. I'm afraid of standing in front of the Big Y forever, but I'm afraid of leaving, too. I'm afraid it'll be a snowy mess already at the bus stop. I'm afraid I didn't wear the right shoes. I'm afraid I don't know if Julie takes the bus home from school. I'm afraid of home. Mine and hers. They're different now. But her home used to be my home. Julie calls my mother Gran. Gran won't shop the Big Y anymore.

I'm still humming the song, through the tip of the cigarette now.

Christ, you know it ain't easy.

You sing it, girl.

After the Big Y, I don't go home. I take the bus to Tony's place instead. Dumb-ass gave me a key. I put on a pair of his boots that are way too big. I drink a beer out of his fridge and pretend to eat some of his food. I check his bedroom dresser drawers for cash. Find the fist-sized handgun he's waved in my face more than once and a wadded-up thirty-six dollars, which isn't enough.

I'm not staying long. I have to go to the house again tonight. I have no choice. Living without choice is easier.

First I jump on Tony's computer and go online to the User Forum. It's a message board. It's anonymous and free. Both are good, because, you know, it's up to me to keep me safe, to keep me not dead. My handle is notreallyhere and yesterday I posted a question.

notreallyhere

eating meth

swim wants to know if swallowing yaba messes up your stomach
bad. swim or people swim knows eat it occasionally, sometimes
on an empty stomach, which probably isn't good, or swim knows
it isn't good but wants to know if it's really as bad as swim thinks.
using toilet paper help? hurt?

I call myself "swim," which stands for *someone who isn't me*. I use
swim even though it's against the forum rules to use it. Everyone else
uses it, too, so swim is kind of a joke. The first response is confusing.

DocBrownstone

Re: eating meth

SWIM has done this before and the toilet paper, too. Little amounts
dont do much and make you constipated. Huge amounts make
you super sick . . . SWIM puked for hours and SWIM buddy had
stomach pumped. So easy to OD this way too. Super harsh, esp. the
stomach. You eat it, it eats you. So play it safe with meth. Dont eat it,
dont stick it in your asshole. You wont like either result.

I don't know if DocBrownstone means little amounts of meth or
little amounts of toilet paper make me constipated. I don't care about
constipation. If it becomes a problem I can cut it with a laxative. I
never eat food anyway. I care only about the stomach pain that bends
me in half like a passed note. There are three other responses.

brainpan

re: eating meth

Better for you health wise to take orally cause it keeps blood serum levels low and keeps neurotoxicity low too. SWIy wants it, oh yes. Pepper some of one's weight in their OJ or coffee in the AM and it's all GO GO GO all day. Did Swibf say its smoother?

enhancion69

re: eating meth

Swim heard eating meth almost gets same IV high. Swim eats and high is longer and stronger, even with smaller amount.

snytheedical

re: eating meth

hey all you little swimmies out of the water. did you see? looks like its not safe anymore.

I can't get past brainpan. He's always all over these message boards and he pisses me off because he's making me nervous and that makes my stomach hurt worse. I mean, there's no way he knows what he's talking about but he's trying to fake it, always faking it. Like he can walk around measuring blood serum and neurotoxicity like ingredients in a batch of cupcakes. I get a twinge of hunger somewhere underneath all the pain. Maybe I should eat something. Maybe thinking about eating cupcakes is all I have to do to make everything better. Then that hunger pang from Christmases past turns into a machete ripping through my guts, and I'm standing up screaming, "Fuck you!" at the computer screen, at brainpan. I stumble back and knock Tony's stupid computer chair over, so I stomp it with his boots, deader than it already is, and I push his keyboard, mouse, and all the stupid little shit he saves on his desktop to the floor and I rampage all over the stuff. I've never been thinner but I crush everything under my mighty mighty weight, and I'm still grinding it all under my heels when everything goes dark.

I tell Julie that a transformer blew out and it's why there's no electricity anywhere in town, and it's why I came to get her, too.

I tell Julie there's nothing to be afraid of.

I ask Julie if she remembers the Ewings and their tiny red house. It was even smaller than Gran's house, but kept nicer. It used to be in the spot where we are now. Their house postage-stamped this big, hilly, wooded lot across the way from Gran's. Mr. Ewing died six years ago, maybe seven, and Mrs. Ewing was shipped to a nursing home. Alzheimer's. Her kids sold the house and plots of land to a local contractor. He knocked the little red house down, ripped out just about all the trees, leveled off and terraced the lot, and is building this huge twenty-five-hundred-square-foot colonial on the top of the hill. For months, I've been checking out the place, watching the progress. Makes me so sad for the Ewings. The contractor keeps the house key in the plastic molding that protects an outdoor outlet near the garage. I show Julie the bright blue key sleeve.

I tell Julie that when I was her age I used to run away from Gran's house all the time, but I'd go only as far as across our street, past the corner, onto Pinewood Road, and to the Ewings' house. The Ewings had five kids, but they were all grown and living on their own. I hardly ever saw them. After I hid from Gran and climbed trees in the Ewings' yard for a bit, Mrs. Ewing would let me in and I'd chase her cat Pins around. Such a small house, one floor with only three bedrooms, and the kids' beds still double-stacked up against the walls like planks. Pillows fluffed and sheets tightly made. It was like being in a giant dollhouse.

I tell Julie that Pins the cat loved when I chased her from bed to bed, up the walls and down. That black and white cat had a snaggletooth that stuck out beneath its upper lip. Pins let me touch the tooth, and it was sharp, but not like a pin, you know? I tell her that sometimes I pressed too hard on the tooth and we'd both cry out and then I'd say sorry and shush us both and say everything was fine.

I tell Julie I don't think Mr. Ewing trusted me much and blamed me for the missing loose change jar he kept on his bureau and wanted to send me home whenever he could, but Mrs. Ewing was so nice and would say, "Bill," all singsong. That way she said "Bill" made my ears and cheeks go red because she was really saying something about me, or me and your gran. I didn't understand what it was back then. Then Mrs. Ewing would make me PB and J sandwiches. She must've bought the apple jelly just for me since her kids were long gone.

I tell Julie we'll get some food later. Mrs. Ewing used to always say I should smile more because I was so pretty, and she'd use that same singsong Bill style, though, which again, I knew but didn't really know it meant something extra. I'm smart enough to not tell Julie she should smile now. She's eight and too hip for that now, yeah?

I'm not sure if I'm making a whole lot of sense to Julie. I'm just so happy to be here with her. Here is the half-finished house. Walls and windows are in. Floors are still just plywood and there's sawdust and plaster everywhere. We're in a giant room he's building above a two-car garage. Twelve-foot-high ceilings with enough angles to get lost in. Our shuffling feet and rustling blankets echo. It's like we're the last two people left in the world.

It's snowing hard outside. It's too dark and cold in here to do much besides huddle under the blankets, talk, watch, and listen. My arms itch and shake but not because of the cold. Julie is big enough to fit into me like I'm an old rocking chair. I hold her instead of scratching my arms. I hum the family song until I think she's asleep. But I can't sleep. Not anymore.

The wind kicks up and this skeleton house groans and rattles. There's a rumbling under the howling wind, and it vibrates through my chilled toes. I'm leaning with my back against the wall, arms and legs wrapped in bows around Julie. I tell Julie those aren't explosions or anything like that, and that sometimes you can get thunder in a nor'easter. I'm talking out of my ass, and it's so something a mom would say, right?

We get up off the floor. Julie is quicker than me. My bones are fossilized to their rusty joints and I need a smoke real bad again. Maybe I need more. There's no maybe about it.

Julie stands at a window, nose just about against the glass. Because we're higher up than the rest of the neighborhood, we can see Gran's house down the hill and across the way. It looks so small, made of dented cardboard and tape, and it disappears as Julie fogs up the window, putting a ghost on everything outside where it's all dark and white.

The rumbling is louder, and lower-sounding than thunder. By lower I mean closer to the ground, you know? It doesn't stop, fade, or become an echo, a memory. It turns our plywood floors into a drumhead. A power saw with its sharp angry teeth shakes and rattles on the contractor's makeshift worktable in the middle of the room. Then something bounces hard off the window behind us, and Julie screams and dives down into the blankets. I tell her to calm down, to stay there, that I'll be right back.

I glide through the darkened house. Been in here enough times I've already memorized the layout. Practice, baby, practice. Julie's soccer coach approves of practice, yeah? Straight out of the great room for ten steps, past the dining room, take that second left off the kitchen, no marble countertops yet but dumb-ass left some copper piping out, which I should probably take and sell, then a quick right, eleven stairs down into the basement, left, then through a door into the two-car garage, left again and step out the side door, into the swirling wind that pickpockets my breath.

Four, maybe five inches of snow on the ground, enough to cover the toes of Tony's boots. My feet are lost in the boots and can't keep themselves warm. Losers. My shaking hands fish for my cigarette pack. I only have one left, and *one* left. The world sighs, breathes, and it's so loud, like a whale breaching in my head. Trees crack and fall all over the neighborhood, London Bridge falling down around our new house on the hill. Sirens somewhere in the distance, in town, probably. More rumbling, more stuff crashing down, cratering into the ground, shaking everything. And that world-sighing stuff, it isn't just in my head, you know. That slow inhale and percussive exhale sound gets louder and has company. Like more than one whale breaching. Beanstalk-high above Gran's house, almost lost in the dark, are thick plumes of white air, exploding along with the rhythmic deep breathing. Three, no four, separate clouds from walking smokestacks. Holy Christ, Darlene's video. They're here and they're walking and breathing somewhere above everything. A front section of Gran's roof is gone. Most of the roof is covered in white, but there's a section that's a dark nothing space. Then those walking smokestacks move in and more of Gran's roof rips up and away, shingles flutter around Gran's yard like dying blackbirds, the ones that are always falling out of the sky dead somewhere down south, always south, and I think I know how that feels. The monsters are giant shadows with giant boulders attached to giant arms or giant legs, I don't know which, and they pile-drive into the house, smashing the chimney and walls, glass shattering, wood exploding, and always those white plumes of breath above it all, breathing slow, but loud, and constant, like they'll never stop.

Julie opens the window above me and starts screaming for Gran. I stick my head inside the garage, into more darkness, and I scream and yell at her, making sure I'm loud enough so I can't hear that goddamn breathing and the end of Gran's house, so I scream and I yell for her to shut up, to stop being a baby, why are you so stupid, they'll hear you.

Swim wants to know if it's as bad as swim thinks.

The ground shakes worse than ever because they're all around us.

My stomach is dead and it hurts to talk, but I tell Julie to stop looking out the window. I tell her that they'll see her. I say it in my quiet, I'm-sorry voice.

I tell Julie that I'd been walking by Gran's house for a while now and I'd heard Gran yelling at her, calling her stupid and so bad, like she used to yell at me, and it's why I'd always run away to the Ewings—remember the Ewings?—and they're not here anymore, you know, so that's why I went and got her out of the house tonight, got her away from Gran.

Julie hasn't said anything to me since we got here, but then from under the pile of blankets and the pile of bones that are my arms and legs, she asks me if I still have the gun.

I tell her my mom became Gran to me the day they let her take you away from me.

And then I tell Julie about that first time, a little more than seven years ago, I went and got her when she was only eight months old. I was downtown by myself, and Joey, that prick, him and his bleeding gums and cigarette burns, he was so long gone it was like he was never even there, and I remember not being able to see Julie at all, right away, and worse, not being able to remember what she looked like or what her chubby little hands and feet felt like, how that must've been the worst pain in the world, right?—I mean, what else could've mattered to me?—so when the pain wouldn't go away I went over to Mom's house, *Gran's* house, and I can't remember if I really remember because what I remember now is how they explained it all when I was in the courtroom, how the lawyers talked about me and what I did before me and Julie went south where everything was green. I remember them saying how I walked into my old house, calm as a summer's day (was how the lawyer said it, someone objected), me and a big knife, scooped up Julie out of the crib, though I don't know how it was I held her and a big knife at the same time, right? That doesn't make sense to me. I'd be more careful than that. So yeah, Mom wasn't my mom anymore but your gran, which means she became someone else, and her stupid twelve-pack boyfriend, whoever he was, the one with the junky red truck and a rusted plow blade hanging off the grille too low, the one with the easy greasy hands, the one who'd walk in on you if you were in the bathroom, he wasn't there, I was there, so was a knife, apparently, and this new Gran, she looked so angry, tough as a leather jacket, fists clenched, hair cut too short and tight like a helmet, and no, wait, she looked like she wanted to give up, so old, thin, dry-boned, but she was screaming at me fine, like she was fine, just fine, like normal, or no, that's not right because then she was crying about how she couldn't take it, any of it, anymore, saying that she had cancer in her liver now, and go ahead she said, go ahead and do it she said, do it, and I ask Julie if she remembers Gran saying that and, and dammit I'm mixing up what happened when Julie was a baby with happened tonight. How do you keep everything that happened in order anyway? Doesn't seem like order matters much because it doesn't change what happened.

I tell Julie that swim didn't think this was going to happen.

We listen to sirens coming closer and we listen to breathing and stomping and everything outside. So loud, it's like we're in their bellies already.

I tell Julie there's nothing to be afraid of. I tell her that when it's morning everything will be all done. I tell her that all the houses around us and in the rest of the world will be gone, stomped and mashed flat, but we'll be okay. I tell her that we'll ride on the back of one of the monsters. Its back plates and scales will be softer than they look. We'll feel the earth rumbling beneath us and we'll be above everything. I tell her it'll know where to go, where to take us, and it'll take us where it's safe, safe for swims. I tell her that I know she doesn't remember the first time but we'll ride it south again. The monster will follow the dotted white lines and instead of trees lining the roads there'll be all the rest of the monsters destroying everything else, watching us, leading the way south, not sure why south, swim south, but maybe it's as simple and stupid as that's where everything is green, because south isn't here, because south is as good or bad as any other place.

Outside there's flashing lights, sirens, pounding on the doors, walls, and roof. Dust and chunks of plastic rain down on our heads and we fall and roll into the middle of the room. Julie's yelling and crying and I brush away hair from her ear with one hand so I can whisper inside her head. Tony's gun is in my other hand.

I tell Julie, Shh, baby. Don't you worry about nothing. Your mom's here.

SOMETHING ABOUT BIRDS

The New Dark Review **Presents "Something About William Wheatley: An Interview with William Wheatley," by Benjamin D. Piotrowski**

William Wheatley's *The Artist Starve* is a collection of five loosely interconnected novelettes and novellas published in 1971 by the University of Massachusetts Press, the book having won its Juniper Prize for Fiction. In an era that certainly predated usage of YA as a marketing category, his stories were told from the POV of young adults, ranging from the fourteen-year-old Maggie Holtz, who runs away from home, taking her six-year-old brother Thomas into the local woods, during the twelve days of the Cuban Missile Crisis, to the last story, a near-future extrapolation of the Vietnam War having continued into the year 1980, the draft age dropped to sixteen, and an exhausted and radiation-sick platoon of teenagers conspires to kill the increasingly unhinged Sergeant Thomas Holtz. *The Artist Starve* was a prescient and visceral (if not too earnest) book embracing the chaotic social and global politics of the early 1970s. An unexpected critical and commercial smash, particularly on college campuses, *The Artist Starve* was one of three books forwarded to the Pulitzer Prize board, who ultimately decided not to award a prize for the year 1971. That *The Artist Starve* is largely forgotten whereas the last short story Wheatley ever wrote, "Something About Birds," first published in a DIY zine called *Steam* in 1977 and oft-reprinted, continues to stir debate and win admirers within the horror/weird fiction community is an irony that is not lost upon the avuncular, seventy-five-year-old Wheatley.

BP: Thank you for agreeing to this interview, Mr. Wheatley.

WW: The pleasure is all mine, Benjamin.

BP: Before we discuss "Something About Birds," which is my all-time favorite short story, by the way—

WW: You're too kind. Thank you.

BP: I wanted to ask if *The Artist Starve* is going to be reprinted. I've heard rumors.

WW: You have? Well, that would be news to me. While I suppose it would be nice to have one's work rediscovered by a new generation, I'm not holding my breath, nor am I actively seeking to get the book back in print. It already served its purpose. It was an important book when it came out, I think, but it is a book very much of its time. So much so I'm afraid it wouldn't translate very well to the now.

BP: There was a considerable gap, six years, between *The Artist Starve* and "Something About Birds." In the interim, were you working on other writing projects or projects that didn't involve writing?

WW: When you get to my age—oh, that sounds terribly cliché, doesn't it? Let me rephrase: When you get to my *perspective,* six years doesn't seem so considerable. Point taken, however. I'll try to be brief. I will admit to some churlish, petulant behavior, as given the overwhelming response to my first book I expected the publishing industry to then roll out the red carpet to whatever it was I might've scribbled on a napkin. And maybe that would've happened had I won the Pulitzer, yes? Instead, I took the no-award designation as a terrible, final judgment on my work. Silly, I know, but at the risk of sounding paranoid, the no-award announcement all but shut down further notice for the book. I spent a year or so nursing my battered ego and speaking at colleges and universities before even considering writing another story. I then spent more than two years researching the burgeoning fuel crisis and overpopulation fears. I traveled quite a bit as well: Ecuador, Peru, Japan, India, South Africa. While traveling I started bird-watching, of course. Total novice, and I remain one. Anyway, I'd planned to turn my research into a novel of some sort. That book never materialized. I never even wrote an opening paragraph. I'm not a novelist. I never was. To make a long, not-all-that-exciting story short, upon returning home and very much travel weary, I became interested in antiquities and, in 1976, bought the very same antique shop that is below us now. I wrote "Something About Birds" shortly after opening the shop, thinking it might be the first story in another cycle, all stories involving birds in some way. The story itself was unlike anything I'd ever written; oblique, yes, bizarre to many, I'm sure, but somehow, it hits closer to an ineffable truth than anything else I've written. To my great disappointment, the story was summarily rejected by all the glossy magazines and I was ignorant of the genre fiction market, so I decided to allow a friend who was in a local punk band to publish it in her zine. I remain grateful and pleased that the story has had many other lives since.

BP: Speaking for all the readers who adore "Something About Birds," let me say that we'd kill for a short-story cycle built around it.

WW: Oh, I've given up on writing. "Something About Birds" is a fitting conclusion to my little writing career, as that story continues to do its job, Benjamin.

Mr. Wheatley says, "That went well, didn't it?"

Wheatley is shorter than Ben but not short, and is broad in the chest and shoulders, a wrestler's build. His skin is pallid and his dark brown eyes focused, attentive, and determined. His hair has thinned but he still has most of it, and most of it is dark, almost black. He wears a tweed sports coat, gray wool pants, a plum-colored sweater vest, a white shirt, a slate bow tie that presses against his throat tightly as though it were gauze being applied to a wound. He smiled throughout the interview. He is smiling now.

"You were great, Mr. Wheatley. I cannot thank you enough for the opportunity to talk with you about my favorite story."

"You are too kind." Wheatley drums his fingers on the dining room table at which they are sitting and narrows his eyes at Ben, as though trying to bring him into better focus. "Before you leave, Benjamin, I have something for you."

Ben swirls the last of his room-temperature Earl Grey tea around the bottom of his cup and decides against finishing it. Ben stands as Wheatley stands, and he checks his pocket for his phone and his recorder. "Oh, please, Mr. Wheatley, you've been more than gracious—"

"Nonsense. You are doing me a great service with the interview. It won't be but a moment. I will not take no for an answer." Wheatley continues to talk as he disappears into one of the three other rooms with closed doors that spoke out from the wheel of the impeccable and brightly lit living/dining room. The oval dining room table is the centerpiece of the space and is made of a darkly stained wood, the tabletop held up by a single post as thick as a telephone pole. The wall adjacent to the kitchen houses a built-in bookcase, the shelves filled to capacity; across the top perch vases and brass candelabras. On the far wall rectangular, monolithic windows, their blue drapes pulled wide open, vault toward the height of the cathedral ceiling, their advance halted by the crown molding. The third-floor view overlooks Dunham

Street, and when Ben stands in front of a window he can see the red awning of Wheatley's antiques shop below. The room is beautiful, smartly decorated, full of antiques that Ben is unable to identify; his furniture and décor experience doesn't extend beyond IKEA and his almost pathological inability to put anything together more complex than a nightstand.

Wheatley reemerges from behind a closed door. He has an envelope in one hand and something small and strikingly red cupped in the palm of the other.

"I hope you're willing to indulge an old man's eccentricity." He pauses and looks around the room. "I thought I brought up a stash of small white paper bags. I guess I didn't. Benjamin, forgive the Swiss-cheese memory. We can get a bag on our way out if you prefer. Anyway, I'd like you to have this. Hold out your hands, please."

"What is it?"

Wheatley gently places a bird head into Ben's hands. The head is small, the size of a half-dollar coin. Its shock of red feathers is so bright, a red he's never seen, only something living could be that vivid, and for a moment Ben is not sure if he should pat the bird head and coo soothingly or flip the thing out of his hands before it nips him. The head has a prominent brown-yellow beak, proportionally thick, and as long as the length of the head from the top to its base. The beak is outlined in shorter black feathers that curl around the eyes as well. The bird's pitch-black irises float in a sea of a more subdued red.

"Thank you, Mr. Wheatley. I don't know what to say. Is it—is it real?"

"This is a red-headed barbet from northern South America. Lovely creature. Its bill is described as horn colored. It looks like a horn, doesn't it? It feeds on fruit, but it also eats insects as well. Fierce little bird, one befitting your personality, I think, Benjamin."

"Wow. Thank you. I can't accept this. This is too much—"

"Nonsense. I insist." He then gives Ben an envelope. "An invitation to an all-too-infrequent social gathering I host here. There will be six of us, you and I included. It's in—oh my—three days. Short notice, I know. The date, time, and instructions are inside the envelope. You must bring the red-headed barbet with you, Benjamin. It is your

ticket to admittance, and you will not be allowed entrance without it."
Wheatley chuckles softly and Ben does not know whether or not he is
serious.

BP: There's so much wonderful ambiguity and potential for different meanings. Let's start in the beginning, with the strange funeral
procession of "Something About Birds." An adult, Mr. H_____,
is presumably the father of one of the children, who slips up and calls
him "Dad."

WW: Yes, of course. "It's too hot for costumes, Dad."

BP: That line is buried in a pages-long stream-of-consciousness
paragraph with the children excitedly describing the beautiful day
and the desiccated, insect-ridden body of the dead bird. It's an effective juxtaposition and wonderfully disorienting use of omniscient
POV, and I have to admit, when I first read the story, I didn't see the
word "Dad" there. I was surprised to find it on the second read. Many
readers report having had the same experience. Did you anticipate
that happening?

WW: I like when stories drop important clues in a nonchalant or
nondramatic way. That he is the father of one, possibly more of the
children, and that he is simply staging this funeral, or celebration,
for a bird, a beloved family pet, and all the potential strangeness and
darkness is the result of the imagination of the children is one possible read. Or maybe that is all pretend, too, part of the game, and
Mr. H_____ is someone else entirely. I'm sorry, I'm not going to
give you definitive answers, and I will purposefully lead you astray if
you let me.

BP: Duly noted. Mr. H_____ leads the children into the woods
behind an old, abandoned schoolhouse—

WW: Or perhaps school is only out for the summer, Benjamin.

BP: Okay, wow. I'm going to include my "wow" in the interview, by the way. I'd like to discuss the children's names. Or the names they are given once they reach the clearing: The Admiral, The Crow, Copper, The Surveyor, and of course, poor Kittypants.

WW: Perhaps Kittypants isn't so poor after all, is he?

There is a loud knocking on Ben's apartment door at 12:35 A.M.

Ben lives alone in a small one-bedroom apartment in the basement of a run-down brownstone, in a neighborhood that was supposed to be the next *it* neighborhood. The sparsely furnished apartment meets his needs, but he does wish there was more natural light. There are days, particularly in the winter, when he stands with his face pressed against the glass of his front window, a secret behind a set of black wrought-iron bars.

Whoever is knocking continues knocking. Ben awkwardly pulls on a pair of jeans, grabs a forearm-length metal pipe that leans against his nightstand (not that he would ever use it, not that he has been in a physical altercation since fifth grade), and stalks into the combined living area/kitchen. He's hesitant to turn on the light and debates whether he should ignore the knocking or phone the police.

A voice calls out from behind the thick wooden front door. "Benjamin Piotrowsky? Please, Mr. Piotrowsky. I know it's late, but we need to talk."

Ben shuffles across the room and turns on the outside light above the entrance. He peeks out his front window. There's a woman standing on his front stoop, dressed in jeans and a black hooded sweatshirt. He does not recognize her and he is unsure of what to do. He turns on the overhead light in the living area and shouts through the door, "Do I know you? Who are you?"

"My name is Marnie, I am a friend of Mr. Wheatley, and I'm here on his behalf. Please open the door."

Somehow her identification makes perfect sense, that she is who she says she is and yes, of course, she is here because of Mr. Wheatley, yet Ben has never been more fearful for his safety. He unlocks and opens the door against his better judgment.

Marnie walks inside, shuts the door, and says, "Don't worry, I won't be long." Her movements are easy and athletic and she rests her hands on her hips. She is taller than Ben, perhaps only an inch or two under six feet. She has dark shoulder-length hair and eyes that aren't quite symmetrical, with her left smaller and slightly lower than her right. Her age is indeterminate, anywhere from late twenties to early forties. As someone who is self-conscious about his own youthful, childlike appearance (ruddy complexion, inability to grow even a shadow of facial hair), Ben suspects she's older than she looks.

Ben asks, "Would you like a glass of water, or something, uh, Marnie, right?"

"No, thank you. Doing some late-night plumbing?"

"What? Oh." Ben hides the pipe behind his back. "No. It's um, my little piece of security, I guess. I, um, I thought someone might be breaking in."

"Knocking on your door equates to a break-in, does it?" Marnie smiles, but it's a bully's smile, a politician's smile. "I'm sorry to have woken you and I will get right to the point. Mr. Wheatley doesn't appreciate you posting a picture of your admission ticket on Facebook."

Ben blinks madly, as though he was a captured spy put under the bright lamp. "I'm sorry?"

"You posted a picture of the admission ticket at nine forty-six this evening. It currently has three hundred and ten likes, eighty-two comments, and thirteen shares."

The bird head. Between bouts of transcribing the interview and ignoring calls from the restaurant (that asshole Shea was calling to swap shifts, again), Ben fawned over the bird head. He marveled at how simultaneously light and heavy it was in his palm. He spent more than an hour staging photographs of the head, intending to use one with the publication of the interview. Ben placed the bird head in the spine of an open notebook, the notebook in which he'd written notes from the interview. The head was slightly turned so the length of the beak could be admired. The picture was too obvious and not strange enough. The rest of his photographs were studies in incongruity; the bird head in the middle of a white plate, resting in the bowl of a large spoon, entangled in the blue laces of his Chuck Taylors, perched on top of his refrigerator, and on the windowsill framed by the black bars. He settled on a close-up of the bird head on the cracked hardwood floor so its black eye, red feathers, and horn-colored beak filled the shot. For the viewer, the bird head's size would be difficult to determine due to the lack of foreground or scale within the photograph. That was the shot. He posted it along with the text "Coming soon to The New Dark Review: Something About William Wheatley" (which he thought was endlessly clever). Of course many of his friends (were they friends, really? did the pixelated collection of pictures, avatars, and opinions never met in person even qualify as acquaintances?) within the online horror writing and fan community enthusiastically commented upon the photo. Ben sat in front of his laptop, watching the likes, comments, and shares piling up. He engaged with each comment and post share, and couldn't help but imagine the traffic this picture would bring to his *The New Dark Review.* He was aware enough to feel silly for thinking it, but he couldn't remember feeling more successful or happy.

Ben says, "Oh, right. The picture of the bird head. Jeez, I'm sorry. I didn't know I wasn't supposed to, I mean, I didn't realize—"

"We understand your enthusiasm for Mr. Wheatley and his work, but you didn't honestly give a second thought to sharing publicly a picture of an admission ticket to a private gathering, one hosted by someone who clearly values his privacy?"

"No, I guess I didn't. I never mentioned anything about the party, I swear, but now I feel stupid and awful." He is telling the truth; he does feel stupid and awful, but mostly because he understands Marnie is here to ask him to take down his most popular Facebook post. "I'm so sorry for that."

"Do you always react this way when someone shares an invitation to a private party? When they share such a personal gift?"

"No. God, no. It wasn't like that. I posted it to, you know, drum up some pre-interest, um, buzz, for the interview that I'm going to publish tomorrow. A teaser, right? That's all. I don't think Mr. Wheatley realizes how much people in the horror community love 'Something About Birds' and how much they want to know about him and hear from him."

"Are there going to be further problems?"

"Problems?"

"Issues."

"No. I don't think so."

"You don't think so?"

"No. No problems or issues. I promise." Ben backs away unconsciously and bumps into the small island in his kitchen. He drops the pipe and it clatters to the floor.

"You will not post any more pictures on social media, nor will you include the picture or any mention of the invitation and the gathering itself when you publish the interview."

"I won't. I swear."

"We'd like you to take down the photo, please."

Everything in him screams no and wants to argue that they don't understand how much the picture will help bring eyeballs and readers to the interview, how it will help everyone involved. Instead, Ben says, "Yes, of course."

"Now, please. Take it down, and I'd like to watch you take it down."

"Yeah, okay." He pulls his phone from out of his pocket and walks toward Marnie. She watches his finger and thumb strokes as he deletes the post.

Marnie says, "Thank you. I am sorry to have disrupted your evening." She walks to the front door. She pauses, turns, and says, "Are you sure about accepting the invitation, Benjamin?"

"What do you mean?"

"You can give back the admission ticket to me if you don't think you can handle the responsibility. Mr. Wheatley would understand."

The thought of giving her the bird head never once crosses his mind as a possibility. "No, that's okay. I'm keeping it. I'd like to keep it, please, I mean. I understand why he's upset and I won't betray his trust again. I promise."

Marnie starts to talk, and much of the rest of the strangely personal conversation passes like a dream.

WW: I'm well aware of the role of birds within pagan lore and that they are linked with the concept of freedom, of the ability to transcend the mundane, to leave it behind.

BP: Sounds like an apt description of weird fiction to me, Mr. Wheatley. I want you talk a little about the odd character names of the children. Sometimes I'm of the mind that the children are filling the roles of *familiars* to Mr. H_____. They are his companions, of course, and are assisting him in some task . . . a healing, perhaps, as Mr. H_____ is described as having a painful limp in the beginning of the story, a limp that doesn't seem to be there when, later, he follows the children into the woods.

WW: (laughs) I do love hearing all the different theories about the story.

BP: Are you laughing because I'm way off?

WW: No, not at all. I tried to build in as many interpretations as possible, and in doing so, I've been pleased to find many more interpretations I didn't realize were there. Or I didn't consciously realize, if that makes sense. In the spirit of fair play, I will admit, for the first time publicly, Benjamin, from where I got the children's names. They are named after songs from my friend Liz's obscure little punk band. I hope that's not a disappointment.

BP: Not at all. I think it's amazingly cool.

WW: An inside joke, yes, but the seemingly random names have taken on meaning, too. At least they have for me.

BP: Let me hit you with one more allegorical reading: I've read a fellow critic who argues there's a classical story going on among all the weirdness. She argues The Admiral, The Crow, and Kittypants specifically are playing out a syncretic version of the Horus, Osiris, and Set myth of Egypt, with Mr. H_____ representing Huitzilopochtli, the bird-headed Mexican god of war. Is she onto something?

WW: The references to those cultural myths involving gods with human bodies and bird heads were not conscious on my part. But that doesn't mean they're not there. I grew up reading those stories of ancient gods and mythologies, and they are a part of me as they are a part of us all, even if we don't realize it. That's the true power of story. That it can find the secrets both writer and reader didn't know they had within themselves.

Ben doesn't wake until after one P.M. His dreams were replays of his protracted late-night conversation with Marnie. They stood in the living area. Neither sat or made themselves more comfortable. He remembers part of their conversation going like this:

"When did you first read 'Something About Birds?'" "Five years ago, I think." "When did you move to the city?" "Three years ago, I think?" "You think?" "I'm sorry, it was two years ago, last September. It seems like I've been here longer. I don't know why I was confused by that question." "As an adult, have you always lived alone?" "Yes." "How many miles away do you currently live from your mother?" "I'm not sure of the exact mileage, but she's in another time zone from me." "Tell me why you hate your job at the restaurant." "It's having to fake pleasantness that makes me feel both worthless and lonely." "Have you had many lovers?" "Only two. Both relationships lasted less than two months. And it's been a while, unfortunately." "What has been a while?" "Since I've had a lover, as you put it." "Have you ever held a live bird cupped in your hands and felt its fragility or had a large one perch on your arm or shoulder and felt its barely contained strength?" "No. Neither." "Would you prefer talons or beak?" "I would prefer wings." "You can't choose wings, Benjamin. Talons or beak?" "Neither? Both?" And so on.

Ben does not go into work and he doesn't call in. His phone vibrates with the agitated where-are-yous and are-you-coming-ins. He hopes that asshole Shea is being called in to cover for him. He says at his ringing phone, "*The New Dark Review* will be my job." He decides severing his already fraying economic safety line is the motive necessary to truly make a go at the career he now wants. He says, "Sink or swim," then playfully chides himself for not having a proper bird analogy instead. Isn't there a bird species that lays eggs on cliffs in or near Ireland, and the mothers push the hatchlings out of the nest and as they tumble down the side of the craggy rock they either learn to fly or perish? Ben resolves to turn his own zine devoted to essays about obscure and contemporary horror and weird fiction into a career. He's not so clueless as to believe the zine will ever be able to sustain him financially, but perhaps it could elevate his name and stature within the field and parlay that into something more. He could pitch/sell ad space to publishers and research paying e-book subscription-based models. Despite himself, he fantasizes *The New Dark Review* winning publishing industry awards. With its success he could then helm an anthology of stories dedicated to Wheatley, a cycle of stories by other famous writers centered around "Something About Birds." If only he hadn't been told to take down the bird head photo from Facebook. He fears a real opportunity has been lost, and the messages and e-mails asking why he took down the photo aren't helping.

Instead of following up on his revenue-generating and promotional ideas for *The New Dark Review*, Ben googles the Irish cliff birds and finds the guillemot chicks. They aren't kicked out of the nest. They are encouraged by calls from their father below the cliffs. And they don't fly. The chicks plummet and bounce off the rocks, and if they manage to survive, they swim out to sea with their parents.

Ben transcribes the rest of the interview and publishes it. He shares the link over various platforms but the interview does not engender the same enthusiastic response the bird head photo received. He resolves to craft a long-term campaign to promote the interview, give it a long life, one with a tail (a publishing/marketing term, of course). He'll follow up the interview with a long-form critical essay about Wheatley's work. He reads "Something About Birds" eight more times. He tacks a poster board to a wall in the living area. He creates timelines and a map of the story's setting, stages the characters and creates dossiers, uses lengths of string and thread to make connections. He tacks up note cards with quotes from Wheatley. He draws bird heads, too.

That night there is a repeat of the knocking on his front door. Only Ben isn't sure if the knocking is real or if he's only dreaming. The knocking is lighter this time, a tapping more than a knock. He might've welcomed another visit from Marnie earlier, while he was working on his new essay, but now he pulls the bedcovers over his head. The tapping stops eventually.

Later there is a great wind outside, and rain, and his apartment sings with all manner of noises not unlike the beating of hundreds of wings.

WW: Well, that's the question, isn't it? It's the question the title of the story all but asks. I've always been fascinated by birds, and prior to writing the story, I'd never been able to fully articulate why. Yes, the story is strange, playful, perhaps macabre, and yet it really is about my love, for lack of a better term, of birds. I'm flailing around for an answer, I'm sorry. Let me try again: Our fascination with birds is more than some dime-store, new-age, spiritual longing, more than the worst of us believing these magnificent animals serve as an avatar for our black-hearted, nearsighted souls, if we've ever had such a thing as a soul. There's this otherness about birds, isn't there? Thank goodness for that. It's as though they're in possession of knowledge totally alien to us. I don't think I'm explaining this very well, and that's why I wrote the story. The story gets at what I'm trying to say about birds better than I can now. I've always felt, as a humble observer, that the proper emotion within a bird's presence is awe. Awe is as fearsome and terrible as it is ecstatic.

Ben wakes up to his phone vibrating with more calls from the restaurant. His bedroom is dark. As far as he can tell from his cavelike confines, it is dark outside as well. Ben fumbles to turn on his nightstand lamp and the light makes everything worse. Across from the foot of his bed is his dresser. It's his dresser from childhood, and the wood is scarred with careless gouges and pocked with white, tattered remnants of what were once Pokémon stickers. On top of the dresser is a bird head, and it's as large as his own head. Bigger, actually. Its coloring is the same as the red-headed barbet. The red feathers, at this size, are shockingly red, as though red never existed before this grotesquely beautiful plumage. He understands the color is communication. It's a warning. A threat. So too the brown-yellow beak, which is as thick and prominent as a rhino's horn, stabbing out menacingly into his bedroom. The bird's eyes are bigger than his fists, and the black irises are ringed in more red.

He scrambles for his length of metal pipe and squeezes it tightly in both hands, holding it like a comically stubby and ineffective baseball bat. He shouts, "Who's there?" repeatedly, as though if he shouts it enough times, there will be an unequivocal answer to the query. No answer comes. He runs into the living room shouting, "Marnie?" and opens his bathroom and closet doors and finds no one. He checks the front door. It is unlocked. Did he leave it unlocked last night? He opens it with a deep sense of regret and steps out onto his empty front stoop. Outside his apartment is a different world, one crowded with brick buildings, ceaseless traffic, cars parked end-to-end for as far as he can see, and the sidewalks are rivers for pedestrians who don't know or care who he is or what has happened. Going outside was a terrible mistake, and Ben goes back into his apartment and again shouts, "Who's there?"

Ben eventually stops shouting and returns to his bedroom. He circles around to the front of the dresser so as to view the bird head straight on and not in profile. Ben takes a picture with his phone and sends a private group message (photo attached) to a selection of acquaintances within the horror/weird fiction community. He tells them this new photo is not for public consumption. Within thirty minutes he receives responses ranging from "Jealous!" to "Yeah, saw yesterday's pic, but cool" to "I liked yesterday's picture better. Can you send that to me?" Not one of them commented on the head's impossible size, which has to be clear in the photo as it takes up so much of the dresser's top. Did they assume some sort of photo trickery? Did they assume the bird head in yesterday's photo (the close-up of the head on the hardwood floor) was the same size? Did this second photo resize the head they first saw in their minds by the new context? He types in response, "The head wasn't this big yesterday," but deletes it instead of sending. Ben considers posting the head-on-the-dresser photo to his various social media platforms so Marnie might return and admonish him again, and then he could ask why she broke into his apartment and left this monstrous bird head behind. This had to be her doing.

After a lengthy inner dialogue, Ben summons the courage to pick the head up. He's careful, initially, to not touch the beak. To touch that first would be wrong, disrespectful. Dangerous. He girds himself to lift a great weight, even bending his knees, but the head is surprisingly light. That's not to say the head feels fragile. He imagines its lightness is by design so the great bird, despite its size, would be able to fly and strike its prey quickly. With the head in his hands, he scans the dresser's top for any sign of the small head Mr. Wheatley initially gave him. He cannot find it. He assumes Marnie swapped the smaller head for this one, but he also irrationally fears that the head simply grew to this size overnight.

The feathers have a slight oily feel to them and he is careful to not inadvertently get any stuck between his fingers as he manipulates the head and turns it over, upside down. He cannot see inside the head, although it is clearly hollow. A thick forest of red feathers obscures the neck's opening, and when he attempts to pull feathers back or push them aside, other feathers dutifully move in to block the view. There are tantalizing glimpses of darkness between the feathers, as though the depth contained within is boundless.

He sends his right hand inside the head, expecting to feel plaster, or plastic, or wire mesh perhaps, the inner workings of an intricate mask, or maybe even, impossibly, the hard bone of skull. His fingers gently explore the hidden interior perimeter, and he feels warm, moist, pliant clay, or putty, or flesh. He pulls his hand out and rubs his fingers together, and he watches his fingers, expecting to see evidence of dampness. He's talking to himself now, asking if one can see dampness, and he wipes his hand on his shorts. He's nauseated (but pleasantly so), as he imagines his fingers were moments ago exploring the insides of a wound. More boldly, he returns his hand inside the bird head. He presses against the interior walls and those walls yield to his fingers like they're made of the weakening skin of an overripe fruit or vegetable. Fingertips sink deeper into the flesh of the head, and his arm shakes and wrist aches with exertion.

There's a wet sucking sound as Ben pulls his hand out. He roughly flips the head over, momentarily forgetting about the size of the great beak, and its barbed tip scratches a red furrow into his forearm. He wraps his hand around the beak near its base and his fingers are too small to enclose its circumference. He attempts to separate the two halves of beak, a half-assed lion tamer prying open fearsome jaws, but they are fixed in place, closed tightly, like gritted teeth.

Ben takes the head out into the living area and gently places it on the floor. He lies down beside it and runs his fingers through its feathers, careful to not touch the beak again. If he stares hard enough, long enough, he sees himself in miniature, curled up like a field mouse, reflected in the black pools of the bird's eyes.

BP: A quick summary of the ending. Please stop me if I say anything that's inaccurate or misleading. The children, led by The Crow and The Admiral, reappear out of the woods that Mr. H_____ had forbidden them to go into, and you describe The Admiral's fugue wonderfully: "his new self passing over his old self, as though he were an eclipse." When asked (we don't know who the speaker is, do we?) where Kittypants is, The Crow says Kittypants is still in the woods and was waiting to be found and retrieved, he didn't fly away. Someone (again, the speaker not identified) giggles and says his wings are broken. The other children erupt into sounds, chant, and song, eager to go to Kittypants. The dead bird they had brought with them is forgotten. I love how it isn't clear if the kids have finally donned their bird masks or if they've had them on the whole time. Or perhaps they have no masks on at all. Mr. H_____ says they may leave him only after they've finished digging a hole big enough for the little one to fit inside and not ruffle any feathers. The reader is unsure if Mr. H_____ is referring to the dead bird or, in retrospect, if it's a sinister reference to Kittypants, the smallest of their party. The kids leave right away and it's not clear if they have finished digging the hole or not. Perhaps they're going home, the funeral or celebration over, the game over. Mr. H_____ goes into the woods after them and finds his gaggle in a clearing, the setting sun throwing everything into shadow, "a living bas-relief." They are leaping high into the air, arms spread out as wide as the world, and then crashing down into what is described from a distance as a pile of leaves no bigger than a curled-up sleeping child. It's a magnificent image, Mr. Wheatley, one that simultaneously brings to mind the joyous, chaotic, physical play of children and, at the same time, resembles a gathering of carrion birds picking apart a carcass in a frenzy. I have to ask, is the leaf pile just a leaf pile, or is Kittypants inside?

WW: I love that you saw the buzzard imagery in that scene, Benjamin. But oh, I wouldn't dream of ever answering your final question, directly. But I'll play along, a little. Let me ask you this: Do you prefer that Kittypants be under the pile of leaves? If so, why?

Tucked inside the envelope he received from Mr. Wheatley is a typed set of instructions. Benjamin wears black socks, an oxford shirt, and dark pants that were once partners with a double-breasted jacket. He walks twenty-three blocks northwest. He enters the darkened antiques store through a back door, and from there he navigates past narrow shelving and various furniture and taxidermy staging to the stairwell that leads to the second-floor apartment. He does not call out or say anyone's name. All in accordance with the instructions.

The front door to Mr. Wheatley's apartment is closed. Ben places an ear against the door, listening for other people, for their sounds, as varied as they can be. He doesn't hear anything. He cradles the bird head in his left arm and has it pressed gently against his side, the beak supported by his ribs. The head is wrapped tightly in a white sheet. The hooked beak tip threatens to rend the cloth.

Ben opens the door, steps inside the apartment, and closes the door gently behind him, and thus ends the brief set of instructions from the envelope. Benjamin removes the white cloth and holds the bird head in front of his chest like a shield.

There is no one in the living room. The curtains are drawn and three wall sconces are peppered between the windows; their single bulbs give off a weak, almost sepia light. The doors to the other rooms are all closed. He walks to the oval dining room table, the one at which he sat with Mr. Wheatley only three days ago.

Ben is unsure of what he's supposed to do next. His lips and throat are dry, and he's afraid he'll throw up if he opens his mouth to speak. Finally he calls out: "Hello, Mr. Wheatley? It's Ben Piotrowsky."

There's no response or even a sense of movement from elsewhere inside the apartment.

"Our interview went live online already. I'm not sure if you've seen it yet, but I hope you like it. The response has been very positive so far."

Ben shuffles deeper into the room, and it suddenly occurs to him that he could document everything he's experienced (including what he will experience later this evening) and add it to the interview as a bizarre, playful afterword. It's a brilliant idea and something that would only enhance his and Mr. Wheatley's reputations within the weird fiction community. Yes, he will most certainly do this, and Ben imagines the online response as being more rabid than the reaction to the picture of the bird head. There will be argument and discussion as to whether the mysterious afterword is fictional or not, and if fictional, if it had been written by William Wheatley himself. The interview with afterword will be a perfect extension or companion to "Something About Birds." Perhaps Ben can even convince Mr. Wheatley to cowrite the afterword with him. Or, instead, he could pitch this idea to Mr. Wheatley not as an afterword, but as a wraparound story, or framing device, within the interview itself. Yes, not only could this be a new story, but the beginning of a new story cycle, and Ben will be a part of it.

Ben says, "This bird head is lovely, by the way. I mean that. I assume you made it. I'm no expert, but it appears to be masterful work. I'm sure there's a fascinating story behind it we could discuss further." In the silence that follows, Ben adds, "Perhaps your friend Marnie brought it to my apartment. We talked the other night, of course."

Ben's spark of new-story-cycle inspiration and surety fades in the continued silence. Has he arrived before everyone else, or is this some sort of game where the party does not begin until he chooses a door to open, and then—then what? Is this a hazing ritual? Is he to become part of their secret little group? Ben certainly hopes for the latter. Which door of the three will he open first?

Ben asks, "Am I to put the bird head on, Mr. Wheatley? Is that it?"

The very idea of being enclosed within the darkness of the bird head, his cheeks and lips and eyelids pressing against the whatever-it-is on the inside, is a horror. Yet he also wants nothing more than to put the bird head over his own, to have that great beak spill out before his eyes, a baton with which to conduct the will of others. He won't put it on, not until he's sure that is what he's supposed to do.

"What am I supposed to do now, Mr. Wheatley?"

The door to Ben's left opens and four people—two men and two women—wearing bird masks walk out. They are naked and their bodies are hairless, smooth shaven. In the dim lighting their ages are near impossible to determine. There is a crow with feathers so black its beak appears to spring forth from nothingness, an owl with feathers the color of copper and yellow eyes large enough to swallow the room, a sleek falcon with a beak partially open in an avian grin, and the fourth bird head is a cross between a peacock and a parrot, with its garish blue, yellow, and green, the feathers standing high above its eyes like ancient, forbidding towers.

They fan out and walk toward Ben without speaking and without ceremony. The soles of their bare feet gently slap on the hardwood floor. The man in the brightest-colored bird mask must be Mr. Wheatley (and/or Mr. H_____), as there are liver spots, wrinkles, and other evidence of age on his skin, but the muscles beneath are surprisingly taut, defined.

Mr. Wheatley takes the bird head out of Ben's hands and forces it over his head. Ben breathes rapidly, as though prepping for a dive into deep water, and the feathers flit past his eyes, an all-encompassing darkness envelops him, and a warmth in the darkness, one that both suffocates and caresses, and then he can see, although not as he could see before. While the surrounding environment of the apartment dims, viewed through an ultraviolet, film-negative spectrum, the bird feathers become spectacular firework displays of colors; secret colors that he was blind to only a moment ago, colors beyond description. That Ben might never see those colors again is a sudden and great sadness. As beautiful as the bird heads are, their owners' naked human bodies, with their jiggling and swaying body parts, are ugly, weak, flawed, ill designed, and Ben can't help but think of how he could snatch their tender bits in the vise of his beak.

The two men and two women quickly remove Ben's clothes. The Crow says, "Kittypants is waiting to be found and retrieved. He didn't fly away," and they lead him across the living room to the door from which they'd emerged. Ben is terrified that she's talking about him. He is not sure who he is, who he is supposed to be.

Through the door is a room with a king-sized mattress claiming most of the space. There is no bed frame or box spring, only the mattress on the floor. The mattress has not been made up; there are no bedcovers. There is a pile of dried leaves in the middle. Ben watches the pile closely and he believes there is a contour of a shape, of something underneath.

Ben stands at the foot of the mattress while the others move to flank the opposite sides. The lighting is different in this room. Everything is darker but somehow relayed in more detail. Their masks don't look like masks. There no clear lines of demarcation between head and body, between feather and skin. Is he, in fact, in the presence of gods? The feather colors have darkened as well, as though they aren't feathers at all but the skin of chameleons. Ben's relief at not being the character in the leaf pile is offset with the fear that he won't ever be able to remove his own bird head.

The others whisper, titter, and twitch, as though they sense his weakness or lack of commitment. The Crow asks, "Would you prefer talons or beak?" Her beak is mostly black, but a rough, scratchy brown shows through at the beak edges and its tip, as though the black coloring has been worn away from usage.

Ben says, "I would still prefer wings."

Something moves on the bed. Something rustles.

The voice of Mr. Wheatley says, "You cannot choose wings."

THE GETAWAY

There's this thing about living in Wormtown my older brother Joe doesn't get, or he does get it and doesn't want to admit it. We live in Worcester, stuck like a dart in the middle of Massachusetts. This isn't Boston. No ocean, just a river. No quaint historical bullshit that attracts tourists. Just hills, colleges, hospitals, and churches making the urban decay look a little prettier. It's not a good place to be, right? But Joe and the rest of the local artsy types, so desperate for the recognition they'll never get, they pump up and promote the nickname Wormtown like it means Worcester is some legit big city people would actually choose to live in, like Worcester is somehow important or any less damaged than it is because of a fucking name change. They brand themselves Wormtowners like they aren't as doomed as the rest of us. So I still use their fun little nickname, but only because it makes me bust a gut laughing.

It's five A.M. I'm sitting in the driver's seat of Henry's rusty Ford Explorer, tucked behind Ace's Pawnshop, which is on the corner of Main and Wellington. Engine on, tailgate up, interior lights off. Sitting here waiting for what's next.

Joe always says I never think ahead, that I only use my lizard brain. Right. He's a thirty-year-old painter who doesn't sell any paintings. But he's really a busboy at some restaurant over by Clark U., a trendy place that just opened and will probably close within the year. He cleans tables and gets no tips from the rich college kids and their yuppie professors. Joe has two maxed-out credit cards and lives with a between-jobs girlfriend and her five-year-old kid in a one-bedroom apartment. So much for thinking ahead, Joe. I'm the one pointed somewhere with both hands on the goddamn steering wheel.

My window is down when it doesn't need to be. There's nothing that I can't see from behind the glass. Mike asked me to do it. He said pretty please before leaving the SUV and going inside.

Goddamn, it's cold out. Didn't wear the right clothes for this. Just a brown flannel and some black jeans, steel-toed boots laced to the ankle. No jacket, and I left my black hoodie at the apartment. If that's my only fuck-up, we'll be okay. Winter is coming early. The black gloves don't keep my hands warm. I take my hands off the wheel and rub them together, then slouch into the seat.

Gunshots. A quick burst of two. I think. Then a third after a pause long enough to be uncomfortable for everyone. The shots are all muffled, coming from inside the pawnshop, but still, somehow, they sound like city-sized phone books hitting the floor after a big drop. There weren't supposed to be any gunshots. Gunshots mean big trouble. There wasn't supposed to be any big trouble.

I suddenly have to go to the bathroom even though I did what Henry said and skipped my morning coffee. I stop breathing so loud. I can't see anything through the pawnshop's cage-covered windows. Still alone in the SUV in the empty lot, I shift from park to drive; my foot is heavy on the brake, and I put my hands back on the wheel where they're supposed to be. Ten and two.

The back door flies open and they all come running out at once, a group of shadows, arms and legs everywhere. No one shouts, they're not dumb enough to be human alarms, but they hiss and whisper orders at me, their humble driver, subtle shit like "Go, go, go" and "Let's get the fuck outta here."

Yes, sirs. I calmly roll up my window and watch them in the rearview mirror, everything happening slow and fast at the same time. They're circus clowns going backward, getting into the car instead of jumping out. Mike sits his heavy ass in the seat behind me, shaking the car. Greg slides in on the other side and rips off his ski mask like it's burning him, and he throws it on the car floor. He better remember to pick that up later and dump it. Greg isn't exactly known for paying attention to the details, for paying attention to anything. He shouldn't be on this job at all, never mind getting to go inside. Yeah, he grew up on the same street as us, but he's loose with everything, you know? Christ, he was fired from his bartending gig at Irish Times because he was caught skimming on back-to-back nights. Henry was nuts to use him, but you can't tell Henry anything. It's his show. And Henry, his ski mask is still pulled over his ham-sized face. He throws the duffel bag in the trunk, jumps in after it. I take my foot off the brake, start inching forward, still watching Henry, and he kind of flickers in the shadows. He pulls his little jerry-rigged rope and shuts the tailgate behind him.

I roll out of the pawnshop's rear lot, and they're all yelling at me. Mike actually says, "Step on it, Danny." Christ. I turn around to say something smart-ass, something to calm everyone the fuck down because the truth of it is, them all yelling go-go-go has got me on tilt. So scared I feel it in my fingers and toes and my tightening chest. Mike cuffs me in the ear with an open hand, turns me back around. My head rings and everything goes white for a second. Mike hitting me doesn't make me feel any better, but I manage to turn left on Main Street without crashing.

They're trying to talk over each other in the back. My ear burns, and I'm looking all over Main Street for blue and white lights, trying to stay focused, and trying to think ahead. I yell over my shoulder, and have to yell it twice, "You assholes gonna tell me what happened?"

Mike says, "Everything was going fine, got the cage open no problem, and then the tough guy over here decides to chuck the old man over the counter." Mike pauses, daring Greg to say something different. Greg is smart enough to keep quiet.

I can see it happening even though I wasn't there: The three of them jumped the old man at the back door, right? Henry knew the old guy was going to be there. This was Henry's gig. They're always his gigs. So they jumped him and went inside, persuaded the old man to open the front counter's cage. Henry talked to him slowly, calmly, hypnotizing the old man into believing everything would be okay. That's what Henry is good at. When we were kids, he'd talk us into stealing cigarettes and porn mags. So Henry was telling the old man that all was well, no one would get hurt, that he was going to go behind the counter with him, go to the register and then to the jewelry and watches kept in the lockboxes. It was then maybe the old guy said something and Greg didn't like it, or the guy gave Greg an odd look because Greg was always getting odd looks with his too-small-for-his-face eyes and a mouth like a cut on his face, or maybe Greg got some wild itch he had to scratch, or he was trying to prove how tough and crazy he was to Henry, and I won't say it to Mike right now, but it's still Henry's fault for taking Greg, for not planning for what Greg might do, which is throw a semiretired old man over the register counter.

Mike says, "And when the old man got up, he was holding—"

Greg cuts Mike's bedtime story short, and yells, "Hey! Hey!"

I'm looking through the small screen of the rearview mirror again and can't see much, only Greg turned around, kneeling, hands on top of the back seats, and he's looking into the trunk. He moves left, right, dancing around like a dog excited to go for a ride. Or maybe he really has to go to the bathroom like I do.

Greg says, "Where the fuck is Henry?"

Great. The kid is bat-shit crazy. Why doesn't Henry say something to him? Maybe Henry is waiting for Greg to stick his head over the seat so he can sucker-punch him, knock loose a few Chiclets.

Greg starts bitching at me about leaving Henry, about me fucking everything up, and he bounces off the car walls and seats like one of those superballs you can get for a quarter. Now I'm yelling, too, saying, "What do you mean?" and telling him to shut up, telling Mike to shut him up. No one answers me. I wish they would. Mike turns around next, but he's too big to turn completely around. Mostly he twists in his seat and cranes his melon-sized head toward the trunk.

Mike says, "He's not in here." He says it like it's the last line in a movie.

More Greg: "You left him there? You fucking left without him?"

Mike repeats himself. "He's not in here."

"Wait, wait, wait." I say bullshit to all that. "Henry? Henry, quit fucking around!" No answer. He's still fucking around, right? Hiding in the back seat, the duffel bag on top of him. It's something he'd do. He isn't answering me, though.

"What did you do?"

I say, "I watched Henry throw the duffel bag in, and then he climbed into the trunk. I watched him. I swear to fucking god. He used the rope, pulled the tailgate shut behind him."

Greg jams his head between the front seats and screams into my ear, the same one that got cuffed. The ear isn't having a good time. "You didn't see shit. He isn't there."

"Enough," Mike says, and pulls Greg back and sticks him into his seat. "We need to think this through."

Oh goody. I'd do anything for Mike, but he's more of a brute squad kind of guy, more of a cuff-you-in-the-ear kind of guy, not the thinker. Thinking makes him more mad, more likely to start breaking shit.

"Turn around, Danny. We can't just leave him behind," says Greg.

Everything I got inside me drops into my shoes. Goddamn Henry. Him really not being in the car with us sinks in. Henry isn't here and it's my fault. But we can't turn around. "Yeah, brilliant idea, right? We'll swing by, pick him up on the corner, no problem." Then I say to Mike, "No going back, but I'm pulling over."

"Why?"

"I want to see what's in the trunk."

Greg says, "We can't leave Henry, man."

Mike is looking at me. Or the me in the rearview mirror. Maybe that me is different somehow. Mike says, "We're not turning around. You're not pulling over. We can't stop, not yet. Keep driving."

I nod. Maybe I'm wrong and Mike always was our thinker, not Henry. Mike's right. About everything. But if Mike told me to turn around, I would. He's known Henry as long as I have and we both owe him everything.

We pass hotels, the local arena, and the UMass medical center. Highway ramps all around us. I should probably take one, head out of Wormtown. I put on the interior lights instead. "Is the duffel bag there?"

Greg roots around in the trunk. "The shotgun and the duffel are here." He lifts the bag up, and it sounds like a pocket full of change. "There's a ton of blood. Oh man, what the fuck?"

"Did Henry get hit?" Never did hear the end of the pawnshop story, what happened after the old man went over the counter, and then the three gunshots.

Mike says, "The old man got off a shot, some semiautomatic piece of shit, but I didn't think he hit Henry. I was right next to him and he didn't say nothing about getting hit."

I don't ask about the other shots I heard. I see now what I didn't see before. I say, "All right. How did the tailgate get shut, then?"

"Huh?" Mike has his ski mask off. He rubs his shaved bald head and the thick stubble around his goatee. His eyes closed, arms folded across his chest. Greg sits back down, holding his hands out. Showing off the wet paint. It's red.

I say, "The tailgate. How'd it shut? While I was waiting for you guys, it was open. Like it was supposed to be. So I'm thinking I didn't see what I thought I saw, right? Henry was hit, got in the trunk, but because of the blood loss he wasn't strong enough to pull the tailgate closed behind him, and maybe I started moving before it was totally shut and he fell out onto the parking lot. But that doesn't seem right. How'd the tailgate get shut? I mean, what, did Henry get up after he fell out and shut it for us, tap the back twice and wish us bon voyage?"

Greg says, "Oh fuck. Nah, that ain't it. Henry ducked his ass out and he's gonna turn us in, pin the robbery and shooting on us. That blood came off the duffel bag, man. He didn't get hit. That bag was sitting in the old man's blood after Henry took care of him, right, Mike?"

Mike says, "I don't remember. I don't know."

Greg says, "That's gotta be it. He dumped the duffel bag and his shotgun back there to pin the whole thing on us while he slinks away. That fucker."

Mike turns to look at Greg, and looks at him like a kid staring at a real ugly bug about to get squished. "If he did, I don't blame him. It all went to shit because of you."

Greg doesn't fire back. He's scared of Mike. So am I. I drive into a residential neighborhood and early-morning commuters are starting to fill the roads. Maybe that's good. We can lose ourselves in the everyday traffic.

Greg says, "So what do we do now, boys? Where we gonna go?"

We're supposed to drive across Wormtown, into Auburn, to Henry's old girlfriend's farmhouse. Seemed like a good plan at the time. Now I can see all the gaping cartoon-mouse holes in everything. Maybe my brother Joe was right. I don't think ahead.

Mike says, "We're not going to her house. We're gonna play it like Henry is ratting us out."

"What if he isn't?" I say. I mean it, too. Because it doesn't feel right. It doesn't feel like Henry. Even with Greg blowing it all up like he did, Henry wouldn't play us. Henry has always taken care of us. He's fifteen years older than me and he worked at the Mobil a few blocks from where I grew up. Him and his early gray hair. He looked like someone's dad. He saved us a couple of times when me and Mike were walking home from school and got jumped by some kids. The second time they jumped us, he busted their heads open with a bike chain. So Henry kept us safe, took us for rides around Worcester, would sit and watch as we bent car antennas and broke windows near the Holy Cross and Clark campuses. Henry would sell us weed, and eventually, we helped him sell to our friends. By *we* I mean me and Mike. My brother Joe didn't like or trust Henry, wouldn't come out with us ever. I tried telling him that Henry was a good guy, that he was fun, that he was one of us, but Joe didn't care, wouldn't listen to me. He never listened to me. Stubborn ass would pull the oldest-in-the-family bullshit about knowing what was best. So I went out with Mike and Henry, and Joe, he stayed home with Grandma and painted his goddamn pictures while she watched TV.

Mike says, "Even if he isn't, we still can't show up at that farmhouse without him."

Greg starts swearing and crying into his hands. Like that'll help. Then he gets back into his old tune. "Fuck. What if we left him? We can't just leave him. Maybe he's hiding in a Dumpster or something, back near the pawnshop, waiting for us to come back. Someone call him. Mike, you call him."

"We can't. No calls."

Mike is right again. Especially if we left a bloody Henry in the parking lot. Cops and/or ambulance would definitely have him by now. We can't be on any phone records today.

Then it hits me, suddenly. Where we can go. Good a place as any for a half-assed getaway, or some kind of last stand.

I say, "I know where we can go, boys."

The trip is going to be longer than it has to be. Need to avoid the Mass Pike and its tollbooths and cameras. So we go north on 190, then we'll hit Route 2 West, then 91 North, then over the river and through the woods to my grandma's old lake house in Hinsdale, Vermont, a one-cow town outside of Brattleboro. It's not her place anymore, but it's no one's place anymore, either. My great-grandmother had the tiny two-bedroom bungalow built next to a private lake. I don't even remember the lake's name. Something long and with a lot of consonants.

It's not Grandma's place anymore because her family never really owned the land. They got the place on a ninety-year lease. Grandma died two years ago, and so did the lease. The state took the land back, wouldn't offer a new lease, and talked about using the house and lake for some electric company outpost or some shit like that. I didn't take that estate meeting well and left Joe to the room and the lawyers. Two years ago is the last time I was up there with Joe. The two of us and a Dumpster. Didn't save anything.

Far as I know, nothing has been done with the run-down place, and I can't imagine anyone would use it, completely out in the boonies with only a five-mile-long, one-lane dirt road as access to the property. I guess we'll find out.

We've been on 190 for almost half an hour. Finally turning onto Route 2. We've left our cell phones on in case Henry decides to call or text us. Nothing. Same kind of nothing on the radio, too.

I pull my cell out of my pocket and stare at the screen. I kinda want Joe to call, too. Not that I could answer his call or anything. Not that we've talked to each other in a month or so. Not after the last time I called him, and he bitched me out for having no real job and still hanging around Henry.

Greg can't be quiet for too long, so he starts in on another of his cute little rants. Mike's gonna pop Greg's head off like he's a dandelion if he keeps it up. Greg says, "This is a big mistake. Going to a place we don't even know we can go to. Great fucking plan."

Mike says, "It'll work out."

Greg rubs his head and face. "I feel like shit and you two idiots are making it worse." He's lathering himself up, breathing heavy, blinking like his eyelids are hummingbirds, in total freak-out mode. He says, "How about we pull over at a rest stop, dump the shotgun and bag, instead of carrying the shit around with us? Might as well be driving with 'we did it' painted on the windows."

We should think about dumping that stuff. Mike won't have any of it, would never admit that Greg was right about anything.

Mike says, "We ain't stopping. We'll dump the stuff when we get up there."

Greg closes his eyes, holds a hand to his mouth almost like he's going to puke. "Dump it at the lake house? That's fucking retarded!"

I say, "Easy, Greg."

"Even if we get there, which we won't, and find the place empty, which we fucking won't, we're gonna do what? Set up a happy house and then dump the shit in the lake? At the same lake we're staying at? Nice. They'd never find that shit, right?" Greg's voice goes higher and louder, getting shrill, his face turning red.

I turn around because I want to actually see Mike punch him instead of watching it in the rearview mirror. And then Greg's voice cuts out, midrant. He looks at us, mouth open, eyes wide, and his face crumbles, slides away, like something broke, and I turn back around fast, because that look on his face, I can't watch that, can't, and whatever happens next will be better seen from the safety of my rearview mirror.

So now I'm looking in that glass and I've lost Greg. Can't find him. Then he's there again, and he flickers. In and out of the mirror. He's not moving. He flickers like a goddamn lightbulb.

I turn back around. Greg's throat is gone. It's all just red pulp. Blood leaks out of Greg's eyes, nose, and ears, and his mouth is open and keeps opening, a silent scream, and how does his mouth keep going like that? and his eyes opening too, the whites gone all red, then worse than a scream, this horrible whisper from his ruined throat, a hiss, a leaking of air, and he winks out. No more flickering light. Blood mists the rear passenger window and Greg's seat, but he's not sitting in the back seat. He's not there. He's gone.

Mike screams Greg's name and kicks and punches the back of my seat, the door, the ceiling. I turn back around and I'm doing ninety, didn't realize it, and am about to plow into the back of a tractor trailer. I brake and swerve onto the shoulder, rumble strip, then grass and dirt, and manage to stop the SUV. Mike is still screaming. I look at the dash, the speedometer reading zero, the road, but don't really see anything other than Greg's face, before, before he what?

I yell to Mike: "Before he what? Before he what?"

"I don't know, Danny. Just go. Just keep driving."

"What?"

"Keep fucking driving. Just keep driving, keep driving . . ." Mike repeats himself and keeps on repeating himself.

I want to dive out of the car and run away and keep running. But I don't. I listen to Mike. I drive. Pull off the shoulder and onto the highway. I keep driving and try not to look into the rearview.

Overcast. The clouds are low and getting lower. North on I-91 and Mike sits in the middle of the back seat, filling my rearview. He watches himself. Making sure he's still there, maybe. I'm watching him, too, him holding Henry's sawed-off shotgun. Every few minutes his hands get to shaking. The gunmetal vibrates in his hands.

I've tried slowing down, pulling off the road or onto seemingly empty rest areas, but Mike won't have it. He threatens to shoot me in the head if I stop. Says that I have to keep driving. Keep going. I keep going, more because I'm scared and don't know what else to do. I know Mike won't shoot me, would never shoot me. Still.

"Hey, Mike."

"Still here."

"Need to think about this. Back at the pawnshop. Did that old guy shoot Henry?"

"It happened so fast. He jumped up with that gun pointed at us and . . . I can't remember, Danny."

"Did he shoot Greg, too?"

Mike shakes his head, and it turns into a shrug of the shoulders, and that turns into his hands shaking all over again.

I don't ask Mike if he thinks what happened to Greg happened to Henry. I don't ask Mike about the three gunshots I heard. I don't ask Mike if he thinks what happened to Greg will happen to him. I know Mike's answer to the questions. And I know mine.

We cross the border into Vermont. Things feel kind of funny in the car. The air all wrong. Too light. Or too heavy.

Mike says, "Remember that one summer your grandma let me come up to the lake house?"

"What? Yeah, of course I remember. Grandma never called to run it by your mom and you didn't tell your mom you were going and by the time we got back the cops had put up posters on half the telephone poles in Wormtown."

Mike breathes through his nose. Almost sounds like a laugh. He says, "That was the first time I'd ever been in Vermont. This is my second." I watch Mike talking in the rearview mirror. Maybe if I focus hard enough on watching him he won't disappear.

"You need to get out more often."

"Henry or Greg ever go up?"

"Fuck no. Greg would've burnt the place down trying to make toast. Just you, man. And Grandma didn't know about Henry."

"She knew. She told me we shouldn't be spending time with a stranger in the neighborhood that much older than us. She told me it wasn't right."

"When did she tell you that?"

"At the lake house. It was the only time she talked to me the whole week up there." Mike laughs for real this time. "I loved it up there, Danny. I really did. But man, it was really weird, too. Your grandmother would cook us meals and make our beds, but I remember her not talking much at all and spending most of the week smoking her Lucky Strikes on the dock, going for walks by herself, leaving us alone."

I say, "She did the same shit back home." Grandma fed us but would kick me and Joe out of the apartment until it got dark out, and Joe would usually go off on his own, not let me come with him. If it was raining or something and we couldn't go out, she'd stay in her room with a book or her little black-and-white TV. Away from us.

"I'm not feeling right, Danny." Mike rubs a forearm across his forehead. Doesn't let go of the gun. His voice sounds smaller, farther away, coming from another room.

"We're almost there, Mike." I say it without thinking. I don't know what to do.

"I know your grandma ignored us all at your home. But it was different up there, all by ourselves, away from the city and everything. Up there, I really noticed it. I got up earlier than you and your brother a couple of mornings and spied on her. She'd stare into the mountains or into nowhere, really. It was like we weren't even there, Danny. I'm getting fucking worried, maybe we were never there. Oh shit, Danny, I don't feel right."

"I'm pulling over, Mike. You relax. Keep talking to me." We're only ten miles from the exit, not that it matters. I slowly pull over onto the shoulder and I want to believe that if we just get out of the car, then we'll be okay, he'll be okay. But there were three shots.

Mike's eyes are closed and he's concentrating hard on something. Brow folding in on itself, upper lip shaking like an earthquake. He says, "Don't know how she could ignore you and Joe fighting the way you did. You fought over everything. Made me feel really, I don't know, uncomfortable. That probably sounds messed up coming from me. But I don't know, man, it didn't feel right. Wanted to kick both your heads in by the end of the vacation."

"Wish you were here, send us a postcard, right? Mike, listen, the car is stopped. We're going to get out. Walk around. Get some fresh air, all right?" I say, then I lie to him: "It'll help."

"What was the name of the card game you guys always played?"

"Cribbage. Joe always tried cheating me on the counts."

"Nah, you were too dumb to count the points right and Joe would call you on it and—" Mike stops talking and slowly fades out.

I scream his name and he comes back. He looks like Greg did.

Bleeding from everywhere. There's a dime-sized hole in his forehead, and it's growing. He opens his mouth but can't speak.

I call his name, not that his name works anymore, right? I ask him if he's still with me. I ask him to say something.

Mike whimpers like a goddamn dog that had his leg stepped on, and he slides across the back seat, out the door, and onto the shoulder of the highway, carrying the shotgun.

I get out, sprint around the front of the car, my own ears ringing, but not because of the cuff in the head he gave me forever ago. Mike stumbles, turns around aimlessly, his feet lost in a circle. His eyes are rolled back in his head. He puts the barrels of the sawed-off in his mouth. He pulls the trigger and disappears. He disappears and pulls the trigger. Which came first? Fuck if I know, but there's nothing left of him but a fog of blood, and the shotgun drops to the pavement after hovering in the air for an impossible second.

Earlier, after telling Greg and Mike my getaway plan, I was more than a little worried I wouldn't remember how to get to the lake house. But I remember. Every turn.

I'm not feeling so great. Don't know if it's because I watched Greg and Mike (and goddamn Henry, I saw him flicker in the rearview, in the dark, too, you betcha) and I only think I'm feeling what they were feeling. Joe always said I was nothing but a follower. Fucking Joe.

So there's that, and now I'm thinking about the shots I heard. Did I hear three? Or was it four? The first two came in a quick burst, one right after the other, piggybacking. Then a pause. Then a third. But it could've been three shots in that quick burst. And how long was that pause? I really can't remember now.

I drive down the long dirt road. I'm the only one out here. Within sight of both lake and house, there's a small chain-link fence across the road. I plow through it and park next to the house. The white shingles have gone green with mold. The roof is missing tiles and tar and is sunken in parts. The screened porch is missing its screens. If a house falls apart in the woods and nobody's there, will anyone miss it?

This is where I spent so many quiet and solitary summer weeks with Grandma and Joe, but not really with them. Joe painted, and she smoked and walked. This place here, this is where I learned to hate them.

In Wormtown, it was different. I had Mike and Henry. I kept busy and didn't have time to think about how fucked up it all was. I miss Mike. Really miss him already, like he's been gone for years instead of minutes.

Now that I'm here, I'm afraid of the house. Like if I stare at the porch too long, I might see Grandma there, sitting in a chair, looking out over the lake, seeing whatever it was she saw, and smoking those Lucky Strikes. And what if now, right now, she finally turns to look at me, to see me?

I spin the car around and park it so I'm facing the lake instead of the house. It doesn't help. I feel the house and Grandma somewhere behind me.

Not sure if I'll get reception out here, but I take my cell out and call Joe. It goes through. He picks up, says, "Hey."

"Hey."

We don't say anything else. We sit and stew in the quiet. It feels, I don't know, thick. Like it always has. I'm thinking Joe maybe feels it, too. What'd Mike say? Being around me and Joe was uncomfortable. Sounds about right.

He says, "What do you want now, Danny? You want to borrow money that I don't have? Bail you out of jail again? Go call Henry if it is."

"Joe," I say. "Hey, Joe. I got something to tell you. It's important."

I pause and imagine what Henry, Greg, and Mike felt after they were shot and before they disappeared. "Hey, Joe," I say again. "Listen carefully. I'm up in Vermont, at the old place."

I roll down my window. Goddamn, it's cold out. Like I said earlier, didn't wear the right clothes for this. Just a brown flannel and some black jeans, steel-toed boots laced to the ankle. Still no jacket, and I left my black hoodie at the apartment. Too bad all that stuff I left behind won't disappear like they did. Like I might. Three shots or four?

"What?"

"Yeah. I'm here, by myself, Joe. The place looks fucking terrible. Rotting away to nothing."

"What are you doing up there?"

"I don't know. Trying to get away, I guess. Can't, though. Doesn't matter. I'm here, and I decided to call you. Because I'm thinking I should've told you something a long time ago. You listening? Here it is: Fuck you, Joe."

I drop the phone. It disappears somewhere below me. The black gloves I'm still wearing don't keep my hands warm. I rub my hands together, and I slouch into the seat. I'm not feeling good at all. Things getting heavy. Lake getting blurry.

The shotgun is on the seat next to me. I might pick it up, and then fade away.

NINETEEN SNAPSHOTS OF DENNISPORT

ONE

That's me standing on the porch of the summer house we always rented. I drove by the old place today. Sunset Lane, which is off Depot Street. The house still has that aqua-green paint job. Four other summer houses crowd around it, almost like they're boxing it in, or protecting it. I don't remember those other houses being so right on top of each other, taking up the whole lane. Everything seemed bigger back then.

Look at me. Hard to believe how skinny and little I was. She's not in the shot, but my sister Liz, who was one year younger, towered over me and probably outweighed me by a solid twenty pounds. Would you look at that kid? Those legs are skinnier and whiter than the porch slats. This was, what, 1986, so I'd just turned thirteen. This is the first picture on that vacation roll. I always had to be in the roll's first picture by myself. It was my thing.

TWO

That's my mother carrying the towels. She already looks aggravated. I would've been, too. None of us kids helped to unpack. The other woman is her younger sister, my aunt Christine. She was my coolest aunt. She lived in Boston and always liked to play games or take us kids to the movies. I think that's an emergency rainy-day puzzle box tucked under her arm. Aunt Christine and my parents were in their mid-thirties. Jesus, everyone was so young. People don't do that anymore, do they? Have kids so young.

My cheap camera makes everyone look so far away. It broke before the end of the summer. That group of people running away, on the right side of the house, they're hard to make out, but that's my younger brother, Ronnie, slung over my dad's shoulder. He stole Dad's floppy Budweiser hat and tried to make a quick escape. You can kind of see the hat bunched up in one hand. Ronnie was eight and built like a hobbit. Liz was tickling Ronnie, trying to help Dad. She always took his side over ours.

THREE

Here's Ronnie and his summer buzz cut, standing in a big sand pit we spent most of the day digging. Can't really tell in the picture but he had this white patch of hair on the right side of his head. Buzzed that short, it looked like the map of some island country.

The sand at the bottom of that pit was shockingly wet and cold. I couldn't admit it to Ronnie, but we got to a point where I didn't want to stick my head in and reach down to dig anymore. I was a big scaredy cat. Always was, especially compared to Ronnie.

We're on one of those Nantucket Sound beaches off Old Wharf Road. I remember the road as a long string of nameless hotels and motels and restaurants and beaches fitting together, squares on a chessboard. In this picture, we're at the public beach next to what's now called the Edgewater Beach Resort. I don't remember what was there back then. Isn't that terrible? So many of the little details always go missing. Maybe if I hadn't been too preoccupied with taking pictures, I would remember more.

Check this out: I caught it by accident, but those legs there, upper right corner, those are my dad's legs. He was following Aunt Christine to the water, but then he stopped to talk to some big guy wearing long pants, shoes, and a yellow shirt. The yellow shirt I remember vividly. I didn't get a great look at him otherwise, but I remember him being bigger and older than Dad.

I asked Ronnie who Dad was talking to. Ronnie didn't know. We waited for Dad to come back, we wanted to bury him in the pit since it was too deep for either one of us. When he got back and we asked who he was talking to, he said, "Just some guy." We were all used to Dad talking to random people at the grocery store, baseball game, walking down the street, didn't matter to him. Used to embarrass the hell out of us (especially Liz) all the time. Talking to strangers and getting them to laugh or at least smile was simply what he did.

Ronnie and I tried to sneak up behind Dad and push him into the pit. He threw us in instead. I knocked heads with Ronnie. We were fine, but I got real mad at my father, mad like only a new teenager can. Dad didn't care. He held us down and buried us in the sand.

FOUR

Rainy day picture. The choice was go with Dad, who went off by himself to pick up groceries, or stay in the house and work on a puzzle with everyone else. I stayed, but I hated puzzles, so I sat and listened to Def Leppard and the Scorpions on my Walkman.

No one really likes puzzles. Mom, Aunt Christine, Liz, and Ronnie don't look excited or at all happy. You can tell by the way Mom has her arms crossed and is turned away from the table. They were all out of patience and annoyed with one another.

That's how I remember the puzzles ending: nothing getting solved and people walking away muttering to themselves.

FIVE

Here we are playing Wiffle ball with the boys who stayed in the house next to us. I don't remember their names. They were from Jersey. The tall redhead was my age and had terrible acne. Looked like his skin hurt all the time. The short redhead was a couple of years older than Ronnie, had round Mr. Peabody glasses, and instead of acne his face was full of freckles. They were geekier than I was, which is saying something. Back home kids at school and in the neighborhood picked on me a lot, and I never said boo. But Dennisport wasn't home, it was somewhere else, and I became the de facto leader of our little summer group: me, my brother (sis Liz wouldn't be seen with any of us), the Jersey Reds.

The first couple of days we tried following around this girl from Italy, Isabella. *Her* name I remember. She was only twelve, which was younger than my thirteen obviously, but she looked older than me. She didn't speak any English, had curly light brown hair down to her butt, and wore short-shorts with white trim. She tolerated us for a bit but ended up hanging around with a group of kids older than us.

When we weren't following Isabella around, we spied on my father.

SIX

Yeah, I took a picture of my hand holding a glass bottle of Coke. There was this small motel down Old Wharf, right before one of the public beaches, that had an antique Coke bottle vending machine. It was expensive, and the bottles were small, held less than cans, but I was convinced the Coke tasted better in glass bottles.

It was down here at the vending machine where we first started spying on my father. Ronnie saw him walking across the sand-filled motel parking lot. Him in his thick black beard, already tan, and he was muscular in a wiry kind of way. I used to obsess over how different I was from my father.

Us kids instinctively ducked behind a parked car, our group wordlessly deciding we were going to jump out and scare Dad or try and tackle him into some nearby sand dune. No way the four of us could've taken him.

He didn't walk by us, though. He veered off toward a set of motel rooms. He stopped seemingly at random and knocked on a blue door. The door opened and he went inside. No greeting or anything, he just went in and the door shut behind him.

Spying on your dad is a younger kid's game, for sure. But being on vacation, away from home like that, away from who you were (particularly if you didn't like who you were), was like permission to be and act younger. Unless Isabella was around, of course.

So we tried waiting Dad out, but he didn't walk back through that blue door. We got bored and went to the beach.

SEVEN

Ronnie took this picture without me knowing. The younger Jersey Red said that maybe my dad was cheating on my mother with the motel maid. So I jumped him and put him in this headlock and forced him into the water. I remember not feeling all that strong, but he let me hold on and give him his fair share of noogies.

EIGHT

That's the same Coke-bottle motel. Early the next morning Dad said he was going out for a jog. Ronnie and I followed him. We both stayed quiet, taking this much more seriously than the game it supposedly was.

I tried getting a shot with the blue door open, hoping I could see who was behind it, but clearly I failed. I mean, it's partially open and when I first got this picture developed, if you looked hard enough, you could see the ghost of my father's shoulder disappearing in the shadow of the room. But you can't see it anymore.

NINE

We're in some record store in downtown Yarmouth. That's a picture of the wall of T-shirts, and the Scorpions one there in the middle that I couldn't buy. I'd already spent my money on a Sandy Koufax baseball card at the card shop next door. It wasn't his rookie year card, but a 1962 Topps that was still pretty sweet.

That afternoon was kind of a slog through the gift shops and kitsch stores. We tried to be good little tourists. It was hot, the streets were crowded, and other than the candy store (I filled up on saltwater taffy and Nerds), we all wanted to go to different places. I fought with Liz, who didn't want to go anywhere. Mom and Dad fought over where to eat. You could tell Aunt Christine was pissed, because she took Ronnie off on her own. Then Liz and Mom, arguing with each other but quietly at least, went off. I went with Dad to the baseball card store, then the record store, and Dad wouldn't buy me anything.

When we all met back later, Ronnie was smiling and carrying monster movie posters. The kid was taunting me with them. I whined to

Dad how come he wouldn't buy me a lousy T-shirt. Dad asked me how old I was in a way that made everyone go quiet.

TEN

I moved this picture to the end of the album. Notice how the empty rectangle of space is a different shade of green compared to the rest of the page. It's darker. And it's ironic that the original or true color of the photo album page was preserved by the photo, preserved by that piece of the past.

ELEVEN

This one's blurry because Ronnie hit my elbow as I was taking the shot of the movie marquee. He did it on purpose. I punched him in the shoulder and almost went at it with him right there in line. We were on edge because we were both nervous about how scary the movie was going to be. At least, I was on edge. Ronnie had seen tons of horror movies on cable, but this was going to be his first in a theater. He didn't say much as a kid, but he'd been talking about seeing this movie all day long.

Dad and Aunt Christine were taking us to see the remake of *The Fly*. Mom stayed home by herself and played solitaire. She said she didn't like horror movies, but she'd been staying back at the house by herself a lot that vacation.

I arranged it so Liz sat on the aisle, then Ronnie, me, Dad, and Aunt Christine. During the movie Liz and Ronnie whispered jokes to each other, and Dad and Aunt Christine did the same. I hugged my knees to my chest and white-knuckled the whole flick. The slow and inexorable transformation of nice-guy mad scientist Jeff Goldblum into Brundlefly was terrifying, revolting, and really kind of sad in a way I couldn't explain. I'd sneak peeks at Dad to make sure he wasn't changing, wasn't melting before my eyes, and that he looked like he was supposed to.

Then there was that gross end scene, where Brundlefly vomited up his digestive enzymes on the guy's hand and melted it. Man, I lost my breath and my legs started moving like I was going to up and run out of the theater.

I looked away and watched Dad watching the movie instead. And during those screams and other horrible violent sounds of Brundle-fly's demise happening somewhere on that movie screen, I almost asked Dad who he was seeing in that motel.

TWELVE

On Main Street, not too far from our rental, near the corner of routes 28 and 134, there was a pocket of kiddie places: an ice cream shack, an old bumper car place, and a trampoline fun park. It was just me, Ronnie, and Dad. The trampolines were sunk into the ground, surrounded by gravel. When you landed, it felt like you were shrinking or melting away like Brundlefly.

This is a picture of the parking lot at the bumper car place. We did the bumpers before ice cream, but after trampolines. Before this shot, everyone, even people I didn't know, would drive their bumper cars into Dad because he was laughing the loudest, calling people out, being a goof. Like I said, everyone loved him.

Ronnie and I got back in line for a second and third go-round on the bumpers. Dad went out to the parking lot. I couldn't follow him outside without being too obvious. Instead, from the bumper car line, I tried to get a shot of him. I couldn't see who he was talking to, but I heard him talking. All you can see here is a screen window and some cars in the lot. There was a better view of the lot from the bumper car floor, but every time I was close to seeing who he was talking to, I got blindsided, usually by Ronnie.

THIRTEEN

This is a picture of the first and only summer group meeting I called in my bedroom. It's a good action shot. That white blur there is the pillow I threw at the Jersey Reds before snapping the picture.

We started off talking about music. They liked rap, which was typical Jersey, right? Then we talked about Isabella and trying to get her to come with us to the ice cream place on Sea Street. Then we talked about girlfriends back home. None of us had any. But in a fit of personal confession that was clearly out of place, I admitted to having a terrible, hopeless crush on a girl named JJ Katz. The Jersey Reds thought that was the funniest thing they'd ever heard and spent ten minutes shouting *dy-no-mite* like the guy from the TV show *Good Times*. I kind of lost my status as the leader of the group right there.

Then we talked about our theories of what my father was up to. When I say we, I'm not including Ronnie. He sat there and didn't say anything. Most of what was said wasn't serious and was part of the game, Dad as secret agent man kind of stuff, until I opened my yap and was again probably too honest for the moment, too honest for the room. I told them how my father would bet on football in the fall, how he'd bring home from work what he called his football cards. They were white cardboard rectangles, printed with a list of teams and point spreads. He'd pick four teams, or ten teams, or both, and sometimes, he'd let me pick a few of the teams for him.

I didn't really know anything about what was happening with Dad, but I think it sounded like I did.

I remember almost telling them about a few months before that vacation, when I was upstairs in my bedroom listening to my parents arguing in the kitchen, Dad saying, "It'll be okay," and "I'm sorry," and Mom too hysterical for me to understand, until she screamed "Fuck you," ran out of the kitchen, and kicked out one of the small plate-glass windows in the front door.

The Mr. Peabody glasses kid started in again with his your-father-was-hooking-up-with-another-woman theory. He said my father looked like the kind of guy who could get women to go to a hotel with him. Ronnie still didn't say anything, but I could tell he was upset. To be honest, I was kind of proud that my dad looked like that kind of guy, and it somehow meant that I was cooler than I was.

I held out my camera and told the Jersey Reds I had evidence and that it wasn't my dad with some other girl. They asked if I had any pictures of *dy-no-mite* JJ on my camera. That's when I threw the pillow and took the picture.

FOURTEEN

Dad came home from a morning jog with a black eye. He laughed and said he slid on some sand, fell, and hit his face on a duck-shaped mailbox. I was surprised he let me take this picture. I don't think he wanted me to, but what could he say or do with the rest of the family there in the kitchen, pointing and laughing at him?

FIFTEEN

All right, that's a picture of the girl from Italy, Isabella, walking away and waving at us. We'd tracked her down and asked her if she wanted to go for ice cream. She pretended not to understand what we were asking despite the Jersey Reds' embarrassing ice cream pantomime. Which was fine. I got a picture, anyway.

SIXTEEN

There's a time gap here with the pictures. I can't remember if there were more photos and I lost them, or if I didn't take them. Sometimes I wonder how much of this I would have remembered if there were no photos, no proof of what happened.

Here we are eating breakfast at the Egg & I. Everyone looks haggard and frazzled because there were only a few days left to the vacation. The Jersey Reds were gone. It was just us. We were all fighting and annoying one another. And again, maybe it's only the lens of elapsed time making it all clearer, but we were all on edge. Something was going on with Dad, but no one knew what, and no one was talking about it.

Aunt Christine and Mom are looking away from the camera and away from each other. Mom might be staring at the ashtray she filled. Liz has her hand in front of her face, and Ronnie, never quite the exhibitionist anyway, his face is a complete blank. He'd been like that since the morning of Dad's black eye, which was the same morning I told him about the big fight back home and Mom kicking the window out.

They're pissed off at me for taking a stupid picture of the table. Or maybe they were all thinking about Dad and asking themselves why he had to make a call from the pay phone three booths over.

SEVENTEEN

Check out this shot. This was the small private beach for our little Depot Street/Sunset Lane association, a patch of steeply sloped sand next to the big Ocean House restaurant. When it was high tide, it wasn't really even a beach—more like a dune, or a cliff of sand. I went to that beach today and I don't know if it's because of erosion or my memory exaggerated everything, but there's barely a discernible slope back there now.

Ronnie spent our second-to-last day of vacation running and jumping off the steep slope, catching major air, and crashing knee-deep into the sand at the bottom. He jumped so much, he had raspberries on his legs after.

I did it with him a few times, but the landing hurt my ankles. It was too steep for me. I went off to the side and climbed up the base of a rock jetty and asked what he thought was going on with Dad, and he said, "I don't know." I asked if he was going to get up wicked early with me to follow him on his jog. He said, "I don't know." And that was it. He jumped, climbed back up, and jumped.

This is a great shot of Ronnie in midjump, arms extended behind him, feet out in front, eyes closed. You look at this long enough, you start to expect him to land.

EIGHTEEN

There isn't much to see in this one, right? Too dark.

I woke up with the front screen door shutting. It bounced in the frame, hinges squeaking. That door is still squeaking as far as I am concerned. It was dark out, but I didn't look at a clock, didn't wake up Ronnie or anyone else. Just threw on my sneakers, grabbed my camera off the nightstand, and ran outside.

It was a cloudy night, and I couldn't see the moon or any stars. I didn't see Dad anywhere and was worried I had been too slow. The

streets were empty and so were the beaches and the restaurant parking lots. I headed toward the Coke-bottle motel and didn't see him
there either. But that room he usually went to, the motel door was
wide open, and inside, the lights were off. I ran as quietly as I could
across Old Wharf, then through the parking lot to another section of
the motel off to the right of the open door. I crept up to it with my back
pressed against the motel, camera held out. I was going to walk by the
open door, snap a picture, and bolt.

Then I heard something. It sounded far away, like it was carried
in by the ocean. It was someone crying. I knew it was Dad, even if I'd
never heard him like that before.

I ran to the motel beach but didn't see anything, so I worked my
way back to the Ocean House restaurant, to our little private beach
with its steep slope and rock jetty, and I ducked behind the jetty as I
found him. Only he wasn't alone. Another man was leading him into
the water.

It was too dark to see details, but I think there was a bag over Dad's
head. The other guy had something in his hand, a gun maybe. I don't
know. It was low tide, and they were walking way out there, were past
the jetty already, but only waist deep in water.

I didn't know what to do, so I took a picture. I don't know if either
of them saw the flash.

I didn't see the end, either. It was too dark and they were too far out.
Only the other man came back to the beach. I ducked down behind
the jetty. He walked by, a few feet away on the other side of the rocks.
I heard him breathing heavily.

I barely remember the rest of the night. Don't remember if I went
to the beach to look for Dad. I don't remember how long I stayed huddled behind the jetty and don't remember walking back to the house
and crawling into bed next to Ronnie. That was where I woke the next
morning. I didn't tell anyone what I saw. I was in shock. I was only
thirteen years old.

Two days later, his body washed up on shore. All the stories in the
papers were about a tourist drowning on a late-night swim.

After we were home, after the funeral, when I picked up my developed pictures, I thought then I'd go to the police, tell them everything,

show them everything. But the pictures didn't show anything, really, and too much time had passed, I was still afraid, and to be honest, I was mad at my father, mad he'd let something like that happen to him.

So, this picture. There isn't much to see in it, right? Too dark. When I looked at this—and I looked at this for years and years, every night before I went to bed, like the first picture of the motel room door I showed you—I thought if I looked hard enough, I could see him there in the picture. But you can only make out black water, the outline of the beach and the jetty. Nothing else. You can't see anything.

There's another picture I've been staring at for years, too.

TEN

This is what I moved to the last page. I took this after the T-shirt place, but before we all met back up again, so it was just me and Dad. A random picture of my father on the sidewalk of downtown Yarmouth, right? Look closer. Over his left shoulder. See that huge guy two store-fronts away, hiding under an awning, but not hiding? He's watching from behind reflective sunglasses and wearing a tight white polo shirt, wearing it like a threat, wearing it the same way he wore that yellow shirt. That's the same yellow-shirt guy from the beach Dad was talking to on our first day of vacation.

I've been staring at this picture of you for almost twenty-five years, a quarter of a century. It's hard to understand how all that time passed so quickly. In many ways, I'm still that kid cowering behind the jetty. In other ways, I'm clearly not.

The funny thing is, I never planned for this. It's not like I've been searching for you all this time. I wasn't even looking for you when I saw you.

NINETEEN

The thing of it is, I don't even want to know why you did what you did. It does and it doesn't matter. Okay, I think I already know why. It's not that hard to figure out. And sure, a few years ago, I asked my mother about the big fight I'd heard and why she kicked out the window on the front door. She said that Dad had blown four grand to a bookie. Four grand was a lot of money in 1986, right? Sure it was.

You see this camera? It used to belong to my grandfather. You're probably about the same age as he was when he died. Anyway, I kept the camera in working condition. Do you remember Polaroids? I'm sure you do. I'm sure you remember lots of things.

So this is you, duct-taped to a chair in our hotel room. It's hard to see with the tape over your mouth, the bruises, the dried blood, but it's you. I know, compared to the you in the other picture, this you is the grotesque Brundlefly. But this was and is you, even if you are so much smaller than you used to be.

I've brought you back down to Dennisport. Just like old times, right? We're at the Sea Shell Hotel next to the Ocean House restaurant. I put the room on your card, but don't worry, it's off-season, so I got a great room rate.

This is the last picture on the last page of my album. I took this picture while you weren't awake. Even for someone of your advanced age, you sure do sleep at lot.

I'm not 100 percent sure what I want out of this. I could leave you here and go back home to my wife and kid. Maybe you'd call the police or come after me yourself, or come after me with a little help. Maybe you wouldn't do anything. Maybe everything would be okay if I unwrapped you and watched you limp out of here, old man that you are, and more than a little broken. That might be enough for me.

Maybe later tonight, I'll take you by the hand, the one that's shaking even now when it's taped behind your back, and we'll take a walk together out into the water, the very same water. But it's not the same water, it's different. Maybe that's okay.

So maybe we'll walk out there, past the jetty, up to our waists in water, and just stand there and feel the cold all around us. Then maybe, at the very least, you'll admit who you are and what you did to him and what you did to me.

WHERE WE ALL WILL BE

Zane is lying on the couch, wrapped only in a faded yellow sheet, with the TV on and muted. More troubling than an aching back and congested head is that relocating from the bedroom to the couch isn't a decision he remembers making.

The old couch has frayed holes in the upholstery and more than a few loose springs. Whenever he shifts his body weight, metallic gongs echo as though there's a cavernous space, a hidden passageway somewhere beneath the tattered cushions.

The weak light of a low, winter-morning sun colors the room in muted tones. He could simply fall back asleep, but the thought of sleeping more, out in the open, in the living room, seems decadent.

Yawning and still wrapped in the sheet, Zane shuffles into the kitchen. He wants coffee, his stimulant of choice now that he's been off Ritalin since late spring. There's no coffee, so orange juice filled with pulp will have to do. He drinks a glass, looking out the kitchen window. His parents must've left for work already. Neither car is in the driveway.

Zane assumed his parents would redecorate the house the nanosecond he left for college. He didn't anticipate the house being preserved, mothballed. Everything has changed and nothing has changed. They can't possibly be sentimental about the couch, can they? Maybe their keeping it prominently displayed in the living room isn't an act of preservation, but of perseveration.

Zane is home on his first winter break from Assumption College. He likes his classes and professors, who have been more accommodating to him and his academic needs than he was led to believe they would be.

His two roommates are typically spoiled assholes from affluent Wellesley, but harmless ones. Zane made other friends easily enough, like always. Zane would describe his friends as he would describe himself: laid-back to the point of being unsure, sometimes painfully and annoyingly so; hardworking but not overly ambitious; loyal to some; distrustful to most.

There were times during the semester while attending the requisite parties, standing in a circle, everyone holding a red plastic cup of beer or Kool-Aid mixed with cheap vodka, when Zane couldn't help but feel they were all looking at one another and thinking: What are we doing here? Why am I here with you? What are we going to do next?

Zane returns to the couch with his pulpy orange juice and unmutes the TV. A British woman teaches a squat older couple how to train their willful Yorkshire terrier. He was watching *Animal Planet* in his sleep, apparently.

It's odd neither of his parents shut the TV off before leaving for work. Maybe they didn't want to disturb him.

He changes the channel to one of the twenty-four-hour cable news networks. There, the video is paused, or mostly paused; two flickering frames stuck in a loop. The quivering set of images is of a reporter, standing outdoors. There's a crowd behind her in a large field or some other vast space. The sky above is wide and grayish blue.

The reporter's blond head is askew, or goes askew as the images flicker. She faces the camera one moment; then the next, her head is turned, or caught in midturn. She's trying to see what's over her shoulder or what's behind her.

Her hands change positions as well. In one shot she holds an oversized but drooping microphone under her chin, and the next, her hands are at her side and empty. The news ticker at the bottom of the screen is illegible. Yellow letters and symbols overlap and blur.

Zane tries changing the channel and flipping it back, but the same schizophrenic scene remains. He tries the other news channels and gets only blank black screens. He quickly spins through the spectrum of pay TV. More than half of the channels are blacked out.

In the midst of his channel-hopping, Zane's father abruptly walks into the house and storms through the living room and into the kitchen. He comes in with such speed and purpose, Zane reacts as if he's been caught doing something wrong. He drops the remote control and sits up quick and straight, jostling the glass in his lap, spilling orange juice onto the sheet.

"Jesus, Dad? Did you, um, forget something?" Zane wipes the spill, balls up the yellow sheet, and carries it with him into the kitchen.

His father is a high school history teacher and track coach. He has been doing both for more than twenty years, famous for having missed only one day of school, for the birth of his son. So, why is he home now?

Hurrying around the room, his father opens cabinets and drawers and closes them just as quickly. When he finally sees Zane, he says, "I—I don't. I don't." His face contorts into a pained expression and he rubs his graying head with his hands.

Zane instantly calculates his father is only fifty-two years old, which he presumes is too young for Alzheimer's, although he can't be sure. Feeling as worried and confused as his father appears, Zane aches to do something helpful. He only thinks to say, "Hey, Dad, there's something wrong with the cable, I think. Got a number I should call? I can, you know, take care of that, if you want."

"What? No, no." His father's face flashes anger, and it's a face that's still scary and intimidating, if not somewhat diminished. His once-chiseled features have softened in age. "Not what—I don't. We. We don't, I mean, we do—" Then he sighs. His furrowed brow returns, and then he leaves the kitchen and wanders into his bedroom.

Zane follows, completely terrified, now thinking *stroke* or *aneurysm* or some horribly rare degenerative cognitive disorder. He has to get his cell phone, call Mom, ask her what he should do.

Inside his parents' bedroom all the bureau drawers are open, socks and parts of T-shirts hanging out like swollen tongues. His father is half inside the walk-in closet.

"Dad? Are you feeling okay? Do you need help?"

His father comes out, grabs Zane by the shoulders. His hands are still cold from being outside.

"Are you okay? Dad?"

His father squeezes Zane's shoulders. He's still a very strong man. He shakes his head and says, "I'm fine. We just. We just have to go, Zane. We have to go. Now." His shadow stretches over Zane, loosely fitting like a hand-me-down suit.

Zane twitches his head and long curly bangs fall over his eyes. "Where?"

His father sighs and growls, throws his hands up, so clearly frustrated Zane doesn't get it, never gets it. He says, "Come on. You—you know. Where we all will be."

It was early December nine years ago when Zane and his parents attended their introductory consultation with the Child Development Group. Zane was ten, in fourth grade, and struggling to finish almost all his in-school assignments on time. New behavioral issues were cropping up as well; harmless stuff, really, but increasingly described by his teacher as "impulsive."

The Group was a collection of three small offices tucked away in the corner of a three-story brick building in some town Zane had never been to before. The carpeting was green, like pool-table felt.

Dr. Colton requested that Zane take off his baseball hat while in her office. She smiled when she said it was her only rule. Zane tried to smile back, but he sort of shrugged his shoulders instead.

He held the hat in his lap. At one point during the meeting, the three adults in the room nodded their heads at Zane as they watched his fingers tapping and manipulating the baseball pins tacked to the brim, as if they'd discovered proof of who he was, who he was going to be.

The doctor's initial questions made him more uncomfortable because she asked if he thought he needed help with school. He didn't think he did, and when he said that, his parents' silence became another, wholly distinct and physical presence in the room.

After the first round of questions, Dr. Colton took out a rainbow-colored brain made of foam. The colors correlated to the brain's anatomy, and she explained to Zane which parts controlled what functions. She said that it was very likely that parts of his brain were simply wired differently from everyone else's.

He liked that she talked directly to him, but he found her gaze too intense to meet. He kept his head mostly down and stared at the green carpet.

There was talk of executive function skills, initiation, working memory, and impulse control. Dr. Colton asked him about his interests before sending him out into the waiting area so she could talk to his parents.

While sitting in the waiting area, Zane imagined he was shrinking in his chair, disappearing down into his shoes. They wouldn't know where he was when they came out to get him, and maybe they'd just take the empty shoes home.

The entire consultation took an hour. It ended with handshakes, smiles, and reassurances. Of course, there would be tests to come; tests that would require multiple dismissals from school and trips back to the town Zane had never been to before.

Zane and his father drove back home by themselves. Mom, having come straight from work, had her own car, and she planned to stop at the pharmacy on the way home. His father let Zane sit in the front seat. He patted Zane's leg and tousled his hair. The combination was his go-to form of affection now that Zane was older.

His father said, "You were great in there. Really great."

Zane shrugged. "Yeah."

"I think it's a good thing your brain is different from everyone else's."

Zane showed a quick curl of a smile and hid it under the brim of his baseball hat.

"So, buddy, what do you think? The doctor was nice, right? Think she can help?"

Zane said "Yeah" again, although he wasn't sure how she could help, or what exactly needed help. And what he really thought was too big, scary, and messy to describe. Zane looked out the car window and absently tugged at his seat belt.

"I'm proud of you, you know that, right?"

"Yeah." If his father didn't stop talking, he was going to start crying. He didn't know exactly why he would cry. He knew only that he would.

Likely sensing that an emotional storm from Zane was building, his father stopped asking questions. He patted Zane's leg again and let him pick songs to listen to from his phone. Zane picked the loudest and heaviest songs.

They didn't speak to each other again until they were almost home. It was dark out by the time they turned onto their street.

"Dad, put the high beams on." Zane sat up and scooted to the edge of the seat. Both hands went on the dash and the seat belt pulled tight across his chest.

That a car had high beams was a recent discovery, and Zane asking for his father to turn them on whenever they were on their street had become an obsession. He imagined all that extra light filled the dark spaces in his head. And, for no reason he could explain, he loved the little blue high-beam symbol in the dashboard.

His father complied, but said, "You make me crazy with the high beams."

Instead of spotlighting the section of woods across the street from their sleepy little house, the light reflected countless white dots floating in the air. His father had once said you couldn't really use the high beams in a snowstorm, that the extra light didn't help you see any better because the snow got in the way. But it wasn't snowing now.

"Man, look at all those moths," his father said, and he slowed the car down, creeping alongside the curve of their front yard.

"Wow. Why are there so many?" Zane had his right cheek pressed against the window, trying see how high up they went. The air was thick with thousands of white moths, each the size of a nickel. They were fluttering pieces of paper, bits of stuff leaking out of a teddy bear.

"It's too warm out. This is supposed to be December in New England, right? And it's, what"—his father tapped the digital temperature display on the car—"fifty-five degrees? That's just ridiculous."

Zane hadn't minded that it wasn't cold out today. But now, listening to his father, to how agitated he was becoming, he wasn't so sure.

Even at age ten, Zane was still sure his dad was the smartest guy in the world. If he said the warm weather was wrong, then it was wrong.

"So, because it's warm out when it shouldn't be, these moths were fooled into hatching or de-hibernating, or whatever it is they were doing. I mean, they shouldn't be out, flying around like this."

They pulled into their driveway and his father shifted into park but didn't shut the engine off. They sat in the idling car.

The high beams were on and the extra light trapped the swirling mass of moths like a tractor beam from some science fiction movie. Zane would've preferred the sci-fi explanation over what his father was telling him: there was something wrong with the weather, there was something wrong out there.

Zane suddenly felt like he was sinking again, this time into the car seat instead of his sneakers. He said, "So what's going to happen to all the moths?"

In the mad dash to keep up with his increasingly erratic father, Zane leaves his cell phone behind. He only has time to jump into jeans and sneakers and then grab his black hooded sweatshirt before sprinting out the front door.

Obviously, there's no way his father should be driving. After their standoff in his parents' bedroom and after his father told Zane to get ready because they had to go, Zane said he would go with him, but only if he was driving. Of course, there his father is, in the car by himself, already behind the wheel, honking the horn.

Twenty minutes later, they're on the interstate, stuck in traffic even though it's not rush hour. On both the northbound and southbound sides, the lanes are full, including the breakdown lanes.

There must be an accident up ahead. Zane tries the radio and gets only static. He leaves the radio on, hoping to elicit some sort of reaction from his father. The constant hiss is maddening.

Zane taps the dashboard nervously and wishes he had a steaming cup of coffee to fill his hands. He didn't tell his parents he is self-medicating with caffeine now; they think he is relying solely on study techniques and the college's academic support.

Zane says, "Dad, you have to answer me. Where are we going?"

"It'll be all right." The spaces between his words elongate. The radio's hiss bunches up in those gaps, gumming up his sentences like misplaced punctuation marks. "You'll see when you get there."

"Dad!"

"It's important. Okay? It's like this. It's like something. Something we all have to do. . . ." He trails off into mumbles again. His bits of nonsensical phrases and shards of broken words act as a simulacrum of speech; something his father might've said to him a long time ago.

He wonders why it's so hard to intervene, to tell his father that he's not well, demand that he pull over and let him take him home or to the hospital. He wonders why he can't simply tell his father that he's wrong.

The all-too-familiar feelings of disorientation and shame return because of his indecision. It's only being exacerbated by everything in the periphery not making sense: the blacked-out TV, the fuzzed-out radio, the endless traffic jam.

There's also this part of Zane, the kernel of him formed long ago, that wants to believe his father, wants to believe *in* his father, wants now to be like all those times they used to drive around together, just the two of them, with his father telling Zane the why and how of everything even when he didn't want to hear it.

"Hey, where's Mom? What about Mom?"

His father says, "She'll be—" There's a great and terrible pause. The radio is still on, and it sounds louder, as if one of them had turned it up. Neither of them has made a move toward the volume button.

Zane finishes the sentence. "Fine? How do you know she'll be fine?"

"No!" His father slams a fist down on the steering wheel. He sighs. The sighs become grunts and the grunts become words. "She'll be there. She'll be there already."

"*There?*" Zane is yelling now, overwhelmed, and on the verge of losing control.

"There!" His father turns toward Zane. He's wild eyed and smiling; it's a look of manic relief. "There. It's—you understand, don't you? You have to."

"No, I don't understand. Just tell me, Dad. Where is *there*, Dad? Where are we going? Where's everyone going?"

Zane looks away, out his window, at the other cars and their drivers. Many of them are alone. They stare straight ahead through their windshields. Some talk to themselves, mouths moving and their words forever trapped behind glass.

The moths. There were so many, fluttering into and over each other. They flew like they were panicking, like they knew the warm weather was some kind of dirty trick.

His father said, "Can they re-hibernate? Probably not, right? It's supposed to get cold again tomorrow. Or, you know, back to normal."

Then he said something else, which was so obvious, but horrible in its obviousness; a secret knowledge that was never a real secret.

What his father said, it sent Zane exploding out of the car and sprinting across the gravel driveway. The stones crunched under his feet.

He tried to run fast enough so that none of the moths would touch his skin. There were too many. Not touching them was an impossibility. Their slight bodies crashed into his head, brushed against his skin and lips, and got caught in the weave of his jacket.

Zane knew this wasn't right, none of this was right, and he was sure the moths, in their alien intelligence, knew it, too. Zane could not articulate these feelings, just as he could not tell his parents or Dr. Colton how he'd felt earlier.

He stood under the single-bulb lamp above his front door. The moths swarmed the fixture. They landed on the door and stuck to the glass panes that had collected condensation in the unusually warm and humid weather.

Zane tried to brush the moths off the glass. They were too frail and crumbled to pieces at his clumsy touch.

Standing there under the lamp, in a cloud of moths, Zane imagined that the collective beating of their thin wings formed a primitive song with a repetitive rhythm and a simple melody, one that was sweet, oddly familiar, yet made to be easily forgotten.

Later that night, after a pizza dinner, Zane sat on the couch next to his mother and ate popcorn, and they watched a rerun of *America's Funniest Home Videos*. She didn't press him with questions. They stayed up late together, with the two of them in his bed, under the covers. Using a small book light, they read comics about a boy and a tiger, and they talked quietly until he fell asleep.

Zane didn't tell her about Dad in the car saying it was good his brain was different from everyone else's. Zane didn't tell her about the moths or what Dad had said in the car, about how most of the moths would be dead in a few hours. How they'd all be dead by morning.

The traffic slows to a stop that doesn't start again. They abandon their car like everyone else.

They walk on the highway with hundreds and thousands of others. Zane tries to get his father to stop, to explain, to refute, to reject, to turn around. He doesn't.

Zane follows his father, finally giving in. The clear and focused will of everyone else around him is too much to deny.

There's no buzz or drone of conversation. No one talks. There are only the collective sounds of footprints, expelled breaths, groans of exertion from those having trouble walking such a distance. They walk for hours.

The sky is more purple than blue, more gray than purple. An inkblot sky, it's the color of static. Zane has lost track of time. He thinks the sun should be higher than it is, which is presumably hidden somewhere behind a strip of clouds ringing the horizon.

Eventually, the crowd veers off the highway, heading east. They don't use an exit ramp. Instead, they pour through the knocked-down soundproof barrier fencing, which has already been crushed and broken into pieces that will never be put back together again.

The ravenous crowd tosses aside parked cars like the afterthoughts they've become. They march over and through swing sets, storage sheds, and amateur gardens. Only the biggest trees and structures serve as obstacles in the inexorable path eastward.

This great migration cuts a swath through small woodlands, through suburban back and front yards, through industrial parks and strip mall lots. Manicured landscaping, fences, and other flimsy man-made delineators of land, property, and culture are destroyed, ground into the soil, rendered to be nothing more than the dead skin of history.

Zane struggles to keep pace with his father. He stumbles a few times and grabs his father's hand. His father doesn't acknowledge that his son is still there. He mumbles and sways left and right to some secret rhythm.

Zane is not tall and he cannot see above or beyond the people surrounding him without jumping up, without dowsing the increasingly infrequent gaps of space between swaying heads and bodies. The crowd continues to swell. Zane can't see its end in any direction.

There are very few landmarks with which to determine direction, position, or place. They could be anywhere. They could be nowhere.

Eventually, the air changes. It's no longer the stagnant air used and discarded by the thousands of pairs of indiscriminate lungs. This new air moves. An insistent wind blows in their faces and over their heads, out of the east. The wind brings the unmistakable smell and taste of salt and brine. The ocean is very close.

The ground under Zane's feet has gone soft, not that he can see his feet anymore while in the thick of the crowd. The people ahead of him are slowly making their way up a large hill. Sand dunes, perhaps.

Zane reaches to his left, for his father, and grabs hold of his sleeve. Only, that sleeve belongs to someone else: a tall, thin woman with a sharp nose wearing glasses and a black overcoat.

He thinks of his mother and feels guilty for not having looked for her. He is heartbroken, and he quickly apologizes to the woman for grabbing her sleeve. She doesn't say anything, doesn't even look at him.

Zane yells, "Dad!" and scans the crowd. There are too many people to focus upon any single one. Zane is weak-kneed with panic, even after he thinks he sees his father ahead of and above him, near the top of the dune.

Zane tries to pass and squeeze through the people ahead of him, but the sledding, as his father used to say, is tough. Walking uphill in the sand has become supremely difficult. The constant pushing and pressure from all sides challenge his equilibrium.

Zane finally crests the dune, and while standing at the top there's an explosion of sounds. There are the crashing waves, yes, but there's also the low and warbling thrum of the surrounding mass of humanity, of their moans and cries.

And below that wall of sound, underneath it all, Zane faintly hears what sounds like the high-pitched, discordant whine of microphone feedback. He tries to focus on it and gets the sense there's a pattern there, somewhere, but it's elusive. He can't track it.

While he is on the top of the dune for the briefest of moments, his vision isn't blocked or obscured. The people directly in front of him are now all below him. And below him, there is no beach, no jetties, only people: people up and down the coastline, people thrashing about in the choppy and icy water.

Zane has lost sight of his father again. There's a massive push from behind. He lurches forward and is pinned against the back of the person ahead of him. He loses his breath in a rush, his chest constricting with each attempted breath.

The pressure breaks when the person he's pressed up against falls and is swallowed up by the advancing crowd. Zane quickly bends and reaches down in an attempt to help, and he sees a terrible glimpse of the beach that is not the beach. The *soft* he's been walking upon is not in fact sand.

Zane is caught in a competing tide and is again rushed forward. The great, cascading roar is ahead of him: the pounding surf, last breaths, lost breaths, and a fragmented chant of *There. There.*

Frigid water licks his ankles. He tries to lift his feet out of the water, but there's nowhere else to put them. He screams for his father. Everyone pushes and converges from every direction.

When he is in water up past his knees, his feet go numb. The people ahead of him never turn around or away from the sea. There's no mass desperate lizard-brained attempt to keep from drowning.

A large wave crashes through Zane's section of the crowd. He manages to remain standing; others topple like bowling pins. Some get up. Some don't. The woman in the black overcoat is gone.

Zane scrambles around and presses his back into the remaining people in front of him for leverage. Now that he's turned around, he's face-to-face with the crowd. Their identical sets of unblinking eyes look through and beyond him.

The undertow tugs at Zane's legs and feet. He stumbles backward and comes precariously close to falling face-first into the water. There's someone directly beneath him. He can't see who it is.

Zane stops looking at their faces. He can't do it anymore. He reaches out, plants his hands on someone's shoulders, and he jumps and kicks and pulls himself up. He scrambles out of the water, above the water, using their flesh as hand- and footholds. He's out of the water and on top of the crowd.

Zane fights upstream. The wind buffeting him helps as he kicks and pulls. The crowd bears his weight like he's not there, a river carrying a log. However, his muscles quickly burn with exhaustion.

He rolls onto his back and finds that he hasn't progressed very far. The sea continues to gather its dead. Still on his back, resting and watching, Zane doesn't dwell on any single floating body too long for fear that he'll find either of his parents, for fear that he'll decide to join them.

Zane looks out past the static-colored sky and toward the edge of the darkening horizon. The color of it all is wrong. And now there are inky, oblong-shaped shadows coloring the ocean swells and gliding beneath the water's surface. Those shadows are the size of submarines.

He flips onto his stomach. There are large splashes or breaches in the water behind him; they sound like detonations. And then there's screaming and the microphone-feedback sound changes pitch and volume.

Zane does not turn around again. He is determined to fight for his life, to scrabble and crawl his way back up the beach, to the dunes, and then away. He daydreams of crawling back in time, somehow; going all the way back to the day of his first meeting with Dr. Colton and its night filled with moths. Zane has always remembered that day (and night) so vividly, it's as though he must surely know the way to get back there.

The morning after, there will be a dark purple sunrise, and the sky will remain that color for the length of the day. The tide will be coming in, the surf swelling well past its usual heights. The water will be bloodred. The water will still be thick with countless bodies and the large shadows underneath.

Zane will return to the beach. He will clear the dead off the top of the tallest sand dune; rolling bodies down into the crashing waves. He will be alone. He will remember his father telling him how it was good his brain was different from everyone else's. Then, in the new silence of the world, he will sit and listen for the high-pitched feedback sound, the one that will continue to be beyond his reach.

THE TEACHER

We loved him before we walked into the room. We loved him when we saw his name on our schedules. Mr. Sorent says, "All right, this is going to be a special class." We love him because of the music and movie posters on his walls, the black stud earring in his left ear, his shoulder-length hair. We love him because of those black horn-rimmed glasses, the same glasses we see people wearing on TV and in movies. We love him because he looks like us.

He stands at his podium. We love him because bumper stickers, many with political messages we want to understand, cover that podium. He says, "Because you guys are seniors and you're going to be outta here and out *there*"—and he points out the window with his miniature baseball bat, and we love him for that, too—"we're going to learn more than AP American History." We love him because he wears jeans. We love him because he makes fun of teachers we don't like. We love him because he plays guitar and he knows our songs.

There are only eight of us in his very special class. Four girls and four boys. We sit at a circular table. There are no desks. His is the only room in the school designed this way. He passes that smile around the circle. That smile we share, that smile we hoard for ourselves. He says, "We will be doing things outside of the book: special lessons. These lessons won't be every day or even every week, but they will be important. They will have weight and meaning. Certainly more meaning than the AP test you'll take in May."

We love him because he tells us the truth. Mr. Sorent leaves the podium and sits on a stool. "Know the after-school rules apply to our special lessons." We love him because he lets us talk to him after school. He lets us be confidential. He lets us talk about beer and parties and drugs and parents and abortions. "This is so exciting. I really can't wait. Maybe we'll have a lesson tomorrow." We love him because he is the promise that growing old doesn't mean becoming irrelevant.

At dinner Mom asks me about my soccer game even though she watched it. She's dressed in a sweatsuit as bright yellow as our kitchen. She leans over her plate to hear my answer. She's eager. She wants the coach to put her in the game. I tell her it was good because we won. Mom then answers her own question by announcing that those girls on the other team were playing dirty. Dad apologizes for missing the first game of the year, but it's perfunctory. He's wearing a yellow sweatsuit, too. He doesn't want to be left out. I tell him it's okay and there'll be other games. My brother, Lance, is six years old and stirs around the unwanted green beans. I stare at his dinosaur plate and Spider-Man fork and wonder why everything has to be something. It's my turn to ask Lance how was his day. This is what we do at dinner. We ask about each other's day as if it were an actual object, something that could be held and presented. Lance giggles, covers his face, and tells us normal stuff happened. Everyone smiles even though we have no idea what normal stuff is. Dad asks me more questions and I try some humor; I say, "How could I possibly describe my day in a manner that would truly communicate my individual experience and worldview concerning what had happened in that randomly delineated time period?" My parents laugh and make we're-impressed faces. Dad says, "Did you learn that in school today, Kate?" He manages enough sarcasm for my approval. Mom shakes her head, then grabs my nose. Her fingers are cold. I look just like Mom. Right there, in the middle of my stir-fry, I make a solemn promise to never color my brown hair auburn or wear a yellow sweatsuit.

After dinner, I go to my room to do homework and Snapchat my friends. We don't capitalize. We use bad grammar and code words. We chat about who is seeing whom and how far each couple has gone. We chat about TV and we chat about Mr. Sorent. We chat about weekends past and future and we chat about nothing, and it's a comfort. I don't hear my friends' voices but I know all their secret names.

A TV on a rolling stand replaces his podium. Mr. Sorent is a live wire. His hands are pissed-off birds that keep landing on his face and then flying away. We sit and whisper jokes about Molly's short skirt and Miles's porn mustache, but we don't take our eyes off Mr. Sorent.

He says, "There will be more films and even some live demonstrations, but today's clip is the arc of the course." One of us turns out the lights without being asked, and the TV turns on.

A black-and-white security video of a classroom. There are finger paintings and posters with big happy letters on the walls. Stacks of blocks and toys and chairs that look like toys are strewn on the floor. There is no sound with the video, and we don't make any sounds. Five preschoolers run around the room; two more are standing on chairs and trying to knock each other off. The teacher is a young woman. She wears white, unflattering chinos and a collared shirt with the school's logo above the breast. Her hair is tied up tight behind her head, a fistful of piano wire. She breaks up the fight on the chairs, and then another child runs into her leg and falls to the ground. She picks up the squirming child, grabbing one arm and leg. She spins, giving a brief airplane ride, but then she lets go. Mr. Sorent pauses the video, and we know the teacher did not simply let go.

Mr. Sorent doesn't say anything until we're all looking at him. He says, "I don't want to say too much about this." He edges the video ahead by one frame. The airborne child is a boy with straight blond hair. We can't see his face, and he's horizontal, trapped in the black-and-white ether three feet above the carpeted floor. "Your individual reactions will be your guide, your teacher." The video goes ahead another frame. The boy's classmates haven't had time to react. The teacher still has her arms extended out. If someone were to walk in now and see this, I imagine they'd want to believe she was readying to catch the child. Not the opposite, not what really happened. Mr. Sorent moves the video ahead another frame and a wall comes into view, stage right. Class ends, and none of us will go see Mr. Sorent after school.

At dinner we eat spaghetti, and we're quiet. Everyone's day is a guarded secret. My parents missed my soccer game, and when they ask about it, I tell them I scored a goal when I didn't. I think they know I'm making it up; my parents are smart, but they don't call me on it. They're still dressed in their work clothes, not their usual sweatsuit dining wear. Mom sits up straight and I can almost hear her spine straining into its perfect posture. Dad crouches behind a glass of water. Lance won't speak to us. He shrugs and grunts when we ask him questions. Dad sighs, which means he is pissed. Mom tells Lance it's okay to have a cranky day. I imagine Lance flying through the air, toward a wall, and I get the same stomach-dropping feeling I get sometimes when I think about the future.

I don't eat much and I go up to my room. My friends are all here on my phone. No one talks about the video. We know the rules. But no one knows what they're supposed to write in their notebooks. Mr. Sorent handed us special-lesson composition notebooks that he wants us to decorate. We're supposed to write down diary entries or essays or stories or doodles or anything we're moved to do after reflecting upon the lesson. My notebook is open but empty, a pen lying in the spine. I've tried to write something, but there's nothing, and I get that afraid-of-the-future feeling again.

Days and weeks pass without another special lesson. We've had plenty of time to waste. Our first-term grades are good and we lose ourselves in the responsibilities of senior year: college recommendations and applications and social requirements.

On the first day of winter term the TV returns. Mr. Sorent doesn't have to tell us what to do. We pull our chairs in tight and put away our books. Mr. Sorent says, "Lesson Two, gang."

There is a collage of clips and images—nothing in focus for more than a second or two—of car accidents. The kind of stuff some of us saw in driver's ed. The images of crushed and limbless and decapitated bodies are intercut with scenes from funerals, and there are red-eyed family members, the ones who never saw any of it coming, wailing and crying and breaking apart. Then the video ends with a teenage boy, alone in his room. There's no sound. His head is shaved to black stubble and he wears a sleeveless white T-shirt. The room is dark, and he scowls. There's no warning and he puts a handgun in his mouth and pulls the trigger. A dark mist forms behind his head and then he falls out of the picture. Mr. Sorent switches to the preschool video, still paused where he left it. He runs the video for a frame, then a second. The boy is still floating and horizontal, but getting closer to the wall. On the wall, bottoms of the finger paintings are curling up, heading toward the ceiling as if everything can fly. None of the boy's classmates know what is happening yet. But we know.

Mr. Sorent says, "Don't forget to do your homework."

There was this time I was waiting for Mom to come home. I had a Little League game in an hour. I wore my white uniform and black cleats, ponytail sticking through the back of my hat. I was in front of my house skipping rope, even though I didn't like skipping rope, but I liked the sounds my cleats made on the pavement. I was nine years old, but if anyone asked I pretended I was ten. Three neighborhood boys, three teammates dressed in their white baseball uniforms, came by, grabbed me, and forced me into one of their backyards. I didn't resist much as they used the jump rope to tie my arms behind my back, but I screamed a little, enough to let them know I didn't fully approve, especially since they never talked to me at baseball practice or games because I was a girl. They led me toward the edge of a stranger's wooded property, to a woodpile buried in dried pine needles and spiderwebs. They'd hanged a bullfrog by its neck from a piece of twine. It was as big as a puppy, kicking its legs out and covering itself in web and debris. The jump rope went slack on my arms but the boys didn't care. They told me to watch. They threw rocks. They had a BB gun and shot out one of the frog's eyes. Then they took turns pulling and pinching the frog, dancing at the base of the woodpile in their bright white baseball uniforms. Everything was white. They had a book of matches.

I left the jump rope in the grass like a dead snake and walked home and sat down in front of the TV. Nothing was on. Mom was late coming home and we missed the first inning of my game. When it was my turn to be the pitcher, I closed my eyes before releasing every pitch, afraid of what might happen.

Jake sits in a chair at the front of the room. Jake is elderly and has no hair. His face is a rotting fruit, and he moves like a marionette with tangled strings. He grins. Big yellow teeth break through his purple lips. He wears only a hospital gown, blue and white socks, and brown slippers. None of us wants to be here. Jake says, "Thanks to the loving support of family and friends, even if I don't beat this disease, I'll still have won, you know what I mean?" We don't know what he means. We couldn't possibly know. He says more heroic things, things that win us over, things that speak to the indomitable human spirit we always hear about, things that inspire us, that make us want to be better people, things that make us believe.

Then Mr. Sorent says, "Okay, Jake." Jake drops the curtain on his yellow teeth and he slouches into his chair, his marionette strings cut. He tells us everything he said is bullshit. He tells us to fuck off. He hates our fucking guts because of our health and youth and beauty. He hates us because we expect and demand him to be brave in facing his own withering existence, because we expect him to make our own lives seem better, or tolerable. He tells us we're selfish and he'll die angry and bitter if he wants, that he's not here to die the right way for us, fuck you, you fucks, he tells us, he doesn't give two shits about us and he tells us that we'll all die the same way he will. Alone. He limps out of the room, limbs shaking and moving in the wrong directions.

Mr. Sorent says, "Look here," and he points with his bat. We hate that stupid bat now. We want to steal it or break it or burn it. It's meaningless to us. The bat points at the TV screen tucked away in a corner of the room, framed by all those posters that are no longer cool, but trying too hard to be cool. We want to destroy those, too. We want to destroy everything. Mr. Sorent is still pointing with that ridiculous bat at the floating-boy video. It moves ahead another frame. Class dismissed.

I help Lance with his homework. Lance sighs like Dad whenever we finish a problem, as if he completed the world's most demanding task. I tell him he'd better get used to it. His eyebrows are two little caterpillars fighting on his forehead. I want to tell him about the bullfrog and about pitching with your eyes closed.

My cell phone rings and Lance ducks under the couch cushions. He thinks he's funny. Caller ID says it's Tom, my boyfriend, and I crawl under the cushions next to Lance. Lance giggles and tries to push me out, kicking me in the head and chest. Tom hasn't called me all week. I hold the ringing phone against Lance's ear, and mock screams mix with his giggles. My last date with Tom was a movie. We watched the previews intently. During the movie, I wouldn't let him stick his hand into my jeans. I told him to stick his hand in his own pants. I thought I was funny. He pouted the rest of the night. I don't and won't answer Tom's phone call. I'm going to break up with him. He's starting to scare me. Lance and I emerge from the couch after the phone stops ringing, and Lance rushes through the rest of his assignment, his eights looking like crumbling buildings.

I go upstairs and Snapchat. I tell everyone that I'm going to break up with Tom before I tell Tom. Tom hears it from somebody else and he yells at me through cyberspace: capital letters and multiple exclamation marks and no smiley faces. I make jokes about him masturbating to porn. I make jokes about the size and smell of his dick. I don't do any homework for Mr. Sorent's class.

All eight of us in Mr. Sorent's special class, our grades aren't good anymore. We are not in good academic standing. Some of us drink. Some of us smoke. Some of us will fuck anyone and everyone, or we punch and kick and destroy, or we drive really fast and late at night, or we stay locked in our rooms. Teachers openly talk about the changes, our senior slides, our early spring fever, and they pretend to be more knowing than they are. But they don't know anything and they won't do anything.

Mr. Sorent has stopped teaching us AP American History because we don't listen. Most days he sits at his desk and reads the paper, smelling of old cigarettes and something else, something organic none of us cares to identify. His hair is greasy and formless. His jeans don't fit his waist correctly, not cut to the length and style we want. He doesn't shave and his beard grows in patchy and rough. He wears old glasses now, the lenses too big. He is an old man trying to act young. He's a fraud. He knows nothing. He can teach us nothing. We know this now, even if we didn't know it then. We've stripped his podium of the bumper stickers, stolen his CDs and his miniature bat.

We listen to Mr. Sorent only during the special lessons. One class he showed us a PowerPoint presentation of crime scene photos: there was a man beaten to death with a bat, only his sausage-sized lips a recognizable part of his face, and there was an old man hacked to death with a samurai sword, and there was a woman who shot herself in the chest with a shotgun, she was a junkie and so withered you couldn't tell she was female, even with her shirt off. Another class was war footage, soldiers and civilians in pieces and burnt and eaten away by the chemicals neither side was using. Another class was snuff and torture films and the sound was the worst part. In other classes we saw the Columbine video, terrorists beheading kidnap victims, grainy newsreel stuff from Chernobyl and Hiroshima, and from Auschwitz and Cambodia and Rwanda and Kosovo and their endless piles of bodies.

And there's still the floating-boy video. Moving only frame to frame with each new day. Some days we can believe there has been no progress, as if that boy will be trapped in the amber of TV forever, but that's not right. He has progressed. He's almost at the wall.

No one talks at dinner. Just forks on plates. Mom says she already ate and then goes out wearing heels and sunglasses and not her yellow sweatsuit. Dad takes off his tie and unbuttons his shirt and dumps Lance in front of the TV with his dinosaur plate and Spider-Man fork. Lance has dark purple circles under his eyes, his skin carrying something heavy. In all the hours of TV Lance has already logged, I wonder if he's seen the floating boy. Dad disappears into his bedroom, then the master bathroom. Both doors shut at the same time. I'm the only one eating at the table. Maybe this is how it always was. I go upstairs. I find my friends in my phone and arguing without me. Tomorrow is our last class with Mr. Sorent. Its arrival will be unheralded and inevitable. I still haven't written anything in my notebook. I can't decide if I want that to mean anything. If I were to write something down, I'd tell Mr. Sorent about the bullfrog. No, maybe I'd tell him about me pitching in the Little League game. Tell him how when I closed my eyes, I hoped the ball would stop somewhere between me and the catcher and float. I would hope so hard I'd believe it was really happening. With my eyes closed, I'd see that ball hovering and spinning and I'd follow the path of those angry red stitches along with everyone else; we'd all stare it for hours, even when it got dark. But then I would hear the ball hitting the catcher's mitt, or the bat, or the dull thud of the ball smacking into the batter's back, and open my eyes.

Mr. Sorent has shaved and cleaned himself up, has a new mini bat, bumper stickers back on his podium. He's a cicada, emerging fresh from his seven-year sleep. He says, "You think you know why I'm doing this. But you don't," which is something so teacherly to say and utterly void of credibility or relevance. "So let's begin again."

We're tired and old, and we've experienced more and know more than he does. We know we can't ever begin again. We hand in our special notebooks. They are decorated and filled with our blood, except for one notebook that is empty. One of us closes our eyes after releasing the empty notebook, refusing to watch its path to the teacher's desk.

Mr. Sorent turns on the TV and the floating-boy video. The boy's head is only inches away from the wall. Some of his classmates are watching now, but they probably don't know what is really going on, or even what is going to happen. We hope they don't know. We hope they aren't like us. The teacher has retracted her arms and is facing the boy and the wall. Her face is blurry, and because we haven't seen the entire video at normal speed, we don't know if this means she's trying to look away or if it's a quirk of the video or if there's some other meaning that we haven't unearthed, or if it's all meaningless.

Mr. Sorent rewinds the video, the boy flies backward and into the teacher's embrace. We know it won't last. He says, "I need a volunteer."

This isn't fair. He is trying to break us apart, turning *we* into *me*. Doesn't he know that we'll hate the volunteer? The volunteer won't be able to rewind back into the *we*. We will never be the same. Maybe we are being melodramatic, but we don't care. We believe the volunteer to be irreversible; there is no begin again, Mr. Sorent, why can't you understand that? But I volunteer anyway.

I leave our circle and it becomes *their* circle. I walk to the front of the class, next to the TV, and I imagine the floating boy finally hitting his wall and then smashing through the right side of the television and into me, into my arms.

"Stand here and face that wall."

I do as he says. I feel their eyes on me. *They* who used to be *we*.

"Please walk halfway toward the wall. Everyone else watch the video." I take four steps and stop; the TV is behind me so I can't see the screen. "Please halve the distance again, Kate." I take two steps. When I move I hear the DVD player whir into action and then pause when I pause. "Again, Kate." I take one step. I could touch the wall now, if I wanted, and rip down the movie posters we already tore down once.

"If you keep halving the distance, Kate, will you ever get there? Is forever that far away, or that close? What do you think, class?" He says *class* like it's the dirtiest of words. I close my eyes, and take a half step, then a quarter step, an eighth step, and I still haven't hit the wall.

"That's good enough, Kate." I don't move, but not because of what he said.

"Go back to your seat and we'll let you decide whether or not this little boy will ever hit the wall." I don't move. My eyes are still closed and I'll stay here until I'm removed. I haven't touched it yet, but the wall is intimately close. It's impending, and it's always there. Mr. Sorent says something to me, but I'm not listening and I'm not going to move. I'll stay here with my eyes closed and pretend that where I am is where I'll always be. Where am I? I'm at the dinner table discussing days with my dissatisfied parents. I'm helping Lance and his caterpillars with homework. I'm on my phone messaging secrets to secret friends.

"Return to your seat so we may finally watch the video, Kate."

No. I'm staying where I am. I'm the baseball pitch that stops before home. I'm an empty notebook. I'm half the distance to the wall. I'm the video with an ending I won't ever watch.

NOTES FOR "THE BARN IN THE WILD"

A brief note from the editors:

In transcribing the following handwritten notebook pages, notes written in the margins and between the lines are represented as footnotes. Italics represent a clear change in handwriting. Everything else has been transcribed as written, including cross-outs, grammar, and underlines.

If found please return to Nick Brach, _____, Nederland, CO, 46926, email: n.brach@gmail.com

Can I be frank with you, Ms./Mr. Finders Keepers? If this notebook is lost, it means I'm lost. I am not overstating this. Please save me.*

BLUE notebook. Notes for (working title) <u>The Barn in the Wild</u>.

Here's hoping that BLUE brings better luck than the RED notebook did on Everest.†

---

*   *editors' note* Name, address (partially redacted), and passage was written on the inside cover of the notebook.
†   When will I learn to keep my big trap shut?

Twenty-five-year-old Thomas "Tommy" Hovsepian was a gifted mathematics student. He left his graduate program at the University of Vermont March 5, 2013, two weeks before he was to take his oral exams. He told no one of his plans,* including his friends and family. His parents (and the university) thought that Tommy was going to continue on to the Ph.D. program. Tommy was not your stereotypical mathematics Ph.D. candidate. From a small town (Ryder, PA, population 8,450), he was an undersized but tenacious star on the high school basketball team. As an undergrad, he tried walking on the team at the University of Vermont but didn't make the cut. He grew his dirty-blond hair long, was a serious Dead Head, worked as a bartender at the popular bar/music club called the Metronome, and grew small marijuana plants in his apartment in downtown Burlington. Tommy was gregarious, outgoing, charismatic. His roommate (Rob Poodiack) told me Tommy could've run for mayor of Burlington and won.† Instead of thumbing across the continental United States (which is what most twenty-something self-described free spirits do, right? I did it when I was his age—Christ, I sound like my father), Tommy traveled north into Canada. Why Canada? And ultimately, why end up in freaking Labrador of all places? What paperback romantic hitches out his thumb and says, "All right, screw the sunny shores of California and the wild-wild-northwest of Jack London's Alaska, the tundra of Labrador it is"? Tommy took some odd jobs, living out of cheap hotels as he made his way up north through Quebec province. On May 4 he landed in Happy Valley–Goose Bay.

to do: Travel expense report, make contact/set up interviews with coworkers, follow up with Royal Newfoundland Constabulary, local wilderness guide?, ~~explain to Scott that I'm not really going off into the wild by myself again~~‡

---

*   What were Tommy's plans? Backpacking? Living off the grid? Disappearing?
†   Why leave Burlington? And choose to leave in the manner he chose to leave?
‡   That didn't go well, did it?

june 30

Hello from Happy Valley–Goose Bay's library! Subarctic climate, but it's sunny and pushing into T-shirt weather. Town sits at the southwestern end of Lake Melville (a town/lake only a Calvinist would love) and at the mouth of Churchill River. It's not much of a city, with a population equivalent to Tommy's hometown of Ryder. A WWII boomtown, founded by sticking an air force base out here. Runway is long enough to have once served as an alternate landing spot for NASA's space shuttles. First nonmilitary settlers were led by a Rev. Lawrence B. Klein, who was appointed as the first resident United Church of Canada minister (1953–1954). Reverend Klein and his wife Johanna organized nondenominational community meetings that eventually led to Happy Valley being officially registered as a municipality in 1953. There were 106 charter families: 45 United Church, 24 Anglican, 21 Moravian, 12 Pentecostal, 4 Catholic. Metis and Inuit now make up close to 40 percent of the town's population.

july 1

Jeffrey Stephens, Royal Newfoundland Constabulary: tall, rail thin, pale skin, strong-man contest handshake. Dark blue dress shirt pressed to within an inch of its life with light blue Constabulary crest patch on left arm. Big window overlooks the bay behind him and his desk. Pleasant enough. Chitchatted. Stammered through saying he enjoyed my book on Everest, well, not that he enjoyed the parts where so many others in my party died, "Jeez, must've been rough. When all hell broke loose and you tripped over the dead climber in the snow on your way down to camp, man, that's something that stuck with me." I told him it was rough and thanked him for reading the book. To ease the mood, I pointed at the pic of his young wife and a baby and told him he has a beautiful family. He didn't ask about my family and he clearly didn't want to be talking to me about Tommy. Maybe reading too much into vibe and his clearly defensive posture (Scott* says it's one of my less endearing features, but I'm a journalist and can't help that).

---

* He hasn't responded to my "Wish you were here" texts.

Tommy's body was found by Antoine and Brandon LaForge (father and son snowmobilers) on March 24. Stephens presented me a photo of the body. Tommy's all curled up in a tight ball, lost inside his puffy anorak. Adjacent to him are the dead coals and black ash of a spent fire pit. Tommy likely died of starvation sometime during the previous fall. Five fingers on his right hand were missing. The coroner was unable to determine if fingers were removed by critters postmortem because of the advanced state of decay of the body.

<u>Were any other body parts missing?</u>

"No."

<u>Isn't it odd that animals didn't take anything else?</u>

"Who knows why animals do anything they do?"

Tommy's hands look to be hidden tight into that ball of rigor mortis. Stephens agreed. There was evidence of frostbite in Tommy's toes, and Stephens suggested (admitted it wasn't likely) that perhaps Tommy cut his fingers off himself after suffering from severe frostbite.* Next an itemized list of the meager supplies found in Tommy's possession, including a camera. They were able to produce only a handful of pictures from the film in his pack and in his camera; the rest were washouts: one photo of a woman in a small apartment kitchen, hiding her face behind a dish towel;† three photos of woods, the hiking trails nearly indecipherable in the brush; an open field with the barn as a dot in the far background; the last picture a self-portrait of Tommy sitting up against the barn, his hair wild, baby face tufted with facial hair, gaunt and emaciated, facial fat and muscles melting away, replaced by the hard angles of what lies beneath,‡ but he doesn't look like he's suffering or in pain, but with the content, wild, ecstatic look of a zealot. He sits with his back up against the side of the barn but toward the front. Above his head, in the upper right-hand corner, protruding out from the front of the barn is an ornamental structure,

---

*   I've had frostbite, and I've had it at 20,000 feet, but didn't cut off my fingers. I'm partial to them. Do people do that? Apparently yes: see Sir Ranulph Fiennes.

†   Nadia?

‡   Unfortunately, I've seen that face before. *You will see it again.*

like a deer's head in profile, and I do think it's some sort of animalistic avatar or totem, only the neck is elongated, but the head has no antlers, or ears, or much of a snout, it's oval, tapers to a rounded point at the bottom, human?

<u>What's that supposed to be on the front of the barn?</u>

"Not sure. The wood at the end has been all chewed up by woodpeckers."

Early town records are a bit murky on who first built the barn ~~and cleared the area to farm it~~, but one of the town founders[*] took it over and used it to host weekend retreats in the summer. The property was abandoned in the mid-eighties by the family trust, officially condemned, but has been left standing so lost hunters/hikers/snowmobilers can use it for shelter if they get in trouble, and frankly, it's too deep in the woods, the road/trail out to it long overgrown, to bring out wrecking equipment.

"We get kids like Tommy up here all the time looking for freedom, adventure, something to fill the hole in their lives. Many walk into the woods. Some don't walk out." (Subtext: don't know what makes Tommy so special that a famous writer would be writing his story.)

<u>Do you think Tommy knew the barn was there?</u>[†]

"I doubt it."

—Lunch at the Silvertop Diner.[‡] Tommy washed dishes here for a little over a month, alternated crashing with a coworker and staying in a motel.[§] I sit at the counter and ask locals about Tommy. Some

---

[*]   Lawrence B. Klein again.

[†]   *It was waiting for you*

[‡]   Shepherd's pie with lamb and buffalo meat . . . Scott still isn't answering my texts. I don't call him. Let him stew.

[§]   Same hotel I'm staying at. Serviceable. Damp and dark, smelling of never-ending winter, carpeting and wallpaper that seem older than the town itself. (a second note) 2:23 a.m., nightmare, Tommy curled up in the dark corner of my room, I called out to him, he stood, his bones creaked and the tendons strained like climb ropes, he staggered to my bed, walking like flipbook animation, and held up his right hand, no fingers, the skin was smooth, marble, white, eye sockets empty, mouth was a round, dark hole, and then it wasn't him, it was him in my dream but his face belonged to someone else, I'm forgetting (third note: *lies*

remember him as a friendly, smiling kid with an infectious laugh. The owner, Garrett Langan (thick glasses and thicker forearms), didn't have too much to say other than "Nice kid. Wasn't afraid of hard work. Knew he wouldn't stick long. A little squirrelly."

Meeting with cook Nadia Bulkin at 6 p.m. tonight. Another co-worker, Steve Strantzas (unclear if he's a cook or washer or waiter), refuses to meet with me.* "What's there to say? Seemed like a nice enough guy, but had no idea what he was getting into and died because of it. Oldest story in the book."† Pressed him for more, told me he was tired and hung up. (subtext: go fuck yourself, Nick.)

Nadia: Beers with Nadia at the Tavern on the Green. She was the last to see Tommy alive. He left her apartment on the morning of June 14 and hiked into the woods by himself. She's a 34-year-old outdoor sports enthusiast (cross-country skiing, kayaking, and mountain climbing mainly). Sunburned face. Wary smile. She's a weird combination of chin-up/chest-out confidence and nervous twitchiness. Says she's thinking of moving to Vancouver next spring, which is the first thing she told me after shaking hands and telling me she's been stuck here for four years. She met Tommy the first night he showed up in the diner. He looked "as scraggly as a wayward dog and twice as skittish." He drank three cups of coffee and ate two steaks. Didn't take her bait in attempts at small talk but asked about the dishwashing job. He was much more pleasant the next morning when he showed up to work and over the next month he wowed everyone with his tales from the road and his boasts about going to live in the woods by himself for one year, to prove that he could do it. Such a genuinely kind, enthusiastic, earnest kid, though haunted. "There was something there, behind the curtain, you know?" Nadia knew he was low on cash and she let him crash at her apartment.

---

you can never forget and you will always remember) who it was, I can't remember, and my fingers screamed and burned with sharp cold, then Tommy who wasn't Tommy said *cross-out, illegible* we've always been waiting

*   Sounds like a real douche on the phone.
†   *Oh there are older stories*

She stopped there and swirled the last sip of her porter around the bottom of her glass.

You and Tommy got close?

"Yeah. Yeah, you could say that."

I tell her I'm sorry. I know it's hard.

"It is. Did I tell you I'm going to Vancouver next spring? Goddamn it, I am. I am."

Nadia's apartment: One bedroom. Kitchen/living room combo. Clean, but run-down. Skis, boots, weather gear, clips, piled by the front door.

"I wanted him to stay. I think he almost did. I'm not just lying to myself, you know. I could sense that he wanted to. That in some ways it would've been easy to, but there was something else there, making him not stay. Making him go to the woods."

What was it?

"He wanted to be alone. He needed to be alone. When he first got to the Bay, you could see him filling up with all the people around him again, a battery recharging. He was manic during those first few weeks. But then you could see him dimming again, losing the juice. We all weren't enough to sustain him, keep him going."

Did he want you to go with him?

"He asked me to go, but he didn't really mean it. And I didn't want to. It didn't feel right. I'm not much of a trust-your-gut kind of person, but this time, I could feel it." I finessed through a question about her being surprised Tommy was found in some abandoned barn only a few days' hike from civilization. "I knew where he was going."

Where? To the barn? How?

"He had this book with him. This stupid book."

Do you have it?*

"Yes."

---

* Stephens made no mention of a book to me. Nadia didn't answer me for a long time. I mean a long time. Glacial.

<u>Can I see it?</u>
"Only if you take it with you when you leave."

Tommy told her he had purchased the obscure book in a used bookstore back in Burlington, VT. He never came out and said as much, but his obsession with the book was the motivation behind his trip. <u>The Black Guide</u> (Morderor de Caliginis)* is a guidebook. Thin paper, small newspaper kind of font. Table of Contents divided the entire east coast of North America into sections. There are occasional grainy black-and-white photographs, rough illustrations, hand-drawn maps, but the meat of the book comprised colorful/colloquial descriptions/histories of regional oddities, "hidden places of arcana" (sic), and areas of interest for the "discerning tourist." Despite my many travels (including hiking the Appalachian Trail from start to finish) in the region, none of the places in the TOC are familiar to me. There's an entry titled "Labrador: Klein's Barn."
<u>You didn't give this to the Constabulary?</u>
"No."
<u>Why?</u>
She shrugged, said that she "sort of" told them about it. Said that Tommy talked about how he'd read about the barn in a guidebook as an emergency shelter if you get stuck out there in weather. "They didn't ask me if I still had the book, either."†
I ask if I could borrow the book for a few days.‡
"Like I said, I want you to take it.
"Tommy promised me the night before he left. He promised me§

---

*   Copyright 1909, with a seventh edition printed in 1986. Book attributed to <u>Divers Hands</u>, no publisher listed, pocket-sized, bound in black leather, broken red ring on the cover. Call Tracy and ask her to get more info on it.
†   What???? They most certainly should've.
‡   Go back to Stephens to ask if he knows about the guide and its Labrador barn entry?
§   Do I weave my weird personal parallels into the story (blending of memoir and reporting?). Scott finally answered the phone. He didn't say hello. "You promised you wouldn't do this again." <u>I never promised I'd stop working.</u> "No,

that he was going to stay with me, that he wouldn't go out there by himself. I wanted to believe him when he said it. He seemed relieved, like that weight was gone. We went to bed. He woke in the middle of the night, screaming from some nightmare. And I mean he was full-on screaming. It took me forever to wake him up. He wouldn't tell me what the dream was about, only that it was awful but it wasn't a big deal, he'd had the same nightmare before and he'd be fine. He spent the next hour in the bathroom with the light on, sink water running on and off. I couldn't sleep and watched his shadow filling the crack of light under the bathroom door. He didn't say anything when he came back to bed. I wanted to talk, but he said he didn't want to talk about it, wanted to sleep. When we got up the next morning we silently ate breakfast and in the middle of his coffee he said that he had to go. That's what he said. 'I have to go, Nadia. I'm sorry.' He got up and packed his gear. I ran out of the apartment and jogged two miles in my bare feet. He shouted after me, 'I'll be back in the spring.' He was gone when I got back. He left the book on the counter."

<u>After he left, did you consider going out to try and find him, find the barn?</u>

"No. I was angry at him, that whole summer, tried to forget him. This was what he wanted and I'm not a survivalist type. What was I going to do out there with him? And he wasn't going to come back here with me."

(Back at the hotel:)

Cursory web search turns up only one copy of <u>The Black Guide</u> on eBay. No publisher information forthcoming. Waiting to hear back from Tracy with more deets. Most of the entries in the book hint at the occult.

<u>The Black Guide</u> entry, "Labrador: Klein's Barn":

Klein's Barn was built in spring/summer 1955, two years after the

---

that you wouldn't go off by yourself . . ." <u>I'm not climbing a mountain or doing anything dangerous. I swear. I'll just be roughing it for a week in a barn just a two-day hike out into the woods.</u> "Why do you have to keep doing this again and again?" <u>This isn't the same as Everest. You know it's not. And I'm not the same.</u> "You promised." Scott hung up. (second note: *promises are kept with blood and bone*)

Reverend Lawrence B. Klein and his fellow United Church of Canada followers registered Happy Valley as an official municipality. They wanted to hold religious retreats in the heart of nature and away from the prying eyes of the military stationed in and around Goose Bay. During a brief but eye-opening trip to France in the winter of 1956, Klein became obsessed with the Grand Guignol Theater in Paris. The theater's popularity was beginning to wane, but its history intrigued Klein; particularly the work of André de Lorde, who collaborated with an experimental psychologist Alfred Binet to write almost 100 plays, a handful of which featured a nameless and rapacious ancient deity with fervent followers who devolved into grotesqueries remade in the deity's likeness. Klein admitted to being absolutely terrified by the plays, but became intrigued with the idea of crossing the lurid aesthetics of Grand Guignol with the ecstasy of old-time religion, of good old hellfire and brimstone. Upon his return from France, Klein wrote morality plays that always ended with the gory tortures of hell and with Satan portrayed as an insatiable, wormlike creature. How many of these plays were performed is not known. Whatever run they enjoyed was short, and his plays morphed into bizarre ceremonies and rites devoted to the nameless deity. The odd, long-necked carving that hangs above the entrance to the barn was apparently carved in its likeness. Klein's wife, Johanna, and a number of other players were seriously injured with a fire stunt and shortly thereafter relocated to Europe and promptly disappeared.

Drank ~~one~~ ~~two~~ three scotches after talking with Scott. Sorry. To-do list: drink more scotch, fuck waiting around, call publisher, arrange a drop and pickup, supplies supplies supplies, more scotch[*]

july 3

Stephens dropped me at the bush line on a stretch of the Trans-Labrador Highway at one of the many snowmobile/ATV trails. I set the GPS for my rendezvous point with Stephens in seven days. Two days' hike in, two days out, three at the barn. Left a message for Scott (he wouldn't

---

[*]   more scotch was achieved, much to my detriment

answer his phone) and told him that I'd have a guide with me in the bush. It's not a full-on lie. I have <u>The Black Guide.</u>* Supplies enough for more than a week. The weather is supposed to be good (always subject to change in these parts, so I'm told). Feels good having a pack on my back again. I think Tommy and I probably had a lot in common. Maybe Tommy shares my pop-psych byline: overachieving and overbearing father who had mapped out his life for him from birth, and after reading Vonnegut, the beats, and Hunter S. Thompson, he rebelled. Right? Scott asks why do I keep doing this. This: dropping out of college to backpack in the U.S., Europe, South America, collecting friends and experiences and stories, and then all the mountains, collecting craggy peaks like coins, each more dangerous and extreme than the last, falling into a crevasse at McKinley and being airlifted out didn't stop me, then on Everest and everyone who died around me. I'm forty-five and that was supposed to be the last adventure for me.†

Night. Tent. Another nightmare. Still shaking. In the barn with Tommy. He was all curled up around a weak fire. Tried to help him, brushed snow off his face, and it was the dead Everest climber, German, from another party, met him briefly at base camp, I said his name, Karl Sidenberg,‡ kept saying it until his name sounded like something else, it was something else, couldn't control my tongue, horrible sounds, hard and then slithery, his frozen mouth opened and kept opening until it was as wide as the world.

july 4

Where are all the fireworks? Dreary morning. Trouble shaking off the night before. Mood improved after I found the clearing of yellowing grass, prickly weeds, and dandelions as tall as cornstalks. The clear-

---

* No word from Tracy on the book. She usually works quick, too. Showed Stephens the book. Didn't tell him it was Tommy's or that Nadia had it. "I've lived here seven years, never heard any stories about the barn like that."

† This hike to the barn is just a stroll down the street to the market by comparison, but I can feel it starting again. That need, that emptiness that knows no other way to be filled.

‡ *he is so hungry*

ing pitches up a small hill and the barn is on the top with more hills behind it. It's bigger than I expected. Strange to find such a large building out in the middle of the bush. I approached from its side. Had to resist the urge to call out "hello," make sure I wasn't trespassing on someone's property. The wooden planks are a bleached-out gray, but it's in damn good shape given the number of Northern Canadian winters it has endured. The roof has a few dips and waves in it, like ripples in a lazy pond, but from what I can see, there are only a handful of slate shingles cracked or missing. The barn is beautiful except for the carving over the front double doors. The carving is a monstrosity. The V-shaped head has a deep indentation that could be a mouth, but whatever else might've been its original features have been obliterated by woodpecker holes. A long, girthy, and frankly lewd wooden neck holds the head out away from the barn.

Inside: As much evident care went into a sturdy, weather-proof exterior, it's bare bones on the inside. No loft. No stalls. No rooms. Just a vast enclosed space. Looking up at the roof with all its beams it looks like a chest cavity, belly of the beast. White Whale and Melville again, right? Is my life becoming that obviously a literary trope? Fuck. Thick support posts line the perimeter. ~~Fells~~ Feels more like a big top, a circus tent, than a barn. The floor is hard-packed dirt with only the occasional dry weed poking through. Evidence of the barn being used as a temporary shelter abounds. Empty coolers and beer cans, tarps, bags, rusted traps, shotgun shell casings, torn-up blankets and socks. Evidence of its last occupant: the rock outline of Tommy's campfire in the middle of the floor, a black stain, a hole.

Back wall is covered in graffiti and names and dates gouged into the wood. The older markings look like gibberish, a combination of swooping marks and hard slashes, fist-sized circles dot the walls everywhere, some of them colored in or gouged out so they look like holes in the walls, and there are broken rings that look like the one on the cover of The Black Guide. Quotes from Vonnegut ("so it goes"), Hemingway, Plath, an ode to Jack London,* this bit from the book of

---

* "Jack London is king! All Hail his Dominant Primordial Beast."

Job: "Can you pull in Leviathan . . . tie down its tongue with a rope? Will it keep beging you for mercy? Will it speak to you with gentel words?" (sic)

In big block letters: "Tommy H. walked into the wild, June 2013 and forever."

Fire started. Tired. An hour left of sunlight. Hopefully sleep will follow. Will explore the surrounding area more fully tomorrow. I'll search for wild edibles Tommy might've eaten (or non-edibles), try to think like Tommy instead of dwelling on all my stuff. Keep busy. When alone like this, the trick is to not get hopelessly lost in your own headspace. Find another place. Looks like the BLUE notebook* has turned into a diary too. . . . Man, I'm such a pathetic, angsty teenager still. FUCK THE MAN! DON'T TRUST ANYONE OLDER THAN ~~30~~ 50! Cooler night than anticipated. Outside is a symphony of insect calls. It's beautiful. It's always been beautiful to me.

july 5

Up with the sun. Done the rounds on the grounds. Cool and cloudy. Nothing out of the ordinary. No trouble finding wild edibles, but it's July. Finding food a few months from now would be a vastly different story.

~~intro paragraph? Tommy Hovsepian and I both made promises to our loved ones. We were not lying and we both meant them with all our hearts and souls at the time we said them. How could I know that? All promises of "I'm staying" are the same and are made to be broken. We've already been promised to (illegible)~~

Probably should knock this shit off. Publisher won't be happy with memoir/nonfiction hybrid.

Considered setting up some small-game traps, trip wires and the like, if for nothing else to keep my mind occupied. But I have enough food. No need to kill any critters for the hell of it. Spent afternoon reading <u>The Black Guide</u> instead. As one of my favorite foul-mouthed lit professors used to say, "Man, that's some fucked-up shit right there."

---

*   Like the RED one and the GREEN one and the YELLOW one before it.

Looking forward to hearing from Tracy when I get back, see what she dug up on this crazy book.

Okay. Fuck. I'm spooked and rattled. Last light fading and I flipped through old BLUE here and found a bunch of notes that I didn't write. They're not mine. Not my handwriting. Fuck. Can't remember leaving my notebook out lying around in Happy Valley. Hotel maid with a weird sense of humor? No. No, there's some of those same fucked-up symbols, dark circles, broken rings from the barn's back wall, and "he's so hungry" is written between the lines of the July 3 entry. I wrote that entry in the tent. Out here. I mean, what, I'm writing shit in my sleep now? Creepy-ass shit too. Has to be what it is. No one's out here, no one's following me. I'm sleepwriting, or something. Using my left hand, even? *This is my left hand.* Looks like the other notes, yeah? It does. It does. Fuck! Scott was right. Shouldn't be out here by myself anymore. I thought I could still do this. Will pack up and leave a day early. If I can't get Stephens to come out a day early, I'll thumb it back to Happy Valley. Fuck fuck fuck.

Asleep next to the fire, and those slithery sounds from earlier dreams woke me up, they filled the barn. Wet things wiggling and dragging through the dirt. Filled my head. Puked on myself. I pulled my little camper's hatchet out of my pack and called out. Movement. Shadows were alive. I circled around the fire, trying to see what was out there and where I could run. I could always run. I ran at Everest. I crouched down next to my pack, started emptying it out, keeping only what I'd need after making a break for the doors. Two thick, albino white appendages wrapped around my ankles and pulled me off my feet, dragged me away from the fire. Light and heat were gone and I was so cold, I was on the white mountain again. I thrashed and punched, then my arms were pinned down, too. I couldn't move. The dying fire threw flickering images, albino white monsters writhing all around me, their arms, legs, necks, intertwined, a mass of worms. Tommy's melted rounded distorted transformed face hovered over my legs. My right hand was held out above my chest and close to my face, and another face telescoped from the writhing mass to me, and the face was no longer a face. The face, it was stupidly blind and all mouth, a wide, black hole that would never be filled. The face, it once belonged to the dead climber I left on Everest. I screamed I said his name Karl I said that I was sorry that I left him there all alone to die I was sorry that I didn't help him when he asked for help his frozen lips couldn't really move but he asked me for help. He put my fingers in his mouth slowly, fingertips passed through an impossibly cold membrane. I screamed I was sorry again and if I'd stopped and tried to help him both us of would've died he was too far gone I wasn't strong enough to help him down there was no way he could've made it no way he could've survived I had no choice. The mouth slid over my fingers down to the knuckle and then suddenly in the soft, wet, cold mouth, there were teeth, and it was wonderful.

july 25
At Labrador Grenfell-Health.*

Rescue team led by Stephens came out to the barn two days after we missed our rendezvous date. I was airlifted out. Vaguely remember bright sunlight, the sound of rotors, and their mechanical wind on my face. Don't remember anything else of the rescue. Stephens said he found me with my right hand badly burnt, so badly burnt that my fingers were blackened stubs, smoking embers, like I'd fallen asleep with my hand in the fire all night long. Infection was already raging, so was a fever, and I spoke nothing but gibberish. The doctors had to amputate the hand at the wrist. I still feel the hand that isn't there.

I didn't answer Stephens's or anyone else's questions. Told them I couldn't remember what happened or how I burnt myself, and I certainly don't remember writing that last entry in the BLUE notebook. I don't think Stephens and friends believe me and I don't care. They finally gave me back my BLUE notebook this morning. Stephens claimed he didn't find The Black Guide in my belongings. I think Stephens pocketed it. I do.

No matter. My old book, the one about Tommy and me, is dead. I'm not going to write it. This BLUE notebook will now become something else. A new kind of guide perhaps.

My lovely Scott is asleep in the chair next to my hospital bed. He looks ten years older than he did when I left him in June. I've promised Scott that

---

*   *Writing with my left hand really sucks.*

I'll never leave him again. Planning a new backyard project to keep me home. We'll use it to host parties, local author readings, spoken word, folk artists, maybe even some off-off-off-Broadway style performances.

(Note from the editors: The notebook ends with a rough map of Nick Brach's home and expansive land, and includes a schematic/outline of a rectangular building that would be twenty feet wide, fifty feet long. It is labeled, simply, BARN.)

For Laird Barron

She says, "Hi, honey," loud enough to turn the heads of all the moms at the pond's small beach.

I do my own comically exaggerated double take. She sidles up next to me, gives me a quick kiss. If this had happened to the teenager-me (alas, that nerdy kid was lost to the world so long ago, and replaced by this older, crankier model), he would've instantly vowed to never wash his cheek, and then locked himself in the bathroom *not* washing his cheek.

"Um, wow, okay. Hi?" I stay rooted in my chair under the shade of a skinny tree, slouched like Sasquatch on injured reserve.

She laughs. "Nice to see you, too. Jeez. Aren't you surprised to see me?"

"Well, yeah. Of course." The spot where she kissed me feels pleasantly swollen.

"It's too nice out and I'm jealous you get to be out here on a Wednesday while I'm stuck at work, so I left. I'm playing hooky. Shh, don't tell anyone." She winks and smiles.

"I won't tell. Dig the bathing suit, by the way."

"Har-har, funny guy. I jogged down here. Four point six miles. Aren't you proud of me?" Standing spotlighted in a sunbeam that burns its way through the thinning tree branches, she strikes a runner's pose. I smile. Or I leer. No, I smile and I leer like some smiling, leering, drunken, douchey frat boy. Seriously, I have no idea what's going on or what it is she's doing and what it is I'm doing. She wears black yoga/running pants (I don't know the difference) and a baggy white T-shirt that modestly cover the *wonderful* (trying to be less of that frat boy, yeah?) swell of her butt. The tee has some logo above her breast that I don't recognize. Her brown hair flecked with gray is tied up in a ponytail and I long to know what her hair looks like when let down. She's fit, pretty in an everyday way, and she doesn't look anything like my wife, Shelley.

I say, "Very. I'm impressed," and I do a quick impression of a cheering crowd and clap my hands together manically over my head, but then I get all self-conscious of my sun-starved skin, the arm-jiggle of my shoestring arms, and even my faded concert T-shirt, the band long forgotten. So, yeah, my half-assed push-ups and burpees three days a week aren't exactly remolding my clay. I sit up straight and pretend not to hear the beach chair's creaks and groans. Crossing my arms awkwardly over my chest, I say, "I get winded even driving that distance."

"Hot. Why are you sitting under the tree, in the shade? I mean, why bother coming to the beach?"

"What do you mean? I'm being sun responsible. Protecting my precious, delicate skin. And it's not like there's a line of willing volunteers to slather me in sun lotion. *It puts the lotion in the basket,*" I say, doing my best Buffalo Bill from *Silence of the Lambs,* and I die inside a little bit because I realize that even my witty pop culture references are middle-aged.

"Ew. You're so creepy," she says but laughs.

"When we get here the kids sprint ahead of me, kick off their flip-flops, and crop-dust the beach, dropping their shit everywhere on their way to the water. If I shout, 'Treeeee!' after them like a madman, then at least they somewhat group their stuff near this spot." I'm talking a mile a minute, and it's already the longest conversation I've had with another adult at this beach.

I pat the tree next to my chair. The pocked and scarred trunk crawls with big black ants. On cue, I twitch, flail, and then flick an ant the size of a dachshund off my leg, and I look so amazingly macho doing so.

"You don't have to justify your life choices to me, hon. How are the swimming lessons going?"

"Great. But I already know how to swim."

"Is Michael on the other side of the dock with the older kids? I can't tell who he is out there. All I see are heads bobbing in the water. Where's Olivia? Oh, there she is. Think she saw me walk in?" She waves.

Olivia happens to be looking at us both. She returns a distracted and hesitant wave back. Olivia has always been friendly, too friendly, really; her enthusiastically returning a hand-wave is generally as autonomic as breathing.

The woman says, "Oh my god, she's like a little teenager already. She's embarrassed I called out to her. That's not supposed to happen yet."

Olivia dives forward into the water at the command of the instructor.

The woman shouts, "You're doing great, honey!"

I cringe at how loud she is, and I do my best to ignore the reverberating shocks of her easy familiarity, of her kiss, and of her knowing who my kids are. The strangers on the beach are one thing (I don't really care what they think), but what am I going tell Olivia and Michael about this woman? Maybe the kids met her at the Matthewses' party and I don't remember? It's possible, yeah? I hope. Doesn't explain why she's acting like she's my wife and acting like she's their fawning mom and why I'm playing along.

Whatever strange act we're spontaneously creating together, it's wrong, very wrong, but my head is pleasantly drunk with it.

Olivia struggles to freestyle-swim toward the young instructor. The woman says, under her breath so only I can hear her, "Olivia's arms are as stiff as boards. Shouldn't the instructor tell her to, I don't know, bend her arms?" She pantomimes the correct swimming motion.

"You'd think you'd get more from fifty-dollar swimming lessons at the Ames Pond, right?"

"Yeah. Where else can you get your kids two weeks of sun, doggy paddle, and *E. coli* exposure?"

"When you put it that way, it sounds like a bargain."

"Ugh, I can't watch this. Can I go down there and help her?"

"She's fine."

"How old do you think the instructor is?"

"Dunno. Eighteen?"

"You wish."

Olivia's swim instructor, like the rest of the pond's lifeguards (who also serve as the swimming instructors), is thin, tanned, wears a tight red bathing suit, and moves with the coltish combination of gangliness and grace of late-high-school- and college-aged kids. And it's so goddamn depressing that my son Michael is only a handful of years and the great and terrible yawning divide of puberty away from being one of them. It's to the point where I try not to look at him when he's shirtless, afraid I'll see a dark patch of hair under his arms. Because then it'll be all over.

I say, "I'm going to ignore that creepy but accurate remark. And I can honestly say I do not wish to be eighteen ever again."

"Yeah, me neither." She steps confidently in front of my chair and sits to my right, on Michael's and Olivia's beach blanket. The blanket is pink and when folded up, looks like a piece of sliced watermelon. It's such a clever blanket. She looks around at all the beachgoers and says, "You really are the only guy, the only *dad* on the whole beach. Lucky you. But come on, wearing those mirrored sunglasses outs you as a total perv. Or a narc."

My face fills with blood and heat, and I sputter into what's supposed to be self-deprecating laughter but probably sounds like emphysema. Christ, I'm melting into my chair like I'm a bowl of ice cream. I'm embarrassed not because it's clear she knows I've been . . . shall we say . . . *ogling* the teen lifeguards and beach moms, but because my patheticness is so predictable and obvious.

Mortally wounded, I say, "No one says 'narc' anymore. You're so not hip. And sunglasses are the windows to the soul."

She reaches across my lap and tickles my knee playfully. Her hand and forearm are soft and she smells like plums, or a sweet tea, or those purple flowers that used to grow along the fence at my grandparents' house. I don't remember the flowers' real name, but Grammy called them her garden mums. And I don't know why I'm thinking about Grammy's flowers when I should be simultaneously enraptured and terrified by the not-so-innocent touch of a strange woman.

"My hubby, the dirty old man." She holds her hands out and nearly shouts to the rest of the beach, "Stand back, ladies! He's all mine!" She laughs at her own joke.

The moms sharing the beach in our vicinity: they pretend to watch their toddlers running amok on other people's blankets and throwing sand (that fucking kid with the sharks on his bathing suit is such a pain in the ass, I seriously considered tripping him on the sly yesterday); or they bury their faces in magazines and beat-up paperbacks they bought at the grocery store; or they look at the pond pretending to be intently watching their kid ignore and give attitude to the swimming instructor; or they blankly look up at the blue sky for the clouds that will one day approach. I'm not being paranoid (okay, I am), but they don't look at me and certainly don't look at the woman. I swear they're actively avoiding looking at us. I feel them *not* looking at me, which of course means they are judging me, saying in their heads *we don't know you and we may not have ever met her, but we know she's not your wife.* I know better, but goddamn me, it's not an entirely unpleasant feeling.

I say, "The dirty old man says that's not nice at all, and take off your shirt." I think about returning her touch. A light tap on her shoulder, or maybe letting my hand linger there, to see if it feels different than when I touch Shelley.

She says, "I'm not nice, but that's why you love me."

"I guess so."

"Oh, don't be so glum, perv. Hey, remember that game we used play when we started dating? We'd be in a bar and one of us would say, okay, the world outside just ended, everyone disappeared or died or whatever, and all that's left is us and the rest of the schmoes in the bar." She pauses so I can remember, so I can cognitively catch up to her in the memory. Of course I don't remember something that's never happened, but I nod like I do. I nod like I'm so pleased and satisfied that anything of what I said or did in the earliest days of our relationship was something worth remembering. I nod because she's offering proof that I still mean something to her.

"Yeah, wow. I remember."

"Then we'd ask each other to rank ourselves in terms of mate-worthiness."

"You were always top five," I say, and then I add a detail, an anec-
dote that belongs to Shelley and me. "Especially at that friend's wed-
ding where that woman showed up wearing a tiny Day-Glo turquoise
skirt and a pink North Face fleece."

"You're so awful. You can't make fun of her, she had—issues."

"Don't we all."

"Look around, though. If the world ended right now, and it was just
all of us here on the beach left, then you'd be a lucky guy. You'd be—
top three, easy."

"Gee, thanks. So you're saying I'm third in a three-man race behind
the teen Adonis lifeguards."

"You're sort of Adonis-like, kind of. If you averaged those two kids
together, maybe?"

"So I'm average-Adonis."

"Don't I know it."

"Yeah. I don't think they'd need my help to repopulate the species."

"Hey, you never know. I bet some of the moms here would go for
the more mature look. And top three is top three. What about me? Be
honest. Where would I rank?"

Before today, this past weekend's party at the Matthewses' house
was the only other time I've seen her (and by *seen* I mean its literal,
nondating or nonaffair usage; as in I *saw* her standing on the other
side of the room, far away from me). The Matthewses are the first family we've really gotten friendly with since moving to Ames three years
ago. Michael and Olivia are approximately the same ages as their kids
and they all get along very well. Emily Matthews thinks Shelley is a
hoot, and I get along great with Richard; we're planning to coach our
sons' flag football team in the fall even though I know nothing about
football, or flags. Future flag football fun aside, the move to Ames
hasn't gone as expected. Our kids have had no problem uprooting and
going to a new town and making new friends, but for Shelley and me,
becoming friends with other local parents and families hasn't been
easy. Branching out and being more social in the community is one of
our family goals of the summer (we're so cutely lame, we even wrote
out our goals on a piece of yellow paper; the list is stuck to the fridge
with a magnet).

So we went to the party and I tried my best to smile and join in on the conversations about lawns and building stuff that I can't build. I don't know why it was such hard work. That's not true; I do know why it was hard work: whenever I was asked what I did for work (stay-at-home dad with some SAT prep tutoring on the side), the blank stares and jokes were all the same. So I mostly kept to myself and kept a full beer constantly in one hand. I was totally blitzed by the end of the night. And not coincidentally, at that same end of the night, the woman walked in the front door along with a guy named Terrance. According to Richard, Terrance was a *good guy* and a recent divorcé. The break was not a clean one. The Matthewses and just about everyone else at the party were good friends with both Terrance and his ex-wife, Mary. Mary wasn't at the party, much to Emily Matthews's chagrin (I'd heard her complaining to my Shells about it as they worked their way through a bottle of red wine).

Anyway, I remember the woman walking in, wearing cutoff jean shorts and a white T-shirt and her hair was up like it is now, and she held Terrance's hand. After an awkward initial introduction ("Everybody, this is _____, and _____, this is everybody"), the party continued to go on around them as if they'd never arrived. I'm serious. Granted, I was all in the bag (see what I did there? as opposed to half in the bag?), but I'm not exaggerating when I say that the party people, they shunned the new couple as though they were Dimmesdale and Prynne. Terrance and the woman banished themselves to the corner. The only person I remember talking to the woman was Shelley. Shells went right up to her and they chatted while I stumbled around looking for shoes (it was that kind of night) and my kids, and not necessarily in that order. I was going to ask Shells what she and the woman were talking about when we got into the car, but I passed out.

I say to the woman, "On this and any beach at the end of the world, you are number one."

"Yay!" She holds up a celebratory I'm-number-one finger. "You're a horrible liar, but I'll take it."

"Do you mean I am horrible in addition to being a liar, or that I'm not proficient at lying?"

"Now I mean both."

"Fair enough."

Our playful conversation ends with the blowing of the lifeguard's whistle. The swimming lessons are over. Half of the kids run out of the water like someone spotted a shark; others stay and thrash around. Olivia stands waist deep in the pond, arms wrapped around herself. She's shivering and her lips are blue, but she won't come out of the water. You have to drag her out, or at least dangle a towel in front of her.

The lifeguard's trilling whistle explodes in my head and ends in a sharp stabbing point inside my ear. My head feels stuffy all of a sudden. Maybe I'm getting one of those summer colds. Wouldn't that be convenient? I try coughing; a precursor to an excuse. It sounds fake and as forced as the sheepish shrug and smile I offer to the woman, who suddenly seems equally unsure of herself.

A shiver passes through me, as though I'm empathically feeling Olivia's coldness. I say, "All right, I think we'll dry off and head out. Go home. It's noon already. Leftovers, more juice boxes, sandwiches, two pizza slices left . . ." and I trail off in volume, my speech degenerating into a weird, bipolar lunch-word association game. I grab Olivia's Harry Potter towel and shake out the ants. "It was nice—" and I'm going to say *talking to you.*

The woman stands up quickly, brushes sand off her legs, and says, "It's okay. You stay. I'll bring her the towel." She takes Olivia's towel out of my hands and grabs a second towel out of my beach bag.

She hustles away from my shady spot and I hold my hand out like I can reach out and grab her, pull her back and keep her chatting and sitting next to me on the blanket, because that was all harmless fun. We were all safe that way. But not now: anything that happens next will be irrevocable. And as she walks away and grows smaller from distance and perspective, I briefly pretend my hand covers her up, a rare back-of-my-hand eclipse, and because I can no longer see her that means she's not really there and I've imagined her. It's the only scenario that won't end badly.

My head buzzes and swims, gets thicker. Maybe I'm becoming the hypochondriac Shells always accuses me of being; I open and close my jaw, pop my ears, and shake my head and nothing feels like it works right. My neck muscles are tight and stiff, the ligaments turning to bamboo.

Olivia comes running out of the water and into the open towel that the woman holds out for her. Olivia doesn't hesitate. The woman kisses the top of Olivia's head, then rubs the towel all over, drying her off. She says, "Go see your father. He'll help you get dressed." She wraps Olivia up tight in the towel, brushes the wet hair out of her face, and tucks loose strands behind Olivia's ears. The woman points at me sitting in my chair, and that's all I'm doing, sitting, watching. Olivia stumbles up the beach, wrapped in a towel cocoon. She's shivering when she reaches me. Her teeth click together.

I say, "You okay, Liv? Your teeth weren't made to smash into each other like that, you know."

"I'm cold." She worms an arm out of the towel and scratches behind one of her ears. Her hair falls in front of her face. She won't look at me. I don't blame her.

"Let's get you dressed. We'll get lunch at home. Okay?"

I hold up the towel around her as she peels out of her two-piece and struggles into underwear, shorts, and a T-shirt. She's still wet.

The woman is down at the shore and no one stands within ten feet of her. She's like a human crop circle, which would be a funny joke to tell her if it wasn't true. I suddenly want to take Olivia up into my arms and run. Fuck the car and fuck this town and run and never stop running until I'm somewhere else, nobody knows where, and only then will I maybe call Shells and tell her that I'm sorry for the rest of my life.

Michael comes out of the water and the woman gives him a coy little wave. He smirks at her, that look that says he sees you, doesn't want to talk to you, not in front of anyone else, but he's still glad you're there. The woman sneaks up beside him and in one motion, drapes the towel over his thickening shoulders and sneaks in a quick hug around his neck. He's already almost as tall as she is. He says, "Stop it," but smiles and gives an embarrassed little laugh. He rubs a spot on the side of his neck absently. He's always been a distracted, twitchy little kid, and now he's a charmingly distracted, twitchy big kid, just like Shells. It's amazing how much he looks and acts like her. Michael lifts the towel off his shoulders and drapes it over his head. The woman walks next to him and bumps her hip into his. From under his towel-hood, he laughs and says, "Stop," again.

I turn my back to them; I can't watch anymore and can't think anymore. I hurriedly fold up the watermelon blanket, doing it all wrong, and it ends up as misshapen as an asteroid. I stuff it and rest of the kids' things into the green beach bag. If I grab Olivia now and run, would Michael know enough to follow me? The left side of my face feels swollen, like I've been punched, and slack, too, and Christ, am I having a stroke?

Michael's shadow falls over me. His is the only shadow there. He's alone, I think. If she's there she's not saying anything. I'm not going to look for her. When did this (this being whatever it was I thought I was doing, I don't know, I don't know) become such a horror show? Has it always been a horror show?

I tell the kids we're going home. I don't give them the option of *not* going home. Olivia and Michael walk around in front of me but don't say anything and they don't look back at me. My eyes fill with tears and my chest is tight with panic, everything in my head spinning so fast, it can only fly off its track and smash into a million pieces.

Michael doesn't bother changing into his dry shorts and T-shirt. He'll sit in the car on his wet towel. Even though Olivia changed into her clothes, her wet towel hangs loosely over her shoulders, a limp, sagging cape.

"Come on," I tell them. I'm impatient. It's how I lie to them: Yes, Dad has done something recklessly stupid, but he can fix it when we leave here, when we get home. "Come on, now! Walk. Move. Let's get home, okay?" I don't ask them to help me carry anything, so my arms are full of all the stuff. We stagger up the small, sandy hill, and then through the fence to the parking lot.

The woman calls out to us from behind. We stop. She stands next to a boulder that demarcates one section of the parking lot. We're five cars away from our car. She holds up surrender hands. Her smile stretches out across the rest of the lazy summer afternoon, yes, but there's something sad in her smile, too. It's an all-good-things-must-come-to-an-end look. I know that look, I do.

She says, "Hey, guys, forgetting something? You really going to make me jog back home?"

We wait and she catches up to us. She says, "You guys are so mean to Mommy." She pats my butt, reaches into my bathing suit pocket, and grabs the car keys. "I'll drive."

We fall in step behind her. She opens the trunk and I dump the chair and everything else inside. The kids dutifully climb into the back seat. They don't argue about who gets to go into the car first and who sits on what side like they normally do.

Earlier, when I parked, I forgot to leave the windows open a crack. The car is a sauna. I sit heavily in the passenger seat and sweat instantly pours off my face. I catch a glimpse of my left cheek in the side-view mirror: there's a puffy mass as red as a boiled lobster. My right eye is closing up.

There's an ant on my thigh. I try to pinch it between my fingers but I keep missing it. I brush it off my leg to the floor of the car. We've already pulled out of the lot and onto the street. I hadn't noticed we were moving.

The windows are down. The woman is driving. I look at her. She's been crying, or maybe still is crying because she wipes tears off her face. She looks an awful lot like Shelley does when she cries but pretends not to be.

She says, "So, um, how were the swimming lessons, kids?" Her voice is bright and cheery.

They don't say anything. I turn around and look at Michael. He's sitting ramrod straight in his seat, eyes open as wide as an ocean, and they are fixed on the woman in the driver's seat. His neck is patchy red, like he's breaking out in hives, and he shivers despite the heat. His bathing suit goes dark in the crotch as piss trickles down off the car seat and onto the floorboards.

I yell, "Jesus, Michael! Are you okay? I think he had—had an accident?" My own voice sounds like it's coming from so far away. I look over at Olivia and she's like her brother. They twitch and convulse together like partners in a dance. Her shorts—

There's a sharp sting on my neck. Everything goes darker and fuzzier at the edges. I settle back in my seat. The woman's hand hesitantly returns to the steering wheel, and maybe I see something protruding from the pad of her thumb before she vines that hand around the steering wheel.

She says, "Don't worry, they're all right. They'll be fine." Her voice wavers and is at the edge of breaking. She covers her mouth and blinks back tears.

I shake and shiver, and it hurts in my bones, like I'm shaking hard enough that I might fall apart on my own.

She takes a deep breath, composing herself, and says brightly, "They probably need something to drink, something to eat. Is anyone else hungry? I don't know about you guys, but I'm starving."

OUR TOWN'S MONSTER

The waning light of dusk filters through treetops and colors the sunroom a gentle gold, as if on cue. The Realtor smiles at the young couple and readies his end-game pitch.

"Gorgeous view, isn't it? At the back of the property is the northeast edge of Tiller's Swamp. The swamp is rather large, about two square miles."

The couple smiles, hugs, and even coos as if they'd been shown a particularly adorable puppy. The male half of the couple wears a suit with a black tie that doesn't waver, doesn't so much as twitch. His name is Brent and his hair is strategically brown and coarse. The woman half of the couple is named Hannah, and she has on a sensible dress neutrally colored to match any house she might be shown. Her shoes are sensible as well, as far as house hunting goes. Not so sensible were she to walk to or near Tiller's Swamp.

This house, which has been on the market for five months, much to the Realtor's dismay, is an antique colonial, originally built in the late 1700s. The kitchen has been updated, the floors are hardwood, the molding is maple, and the exterior is a stately blue and gray.

After blathering about how the town only occasionally sprays the area for mosquitoes due to eastern equine encephalitis fears, the Realtor says, "There's a monster in the swamp. It eats cats and dogs; small, unwanted children, you know the type; and the occasional beautiful woman. Only rarely, so far, once a century, will it devour the angry torch-wielding villagers—your potential neighbors." The Realtor brightens, positively beams at the prospect. "The monster generally keeps to itself and tolerates us more times than not. It's really quite a charming monster, if you think about it. It gives our town character."

The couple laughs. Brent asks, "What's it look like?"

"Humanoid, I suppose, insofar as it walks upright. Two arms, two legs, that whole bit. Large in the shoulders and chest. Brackish and dark, the color of decay, really."

Hannah makes a *tsk* sound, or maybe it's an I'm-bored sound, and says, "So it's not green, then?"

"Not currently, no." The Realtor stretches out the sentence, as if his inserted spaces between words and syllables will assuage her disappointment.

She says, "Doesn't sound as if the swamp is very healthy then. Right, honey?"

Brent says, "Oh, I don't know if there's a correlation."

"I'm quite confident there is no correlation and the swamp is healthy and vibrant, passes all the water health and bacterial tests. All of which, of course, is a matter of town pride."

Hannah says, "Green is a proper color for a swamp monster, I think."

The Realtor detects a hint of British accent in her voice, one he concludes is fake given the couple's personal histories detailed on the loan application he wasn't supposed to see. He also concludes the couple won't last two years, but he would admit to allowing personal distaste to cloud any judgment he might make. "I am by no means an expert, but I think its coloring might be regional."

Brent nearly shouts, "Equatorial?"

"Perhaps," says the Realtor, despite not knowing what the man means by such an odd remark.

Hannah then asks what she presumes is a most sensible question: "What about sex?"

"Excuse me?"

"Does sex bother the swamp monster?"

"Well, to be honest, that question has never come up before. No, I don't think that would be advisable at all."

Brent laughs and says, "Jesus, you asshole, she's not asking if either of us can have sex with the monster."

Hannah leans in close to the Realtor with her mouth wide open. She isn't subtle in mocking him. "Is that what you thought?"

Everyone laughs as if there were no monsters anywhere, never mind in the swamp at the edge of the prospective property. The Realtor says, "I am sorry. Do forgive my misinterpretation."

Hannah tries again. "What I meant was would *our* being intimate, shall we say, bother the swamp monster?"

The Realtor remains puzzled, then, in a fit of unbecoming unprofessionalism, he attempts a joke in poor taste. "By *our being intimate*, do you mean me and you?"

The Realtor spends the next two and a half minutes trying to pry Brent's fingers off his lapels. The Realtor grovels, attempting to convince the now frothing, bullheaded mass of testosterone that it was a harmless joke, an homage to the classic Who's-on-First type of humor that was simply building upon their previous sex-with-the-monster misunderstanding, which everyone had agreed was hilarious.

After the near assault, the Realtor, red-faced and humiliated, particularly as he doesn't like anyone or anything touching him, says, "My apologies, again. I don't see why you two being intimate should bother the monster. I suppose it wouldn't approve of it, given a choice, as it is a disagreeable creature by its very nature. However, I don't think it objects to sex as a general rule. There's no evidence to point to its objecting." By *evidence* the Realtor means the public records, generations of collected anecdotes, legends, and eyewitness accounts of the monster's behavior. He doesn't elaborate on his meaning of evidence, as he hopes the simple word choice has the ring of a scientific, backed-by-data truth.

Hannah says, "Well, I just thought that in all those movies, whenever an attractive young couple—like ourselves—have sex, that's when the monster gets them." She smooths her dress over her thighs, drawing attention to her authoritative attractiveness.

The Realtor says, "Yes, I see. I think you're confusing monsters with slashers. A common mistake."

Brent waves his hands, shooing away the words, and likely the Realtor. "Same thing, right?"

Instead of continuing the discussion, the Realtor ends it with: "Regardless, I can all but guarantee the swamp monster won't devour you simply because you choose to be intimate. I hesitate to speak for the residents of our fair town, but I'm quite certain many if not most are having sex as well, and the collective sex lives of our citizenry has only yielded new generations of inhabitants and has yet to incite a monstrous rampage from the—well, from the monster, as it were."

The couple buys the house and lives there happily for two weeks.

Besides the swamp and its monster cottage industry, which includes guided tours, night watches, monthly fan club meetings, and an elaborate gift shop, the old schoolhouse is our town's only other tourist spot. It's an austere one-room schoolhouse: red, and replete with a bell tower and a still-operating bell.

Mr. William Butler—a spry 102 years old, the school's last teacher (so claim our pamphlets and website)—gives the tours and a lively PowerPoint presentation. Children from all over the state take field trips to the Little Red Schoolhouse. Invariably, because of where our town is and who we are, the talk of the one-room education of yore turns to monsters.

Mr. Butler says, "There's a monster in this schoolhouse. Can anybody see it?"

The children sitting at the authentically wooden school desks shuffle their feet and hold back giggles. And they hold back screams. Their eyes are wide, and hopeful in a way, because they already know the world is full of monsters.

"It's not our most famous swamp monster. And I know you're thinking there isn't a lot of room to hide in here, and no, I don't see the monster under your chair. Maybe, at the end, you'll be able to help me find it."

Mr. Butler sits down on top of his teacher's desk, which is terribly small. He explained earlier that the desks were small because people back then were smaller. He starts in, seemingly in the middle of some speech, one that is missing an introduction and the aid of visual media.

"The body becomes monstrous." His voice is still strong, and his pauses are ones of confidence, not indecision. "Our skin sags, wrinkles, flakes, loses the luster that isn't any color in particular, but is there. Strange bumps and lumps will emerge, like they've been there all along, waiting beneath the surface, biding their time. Our body transforms into this *thing*, this intimate stranger."

Now, Mr. Butler was never actually a schoolteacher. He worked at the paper mill for forty years. Maintenance. He made sure the conveyor belts worked right, and the front loaders loaded and the forklifts lifted. His wife, Vera, was the last teacher at the Little Red Schoolhouse. The Butlers were never able to have children of their own. Vera told everyone that the town's children were hers as well. In truth, Vera spent her last years complaining about how cruel and rude the children were becoming, and in the easy comfort of her husband's company, she often referred to her students as little monsters. A decade after teaching her last class, Vera served as the first tour leader for the schoolhouse. When she died, the town council unanimously decided that Mr. Butler was in fact the school's last teacher and changed the public record to reflect as much.

"For those of us who have had the fortune of experiencing advanced age, the skin is the first thing we notice about our new monster-ness. I've been an old man for a long, long time, but there are still moments when I am sure that this is not my skin. Moments when I am sure that my skin was like your skin just yesterday, or this morning. It's as though my lifetime has occurred during one single day. It was only this morning, after breakfast, that I ran with my friends and I wore bruises and scabs on my knees and elbows like badges of honor. Then, right before lunch, my skin held fast, strong muscles that never knew weakness. Only an hour ago, my wife was tracing little, looping circles on my back that gave me shivers."

Initially, Mr. Butler fought against the town's edict, their blithely bureaucratic elimination of his wife from the town's history. He succumbed to their wishes, eventually, if only to give him something to do with his remaining days. Of course, when he dies, his name will be erased from the town charter and there will be a new last teacher. Mr. Butler looks forward to having his name—and his unfortunate usurping of Vera's life work—erased from the moldy corridors of the town's folklore. He met his two replacement candidates last week. Despite their doctors' notes and claims to having their original hips and teeth, the candidates looked to be in ill health. He's no doctor just like he's no teacher, but they looked worse than he felt.

Mr. Butler says, "There are still moments when I am sure there must be some mistake, some horrible, terrible mistake, and that I have—for some reason that has never been made exactly clear to me—grown the skin of a monster. I guess what I am saying is I'm not sure I deserve this honor, one way or another."

Some of the children laugh nervously, even if they don't quite understand all the words Mr. Butler uses, but they do understand what he means. Most of the kids don't hear a word he says and stare at the large black mole on his left cheek, the one that looks like a hole.

The chaperones fidget like their students and they no longer want to be in the Little Red Schoolhouse. They want to cut the tour and presentation short as they feel the encroaching tightness in their joints, the lower-back pain that worsens when sitting in any one position too long.

The chaperones do not interrupt Mr. Butler. They smile politely and rub their hands together as if something is on them.

The older brother, his name is Teddy, tries to be a stereotype of a disaffected teen. With the help of countless faceless others, his parents have already achieved the full-blown stereotype status belonging to the rural impoverished. Their hopelessness, which has turned so easily to violence and neglect, is as established as a rut in a logging road.

Teddy's hair is dark, greasy, and falls in front of his ferretlike eyes. His limbs are stretched-out tube socks. He wears the Walmart version of what he sees other teens wearing on TV. He swears loudly in public places, especially around the elderly and children. He and his friends smoke marijuana, drink beer, and if there's nothing better to do, they huff glue, gasoline, and Bactine. There's never anything better to do, of course.

Teddy fails in completing his teen stereotype in subtle ways that fill him with shame. His friends once caught a baby squirrel and tortured it with a piece of rope, a bucket, and their disposable lighters. Afterward, Teddy locked himself in his room and cried until he could no longer smell burnt hair.

This afternoon, Teddy leads his seven-year-old brother, Caleb, away from the elementary school playground and into the town graveyard. It's not a large graveyard, or very ornate, or even well kept. Weeds and strawlike grass envelop the smallest stones, most of which are crooked or knocked over. Generations of vandalism at the hands of stereotypically disaffected teens have taken their toll.

Dying pine and birch trees ring the small graveyard. The brothers sit on stones so old that the names and dates have eroded away.

Earlier, Teddy skipped school and spent the late morning fleeing from his friends. The pack had inexplicably turned on him. Although he has always feared they would figure out he was a fraud and, eventually, eat him alive, Teddy does not understand what set them off. One minute they were walking down Elm Street, throwing rocks at mailboxes and calling each other pussies; the next he was fighting to stay off the ground and not be rolled into a big pile of dog shit. His elbows and knees are raspberried from the asphalt.

Like any wounded and self-respecting older brother, Teddy plans on taking it all out on baby brother and scaring the piss out of him. A terrific crash echoes through the valley. A rotted tree falling or something horrible bullying its way through the woods. Either way, it'll serve as a perfect introduction.

Teddy says, "There's a monster in the graveyard."

His brother Caleb doesn't look up and keeps playing his Nintendo DS. Gunshots and squealing tires spill out of the handheld's mini speaker. He's playing some game rated *mature* due to its language, violence, and extreme sexual situations. Teddy stole it for him from Walmart. The idea was that the game, with its mobsters shooting cops in the face and beating prostitutes with bats, would freak his little brother out. Instead, Caleb plays it quietly and obsessively.

"Listen to me, you little douche. I'm serious. There's a monster, and it comes out, like when it first gets dark. New dark, right? It hates everyone and everything, and it'll be so goddamn hungry."

Caleb is the size of an asterisk. He's adrift inside a second-generation hand-me-down Disney T-shirt. He says, "The monster as the other. Did you know every civilization throughout human history has portrayed their enemies, their rivals, the faithless, anyone they hated, as a monster, or as having monstrous qualities? Warring nations, zealots, clashing political parties, high school football rivals, it inevitably boils down to us versus them, and *them* are always the monsters."

Teddy says, "Check it out: this monster has like tentacles for arms and legs. Head is all eyes and shit." He stands up, almost trips over a stone that belongs to a woman who died over 150 years ago. Her succinct inscription once read: *Beloved Mother and Wife*. There are forty-seven other stones like hers. They're like hers in that they share the same date of passing.

Teddy gains his feet and says, "Mostly it eats the dead people, right? Mostly. But not today. Live meat today, brother."

Caleb moves his fingers and thumbs; the pixelated avatar he controls knocks out some other character's teeth with a chain and without remorse. He says, "It wasn't that long ago people thought children born with birth defects were monsters. Think about it: How else was the average person of yore going to explain an extra limb, a missing eye, a Siamese twin? Or an infant born with encephalitis? If the baby survived to childhood, then the unfortunate kid was presented as a freak, as a real live monster in carnival sideshows."

Teddy sneaks up behind Caleb, grabs his shoulders, and shakes him. "Raaar! Okay, seriously, the monster is pissed, man. I can feel it. Can't you feel it? It's gonna rip the shit out of whoever's fuckin' around in the graveyard. We should go. Now!" Teddy runs two steps and then takes an obvious dive. He writhes on the ground, clutching an ankle. He knows none of this is working, but he commits to his plan as if there were honor in simply committing.

Caleb's avatar acquires a grenade launcher. "I have no doubt there's a monster here. There are monsters everywhere. The monster is the id. And the ego. It's philosophy, and religion, and collective will. It's you, me, them. It's us."

Teddy cries, "I think my ankle's broken. Run home and get help. Quick. Please, Caleb. I'm not fuckin' around!" His last try: If Caleb runs, Teddy will outflank him at the other side of the graveyard and scare him. If he doesn't run, Teddy'll get up and beat the shit out of him.

Caleb jumps off his stone, shuts his DS off, scurries next to his brother, and puts a small hand on Tommy's chest. He says, "Shh. Listen. I have my own monster story. It's a short one. Imagine our town was all there was. Our town was everywhere."

Teddy stops thrashing around. He's aware of how much he doesn't want to be in a graveyard listening to his freaky little brother. He tries to get up. "What? Let's just—"

Caleb pushes him back down. He's not that strong, really. "You stay there and wait, okay? I'm saying imagine our town is all there is to existence. There's an unending desert that surrounds our green little happy place. Okay, then. Now: the town is a monster."

Ten thousand years ago, Tiller's Swamp and the surrounding lowlands were formed by glacial retreat. There is argument in local scientific circles as to whether or not Tiller's Swamp is a true swamp or merely a marsh, which is another type of wetland. Such classifications are meaningless, of course, particularly to the monster.

As far as our closely guarded public records are concerned, the true story of Tiller's Swamp and the monster does not begin in the Ice Age, but begins, instead, in the mid-nineteenth century with one Joseph Tiller. Descended from Quakers, Joseph was a small, brutish man with a left leg three inches shorter than his right. His left boot and equilibrium-enabling rawhide lift can be found in our swamp museum. In part inspired by the great landfill projects that shaped the geography of his beloved hometown of Boston, Joseph formed a company of simple-minded recruits and helped to drain parts of the Great Black Swamp in Indiana so it could be converted into valuable farmland. Tiller and his men were among the thousands of workers digging tiers of drainage ditches. The members of the Tiller Company earned distinction by the speed with which they dug and by famously not succumbing to the fevers and shakes associated with the *bad air* of the swamp. Doctors had yet to discover that it was the enormous clouds of mosquitoes and other bloodsucking insects spreading fever and disease, not the swamp air. Regardless, "Tiller was one of the cogs of that great wheel of human progress" (quoting the plaque that accompanies his left boot in our museum).

Upon hearing of Tiller and his heroic deeds, our heady, media-savvy ancestors conceived of a plan: they extended an official invitation to live in our town to Joseph and his men. Our town council offered free plots of land upon which to build homesteads and communicated a somewhat dubious claim that our town had an inordinately high population of unwed young women waiting for the right man, or, as it were, men.

In what was considered a coup, Joseph and his company of men decided to accept our invitation and relocate from Indiana. Upon arrival, they found that their free plots all abutted the nameless swamp, which, ironically enough, was thought to be only a marsh, or even a bog, back then. The unwed women quotient turned out to be a considerable exaggeration as well. Tiller and his men, exhausted from the Great Black Swamp gig and the rigors of mid-nineteenth-century travel, shrugged, threw up their hands in frustration, and stayed anyway, thinking they'd improve their collective lots somehow.

With such improvement in mind, and in an effort to attract media attention (and young singles from the neighboring communities), Joseph and the town council agreed to set up an elaborate marsh-draining ceremony.

The rest, as they say, is history. History records that they ran out of wine and cheese before the ceremony, which was a huge public embarrassment that still resonates with our residents, who now are never without the proper amount of wine and cheese.

Also, the monster decapitated Joseph Tiller before the first tossed shovelful of ceremonial dirt hit the soggy ground. The monster then went on a rampage, razing the town (sparing only the Little Red

Schoolhouse) and laying waste to any living creature in its path. The siege lasted two full days. Luckily, an anonymous heroic citizen thought to save and preserve the left boot and lift of Joseph Tiller for future generations.

For the monster, there is no past, present, or future. There is no time, at least not in the way we conceive of it. The monster measures time in layers of sediment and in blood.

Regardless of what folklore might imply about the monster's territoriality, or some sensationalistic or even salacious notion of its seeking revenge, its consciousness and motivation, for lack of better terms, are totally alien to us. If we're being honest here, we have to admit that we cannot know what or how it thinks, if it can even be said to think at all, at least in terms of how we understand thinking. Let's put it this way: asking why the monster chooses this moment to emerge from Tiller's Swamp is equivalent to asking an earthquake what its favorite color is.

On this day, the monster moves like a tectonic plate. It sloughs an ancient skin of mud and peat, soil and weed. Stagnant water, green and thick with algae and lily pads, bubbles and shifts as the monster rises. Within the swamp, there are now waves where there should not be waves. Water rushes past its boundaries and crashes over the hummocks, the swamp's small dry-land islands, washing out shrubs and other adolescent wooded vegetation that never had a chance.

The monster that finally, irrevocably steps onto dry land is a hulking, featureless, stygian mass. No one is ready for it. Most of us will succumb to it as weakly as the washed-out shrubs and trees. Only a precious few will understand the monster for what it truly is. Brent and Hannah, our new and presumably happy homeowners, will not be counted among those precious few.

Ironically enough, Brent and Hannah are fucking like animals in their new home, in the downstairs guest bedroom, when the monster attacks. We can't know for sure, of course, as previously noted, but it's likely their fucking has no effect on the monster. Their fucking is as inconsequential to it as the dragonfly that briefly rests on its shoulder.

In the throes of their, frankly, impressive passion (aided by a bottle plus of cheap merlot and a porno documentary they watched on HBO), the couple do not hear the monster emerging from the swamp, nor do they notice when it rips open their home. Their sexual position is an athletic variant of missionary. Hannah's eyes are closed, as she doesn't like seeing Brent's facial contortions during lovemaking: he looks old, his hairline exposed as thinning; then he appears angry, gritted teeth and thick veins like tree roots in his neck; then he's someone else, someone she doesn't recognize at all, a stranger, but not a fantasy stranger, not an arousing stranger, certainly not anyone like the Realtor. Although Brent's transformative stranger is a familiar one, if that makes sense. He becomes the same stranger who mindlessly thrusts his hips and clumsily paws at her breasts, and leaves her thinking *Who is this man?* Usually, if she closes her eyes, everything is okay.

We know that everything is not okay. Before her horrifying death, Hannah is the recipient of one final, fleeting, and random bit of fortune. She doesn't see the monster open its swinging-gate maw and she doesn't see the top half of her husband (starting, roughly, at his solar plexus) disappear. In the darkness of her own making, she feels Brent become slight, and she senses his falling away from her. Then, after a blunt-force trauma that crushes her skull, she feels nothing more. Or so we hope.

The monster makes short work of the gift shop, museum, and fan club. The graveyard is the next stop on the monster's frenzied path. The headstones, which serve as a final record of who lived and died in our town, the final statement of who we were, a statement proffered by people who loved us and thought we mattered, turn to dust under the monster's feet.

Caleb finishes telling Teddy his brief monster story. "Okay, then. Now: the town is a monster. It's a Frankenstein-type monster because we created it. The houses and buildings are its blunt teeth, and one day soon, it will close its great mouth and swallow us whole, devouring everyone and everything."

The monster overhears but is unmoved. It picks up Teddy and plucks off appendages as a child might pluck petals off a flower.

Caleb returns to playing his handheld video game but is no longer playing well. He says, "I have another story: the degradations you, the monster, visit upon us are many, too many to be documented. Instead we lavish care on the details of only a few victims. The lucky few, right? Why do we do this? Do we fear that we'd buckle under the weight of all the accumulated sorrow, tragedy, and loss? Perhaps we fear complacency instead of vigilance within the shadow of your destruction and chaos?" Caleb throws the game player behind him and reaches out a small hand to touch the monster. "Or do we only tell some of the victims' stories because we fear not complacency but overexposure; we fear losing a perverse sense of mystery, because then you and we—your victims—wouldn't be special anymore?"

The monster crushes Caleb's complex and terrible brain under its foot. Caleb's flesh mixes with the gravestone dust, making a gory, pasty mess that leaves a trail on the road to the Little Red Schoolhouse.

We will not linger here in the schoolhouse, where there will be no survivors. The chaperones will die first, nobly trying to protect the children. Mr. Butler, confronted with a real monster, not one constructed of self-pity, will not be heard over the screams. He will walk toward the monster, resigned, and saying, "Go away," like the punch line to a long and not particularly funny joke. He'll die in the monster's hands, thinking of Vera and how he'll miss her memory.

As distasteful and unpopular as it is, the children will die horribly. There are no Hansels and Gretels here. Most of the children will die wondering how this could be happening to them. Some will remain convinced this should not be happening to them, thinking it's like Mr. Butler was saying before, *There must be some kind of mistake.* The ones who will be eaten last suffer terribly, having had to watch their classmates eaten before them. Their suffering will be no fair trade, please do not think that, yet these *final* children will be the precious few who come to understand what the monster is and what it means.

Perhaps if we were to actually tell the real monster story and fully confront all the tragedies mentioned above, we might glimpse an awful and beautiful and most elusive wisdom: of how to love and live with each other and with the terrible knowledge of the unknowable, uncaring, and undiscriminating monster.

Of course, it should be noted that the next new-and-improved set of official town records will not document the attack on the school-house. In fact, the next town record will report that the schoolhouse was spared, just as all the previous sets of town records (going all the way back to Joseph Tiller's era) fictitiously, erroneously reported the monster had spared the schoolhouse. Instead, the surviving coun-cil members and the always professional Realtor will concoct a story about how our town's faith and fortitude overcame another attack. Our future locals will spend years discussing and digesting the fictional last-minute heroics of a town selectman and a Methodist minister.

The new official story will go as follows: the two men filled the town selectman's twenty-year-old American-made pickup truck with raw meat and lured the monster away from the school, to the cheers and smiles of the twenty-six little faces they saved. The minister prayed hard and the selectman drove hard, right into the swamp, setting the trap. The monster jumped on top of them, the accumulated weight of monster and machine sank the heroes and their perfectly good pickup truck into the depths of the swamp, and that's where they all stayed.

The future locals will fill in personal details concerning both the selectman and minister, reveling in their past sins and weaknesses, which will serve only to make their sacrifice and ultimate redemption all the more sweet. Some future locals will insist they heard the se-lectman and minister were alive and living happily anonymous lives in another town. In our future pubs and themed family restaurant bars, future beers will be wagered upon whether or not there was a spectacular Hollywood-style explosion when the monster and pickup truck hit the swamp's bottom.

What will not be debated or questioned by the future us is the moral of the town's newest official monster story: don't worry, we'll all be saved and everything will be all right.

A HAUNTED HOUSE IS A WHEEL
UPON WHICH SOME ARE BROKEN

ARRIVAL

Fiona arranged for the house to be empty and for the door to be left
open. She has never lived far from the house. It was there, a comfort,
a threat, a reminder, a Stonehenge, a totem of things that actually
happened to her. The house was old when she was a child. That her
body has aged faster than the house (there are so many kinds of years;
there are dog years and people years and house years and geological
years and cosmic years) is a joke and she laughs at it, with it, even
though all jokes are cruel. The house is a New England colonial, blue
with red and white shutters and trim, recently painted, the first-floor
windows festooned with flower boxes. She stands in the house's considerable shadow. She was once very small, and then she became big,
and now she is becoming small again, and that process is painful but
not without joy and an animal sense of satisfaction that the coming
end is earned. She thinks of endings and beginnings as she climbs
the five steps onto the front porch. Adjacent to the front door and
to her left is a white historical placard with the year 1819 and the
house's name. Her older brother, Sam, said that you could never say
the house's name out loud or you would wake up the ghosts, and she
never did say the name, not even once. The ghosts were there
anyway. Fiona never liked the house's name and thought it was silly,

and worse, because of the name preexisting and now postexisting, it means that the house was never hers. Despite everything, she wanted it to always be hers.

Fiona hesitates to open the front door. (Go to pg 153 THE FRONT DOOR*)*

Fiona decides not to go inside the house after all and walks back to her car. (Go to pg 170 LEAVING THE HOUSE*)*

THE FRONT DOOR

It's like Fiona has always and forever been standing at the front door. She places a hand on the wood and wonders what is on the other side, what has changed, what has remained the same. Change is always on the other side of a door. Open a door. Close a door. Walk in. Walk out. Repeat. It's a loop, or a wheel. She doesn't open the door and instead imagines a practice run; her opening the door and walking through the house, stepping lightly into each of the rooms, careful not to disturb anything, and she is methodical in itemizing and identifying the ghosts. She feels what she thinks she is going to feel, and she doesn't linger in either the basement or her parents' bedroom, and she eventually walks out of the house, and all this is still in her head, and she closes the door, then turns around, stands in the same spot she's standing in now, and places a hand on the wood and wonders what is on the other side, what has changed, what has remained the same.

Fiona opens the door. (Go to pg 154 ENTRANCEWAY)

Fiona is not ready to open the door. (Go to pg 153 THE FRONT DOOR)

Fiona decides to walk back to the car and not go inside the house. (Go to pg 170 LEAVING THE HOUSE)

ENTRANCEWAY

Fiona gently pushes the front door closed, watches it nestle into the frame, and listens for the latching mechanism to click into place before turning her full attention to the house. The house. The house. The house. Sam said because the house was so old and historical (he pronounced it *his-store-ickle* so that it rhymed with *pickle*) there was a ghost in every one of the rooms. He was right. The house is a ghost, too. That's obvious. That all the furniture, light fixtures, and decorations will be different (most of everything will be antique, or made to look antique; the present owners take their caretakers-of-a-living-museum role seriously) and the layout changed from when she lived here won't matter because she's not here to catalog those differences. She'll have eyes only for the ghost house. Fiona says, Hello? because she wants to hear what she sounds like in the house of the terrible now. She says hello again and her voice runs up the stairs and around banisters and bounces off plaster and crown molding and sconces, and she finds the sound of the now-her in the house pleasing and a possible antidote to the poison of nostalgia and regret, so she says hello again, and louder. Satisfied with her reintroduction, Fiona asks, Okay, where should we go first?

Fiona turns to her right and walks into the living room. (Go to pg 155 LIVING ROOM*)*

Fiona walks straight ahead into the dining room. (Go to pg 156 DINING ROOM*)*

The weight of the place and its history and her history is too much; Fiona abruptly turns around and leaves the house. (Go to pg 170 LEAVING THE HOUSE*)*

LIVING ROOM

Dad builds a fire and uses all the old newspaper to do it, and pieces glowing orange at their tips break free and float up into the flue, moving as though they are alive and choosing flight. Fiona and Sam shuffle their feet on the throw rug and then touch the cast-iron radiator, their static electric shocks so big at times, a blue arc is visible. Mom sits on the floor so that Fiona can climb onto the couch and jump onto her back. A bushel and a peck and a hug around the neck. The fire is out and the two of them are by themselves and Sam pokes around in the ashes with a twig. Sam says that Little Laurence Montague was a chimney sweep, the best and smallest in the area, and he cleaned everyone's chimney, but he got stuck and died in this chimney, so stuck, in fact, they would not be able to get his body out without tearing the house apart, so the homeowners built a giant fire that they kept burning for twenty-two days, until there was no more Little Laurence left, not even his awful smell. Sam says that you can see him, or parts of him anyway, all charred and misshapen, sifting through the ash, looking for his pieces, and if you aren't careful, he'll take a piece from you. Fiona makes sure to stay more than an arm's length away from the fireplace. Of all the ghosts, Little Laurence scares her the most, but she likes to watch him pick through the ash, hoping to see him find those pieces of himself. There are so many.

Fiona walks into the dining room. (Go to pg 156 DINING ROOM)

Fiona walks to the kitchen. (Go to pg 157 KITCHEN)

This is already harder than she thought it was going to be; impossible, in fact. Fiona doesn't think she can continue and leaves the house. (Go to pg 170 LEAVING THE HOUSE)

DINING ROOM

Fiona and Sam are under the table and their parents' legs float by like branches flowing down a river. The floorboards underneath groan and whisper and they understand their house, know it as a musical instrument. Dad sits by himself and wants Fiona and Sam to come out from under the table and talk to him; they do and then he doesn't know what to say or how to say it; her father is so young and she never realized how young he is. Mom isn't there. She doesn't want to be there. Sam says there was an eight-year-old girl named Maisy who had the strictest of parents, the kind who insisted children did not speak during dinner, and poor Maisy was choking on a piece of potato from a gloopy beef stew and she was so terrified of what her parents would do if she said anything, made any sort of noise, that she sat and quietly choked to death. Sam says you can see her at the table sitting there with her face turning blue and her eyes as large and white as hard-boiled eggs and if you get too close she will wrap her hands around your neck and you won't be able to call out or say anything until it's too late. Of all the ghosts, Maisy scares Fiona the most, and she watches in horror as Maisy sits at the table trying to be a proper girl.

Fiona walks straight ahead and into the kitchen. (Go to pg 157 KITCHEN*)*

Fiona turns right and walks into the living room. (Go to pg 155 LIVING ROOM*)*

Fiona bypasses the kitchen entirely and goes to the basement. (Go to pg 158 BASEMENT*)*

This is harder than she thought it was going to be; impossible, in fact. Fiona doesn't think she can continue and leaves the house. (Go to pg 170 LEAVING THE HOUSE*)*

KITCHEN

Dad cooks fresh flounder and calls it "fried French" and not fish so that Fiona will eat it. The four of them play card games (cribbage, mainly) at the kitchen table and Fiona leaves the room in tears after being yelled at (Dad says he wasn't yelling, which isn't the same as saying he's sorry) for continually leading into runs and allowing Sam and Mom to peg. Mom sits at the table by herself and says she feels fine and smokes a cigarette. Her mother is so young and Fiona never realized how young she is. Sam screams and cries and smashes glasses and dishes on the hardwood floor and no one stops him. Fiona and Mom stand at the back door and look outside, waiting for the birds to eat the stale bread crumbs they sprinkled about their small backyard. Sam says there was a boy named Percy who was even smaller than Little Laurence. He was so small because the only thing he would eat was blueberry muffins, and he loved those muffins so much, he crawled inside the oven so he could better watch the muffin batter rise and turn golden brown. Sam says that you can see him curled up inside the oven and if you get too close he'll pull you in there with him. Of all the ghosts, Percy scares Fiona the most because of how small he is; she knows it's not polite, but she can't help but stare at his smallness.

Fiona saves the basement for later and walks through the dining room, the living room, and then into the den. (Go to pg 159 DEN)

Fiona backtracks into the dining room. (Go to pg 156 DINING ROOM)

Fiona goes to the living room. (Go to pg 155 LIVING ROOM)

Fiona goes into the basement. (Go to pg 158 BASEMENT)

This is harder than she thought it was going to be; impossible, in fact. Fiona doesn't think she can continue and leaves the house. (Go to pg 170 LEAVING THE HOUSE)

BASEMENT

Fiona is not ready for the basement, not yet.

Fiona saves the basement for later and walks through the dining room, the living room, and then into the den. (Go to pg 159 DEN)

Fiona goes into the kitchen. (Go to pg 157 KITCHEN)

The idea of going into the basement is enough to make her abandon the tour and leave the house. (Go to pg 170 LEAVING THE HOUSE)

DEN

Sam is never delicate closing the French doors, and their little rectangular windows rattle and quiver in their frames. Fiona rearranges the books in the built-in floor-to-ceiling bookshelves: first alphabetical by author, then by title, then by color. Dad shuts the lights off in the rest of the house, leaving only the den well lit; he hides and dares his children to leave the den and find him, and he laughs as they scream with a mix of mock and real terror. Dad and Mom put Sam and Fiona in the den by themselves and shut the French doors (controlled, and careful) because they are having a private talk. Mom watches the evening news with a cup of tea and invites Fiona and Sam to watch with her so that they will know what's going on in the world. Sam and Fiona lay on the floor, on their stomachs, blanket over their heads, watching a scary movie. Sam stands in front of the TV and stiff-arms Fiona away, physically blocking her from changing the channel. Mom lets Fiona take a puff of her cigarette and Fiona's lungs are on fire and she coughs, cries, and nearly throws up, and Mom rubs her back and says remember this so you'll never do it again. Sam says there was a girl named Olivia who liked to climb the bookcases in the walls and wouldn't stop climbing the shelves even after her parents begged her not to, and in an effort to stop her, they filled the bookcases with the heaviest leather-bound books with the largest spines that could squeeze into the shelves. Olivia was determined to still climb the shelves and touch the ceiling like she'd always done, and she almost made it to the top again, but her feet slipped, or maybe it was she couldn't get a good handhold anymore, and she fell and broke her neck. Sam says you can see Olivia high up, close to the ceiling, clinging to the shelves, and if you get too close, Olivia throws books at you, the heaviest ones, the ones that can do the most damage. Of all the ghosts, Olivia scares Fiona the most, but she wants to read the books that Olivia throws at her.

Fiona goes back to the foyer and to the front stairs. (Go to pg 161 THE STAIRS)

Fiona goes into the kitchen. (Go to pg 157 KITCHEN)

The first floor is enough. Fiona doesn't think she can continue and leaves the house. (Go to pg 170 LEAVING THE HOUSE)

THE STAIRS

Sam ties his green army men to pieces of kite string and dangles them from the banister on the second floor and Fiona is on the first floor, pretending to be a tiger that swipes at the army men, and if one is foolishly dropped low enough, she eats the man in one gulp. Fiona counts the stairs and makes a rhyme. Dad falls down the stairs (after being dared by Sam that he can't hop down on only one foot) and punches through the plaster on the first landing with his shoulder; Dad brushes himself off, shakes his head, and points at the hole and says don't tell Mom. Mom walks up the stairs by herself for the last time (Fiona knows there's a last time for everything), moving slowly and breathing heavily, and she looks back at Fiona, who trails behind, pretending not to watch, and Mom rests on the first landing and says there's a kitty cat that seems to be following her, and she says that cat is still with her when she pauses on the second landing. Sam says there was a boy named Timothy who always climbed up the stairs on the outside of the railings, his toes clinging to the edges as though he was at the edges of great cliffs. Climbing over the banister on the second floor was the hardest part, and one morning he fell, bouncing off the railings, and he landed headfirst in the foyer below, and he didn't get up and brush himself off. Sam says that Timothy tries to trip you when you are not careful on the stairs. Of all the ghosts, Timothy scares Fiona the most, but she still walks on the stairs without holding on to the railings.

Fiona walks up the stairs without holding the railing (and actually smiles to herself), and then goes into her bedroom. (Go to pg 162 FIONA'S BEDROOM)

The stairs make Fiona incredibly, inexplicably sad; she doesn't think she can continue and leaves the house. (Go to pg 170 LEAVING THE HOUSE)

FIONA'S BEDROOM

Fiona spies out the window, which is above the front door, and as their house is on top of a hill, it overlooks the rest of the town, and she picks a spot that is almost as far as she can see and wonders what the people there are doing and thinking. Dad reads her *The Tale of Mr. Jeremy Fisher* using a British accent; it's the only storybook for which he uses the accent. Mom takes the cold facecloth off Fiona's forehead, thermometer from her mouth, and says scoot over, I'll be sick with you, okay? There is the night Dad isn't allowed in her room and he knocks quietly and he says that he's sorry if he scared her in the basement and he's sorry about dinner and he's making it right now and please open the door and come out, and he sounds watery, and she's not mad or scared (she is hungry) but tells him to go away. Sam is not allowed in her room but he comes in anyway and gets away with it and he smiles that smile she hates. She misses that smile terribly now, for as much of a pain in the ass as he was as a child, he was a loyal, thoughtful, sensitive, if not melancholy, man. Sam says that there is the ghost of a girl named Wanda in Fiona's closet and no one knows what happened to her or how she got there because she's always been there. Of all the ghosts, Wanda scares Fiona the most because try as she might, she's never been able to talk to her.

Fiona will go to all the second-floor rooms in their proper order, waiting until she's ready to go to her parents' bedroom. (Go to pg 163 SAM'S BEDROOM)

The second floor is indeed too much. Fiona doesn't think she can continue and leaves the house. (Go to pg 170 LEAVING THE HOUSE)

SAM'S BEDROOM

Fiona sits outside Sam's room and the door is shut and Sam and his friends are inside talking about the Boston Red Sox and the Wynne sisters who live two streets over. Fiona finds magazines filled with pictures of naked women under Sam's bed. Dad is inside Sam's room yelling at (and maybe even hitting) Sam because Sam hit Fiona because Fiona took some of his green army men and threw them into the sewer because Sam wouldn't play with her. Sam lets Fiona sleep on the floor in a sleeping bag (she always asked to do this) because they watched a scary movie and she can't sleep but isn't scared and tries to stay awake long enough to notice how different it is sleeping in Sam's room. Mom hides under Sam's piled bedsheets and blankets and they trick Dad into going into Sam's room and she jumps out and scares him so badly he falls down on the floor and holds his chest. Sam tells Fiona to come into his room and she's worried he's going to sneak attack, give her a dead arm or something, and instead he's crying and says that they aren't going to live in this house anymore. Sam says that there aren't any ghosts in his room and tells her to stop asking about it, so Fiona makes one up. She says that there's a boy who got crushed underneath his dirty clothes that piled up to the ceiling and no one ever found the boy and Sam never takes his dirty clothes downstairs because he's afraid of the boy. Of all the ghosts, this one scares Fiona the most because she forgot to name him.

Fiona goes into the bathroom. (Go to pg 164 BATHROOM)

The second floor is indeed too much. Fiona doesn't think she can continue and leaves the house. (Go to pg 170 LEAVING THE HOUSE)

BATHROOM

Dad leaves the bathroom door open when he shaves his face and he says there goes my nose and oops no more lips and I guess I don't need a chin. The shaving foam is so white and puffy when Fiona puts it on her face, and she greedily inhales its minty, menthol smell. Sam is in the bathroom for a long, long time with what he says are his comic books. Mom is strong and she doesn't cry anywhere else in the house, certainly never in front of Fiona or Sam, but she cries when she's by herself and taking a bath and the water is running; the sound of a bath being run never fails to make Fiona think about Mom. Everyone else is in her parents' bedroom and to her great, never-ending shame, Fiona is in the bathroom with the door shut, sitting on the floor, the tile hard and cold on her backside, the bath running, the drain un-stopped so the tub won't fill, and she cries, and Dad knocks gently on the door and asks if she's okay and asks her to come back, but she stays in the bathroom for hours until after it's over. Sam says that there was a boy named Charlie who loved to take baths and stayed in them so long that his toes and feet and hands and everything got so wrinkly that his whole body shriveled and shrank until he eventually slipped right down the drain. Sam says that if you stay in the bath too long Charlie will suck you into the drain with him. Of all the ghosts, Fiona finds Charlie the least scary, and she talks to him in the drain.

Fiona goes into the hallway and stands in front of her parents' bedroom. (Go to pg 165 PARENTS' BEDROOM DOOR)

Fiona stays in the bathroom, as she did those many years ago. (Go to pg 164 BATHROOM)

Fiona doesn't think she can continue and leaves the house. (Go to pg 170 LEAVING THE HOUSE)

PARENTS' BEDROOM DOOR

The door is closed. It's the only door in her haunted house that is closed. Even the door to the basement in the kitchen is open. This door is closed. It's a Saturday afternoon and the door is closed and locked, and Fiona knocks and Mom says please give them a few minutes of privacy and then she giggles from deep down somewhere in her room, and Fiona knocks again and then Dad is yelling at her to get lost. The door is closed because it's almost Christmas and she doesn't believe in Santa anymore but hasn't said anything, and she knows she can't go in there because their presents are wrapped and stacked along one bedroom wall. The door is closed and Mom's smallest voice is telling her that she can come in, but Fiona doesn't want to. Fiona places a hand on the wood and her hand is a ghost of her younger hands. She wonders what is on the other side, what has changed, what has remained the same. Change is always on the other side of a door. Open a door. Close a door. Walk in. Walk out. Repeat. It's a loop, or a wheel. Of all the ghosts, the ones in her parents' bedroom scare her the most because maybe nothing ever changes and even though she's an adult (and likes to think of herself at this age as *beyond-adult* because its connotations are so much more dignified and well earned than the title *elderly*), she's afraid she'll make the same decisions all over again.

Fiona opens the door. (Go to pg 166 PARENTS' BEDROOM)

Fiona returns to the bathroom. (Go to pg 164 BATHROOM)

Fiona doesn't think she can continue and leaves the house. (Go to pg 170 LEAVING THE HOUSE)

PARENTS' BEDROOM

Sam and Fiona wrestle Dad on the bed, with his signature move being a blanket toss over their bodies like a net so that he can tickle them with impunity. Fiona tells Mom that Dad shouldn't have hit Sam because she kind of deserved what he did to her for throwing his army men in the sewer. Mom stands in the room wearing only a loose-fitting bra and underwear, and she yells at her clothes, discarded and piled at the edge of the bed, saying nothing she has fits her anymore, and she says it's all just falling off me. It's Christmas morning and Sam and Fiona sit in the dark on the floor next to Mom's side of the bed, watching the clock, waiting for six A.M. so that they can all go downstairs. Mom is in bed; she's home from the hospital and she says she is not going back. Despite the oppressive heat, Fiona sleeps wedged between her parents during a thunderstorm, counting Mississippis after lightning strikes. Fiona gives Mom ice chips because she can't eat anything else and Mom says thank you after each chip passes between her dried, cracked lips. Dad sets up a mirror opposite the full-length mirror and takes pictures of Fiona and her reflections from different angles with his new camera (she doesn't remember ever seeing the photos). Mom's skin is a yellowish green, the color of pea soup (which Fiona hates), and her eyes, when they are open, are large and terrible, and they are terrible because they are not Mom's, they are Maisy's eyes, and her body has shriveled up like Charlie's and pieces of her have been taken away as if she was Little Laurence and she says nothing like Maisy and Wendy say nothing, and Sam is standing in a corner of the room with his arms wrapped around himself like boa constrictors and Dad sits on the bed, rubbing Mom's hand and asking her if she needs anything, and when a nurse and doctor arrive (she doesn't remember their names and wants to give them ghosts' names) Fiona does not stay in the room with her family, she runs out and goes to the bathroom and sits on the floor and runs a bath and she hasn't forgiven herself (even though she was so young, a child; a frightened and heartbroken and confused and angry child) for not staying in the room with Mom until the end. Sam says there was a girl named Fiona who looked like her and acted like her, and her parents stopped caring for her one day, so Fiona faded away and disappeared.

Sam says if Fiona doesn't stop going into Mom and Dad's room the ghost-Fiona will take her over and she'll disappear, fade away. Of all the ghosts, ghost-Fiona scares her the most, even though she knows Sam is trying to scare her out of the room so he can wrestle Dad by himself, and she thinks there are times when ghost-Fiona takes over her body and the real Fiona goes away, and sometimes she wishes for that to happen.

Fiona is determined to finish her tour and she walks downstairs, walks through the first floor, into the kitchen, ignoring Percy, and then down into the basement. (Go to pg 168 BASEMENT)

Fiona is still reenacting the night her mother died in her bedroom and she goes back to the bathroom. (Go to pg 164 BATHROOM)

Fiona doesn't have to go to the basement. She leaves the house. (Go to pg 170 LEAVING THE HOUSE)

BASEMENT

Fiona does a lap around the basement, sometimes holding her hands above her head or tight against her body so that she won't brush up against the forgotten boxes and sawhorses and piles of wood and roof shingles, and careful to not go near Dad's work area (off limits) with its bitey tools and slippery sawdust, but she has to go fast as Sam is counting and if she doesn't make it back to the stairs before he counts to twenty he kills the light (at some point he'll kill the light anyway). Fiona follows Mom to the silver, cow-sized freezer and watches her struggle to lift out a frozen block of meat. Sam places his green army men on top of the dryer and they make bets about which plastic man will stay on the longest and Fiona doesn't care if she loses because she loves smelling the warm, soft, humid dryer exhaust. Dad has been in the basement all day and they haven't eaten dinner and Sam is not there (she forgets where Sam is, but he's not in the house) and Mom has been gone for exactly one year and Fiona doesn't call out Dad's name and instead creeps down the basement stairs as quietly as she can and the only light on in the basement is the swinging bulb in Dad's work area, and a static-tinged radio plays Motown, and Fiona can't see Dad or his work area from the bottom of the stairs, only the light, so she sneaks in the dark over past the washer/dryer and the freezer, and Dad sits on his stool, his back is to her, his legs splayed out, his right arm pistons up and down like he's hammering a nail but there's no hammering-a-nail sound, and he's breathing heavy, and there are beer cans all over his table, and she says, Dad, are we having dinner? even though she knows she should not say anything and go back up the stairs and find something to eat, and he jumps up from the chair (back still turned to her), and beer cans fall and a magazine flutters to the dirty floor (and if it's not the exact same magazine, it's like one of the naked-girl magazines she found in Sam's room) and so do photos of Mom, and they are black-and-white photos of her and she is by herself and she is young and laughing and she is on the beach, running toward the camera with her arms over her head, and Fiona has always loved those pictures of Mom on the beach, and Dad's shirt is untucked and hanging over his unbuckled pants and instead of getting mad or yelling he talks the way Sam might talk when he's in trouble, a little-boy voice, asking what she's doing down here, and he picks up the magazine and the pictures and he doesn't turn around to face her, and then she asks what was he doing, and he slumps back into his chair and cries, and then he starts throwing the beer cans (empty and full) off the wall, and Fiona runs out of the basement in less than twenty seconds. Sam says that the ghost of every person who ever lived in the house eventually goes to the basement and that some houses have so many ghosts in their basements that they line the walls and they're stacked like cords of wood.

Fiona has finally seen all the ghosts and spent enough time with them, and she can now leave the house. (Go to pg 171 LEAVING THE HOUSE)

Fiona goes back up all the stairs to stand in front of her parents' bedroom door. (Go to pg 165 PARENTS' BEDROOM DOOR)

LEAVING THE HOUSE

It's colder now than it was when she arrived. Fiona walks to her car and won't allow herself to stop and turn and stare at the house. Even with the visit cut short, she knows the ghosts are not trapped in the house, not bound to both the permanence and impermanence of place, as she once foolishly hoped. The ghosts do not follow behind her, in a polite, single-file, Pied Piper line to be cataloged, then archived and forgotten. The ghosts are with her and will be with her always. It is not a comfort because she will not allow it to be a comfort. How can she? As always, Fiona is too hard on herself, and she remains her very own ghost that scares her the most.

Fiona does not forgive herself. (Go to pg 153 THE FRONT DOOR*)*

Fiona returns to the house. (Go to pg 153 THE FRONT DOOR*)*

LEAVING THE HOUSE

It's colder now than it was when she arrived. Fiona walks to her car and won't allow herself to stop and turn and stare at the house. She knows the ghosts are not trapped in the house, not bound to both the permanence and impermanence of place, as she once foolishly hoped. The ghosts do not follow behind her, in a polite, single-file, Pied Piper line to be cataloged, then archived and forgotten. The ghosts are with her, have always been with her, and continue to be with her, and maybe that can be a comfort, a confirmation, if she'll let it. Fiona was ten years old when Mom died from colon cancer. Her father died of cystic fibrosis thirty-seven years later. Dad never remarried and moved to Florida when he got sick and Fiona wrote him letters (he wrote back until he became too weak to do so) and she talked to him every other day on the phone and she spent three of her four weeks of vacation visiting him, and her lovely brother Sam cared for Dad during the last two years of his life. Poor Sam died of pneumonia after suffering a series of strokes five years ago. She doesn't know what to do, so she starts talking. She says to her father (who she knew for much longer and so much more intimately than her mother, yet somehow it feels like she didn't know him as well, as though the glut of father-data confuses and contradicts), I'm sorry we let every day be more awkward and formal than they should've been and I'm sorry I never told you that I don't blame you for anything you did or said in grief, I never did, and I want to say, having outlived my Marcie, that I understand. Then she says to Mom (who she knew for only ten years, less, really, in terms of her ever-shrinking timeline of memory, and of course, somehow, more), I'm sorry I didn't stay, I wish I'd stayed with you, and I can stay with you now if you want me to. Fiona cries old tears, the ones dredged from a bottomless well of a child's never-ending grief. And she cries at the horror and beauty of passed time. And she chides herself for being a sentimental old fool despite having given herself permission to be one. As always, Fiona is too hard on herself, and she remains her very own ghost that scares her the most.

Fiona is still turned away from the house and she feels fingers pulling on the back of her coat, trying to drag her back into the house to go through it

all again. Fiona still cannot forgive herself for not staying in her parents'
bedroom with her mother until the end. She fears that her mother's end
(all ends for that matter) is cruelly eternal and that her mother is still there
alone and waiting for Fiona to finally and forever come back. (Go to pg 153
THE FRONT DOOR)

Fiona is still turned away from the house and she feels fingers pulling on
the back of her coat, trying to drag her back into the house to go through
it all again, or maybe pull her away from everything, pull her away, fi-
nally, until she's hopelessly lost. But she doesn't want to be lost. Fiona walks
around the car, tracing the cold metal frame with one hand, to the driver's-
side door, and gets in the car and starts the engine, which turns over in its
tired mechanical way, and she shifts into first gear. The tires turn slowly,
but they do turn. (Go to pg 173 THE END)

THE END

IT WON'T GO AWAY

I can tell this only in pieces. It's all in pieces. Each piece seems worse than it did the day before or the hour before, as though remembering is a conspiratorial act of further implication, of making *more* worseness.

The last piece arrived today.

Nine days ago, I received an envelope in the mail from Peter. It was exactly one month after he killed himself. I'd been in my new apartment for ten weeks. Time is not an arrow. It is a bottomless bag in which we collect and place things that will be forgotten.

The envelope was blue and greeting card sized. A yellow "notify sender of new address" sticker was plastered diagonally over my old address, a PO box I'd rented during the blurry thirteen months I guest-room-surfed with other writers and artists in the Hudson Valley. Peter's name and return address were a scrawled blotch on the envelope's upper left corner, nearly illegible in black ink, the first of many Rorschach tests. I'd seen enough of his handwriting to determine he was careless and rushed through writing his address. Or maybe he wasn't concentrating, writing on autopilot. Or he was ashamed, and the envelope and its contents were a cry for help I wouldn't hear until it was too late. I've become both expert and failure at finding meaning in the meaningless.

More time again: The postmark date was six days before he killed himself, four days before I left to go to the event in Providence. My shitty one-room efficiency in a shittier neighborhood in Kingston, New York, and his beautiful, newly constructed house in a suburb of Boston were separated by less than 225 miles. (And sometimes more.) If he'd sent the envelope to my new address, I would've received it before I saw Peter that weekend.

The Sunday morning of the reading/book signing, only four hours before he would be dead, I went out to breakfast with Peter, Lauren, and their lovely children (now a teen and a preteen) Steph and Maggie. Steph and I traded New York Yankees/Boston Red Sox quips despite neither of us being big baseball fans. Steph was over six feet tall and armored in his new, easy muscles, but he always carried himself like a smaller child. He was reserved, spoke softly, avoided eye contact, and most of his smiles were fractional, with half-lives measured in seconds. I've wondered what kind of father Peter was and if I was better or worse than him even when I knew the answer was neither. Maggie was flamboyant, manically friendly, an excited electron looking to bounce and charge. When she was younger, she used to draw pictures of me with my beard's length greatly exaggerated and leave the artwork on the floor for me to find when I'd stayed at their house. That morning she had newly pink hair and wanted to talk to me about what horror movies I thought she was old enough to watch.

Peter paid for my coffee and short stack of pancakes. I tried to give him a ten but he wouldn't take my money. The gesture was kind and it was humiliating, even if he didn't intend it to be.

I was the last to leave the breakfast table. Peter stood and walked away after his kids, then Lauren right behind Peter. She ran a hand up and down Peter's back. He turned around and smiled at Lauren. Did that flash of physical affection make him rethink what he was planning to do? Peter briefly surveyed the small dining area filled with patrons and their over-easy eggs and mugs of coffee, and then he looked back at me, or next to me, as though someone else was there sitting in the empty space to my left.

I imagined the envelope contained a letter, encyclopedic in detail about why he did what he did, and then I would have to show it to Lauren and/or someone from the Providence police department.

I carried the unopened envelope to the kitchen table and dropped it there. I cried, briefly, and said, "You asshole," a few times. I knew that wasn't fair. He killed himself because the stew of chemicals in his brain had morphed into a dirty rotten cheat and a liar.

Inside the envelope was a greeting card. Its cover was green with a neon blue cursive *Thank You*. I opened the card and a photo slid out. I assumed the thank-you card wasn't meant to be mocking but simply a vessel for the photo, something Peter grabbed in haste. The photo was printed on regular white paper and not glossy photo stock, so it had a grainy look and the amount of ink curled the paper at its margins.

In the photo, Peter was alone. He stood in front of his bathroom mirror, holding his cell phone in one hand; a little star flash obscured the left half of his expressionless face. He wore black boxer briefs and nothing else. Red and purple acne scars dotted his white skin. His posture was hunched, curved into a cruel kyphosis, like he didn't have the strength to hold up his chest and its vulnerable contents. He was a thin, wiry man, but the exaggerated chest-caved-in posture made his skin sag and melt into rolls that hung over the waistband of his underwear. It appeared he was attempting to make himself look ugly, haggard, grotesque. Seeing him this way, I wanted to cry again, and I wondered why he'd take such a photo of himself. I concluded that in the grips of some dreadful psychological illness this was how he saw himself, how he thought other people saw him. Then I found and read the brief note written inside the thank-you card.

"Lower right of the photo. Can you see it? You can't show it to anyone else."

Peter and I saw each other two or three weekends a year at various writers' conventions and author readings in the Northeast. I stayed at Peter's place for a weekend each February and then we'd drive into Boston for a small science fiction convention that inexplicably invited us horror writers to speak on some panels. We generally talked on the phone once a week. The frequency of calls increased dramatically in the weeks leading up to my divorce as in the weeks after, and during those calls he'd keep me talking and tell me that I would be okay and that the relationship with my son, Dominick, would evolve and survive. Before my divorce, Peter would visit and stay at my house for a few days, usually during his school's spring break, and Dominick reveled in showing off his new karate moves. Dominick is kind, joyously physical in his expression of enthusiasm and curiosity, and as socially awkward as his father, I'm afraid. I see Dominick and his very worried face only every other weekend now. As long as the ponds and rivers aren't frozen over, I take him fishing so that our barely speaking to each other becomes pragmatic instead of soul crushing.

I have plenty of acquaintances and colleagues, maybe too many. Most of them are digital—a collection of avatars, likes, retweets, and e-mails to which I now infrequently respond. Peter and I were friends. I don't say that lightly. He called me his brother less than a minute before he killed himself.

Why didn't he e-mail me the photo or tell me about it on the phone? Why didn't he show me everything when I was right there in his house, or when we were in Providence?

Why hadn't I seen it in the photo for myself (when it is now so clearly *there*) before I read his message in the thank-you card?

A second envelope, same size as the first, arrived a few mornings ago. I haven't opened it yet. The morning it arrived, I let it sit atop a mass of photos I printed out, including the pictures I'd started taking of myself. And those photos of me were a layer of ash on top of printed-out photos of Peter. Those Peter photos were cut up and spliced and taped together, and somewhere under those was the first photo he mailed to me, and under that was the thank-you card and the first envelope, and under that was the kitchen tabletop, and it all connected and it all infected, and this is the cat that killed the rat that ate the malt that lay in the house. . . .

The new envelope. Its postmark date was four days before he killed himself, which was two days after he mailed the first envelope, two days before I left for Providence.

Time is not an arrow. Sometimes it is a deck of cards that you can shuffle. And cut.

In a different universe, the one in which I had received the card and photo before leaving for Providence, I might've assumed Peter was scheming some new and odd viral marketing campaign. He was much more active and social media savvy than I was. His easygoing, friends-to-all persona was naturally geared toward successful online promotion that managed to walk the line between an endearing aw-shucks-isn't-it-cool-that-this-is-happening-to-me and being an annoying spambot.

In his newest novel, only a few months old, characters think they see fleeting dark shapes in corners and empty spaces of rooms and peering into their windows. The dark shapes may be portents of doom, or the shadow of a real person representing the mundanity of evil, or a literal devil, or the echo of guilt and shame, or the avatar of violence following the characters (even the dead ones) into a kind of afterlife, or it's all nothing but the figments of imagination and grief, or something else entirely, or something that's not there at all.

In the photo, to Peter's right, below the marble bathroom sink counter and toward the corner of the wall and linen closet door, is a dark shape. At first glance and second glance, and third, one might have assumed it was the ink-jet printer spasming, unable to re-create the photo flash effect in a darkened bathroom. I kept giving the photo more glances, and the dark blotch of ink seemed to refocus and not quite take a recognizable, organic shape, but come maddeningly close so that it blurred and subtly re-formed the longer I looked at it. But then if I blinked or turned away, it snapped back into whatever form I thought I saw initially.

I turned the photo, flipped it, held it up to the light, thinking I might see a boundary, a line where the darkness began or ended.

Upon arriving in Providence on Saturday around one P.M., I met Peter and Frances at the Trinity Brew Pub, only a block away from the library, one of the venues hosting the Lovecraft Film Festival. Frances was in her early thirties, a decade-plus younger than Peter and me. She was an indie filmmaker adapting one of my short stories into a film. She wanted me to have and take home a large prop made for the movie, a rib bone curling six feet in length from tip to tip. I had no space for it in my apartment, but I toyed with taking it back to give to Dominick. Maybe I would have taken it back for him if everything that happened on Sunday hadn't happened.

Peter and Frances had already secured a table and were two beers deep. We exchanged greeting hugs, something I'm terribly awkward with, particularly when tired, hungry, and stressed out from a long drive. And, to be honest, my social anxiety was one of the reasons why I had decided to stop frequenting conventions and readings, with finances being another reason, and yet another, the notion that I could prevent the inexorable untethering from Dominick if I remained geographically fixed within the Hudson Valley at all times, like an old stone fence in a forgotten stretch of woods.

Peter often made a joke about my awkward greetings, but didn't that afternoon. He said it was great to see me, and he lingered. He lingered there, within arm's length, his large, spidery hands on my shoulders. I shrugged him off and said I'd be more human after food. He asked if I'd received anything from him in the mail.

It's odd now in retrospect that he would ask right then, because depending upon my answer, he would have had to explain to Frances what it was he'd sent, unless he thought he could count on my confusion and/or discretion to not fully detail the contents of what I'd received.

I told Peter there was nothing from him in the mail this week and I asked what he'd sent.

He smirked and side-glanced at me, a mischievous look, or perhaps he wasn't sure if I was telling the truth. He dismissed me to sit in the booth by waving a hand, and then he lied. He said it wasn't a big deal and that it was an extra copy of a new writer's short-story collection.

The three of us fell into an easy conversation about movies and books, and Frances told stories about her screenwriting work on prior films. Peter was engaged, content to listen more than he talked until Frances asked him what he was working on. He mentioned a novel that was in the earliest planning stages but didn't give any plot or character details. I don't recall if he was prompted by a follow-up question or something one of us said, but Peter went on to say he'd been having trouble coming up with an idea for the next novel; he'd struggled with it all spring and now into summer. He said ideas are fleeting like that sometimes, just out of reach, or seeming to always belong to someone else. He said sometimes an idea felt like it had been there in his head since before he was him, and the idea was patiently waiting, plotting for the right time to show itself. He said sometimes an idea was a bully and would take him over, hold him hostage, and he'd be powerless to do anything else but think and worry at it.

I stayed at Frances and Victoria's house in East Providence for five days, not returning home until after Peter's wake and the funeral. I stayed in their guest room and came out only to eat and use the bathroom and apologize for all the whiskey I was drinking. I spent the rest of the time online.

Peter's death and the *how* of it caused an online and offline shit-storm. The small horror-writing community was shocked, devastated, and confused. How could he do that to himself when his life and career were not just going well, but were the envy of most? He'd published his last two horror novels with one of the largest publishing houses in the world, HarperCollins. Both books were optioned by major Hollywood production companies. He'd earned starred reviews in *Publishers Weekly* and *Booklist* and the books were glowingly reviewed in the *New York Times*, on NPR, in *Entertainment Weekly*. So many of the important cultural tastemakers had praised his work. His books sold well, though how well was exaggerated by many, as Peter would be too quick to point out, maintaining he was no bestseller and he wasn't quitting his teaching job anytime soon. Regardless, to most outside observers, Peter was living the horror writer's seemingly unattainable dream.

My social media platforms and e-mail inbox were flooded with messages and questions from other writers and readers. Had Peter been unhappy? Had he been ill? Had something happened to trigger this? Were there things we didn't know about him? Were there any signs? I had no answers for them and I had no answers for myself.

Having been Peter's close friend and coreader at the Providence event, I was inundated with interview requests from all manner of press outlets. I rejected almost all of them. On the first night back to my apartment, slurring drunk, I was on a phone call I didn't remember answering with a reporter from CNN. When he asked if I thought the kind of stuff we wrote might've infected Peter somehow, if this *situation* (the fucking twit actually said "situation") was similar to when heavy metal listeners killed themselves or others, I told him to fuck off, hung up, and committed to breaking all the glasses and dishes in my apartment.

Peter, his life and work, and horror as a genre and as entertainment were discussed on cable networks and online and in print. Less-than-half-baked think pieces sprouted like weeds. Everyone had an opinion, and most of the opinions were speculative, lazy armchair psychiatry and moral-pandering pabulum. I blasted social media missives at articles' authors and created accounts at news websites and platforms in order to scorch the comment sections.

The news cycle chewed up Peter and spat him out in a matter of days. The writing community mourned, lamented, introspected, promised tribute stories and anthologies (the proceeds from which would go to Peter's family, of course), and limped on with their collective lives after a few weeks. Peter's afterlife would be as the horror community's mystery, martyr, and cautionary tale, itself a horror story, a twist on the hoary cliché of *be careful what you wish for.*

Then it all blew up again four days ago, after one of the reading's attendees killed himself. Will, the man who'd set up and maintained the event room's sound system, slit his wrists while his girlfriend was at work.

After I'd finished poring over the photo, the thank-you card, and its message, I cannonballed into a bottle of Maker's Mark and spent the rest of the afternoon and evening scrolling through Peter's Facebook page. He had posted and been tagged in hundreds of pictures. There on my screen was Peter at various readings, book events, and conventions, standing at podiums, sitting at long tables in front of a microphone, pen in hand, book splayed out before him like a treasure map, him and a toothy smile, arm around someone's shoulder, glasses filled with amber liquids in raised hands, and there was Peter with Lauren on a beach, goofy selfies with Maggie sitting on their big green couch, the family on vacation at a rented lake house, at one of Steph's basketball games, at a sibling's house, at nieces' birthday parties. I sank deeper and deeper into the bottle and into those bits of color and image from his life. I couldn't help but think he put too much of himself and his family out there for anyone to gawk at, and I judged him negatively for it as much as I was envious of the attitude that enabled him to share as much as he did. On my phone I had only three photos of Dominick and me together.

I first saw it in a picture of Peter from the night of his latest novel's release event, which was almost exactly two months before he killed himself. The photo was from before the reading/party. He was still at his house and dressed in a black button-down shirt and jeans. He stood in front of a red wall in his dining room, eyebrows arched over his black-framed glasses, lopsided smirk, his new novel in one hand and a Narragansett beer can in the other. Peter was a big *Jaws* fan; he'd dressed as Quint the previous Halloween and the can was part of his costume. Below his bent elbow was the shadow of his arm. The shadow began to look odd, a little off, like it didn't quite fit the space that should've been allotted to it. The longer I looked, the more certain I became, a discovery of what I would ultimately see was imminent, but I did not progress beyond a *feeling* of certainty.

I sifted through his hundreds of Facebook pictures a second time. And a third. A pattern initially emerged within the photos from the two months between the release event and the Providence reading, and a subset of those photos in which Peter was alone. Away from the center of focus, which changed from photo to photo, depending on the foreground, the staging, his posture, his expression, the angle of the camera, the lighting, the environment, there was a bit of darkness, or blankness, and maybe at first glance it was simply shadow, or quirks of the photography, but at more glances, more and more glances, it was something else. There was something there in the photos with Peter. There had to be.

I printed out pictures until I ran out of ink.

I didn't tell Lauren or the Providence police about the thank-you card and the photo he had mailed. I felt and continue to feel guilty about not telling Lauren, but at the same time, I didn't want her to see that picture of Peter. I know that was not my decision to make, but I made it anyway. He asked that I not show anyone else and I felt bound to do as he requested.

A second attendee of the reading killed herself this afternoon. Rachel was a recent college graduate living in Connecticut with her parents, an aspiring writer, and she swallowed a fistful of her mother's sleeping pills.

That night, a Saturday, we left Providence early. After a fine afternoon spent in conversation and walking around downtown Providence with Frances and other writers and fans, we skipped out on both the viewing of ten short films and a local brewery's after-party that was to feature the unveiling of a Lovecraft beer. I'm not a beer guy. My faith is in whiskey.

Peter and I went to his house, which was an easy forty-minute drive. We ate pizza with his family and then we attempted to sneak away into the living room on our own, but Steph wanted to show me a new RPG video game that'd been getting a lot of attention. Peter finally kicked Steph out a little after midnight.

We were both working on a third glass of scotch and halfheartedly started in on more talk about books, movies, and industry gossip. I don't know if Peter had planned to finally tell me about the card and photo I hadn't yet received in the mail, because I didn't give him a chance. Buzzed and melancholy despite my first enjoyable and anxiety-free afternoon in months, or maybe because of it, I launched into a confessional concerning my current economic situation.

I told him that my teaching two writing courses at a community college and royalties paid by a slew of small presses barely covered the rent, utilities, and now alimony payments. Peter stammered through a sorry, and before he could say more, I tried to rescue him by clinking my class against his, saying that I would be okay, but I probably wouldn't be coming to very many conventions or readings for a bit. Then I thanked him for letting me crash and complimented his choice of scotch (single malt, and according to the bottle label, fourteen years old, splitting time between whisky oak and cherry oak casks). Peter looked around that giant living room of his that was perched like the victor on top of his two-car garage. He scratched at his cheeks and had barely breathed out his *thanks*. I assumed he was embarrassed, even if I hadn't fully intended to make him so.

Now, of course, I can't be sure he was embarrassed. Had I derailed his intention to talk to me about what he was going through with my own tale of woe?

I don't know what he was thinking on that night or what he was thinking the next morning at breakfast or the next day back in Providence. I'm afraid to know, or more to the point, I'm afraid that I might know now what he'd been thinking or what he might've seen there in the room with him, or with us.

Patty called and said I was late and where was I?

Dominick. It was my weekend for Dominick. I told her I was sorry, but I was sick, wasn't feeling well, and didn't want him to catch whatever it was I had. I was lying and I wasn't lying. I asked her to put him on the phone and she hung up instead. I called him and he didn't answer. I left a voice mail message and told him that I loved him and that I'd make it up to him. I wasn't lying and I was lying.

I burned through three more ink cartridges. Upon reinspection of all the images (including photos in which Peter wasn't the only person in the picture) from the two months between the release of his novel and the Providence reading, I found darkened areas, and I cut them out, leaving only the photo he sent me untouched. I arranged the cutouts like pieces of a jigsaw puzzle. They came close to fitting together into something, a silhouette, a shape, but there was something missing. I tacked the photos with the cutout holes in them to a wall to help keep track of what photos I'd already used. I printed out more pictures. I taped and spliced the darkly colored bits of paper together. In a fit of inspiration, I attempted to re-create the recurring shadows in three dimensions and constructed a block, then an obelisk, a crooked tower. Something was still missing. I tore it all down. I printed out more photos. Then I made a mask. That seemed to be closer to the truth of things but not fully there.

I took photos of the printed-out photos with my phone. I accidentally flipped the screen on one shot and snapped a picture of my face. My eyes were red and blind. It'd been so long since I'd last trimmed my facial hair, my mouth was hidden somewhere beneath the avalanching mustache. From the upward angle, the skin of my neck rolled, forming multiple chins. I looked at the photo and didn't delete it. And I looked again. I focused on the shadow that hung like mist above my left shoulder, or rested on my shoulder, an abstraction of exhaustion.

There weren't nearly as many pictures of me on my computer. I checked them all. They were okay, and by okay I mean that I wasn't seeing what I saw in Peter's photo and in my accidental selfie.

Did Peter see or feel the shadow, the darkness, before he took the picture of himself in his bathroom, or did he only see it after?

I walked into my bathroom, turned the light off, peered into the corners of things, including myself, and I saw nothing and everything. I aimed my camera at the mirror.

The Arcade Mall in Providence is purportedly the oldest indoor mall in the United States. Its façade features a row of Greek columns and marble stairs that lead into a naturally lit atrium. On nice days, sunlight pours through the metal-framed glass ceiling and reflects off the white tile floor, giving the effect of an aviary. The second and third floors that overlook the mall feature trendy new apartments, what the proprietors call "micro-lofts." The shops and restaurants of the first-floor mall are an eclectic collection of hipster chic. Across from a combo coffee and spirits bar is the box-sized Lovecraft Museum and Bookstore. The bookstore sells horror and occult books, along with curios related to H. P. Lovecraft and weird fiction.

An hour before our reading, fifty or so friends, writers, artists, and fans gathered to buy books and meet and greet. Peter and I sat at café tables in front of the bookstore. We shook hands, signed books, and posed for photos with fans. I was not expecting the level of enthusiasm our reading received, particularly given that we were the only book authors at what was, ostensibly, a film festival. The brightness within the mall atrium reflected our moods.

Ten minutes before the reading began, Niall (one of the owners of the bookstore and a film festival event planner) asked in what order did we want to read. Without hesitating, Peter said he really wanted to go second. He rambled on for quite a bit, saying normally it didn't matter to him, and he apologized to me for making it a big deal, but today he really wanted to go second. He was anxious and afraid, shrinking and receding away from the café table at which I remained seated during our last conversation together. I told Peter it was fine and I would go first, even though it wasn't fine.

The room used for the reading was a small common area hidden behind a row of storefronts. There was a black couch and skeletal collection of gray folding chairs, perhaps enough to seat thirty. The room wasn't well lit despite the two rows of windows. The ceiling was low and white. The walls were stone, stratified, a dark shale. At the back of the room, in the designated reading area, were a red plush chair and a black hooded microphone in a bent metal stand.

After Niall briefly introduced me, I sat in the chair and I read. I read parts of a longer story that I'd written for a bird-themed horror anthology. I've done enough readings to know when a crowd is paying attention. They laughed at the appropriate parts, and when I chanced a look into the audience their eyes were on me and not on the floor or out a window or closed. I read for twenty minutes and answered two questions from the audience, one about the film adaptation and one about what I was working on currently. You always had to have an answer for that question even if the real answer was nothing. Then it was Peter's turn.

I walked to the standing-room-only area along a wall behind the audience and near the room's sole entrance/exit. When Peter and I passed, he said great job and patted my shoulder. I said thanks, and there was a part of me that wanted to say fuck you, I'm not your opening act. I shouldn't have been so petty and angry, but I was. I stood in the back and stewed despite how well the reading and previous hour of book signings had gone. I was a petulant little asshole and I didn't care.

Peter wore a blue *Jaws* T-shirt and cargo shorts. He didn't sit in the chair but stood in front of the microphone. He towered at the front of the room. He started off thanking people and making jokes, but I wasn't really listening. I think he sent a playful jab my way, because there was laughter and then he said, no, seriously, it's an honor reading with Jared and he's like a brother to me. Him saying that pissed me off, too. Was this the kind of faux deference, self-important smarm he peddled now that he was publishing with the big shots?

Peter unshouldered his black bag onto the red chair, bent, and rooted around inside it. His hands emerged holding a black .22. I didn't see him pull out the handgun because I assumed he was retrieving a book from which to read and I was lackadaisically scanning the crowd, picking out who I'd sold and signed books for.

There was a gasp and a few nervous laughs that died so quickly as to have never been. I looked up in time to see him with the barrel in his mouth and his eyes closed. I looked up in time to see him squeeze the trigger and tense up his arms and shoulders and mouth, as though bracing himself.

There was a loud pop and I flinched so hard my teeth clicked together. His body dropped and smoke hung in the air in his place, where he used to be, poof, abracadabra, gone. Peter fell back, knocking into the red chair before landing on the floor. One of his feet must've kicked the mic stand, because it tipped into the attendees in the first row, and when the mic bounced to the floor, feedback shrieked through the speakers. Some of the attendees spilled out of their chairs, trying to scoot back and away from Peter and the gun; others rushed to where his body lay, and I couldn't see him in the immediate aftermath. Everyone was screaming. I pushed through the crowd and stepped over abandoned folding chairs. There was blood on the stone wall at about Peter's height. There was blood on the back of the red chair that he hadn't used. There was blood on the floor under Peter's turned head and his left arm. In my memory that expanding pool of blood resembles a shape that continually shifts.

It's been two days since the second envelope arrived. I haven't opened it yet.

During those two days I found photos of the two reading attendees who killed themselves, photos from before and after the reading. I can't look at either set of photos without crying. There wasn't anything in their before pictures. But there is in their afters.

Two days. I took hundreds more pictures of myself and printed them all out. Every picture had those lingering, lurking, Escher-like shadows, dark forms, or outlines of empty space that weren't in any of my previous pictures. They weren't there until they were. They're there in any new photo of me now no matter how or where or when it's taken; no matter the angle or how bright or how dark. And they're there with me now even if I can only almost see them.

I carefully cut out the shadow pieces from all the photos. I couldn't pretend they were cancerous cells that could be removed, at least not from me, but maybe I could stop this from spreading to anyone else. Maybe this was what Peter had thought, too, back when he'd mailed me his photo. I wanted to call Dominick and explain to him what I was doing, but I couldn't risk it, couldn't risk him.

I was going by feel, by hunch. It was an idea, one that I couldn't shake or stop thinking about, and I had no choice but to see it all the way through. Sometimes ideas are like that.

I stripped down to my underwear and taped and glued the cut-out pieces to my body, covering myself, bit by bit, lining up the edges so that they fit together perfectly. Seamlessly. As in there were no seams. I started by covering my right forearm and it turned to shadow, to space, to nothingness. I spent hours and hours applying the pieces to my body. With only my eyes not covered, I shuffled into the bathroom, slow but as inexorable as an advancing glacier. I stood in front of the mirror. I was not there. I could not see me.

I took a picture and I was not in that, either. I was gone already.

Now I ignore any and all phone calls. I let the battery finally die. There was a knock on my door a few hours ago and I ignored that, too. I am sitting at my small kitchen table. They will find me or they won't find me armored in my suit, scaled with bits of shadow.

I finally decide to open the second envelope, the one that arrived after the first one even though Peter had mailed it two days earlier. Time is not an arrow, and if it ever was, it has been broken into pieces, and then the pieces broken into more pieces, and again and again and again.

My shadow-fingers are clumsy but insistent. Inside the envelope is the same type of thank-you card, one of a set. There's no photo. Two sentences written inside the card.

"I had an idea. It won't go away."

NOTES FROM THE DOG WALKERS

On Mon, Aug 21, 20__ at 2:22 PM, <littlezees2@_____.___> wrote:

Hi!

My name is P___ _____, I'm a local high school teacher and a writer. We have a 7 yr old red mini pin mix, around 15 lbs. She's a rescue and has been with us for over a year now. She loves people, other dogs not so much. We've had a local high school student walk her in the afternoons last spring but he won't be able to do it this fall. I live in _____, less than two miles from your doggy daycare.

We'd be looking for walks for Holly on Tuesday through Thursday. Please give me a call at _____ when you get a chance. Thanks!

P___

On Monday, Aug 21, 20__ at 7:25 PM, <janeR@happydogservices. com> wrote:

Hi, Mr. _____,

Thank you for contacting me. I would love to come and meet you and your fur child. Let me know when you are available for a meet and greet.

Best,
Jane

Jane Rogers
Happy Dog Services
Every day is a great day to be a HAPPY DOG

On Tuesday, Aug 22, 20__ at 8:30 AM, <littlezees2@_____.___> wrote:

Fabulous! Could we do Wednesday or Thursday 3:30 pm or after? If that day doesn't work, we could try Friday.

(address redacted)

Sent from an electronic device destined for Skynet

On Tuesday, Aug 22, 20__ at 9:46 AM, <janeR@happydogservices. com> wrote:

3:30 on Wednesday works great! Please use the form attached to this email to set up our electronic billing. If you can fill it out I can pick it up when we meet.

See you on Wednesday.

Jane

On Thursday, Aug 24, 20__ at 10:13 AM, <janeR@happydogservices
.com> wrote:

It was great meeting you and little Holly. She is a doll.

Also confirming you want the 20 minute walks. I did forget to tell
you that after the walk, the walker leaves a note telling you how
the walk went.

Enjoy your Labor Day weekend and tell Holly we'll see her in a few
weeks!

Jane

—9/12
12:04 to 12:24
Holly did great on her walk today. She's such a sweetheart.
Jane

   Pee: ✓   Poop:

—9/13
1:23 to 1:44
It was raining and Holly didn't want to venture too far out there today,
so she got extra love and belly rubs when we came back inside instead.
Elisa

   Pee: ✓   Poop:

—9/14
12:20 to 12:40
After Holly warmed up to me, we had a nice walk around the block!
She loves watching the wildlife.

Geoff

Pee: ✓   Poop: ✓

—9/19
12:49 to 1:09
Holly and I walked. She was afraid of a leaf twitching in the wind. She peed and crapped all over the place.

KB

Pee: ✓   Poop: ✓

—9/20
12:50 to 1:10
We had a nice walk together. Then inside for Holly's favorite part. Belly rubs! Have a great day.

Elisa

Pee: ✓   Poop:

—9/21
12:19 to 12:39
Holly is afraid of everything. If I were that size I would be jumpy and shaky too, or perhaps my great mammalian brain would've cobbled together coping mechanisms adequate for my miniature existential condition.

KB

Pee: ✓   Poop: ✓

—9/26
1:30 to 1:50
Because of the rain Holly didn't want to walk very far so we came back inside for extra cuddles and belly rubs. We had a nice but real conversation. I like to keep things in perspective, good with the bad, light with dark, so I told her that I don't know who her previous family was

but by the looks of your house she's in a happy place. That's not to say I had a look around your house, but I did have to search the first floor to find her. She was sitting on top of your living room couch like a cat. So cute! I also told her that her family loved her very much, that she is a great dog, a real love, but also that the world is still a cruel place. I don't want to lie to her. That won't help anyone, least of all Holly.

Elisa

Pee: ✓   Poop:

—9/27
1:01 to 1:21

Holly wasn't into the walk today so we cut it short to work on training. I trained her to bark at anyone who wears a hat indoors.

KB

Pee: ✓   Poop:

—9/28
1:16 to 1:36

Holly is still afraid of me when I come inside your house, to be honest, but we're working through it together. She's a trouper. I'm kind of a big dude with a long, bushy beard, and I've been told my eyes are kind of intense. Does Holly not like men or is it just me? Ha! Look, I get it. I know I can be scary looking when you first meet me. Believe me, I get that from people all the time, but they quickly find out I'm a Teddy and not a Grizzly. Holly let me put the leash on when I sang her a song, "Ride Captain Ride," by some classic rock band. Very catchy and soothing. My parents are collectors and they have an antique, vinyl-playing jukebox with the 45 of that song. I collect vinyl too, but mainly metal/deathcore. Maybe I'll play "Ride Captain Ride" for Holly on my phone the next time I come into the house. It'll be our thing. Every relationship needs a thing, right?

Geoff

Pee: ✓   Poop: ✓

—10/3
1:46 to 2:06

Holly has a nemesis, and by proxy, so do you. I'm sure you've encountered him. He's an older man with leathery skin and crinkled-up eyes, and he walks a Goldendoodle. Ugh, I love all dogs—all animals—but not a fan of designer breeds, and that breed in particular. It's like this guy has figured out Holly's walking schedule and only goes out when we go out. His dog barks, growls, snarls, lunges, and leaps into the air, straining against the leash to get at poor Holly. He makes these weird, throaty, rabies-infected or demon-dog-possessed noises that are terrifying even though he's a puffy/curly ridiculous-looking oversized poodle. There's wisdom there, I think. The dog goes literally berserk, or turns Berserker. I have no idea if either breed of the mix has Nordic ancestry but I do according to the online DNA kit I got for a present last Christmas and I've been kind of obsessed with learning Norse folklore since. Poor Holly stands her ground and barks, but it's like bringing a slingshot to a nuclear war. Sorry for that horrific image but there is something apocalyptic about their confrontation. For me, the scariest part is the dog's parent, the leathery-skin guy, because he cackles wildly, like his dog's aggressive reaction to Holly is the funniest thing he's ever seen. He laughs like a supervillain pleased his dastardly plans have finally come to fruition.

Elisa

Pee: ✓   Poop:

—10/4
12:58 to 1:18

I trained Holly to shiver and whine when she hears the phrase "intellectual property." I trained her to huff air out of her snout whenever she feels ennui.

KB

Pee: ✓   Poop:

—10/5

1:16 to 1:36

Holly enjoyed the song when I played it on my phone but was still a bit
shaky when I put the leash on her. Please tell her I'm sorry but I can't
change who I am or what I look like. Our walk was fine, if not tinged
with anxiety and regret.

Geoff

Pee: ✓   Poop:

—10/10

1:02 to 1:22

I trained her to dig up the grass when one says, "Isn't it a beautiful day?"
I trained her to spin and point her left hind paw at obvious hypocrites.

KB

Pee: ✓   Poop:

—10/11

1:30 to 1:50

Your neighbors (not necessarily the people who live directly next to
you but the people who live in your wider neighborhood) are not con-
siderate dog walkers. There is a lot of dog poop out there on the sides of
the roads, especially along the dirt road and the pond's shoreline. Your
neighbors, the most local of co-signees of the greater societal compact,
are not picking up after their pets. It's disgusting and disappointing. I
bet the Goldendoodle guy is the main culprit. I refuse to pick up after
these people. But I've decided to be a visible role model for them. Before Holly and I left your property today, I stuffed a wad of dried leaves
inside one of our biodegradable dog-poop baggies. Authenticity wasn't
the point here, and besides, no one could tell the lump in the bag
wasn't poop. The point was my demonstrating proper dog-walking eti-
quette. I carried the pendulous, partially full baggie as a person might
carry the flag of her nation during an Olympic opening ceremony, not
that I support the concept of nationalism in any way. Everyone who
walked or drove by us, everyone who opened a curtain or lifted a shade

to see who was walking by their house saw me carrying a bag of Holly's waste. They knew I had responsibly cleaned it up so no one would step on it. They would then think I was a fine, trustworthy young person for doing so, and maybe, hopefully, they would be inspired to do the right thing when they walked their own dogs. Holly was brilliant and played right along, looking suitably sheepish, as though the baggie was a reminder of a terrible deed.

Elisa

Pee: ✓   Poop:

—10/12

1:12 to 1:32

I loved Holly's raincoat. She was rather fetching in it! Hey, what have the squirrels ever done to her? Haha! She sure acts like she wants to catch one and tear it to shreds.

Geoff

Pee: ✓   Poop:

—10/17

1:33 to 1:53

I trained her to defecate underneath other people's mailboxes. Are you keeping up with her training? The desired behavior will only take root with consistent training. I also trained her to bare her teeth whenever one isn't being truthful. In the midst of all the training I might have inadvertently trained her to bite you and/or other dog walkers when you will least expect it, but only when you deserve it, so it'll be fine.

KB

Pee: ✓   Poop:

—10/18

12:31 to 12:51

To tell the truth (and I will tell you the truth because I take my job seriously and I value you as the parents of a rescued fur child), Holly did not enjoy her walk today. I can't say that I blame her. Maybe the two of us were in one of those shared moods, but every person we encountered was a stranger and we didn't trust any of them. Each house we walked by was empty, ominous, and had the look of something awful happening inside their darkened rooms, inside their walls. Terrible things do and/or will happen in all the houses; it's only a matter of when. I'm describing one of the many horrors of the suburbs, aren't I? Even the cute pond down the road was full of menace. Yes, the sun was out and it was really warm (but a wrong warm, the kind of warm that makes you think about the melting ice caps, rising seas, droughts and desertification of the land, and the apocalypse around the corner) and the ducks and swans were out but the ducks quacked and gave us the side-eye and the swans hissed and charged us, threatening to drag us into the water and below the surface and down to the cold muck where the boulder-sized snapping turtles lie waiting and dreaming their dinosaur dreams. The walk was fraught with danger when you really think about it. It's a miracle we survive it every day. Sorry, just one of those days when I can't help but feel as small and vulnerable as Holly in the wider world. I should be paid more than minimum wage. I'm taking a year off from school to "figure things out." Ugh, I hate being a cliché, but I told you I was going to tell the truth. I'm not even sure I want to go back. I attend a small liberal arts college but it's not small enough. I hate being herded into the dorms. I don't like being trapped in rooms with other people not of my choosing. Maybe what I need is a wide empty space. I have fantasies of signing up for a months- or years-long research excursion to isolated locales, to corners of the globe so remote they haven't been divvied into state-sanctioned slices of inequity, so remote they haven't been forgotten because no one thinks about them, and if the rest of the civilized world were to blow up, I wouldn't know about it because I was far enough away, or removed. I like that word. Removed. Are there any places left like that in the world? Sometimes I imagine Holly and I are the only two people left alive on our walks, and I have to say, it's a comfort until the spell is broken by a carbon-spewing car or that jackass with his Goldendoodle. When Holly and I got back to the house today, we clung to each other like we'd been through something traumatic. Holly is very expressive and empathic. She has a gift. But since I promised to tell you the truth, I think it's more like a curse.

Elisa

Pee: ✓   Poop:

—10/19
12:19 to 12:39
Holly is going to get her ass kicked by the swans down at the pond if she doesn't smarten up. Her charging at them armed only with her little ineffectual barks is not advisable.

KB

Pee: ✓   Poop:

—10/24
12:23 to 12:43
It was garbage day and Holly was quite brave. Have to give her props. She really doesn't like those garbage trucks. Hates them. She's even more afraid of the trucks than she is of me. (We're working on it!) Whenever one rumbled by, she lost her doggie mind and tried to run away, to run anywhere that wasn't there, and it was all I could do to keep her from bolting into someone's yard or even into the street. I felt so bad for her. I'm guessing she had a bad experience with garbage trucks in her past. But I wonder what happened? She couldn't have been hit by one. She's too small to survive that. Though I guess it's possible she could run under a truck and get bounced around without being squashed. I've seen squirrels come rolling out from under cars like that. It's a hard world for little things. Maybe it's as simple as Holly doesn't like how big and noisy the truck is, and to her it's a big monster coming down the street. I mean, put yourself in her head. What does she think a truck is? This big, smelly, smoke-belching thing rumbles and roars down the street, eating all the garbage. Big dudes hang off the garbage monster's side and jump out onto the street to do the garbage monster's bidding and throw everything in the monster's belly. Holly isn't a fan of the garbage barrels either. That I don't get. She

gives them a wide berth. There was one lying on its side and the wind kicked up and it started rolling back and forth. Holly got her back up and barked like crazy at it. Now I'm wondering what she thinks the barrels are, or maybe it's what could be inside of them that freaks her out. Maybe she knows something we don't know, right?

Geoff

Pee: ✓　　　Poop:

—10/25

1:11 to 1:31

Have you ever given proper depth of thought concerning evolution in regard to how the earliest mammals became the wolf and then the years and years of genetic selection, engineering, and species management that resulted in canis familiaris and your skittish, slightly overweight 16 lb Holly? I took her into the en suite bathroom off your bedroom and weighed her on the scale. She wasn't heavy enough to register and she wouldn't stay sitting on the scale either. I don't blame her. So I weighed myself (fully clothed, not to worry) and then stepped onto the scale with her in my arms and did the math. Holly needs to lose about 3 lbs, which doesn't sound like much, but if you think in terms of percentage of body weight, she's got some work to do. Actually, it's you who has work to do. More walks. Make sure she gets a free run during the day too. No more giving her buttery popcorn. It's advertised as a healthy snack alternative, but that's a lie. I found a couple of pieces under your couch in the living room. In the parlance of the home improvement shows that have become so maddeningly popular, that living space could be described as a "great room" because of its size and the high vaulted ceilings. Perhaps you call it the "great room" amongst family but it's only a living room when friends are over. I hope you're aware, calling it a "great room" would be more than a little obnoxious. That's first-people-against-the-wall-when-the-revolution-comes kind of stuff. Not to worry, it seems you're not into ostentatious displays of class status by the looks of the rest of your place. That is most certainly a compliment. There are no high-end appliances or ridiculous and unnecessary kitchen accoutrements, and I appreciate the homey, lived-in clutter within what I assume is P___'s writing office and the wonderfully stuffed-to-overflowing IKEA bookcases. This shows you are relatively comfortable with who you are and that you don't take yourselves too seriously. However, I wrote "relatively" because you're not free from discomfort, as I think you are struggling with class anxiety and guilt. For example, it's almost as though the kitchen counter is cluttered with junk mail and circulars and the like as a strategic decoration for the benefit of the hired help who come into your home to walk your dog and clean up after her. Just so you know, I threw away the popcorn and didn't let Holly have it, though I let her lick my fingers. She's not picky with who or what she licks. To circle back to the wolf and genetics, how did that kind of behavior (in addition to being servile, working and living only at the whims of a master, for lack of a nicer term) become cellular memory? Yes, I'm dancing around a larger point here. Did you know Holly has the same basic genetic code as Bernese Mountain Dogs, as Leonbergers, as Marmaduke and Clifford (if Marmaduke and Clifford were real)? I tell you what, though, Holly left a Clifford-the-Big-Red-Dog sized present on your neighbor's front lawn today. Didn't think she had it in her. Literally.

KB

Pee: ✓   Poop: ✓✓✓

—10/26
12:46 to 1:06
Today there was an old woman at the pond feeding the ducks and swans. All of them. In the world. She dumped enough bread to feed a small nation of waterfowl. I'm serious. It was like she was landscaping with bread instead of spreading mulch. I rightly worried she was overfeeding them and their little stomachs would fill with bread and explode out between their beaks. I grant you that might be extreme (and gruesome, sorry), but I remember reading somewhere that processed white bread isn't the best food for ducks or birds, which shouldn't be a surprise, as it isn't the best food for us either. It was a challenge to stop Holly from eating bread and keeping her from barking and charging

at the ducks. Her stiff-legged hops of aggression are cute and sad at the same time. Luckily those huge swans were elsewhere. They're as tall as I am when they stretch their necks up. Without even saying hello to me the old woman started talking in medias res, telling me about how all the baby swans, born in the spring, have died. Jeez, I'm doing fine, how are you, right? I know this sounds ageist, but the old woman was more than kind of creepy. I swear it was not because she was old and gray, and hunched, a bit shaky, but it was because of how she looked at me. Her stare wasn't quite vacant, but it was not all there either. She was looking beyond me, to the horrible future we're all doomed to suffer. Her voice was echoey, like a chair creaking in an empty house. And seriously, the sheer volume of torn-up bread on the ground made everything feel off, feel wrong. We tried to move quickly past the scene without getting drawn into a long conversation I did not want to get into. I smiled and nodded and I told the woman that it was too bad about the baby swans. She said the snapping turtles got most of the babies (and that made Holly and me afraid of being dragged underwater and into the dark mud all over again), but last night she heard a coyote howling across the pond and she was sure it got the last swan baby. I told her that it was terrible, it was all terrible and horrible, and it was, but I didn't want to deal with it today, not with the chill in the air and weakening sunlight, and as I walked away she yelled to me that I had to keep a close eye on the dog and not let her get too far away from me. We normally walk past the pond and then curl back to your house, but today we cut the walk short. All I could think about were hungry coyotes as big as cars and they howled and they had bloodied and torn Hollys in their mouths. Holly and I came home, but neither of us was into the belly rubs. We sat together and I let Holly have a good cry instead.

Elisa

Pee: ✓   Poop:

—10/31
12:23 to 12:46
I loved Holly's referee (sorry: rufferee) costume. The black and white stripes are befitting, and she strutted around the neighborhood showing

them off. Holly didn't have a care in a world while I wrestled with whether or not to tell you that I took a piece of candy from your jack-o'-lantern candy bucket. My mom has one just like it, but yours has a cooler, more jagged smile and looks more like a real pumpkin. Obviously I decided to confess to you that I took a peanut butter cup. There was no ill intent and I did it without even thinking. That is not to say I am not constantly aware of treating your place and belongings with professional care and respect. It was this weird natural reaction: I opened your front door and bam, there was all that candy in its shiny packaging practically spilling out of the bucket hanging there on the stairway's front post. I'm not saying it's your fault, and I don't even blame Holly, but it's hard walking into your house sometimes because Holly still barks and skitters away from me and cowers in her little dog bed like I'm the scariest guy ever. That's not my fault, but it doesn't feel good. It's not anyone's fault. It is what it is. I woke up in a great mood today, too, I mean, it being Halloween and everything, but on this day of all days it was a bit much to get barked at again when all I did was open the door with my biggest, goofiest smile, and she wouldn't stop barking. Our song didn't work today. I felt ridiculous having a little dog dressed up in a football referee costume barking her furry face off at me, and, well, I don't like being made to feel ridiculous, and like anyone else, I wanted to feel good, feel better about who I am and what I was doing with my day and yet-to-be-determined direction of my life, so yeah, I took a piece of candy to get the chocolate endorphins kick. And you know what? Unwrapping the peanut butter cup helped Holly too. No, I didn't give her any, but she stopped barking when she smelled the chocolate. Anyway, I feel bad about taking it even though you clearly had enough there to spare and you probably wouldn't have known one piece was gone. I wasn't going to say anything and I figured it wouldn't be a big deal to you at all, but then I didn't know how many pieces you gave to trick-or-treaters. One? Two? A handful? While Holly and I were walking around I couldn't stop imagining you guys running out of candy right when some poor little kid dressed up in a homemade mummy costume rang your bell. That's the costume I wore once because Mom told me I was too tall for a store-bought costume. She was lying to me, and it wasn't because we couldn't afford to buy one. She simply didn't want to go with me to the store. That was it. She couldn't be bothered—one of her favorite phrases. I could tell by the slumped shoulders and sigh in her voice when I asked her, and there was no way Dad could be bothered to take me to Party City, so I wrapped myself up in roll after roll of toilet paper, which pissed my parents off more because I used almost every roll we had. The worst part was that my costume was lame. The TP didn't look like ancient, dusty wrappings. I looked like I was wrapped up in toilet paper. Way too white, soft, and cushy. The stuff didn't stay on my body very well either. I wrapped my head last and Scotch-taped the ends to my face and because I wanted it to look real I made sure my mouth wasn't showing and same with my eyes, and I couldn't breathe or see very well and when I finally went outside I fell a couple times. So because of all that I worried your neighborhood mummy kid wouldn't get your last piece of candy because I took it and I worried that kid would feel worse than he already felt because of me. And I'd hate myself if the kid then did something bad to your house in retaliation. Trick or treat, right? I am sorry, and I'll buy a candy bag and fill up your bowl the next time I come over.

Geoff

Pee: ✓   Poop:

—11/1
1:13 to 1:33
So after I tried on all your clothes and had a fashion show for Holly (kidding!), she took me on a tour of the office/writing room today. I love the red walls, framed (but not hung) horror movie posters (the <u>Nosferatu</u> canvas replica is my favorite) perched atop the back of that small sofa, and the wooden desk overflowing with notes and knickknacks. Enjoyable, understated, and functional décor. That said, I don't get how you've organized the books within the office book-shelves. Aside from one shelf that's all graphic novels, the "brag" shelf of your publications, and on top of the case, above the brag shelf, the crooked stacks of foreign editions, there's no discernible order or rea-son to how the books are shelved. Not alphabetical by title or author,

not by genre, not by copyright date. I can't imagine it would be by purchase date. Not by cover or spine color, which I'm glad you haven't done, as that's annoying. Books aren't bits of mosaics. A book is the mosaic. Although, that's not entirely accurate, as individual stories are pieces to a larger whole of our collective culture. A discussion to revisit at a later date, perhaps. I'm saying the cover art/color in and of itself is not best employed for the purpose of office decoration. How do you find a book that's been shelved if there is no order, no system? Do you stand in front of the bookcases with arms folded across your chest and scan the spines like a bored god? Are you ever paralyzed with the inability to choose and you then stare for hours? Have you ever walked away, overwhelmed by the weight of choice? Do you go to the shelf not looking for a particular book and then simply choose one at random? Do you carefully run a finger along each spine, briefly refamiliarizing yourself with each book and its position within the shelves until you happen upon the one you want? I like the idea of your bookshelf inefficiency, as it forces you to spend quality time with the bookshelves every time you retrieve a book. Is it possible you have the improbable map of books safely contained within your head, and this map only makes sense to you, is only readable to you, and it is organic, rearranging itself into the new daily patterns, growing like a creeping fungus? Color me intrigued!

It was cold outside today, and Holly walked with a slight limp, as though her little tendons and bones foretold the long, hard winter to come.

KB

Pee: ✓   Poop:

—II/2
1:04 to 1:24
Obviously, phrenology is utter quackery (at best) and was monstrous in practice. Palmistry is for suckers and so too are tarot and aura readings, and tasseography is no less a sham but harmless and I rather like my cup of tea in the afternoon. If only there was a term

for determining the character of a person or persons via their book-shelves; piecing together an inner life or mind from the titles and types of books and how they are arranged and cataloged. If there is a term for bookshelf-dowsing or bibliodivination, I am unfamiliar with it. Of the two options, I think bookshelf-dowsing is the lesser descriptor of my talent, as it implies searching the shelves for only one book in particular and not discerning the very nature of the home library curator. Although, ultimately, when any of us looks at a book-shelf, we're always looking for <u>one</u> book; the one to read or the one with which to make a sweeping judgment. Sometimes we search for the lack of a certain book, or the lack of any books at all. I will admit to class privilege at work here, and I assure you, upon finding a home devoid of books I do not presume the inhabitants have the disposable income for a library and choose instead to spend the money on lesser entertainments and effluvium, nor do I assume the inhabitants of a bookless domicile aren't readers and devotees of their local library. I am most careful in my bibliodivinating. With all that in mind, <u>Infinite Jest</u> by David Foster Wallace wasn't the first book I noticed in your shelves and it wasn't the first I flipped through; however, it was <u>the</u> book for which I was looking without knowing I was looking for it. This book is the cipher to your bookshelf encryption. This begins with my finding <u>Infinite Jest</u>. In case you aren't aware (I believe you are deeply aware), the book rests in your left bookcase number two, third shelf, flush against the case's frame on the right, the book merely and meekly peeking around the corner of the black wood. Such a position could mean you are trying to hide the book, like one tries to hide shame. It is not proudly displayed in the middle of the shelf with its thick spine legible from any distance or vantage within your office. (And not for nothing, your positioning of the four tall black shelves—and I can't resist making a filmic reference, here, to the monolith in <u>2001: A Space Odyssey</u>—against the walls opposite your desk and lap-top docking station doesn't go unnoticed.) I don't think you are pur-posefully hiding <u>IJ</u>. Its modest position relative to the rest of the books represents a touch of your practicality showing through. The novel simply fits best there with the wood to slide up against while stolidly serving as a quasi-bookend; the book is big and strong enough to hold up the others, the sentinel of the shelf. It doesn't get in the way of the other books and doesn't selfishly prevent the eye from wandering along the other spines. Its place within the wider galaxy of your shelves is interesting, of course, but not as interesting, or telling, as what I found inside the book. I'm sure I don't have to tell you what I found. In fact, I wouldn't be surprised if you could tell me the pages where the bookmark is located. The first meaning of the bookmark (a repurposed torn-off square of an advertisement for a local donation [clothes, shoes, books] outfit, printed on green card stock) is obvious: you made it only to pages 126–127 of the book and then you gave up. "Gave up" is a little strong and ascribes motive I have yet to fully determine; however, you get the point. Initially, you were excited, as we all are when we start a new book. You knew what you were in for and had committed to the idea of donating months of your reading time to this famous and famously long, sprawling novel. Things were going well early on, but you lost steam; perhaps it was too difficult to read at night before bed, if you are that kind of reader; it is not the kind of book one can read twenty or twenty-five minutes at a time. Or perhaps you lost the thread (which is one of my favorite polite ways of saying you were no longer interested in the story, the characters, the theme, the style, the book), or perhaps your to-be-read pile (which, as an aside, I assume is the impressive pile of books stacked on the floor next to your bookcases; no place for them in the shelves, as they have not yet been read, yes?) began calling to you to indulge in the greedy little thrill of starting another <u>new</u> book and/or you couldn't abide the thought of that to-be-read pile growing larger or being ignored for the duration of what would be a long, long read. Whatever the reason(s), you put <u>IJ</u> back on the shelf (having purposefully chosen its current spot) and you promised yourself you'd get back to it when you had more time. Of course, if you'd truly fallen under the book's spell you would've carved out the time. Now even more time has passed and if you were to pick up that novel again you'd have to start over because there's no way you remember enough of those first one-hundred-twenty-plus pages to be able to pick up the thread(s) (perhaps you remember something about an academic setting and tennis and footnotes, but that's likely it). The bookmark is your confession, and a noble one, I might add. When you are asked if you've read IJ, you do not pretend that you have read it in its entirety and I believe you do answer the question honestly no matter who is in the room, or at the party, or attending the conference. You tell the truth because you have to, you are forced to; the bookmark is there and it doesn't lie. A person who would pretend to have read IJ (and there are plenty who do) would've left the book in a place of prominence, a look-at-what-I-read spot, surrounded by books with thin, unreadable spines, withering in the shadow of the great and terrible book. That is not what you did. I also found Wallace's The Pale King, trade paperback, on the shelf below. It doesn't quite sit in the middle of the shelf but neither is it hiding in a corner. There is no bookmark cleaving its pages. One might assume you haven't read it because you didn't finish IJ, but I looked closer and there are clear signs of the book having been read, including three highlighted passages, the last coming on page 423. The question remains: did you connect with the more "accessible" but unfinished TPK and its Kafkaesque bureaucracy meets twenty-first-century neurosis or did you read it all the way through as a form of penance for quitting on IJ? You've lived your whole life in New England and I wouldn't be surprised to find puritanical shame and guilt playing an oversized role in your decision processes. After the TPK discovery I focused on cataloging the non-genre or mainstream literary books you haven't finished reading as they are similarly bookmarked. I was pleased to find more unfinished works of note, and I wonder if their bookmarks are akin to a reading virus, infecting and proliferating. Further, I am fascinated by some of your author bookmarked/not bookmarked pairings: you read Donna Tartt's The Secret History and The Little Friend, but The Goldfinch on pages 188–189 has a card stock bookmark adorned with pictures of your daughter posed with a soccer ball (TG sits next to Christopher Hitchens's The Portable Atheist, no bookmark, though I am not confident it has been read completely based on the intact paperback spine); Mark Danielewski's Only Revolutions is bookmarked (and not with the spine ribbons but a bookmark from an indie bookstore in Cambridge) on page 92–93, whereas House of Leaves is so well read and worn the cracked spine is falling apart and pages are loose; you made it to pages 244–245 in Roberto Bolaño's The Savage Detectives (pages marked with a folded paycheck stub), but you read <u>2666</u> (many marked passages throughout) to completion. Other notables within the bookmarked/abandoned category include <u>Bless Me, Ultima</u>, <u>Geek Love</u>, <u>Anton Chekhov: Collected Stories</u>, and <u>Pussy, King of the Pirates</u>, while other large and/or challenging works like <u>Mrs. Dalloway</u>, <u>1Q84,</u> <u>Beloved</u>, and <u>Jane Eyre</u> have clearly been read. Though I would allow <u>Jane Eyre</u> might not have been read by P___ as it appears to be an older college text, one in which, judging by the handwriting, L___ wrote notes within the margins. However, a bibliodivinator must operate under the assumption (particularly given the length of your relationship/partnership) of what's yours is hers and what's hers is yours unless contradictory information surfaces at a later date. Call me a romantic, but I would argue that even if you, P___, haven't read <u>Jane Eyre</u>, you've still been informed by L___'s read of the novel. Ah, the magic of the printed word. Note I focused solely on the non-genre (or non-horror, at the very least) books for now. Clearly the majority of the books in the writing office would be categorized as, if not horror, then dark fiction, as one might expect given the nature/concerns of your own published work. I want to familiarize myself with such before making any further comment.

Holly endured the walk with the briefest moments of enthusiasm.

KB

Pee: ✓   Poop:

—11/7
11:08 to 11:28
It was kind of a sad walk as it was my last day with Holly. She could tell what was up today, I think, and even though we started our day together with the usual amount of barking and shivering, we both walked around the neighborhood with our heads high and chests out. Looking back over our times together, our negative energies were caught in a loop, and they fed off one another, no matter how hard we tried to alter it, so I think we're better off if we make a clean break. No hard feelings at all, and it has been an absolute pleasure being

welcomed into your house, your world, your family. Please don't worry about me, I'll be fine, and Holly will be left in good hands. There are two other walkers who seem to be in a competition to fill up Holly's schedule sheet with their names. Honestly, even if I didn't choose to stop being one of her walkers, they would've forced me out. Haha! As it is, I had to convince one of them to let me have this one last day. She wasn't easy to convince, but I told her that it was important to me. Thank you, _____ family. I grew a lot and figured some stuff out about myself, with Holly's help of course. I will never forget her. She's a special dog. I hope you enjoy the bag of candy I left on your counter. Please tell Holly her thoughtful friend brought it for the entire family to enjoy. Take care.

Geoff

Pee: ✓   Poop: ✓

—11/8

2:05 to 2:35

I apologize for walking Holly later in the afternoon than usual. I had a dentist appointment set for much earlier, but everything was all backed up and I had to wait over an hour to be seen. To make up for my lateness to Holly we had bonus time inside the house with belly rubs. She seemed very happy, but I was thrown off by the whole day. I can't tell if it's a mood I'm in or if I'm sensing the coming of something truly horrible. Well, that's not entirely true because I don't think what I'm about to describe is a mood, per se, which is ephemeral by definition. This foreboding feeling has settled in for an ice-age stay. I don't believe that I'm special or that I'm the only one who feels this, nor am I claiming psychic ability or anything like that. I believe everyone is feeling the big bad. That's what I'm calling it. And I can see it on everyone's faces, as our smiles don't last as long as they used to and it's there in our confused and glazed-over looks. It's in the slight hitch in our voices, our extra ums and verbal tics, and it's there in the increased volume and anger of our shouts, and our whispers are quieter and more desperate. We all know the big bad is coming, and there's nothing we can do to stop it, yet we still go to our jobs and we chitchat about nothing important with coworkers and we go to dinner and we go to the mall and we go to our dentist appointments and we buy groceries and we make plans with friends and family and we walk and love our pets and we watch TV or read or sit in the glow of our smartphones, and all we're doing is going through the motions because we can't stop and think and accept that the pit of dread in our stomach is a pit of knowing. The big bad is coming. Holly senses it too. Of course she does. During our walks Holly will stop and look down the road and sniff the air and then look or slink away from that direction and sometimes when I'm in your house with her she'll suddenly look off into a different direction and then tilt her satellite dish ears as though she hears something far away but approaching, and she shivers. So what I'm describing is an animal-brain kind of sensation, a not-tactile sense, one the brutalizing post–Industrial Revolution years have all but ground out of humanity. But now the signal is so strong and insistent us dummies are finally getting it too. It really hit me hard at the dentist's office, of all places. Sure, I was freaking out because my routine cleaning was over an hour late, and yeah, I was pissed, but whatever, right? I would deal with the little setback and things would be okay. I said that ("things will be okay") to myself and that sense I'm talking about answered back with "no it won't." The hygienist was apologetic for everything getting all backed up and I told her it was okay, which was a lie but not because I was mad at her. She didn't try to chat me up during the procedure, so I sat silently in the chair, staring up at the ceiling. Because my mouth was such a mess when I was a teen (cavities, braces, wisdom teeth . . . the works), I've created this stare-at-the-dentist's-ceiling routine: I counted the number of holes or pits in the ceiling tiles. I just looked up "ceiling tiles" on my phone and found them for sale on a home improvement website: acoustical ceiling tile, fissured, made of mineral fiber. Fissured sounds about right. Each tile was a rectangle, as big as a dinner tray. Anyway, I counted the marks not because I was anxious about having my teeth scraped and cleaned, but because I was searching for secret knowledge. No, seriously. No one knows how many of those black dots there are on one of those tiles or how many there are in all the tiles in that room.

Yes, it's totally useless, random knowledge, but that's the kind of stuff I want to know. I used to hope that when I died I'd go into some kind of afterlife where I'd instantly know all these weird statistics like how many heartbeats I had in my life or how many breaths or how many times I said the word "tomato" or how many people thought I was a good person or how many holes there were in the ceiling tiles of my dentist's office. But I didn't count the holes or fissures today. With the big bad pressing down on us, counting the holes seemed even more pointless, and then the very idea of counting represented the pointlessness of everything. I tried to break free of that spiraling thought process by focusing on the overhead lamp instead, the one attached to the ceiling on a mechanical arm. A corporate logo—some name that had been serif-ed within an inch of its life—was stenciled on a plastic knob in the middle of the clear plastic casing. I'd never heard of the company and I have already forgotten its name. But as I sat there, re-clined, my mouth open, a woman's latex-gloved hands in my mouth, I wondered where this lamp-producing company was and if they had multiple locations and how many lamps they produced and who were the individuals responsible for making the lamps and/or the compo-nents, who ordered parts, who communicated with the warehouses and buyers, who installed the lamps, and that whole delicate sche-matic of how the lamp got to be hanging above my head was a willowy spider web in my mind and then I thought about the threads breaking and how easily it would (and will) all come down and how no one will remember that company and no one will remember the people, the employees, and I reached out into the far-flung future and saw some new life-form finding this very lamp in the rubble of our civilization and wondering what it was, why it was, and why it had to be. I'm not normally this nihilistic, but that's what I'm trying to tell you. Tell you it's not just me being like some moping goth teen. We're all feeling it. I know you are too. When the cleaning was completed, I stood up and rinsed one last time at the sink and the lamp was eye level and not shining directly in my face and it looked quite old. It's possible the company that produced the lamp doesn't exist anymore. The prod-uct outlasting the producer seems a fitting fate for our late-capitalism nightmare lives. In the meantime, at least you have a sweetheart of a dog. I really enjoy my fleeting time spent with her.

Elisa

Pee: ✓   Poop:

—11/9

1:11 to 1:32

I've been reading through your oeuvre. You don't need me to tell you whether or not it's any good, so I won't. Based on my reads of your work and my bibliodivination of the office bookcases, I do think that's a question you ask yourself often. "Is my writing any good?" Like I said, I won't give you an answer. However, I do want to thank you for not relying upon the crutch of dreams within your most recent fiction. Nothing makes my eyes roll harder than a dream sequence jammed into a story, excluding dreams that do serve the plot or theme or the general aesthetic of the work. Dream sequence clichés are most associated with genre fiction, science fiction/fantasy/horror in particular, which is not entirely fair. Yes, there are countless examples in horror books and films of dreams included only because there needed to be a jump scare or something spooky or moody or weird and the writer was unable or unwilling to do the work to create the desired effect within the story proper. That is a well-earned criticism, particularly for the works of horror that fail as art. What is <u>not</u> fair is the dearth of criticism mainstream/literary writers receive for their similarly unimaginative, lazy use of dreams as attempts to create an effect their stories are otherwise lacking. And they do it all the time. Even your beloved Roberto Bolaño does it in <u>2666</u>, although his dreams are at least beautifully written. The dream problem, as I see it, is only getting worse. For twenty-first-century writers, particularly American ones, nothing screams hey-I-paid-a-lot-of-money-for-this-MFA-degree-in-writing more than a pointless dream sequence in which the endlessly workshopped, plotless navel gazing is made even more tedious by a dewy Jungian dream about an unmade bed, a glass of soured milk, and/or the burning tree (next time you browse a bookstore [virtual or real] count how many books have burning trees on their covers . . .) outside their bedroom window that can't be seen and can only be <u>sensed</u>. Actually, the dream I described is more interesting than the usual literary fiction dream representation of an upper-class (sub)urbanite's neurotic id and predictably libidinous infidelities. Okay, I'm speaking in hyperbole (mostly), but you get the gist. This is not an anti-intellectual rant and I applaud and encourage those who want to study writing in depth. However . . . My frustration with literary fiction getting a free pass when it comes to bad writing within the larger academic/literary vs. genre debate/divide is rooted in class, which is too often ignored by the genre-is-innately-inferior literary crowd. Most (not all; there are no absolutes here) MFA writing students still have the ability to pay the exorbitant tuitions and do not come from working-class homes. These students are being taught by career academics, many of whom come from similar upper-class economic backgrounds. Many of these same academics, somewhat ironically, lament their salary isn't commensurate with their lofty professional positions as representatives of the finest institutions in all the land that merrily practice exclusion upon the general populace. And these academics were themselves taught that genre fiction was inherently inferior (the dirty genreness of a story somehow invalidates how well it is written), and they were taught that genre fiction was not <u>serious</u> writing, because, well, serious people (the ones born into the means with which to attain the title of "serious person") haven't ever taken, historically speaking, "popular" writing or writing for the unwashed masses seriously because genre stories were not written by nor were they about the <u>serious</u> people. Now you tell me who are the anti-intellectuals. Of all the genres, horror is taken the least seriously, even amongst the other less serious speculative genres (indeed, the worst works of horror, the ones Hollywood has typically spewed out for decades, should be criticized and not taken seriously, particularly the films/stories that trade in misogyny, xenophobia, homophobia, transphobia, and white upper-class suburban fantasies of the other as invading monsters to be expelled; horror is hardly the only genre in which some of its practitioners have sinned as such, but it might be the only genre that is solely and forever damned within the eyes of the mainstream by its worst representatives). Without getting too far afield (this started with dreams, didn't it?), I've taken notice of some of the class concerns within your fiction: the dire economic challenges facing your families in two of your more recent novels; the closing of a toy manufacturing plant and laying off all the employees (something your family apparently experienced firsthand when you were a teenager) is used as backstory in several of your works; within a recent short story, the one in which a writer shoots himself at a reading, the writer is clearly uncomfortable with his perceived level of elevated material success amongst his friends and colleagues. That story features one scene that illustrates the writer's complicated feelings of shame standing in his "great room" and opening an expensive bottle of scotch while in the company of a friend who is mired in economic hardship. Although the story never explicitly makes mention of hired dog walkers, given your purported working-class upbringing and your still being a high school teacher by day, I can easily imagine your discomfort/class guilt at having become someone who can and is willing to pay $21 for 20-minute dog walks three times a week. Am I onto something? Hmm. . . . Well, all the above is to say I appreciate that one of your least-popular novels (measured by copies sold) begins with the line "Elizabeth wasn't dreaming." Despite your using a waking dream sequence later in the novel (one that was brief, not used to scare or cheaply unsettle the reader, and was at least tethered to the character's waking thought process), I thought the opening sentence was a bold proclamation, a dire warning to the reader that the natural and supernatural would be treated the same, that the ambiguities would be real and treated as such. It was a welcome mission statement for the novel and perhaps for your novels and stories to come (if there are to be any more): There are no dreams here. The dreamers will all one day be dead.

Holly lagged behind for most of our walk until we turned around and headed back home. Then she led the way, stretching the leash to its limits.

KB

Pee: ✓   Poop: ✓

—11/14

12:23 to 12:55

I hate to be a tattletale or cause problems where there aren't any, beyond the problems this causes in my own wretched little life, but there's another walker at Happy Dog Services who passive-aggressively and regular-aggressively fills up Holly's entire schedule with their name. I've never met the charming "KB," but they leave little notes on Holly's schedule that are presumably jokes but have come to read as vaguely threatening. Examples: "She's mine. All mine! Muhahahaha!!!" "You're vegan so you can't have the little sausage." "Holly, Holly, Holly, get your adverbs here." "If anyone but me shows up, Holly will bite them in the spleen. Repeatedly." "Holly and KB sitting in a tree." The most recent message being, "Holly requested me yet again and barked epitaphs at all the other walkers." I initially assumed KB meant to write "epithets," but now I'm not so sure. This is no reflection on you, but I haven't cared enough to ask Jane about this person since by her own inaction (the schedule/message board is there in the middle of the day-care common room for all to see) Jane is apparently fine with KB's messages. I don't know if I can lay the following at KB's feet, but it seems too coincidental to actually be coincidental. The day after I was late walking Holly I received bizarre text messages from an unknown number I've since blocked. The messages: "in their underground chambers dead squirrels lie dreaming"; "I can do voices"; "we were in this great and terrible story"; "we can't go on"; "careful or it'll be sassafras and lullabies." The cheerful unhinged-ness of these messages are written in a style similar to KB's message board notes, I think. And I'll admit to being a touch paranoid, but I could've sworn Holly and I were being followed on our walk today. It was beyond the feeling of being watched, which I probably shouldn't discount because it is real and it has weight and if you tell me you've never felt it, then I'll call you a liar. No offense. But in the wooded sections of our walks, I heard branches snapping and rustling leaves and whatever was surreptitiously traipsing through the brush was larger than a squirrel. I love walking Holly, don't get me wrong, but there's only so much above and beyond I'm willing to do for minimum wage. Am I wrong to admit that? People get uncomfortable when they talk about how much they make in a non-braggy way, and it is only culturally acceptable for the braggy rich folks to talk about how much they make. It's totally ass-backwards and screwed up and is a purposeful function of the rigging of the system by the haves, etc. It's important to point out this cultural disparity and important to share salary information among laborers particularly given how toothless the endangered species of unions have become. And for the braggy haves, maybe talking about how little the rest of us make in front of them can be a reality check of sorts. Not that anyone bothers to check on reality very much. Wouldn't that be nice if we had reality checkers, people whose job it was to ensure everything that happened had happened like it was supposed to? Not that I believe our lives are predetermined or anything like that. I imagine the reality checkers would operate in accordance with probabilities. Any event more than three standard deviations away from the expected range of "happening" would be investigated and possibly corrected. Of course there would have to be allowance for unexpected events. Maybe a certain number or quota per month of totally random happenings to keep us on our toes; otherwise the reality checkers swoop in and clean up the messes and make the wrongs right. Inequities would be addressed and corrected. The worst, most senseless accidents and tragedies would largely be abolished. I suppose they'd have to allow a few to satisfy the random quotient. For instance, all those people who slip, fall, and die in showers or bathtubs, I imagine, that number might be cut by half at the very least. The reality checkers would save the lion's share of outdoor cats who die when a careless parent/owner starts the family station wagon without checking to see if the cat was warming herself within the engine block, which happened to my poor cat Parsnip when I was seven. The reality checkers wouldn't be God or gods, despite their essentially doing the vacated job of a deity. For it all to work, the checkers would have to be regular people with regular friends and regular families and they'd have to be protected from powerful people and special interests who would work tirelessly to sway them, to influence them and their probabilities.

We'd pay the reality checkers, but only as much as they'd need, a true and fair living wage that would be published and publicized, and every employee within the larger reality checking system would be paid the same to ensure there would be no undue influence, no gaming of the checking system. I'm sorry if I'm rambling, but Holly is nuzzled in my lap as I write this and I'd like to keep her here with me a little while longer. She's so cute. I love how she rests her head on my forearm, her thin little legs and paws outstretched. I fear this might be my last day with her because there aren't any reality checkers who are going to investigate this obnoxious KB person and what they are all about.

Elisa

Pee: ✓   Poop:

—11/15
1:14 to 1:34
Before all this ends (and it will end, and always sooner than we think it will) I would like to help you, P___. Or at the very least offer a suggestion, or more accurately: a push. You've dabbled with the following concept but haven't fully committed to it. I think you should explicitly create your own interconnected universe of characters/stories. You know you want to and you've already tested those waters, dipped in a toe. The short story of yours we previously discussed made mention of your disappearance novel and posited theories on what the shadowy figure represented. That same novel was referenced (albeit obliquely) in your splashy "home invasion" novel. In this latter instance, you made self-deprecating winks and jokes at the disappearance novel's expense. In 2010 you first published a short story about the uncontrolled apocalyptic growth of vines, which years later became a big part of your maybe-possession novel. The vines story told by the older sister was suitably creepy and hinted at future plot points. Also, a throwaway line buried in one of the possession novel's brilliantly labyrinthine (if you don't mind me saying so) blog posts you referred to "Growing Things" as being written by an obscure author, who was, of course, you. I love it all. You should do more of this, but be

more explicit. Is there anything more satisfyingly self-indulgent than the interconnected literary universe? It's okay. Really, I'm telling you it's okay to go ahead and indulge. One could argue literary careers (especially midlist ones, especially midlist horror ones) have never been shorter or more fickle, so why not have fun with it while you can? A certain level of hubris is a prerequisite for writing. Having the gall to write a story, then presuming other people should spend some of their precious allotment of time reading it and considering whatever it is you have to say, is already a bit of an ask. Hey-look-at-me-look-at-what-I-wrote! I mean, who do you think you are anyway? You might as well make the full-on cannonball splash into the indulgence pool. Come on in, the water is fine (to stick with the metaphor). I realize I previously moaned at length about taking works of horror seriously, but that doesn't mean you should take yourself too seriously. I encourage you to make more connections between books and stories and characters, and for no loftier reason than it would be fun. Is fun so bad? So many of the writers on your shelves (again, including Bolaño) have stories that unfold in the same places/worlds or have stories that aren't sequels or parts of series yet still overlap in timelines and happenings or they have characters that appear and reappear so their prior works function as literary memories. Some might claim the purpose of the interconnected body of work is to inform both the new and previous stories, but if we're being honest, it's almost always more about the author showing how clever she is. I'm only partly joking. The best part for you is that the interconnected literary universe is practically de rigueur in the horror genre. It'd be easier to name horror writers who haven't conjured connections between their stories than those who have. Give them horror people what they want! Your horror fiction reading/writing community, as small as it is, is fervent and self-perpetuating, almost to a fault. In part because of its small size, transgressive themes and interests, at times proud expectation of lack of sales, the horror community can produce true and wonderful outsider art, adhering to a punk aesthetic, which is something, I think, you crave. However the community can also be insular, paranoid, petty, shortsighted, self-defining, and self-defeating. Yes, it is very difficult to sell horror to the big five publishers (most of whom won't dare to use the H-word and will instead call their books thrillers or suspense), and exponentially more difficult for horror writers who are not white cis-gendered men, but how many talented horror writers don't push to break into the big five, don't try to find an agent, and they self-publish or sell their novels/books to the first indie publisher who comes to mind, a publisher who will rarely pay out their royalties on time if ever at all? Simultaneously, there's an oddly exaggerated engagement with the history of the genre that borders on delirium as the members of your community will discuss the "Mount Rushmore" of horror (which must be made of some new form of malleable marble as often as vis-ages would be added and erased), eagerly anointing new writers who have only a handful of published stories to their credit as "masters of horror" (or "the weird," if you prefer), which is incredibly unfair to new writers who then frantically strive to live up to such an impossible standard. Does any other genre do this to its new writers? It occurs to me that part of the appeal of being a member of your madly merry band of enthusiasts is the noble promise of the obscure, overlooked, underappreciated-in-her-day horror writer: your colleagues and com-patriots will champion her work and they will sing her song loud enough and often enough that it will forever echo in the halls of hor-ror. It's the old back door to writing immortality, patented and made famous within the horror genre by H. P. Lovecraft, and I'm convinced it's a corollary to his enduring appeal. Anyway, with all that in mind, I implore thee to continue the fine, interconnected literary universe tradition of your oft-maligned genre. What do you have to lose? Fur-thermore, I've had more than a few days stewing on this and here's a brilliant suggestion (free of charge): Publish a short story collection. Boom, right? You haven't published one in almost ten years, so you're due. It's another horror genre rule: one short story collection every ten years or you get the heave-ho. The paradox, dilemma, conundrum is that the majority of readers don't read short stories. And publishers, the major ones, generally don't publish collections. Maddening, right? In our age of dwindling attention spans, one might think short fiction would be all the rage. Maybe it's not that surprising. Reading a book of stories is harder and asks more from the reader than a novel does. Gen-erally with a novel you have to acclimate to only one set of characters and circumstances. In a collection, you have to suffer through that acclimatizing process for anywhere from ten to fifteen stories and within a compressed amount of reading time, which can be mentally taxing if not exhausting. Am I wrong? I'm not judging anyone. I get it. With each new short story one has to learn about a new set of characters and settings and figure out what's at stake. Also, it's likely the author (subconsciously feeling unencumbered by the demands of the marketplace) dares to be a bit more obtuse and experimental than she would in a novel, and so the stories tend to be even less easily digestible. It is not an accident that in the Western world for well over a hundred years the novel has been the most popular form of written fiction. You can allay some of the short-story anxiety and ensure that at least some readers will not balk at the prospect of reading a collection by writing a few stories making explicit connections to your novels, which mitigates some of the necessary learning curve the reader slogs through with each new tale. Even if the story makes only a glancing connection to a previous novel, you are giving returning readers some easily retrievable context and their reading experience receives a booster shot from the positive memories they have from your earlier work. If readers didn't enjoy your previous work, well then, they're probably not reading these stories anyway. If readers of the collection are reading your work for the first time, there's now an increased chance of their picking through your back catalog. It's a true win-win literary scenario presuming you don't fuck it up and write something that sucks. I propose you write a story about Arnold's uncle, "The Rev," from your disappearance novel. According to Arnold (he could've been lying the whole time, but I don't think he was) The Rev traveled around preaching and healing at revival tents and carnivals, and later led church youth groups of which Arnold was forced to be a member. That kind of preacher can be a bit of a horror trope, but you can't avoid all tropes. It's all in how you use them. How you approach them. Why don't you try this roughly sketched-out idea? Keep in mind, I do think it's best to keep the story short (not a novelette or novella) and episodic, and leave space for the reader to fill in, both in terms of the story and how it ultimately connects to your disappearance novel. The story opens in 2005 with Martin Weeks, aka The Rev, giving an olde-tyme hellfire and brimstone kind of speech at a church-run swap meet/flea market somewhere in central Connecticut. Not the usual setting for this kind of thing, but you can make it work to your advantage. Weeks is in his early sixties and his once fit and athletic frame is at least ten years past its prime. His posture collapses in on itself as though his body is a dilapidated shed or garage. The ravages of decades-long alcohol consumption (wine and vodka mostly) are mapped in red lines on his face. His eyes are icy and sharp, though, like a hawk's eyes (you can come up with a better simile/description when you write it). His tent is only half-full when he starts, but with the power of his voice and his promise of healing and seeing the future, more people trickle in, and the ones who are there already are rapt, rooted to metal folding chairs tilted askew on the uneven ground, legs sinking into the straw. Weeks's voice has an unidentifiable accent, insofar as it's not local, nor belonging to anywhere specifically, though I imagine it might be a strange concoction of fake but subtle nondescript southern twang, Rhode Island long-sounds, and haughty Brahmin Boston. We'll meet Weeks's younger half sister later in the story, but you don't tell us where he came from or tell us any hardships that may have befallen him along the way because I know you, and you want the reader empathizing with all your characters, even the rotten ones, but this is going to be a different kind of story, I think. This scene in the tent starts off being told from an omniscient and detached third-person POV, one that eventually settles into the head of someone watching from the back of the tent, a someone who is clearly a child and is considering ducking out and running away because The Rev (how he looks and moves, how he talks, what he's saying and promising) is scary. That POV finally does leave the tent after The Rev puts his hands on the head and shoulders of a little girl with a lazy eye and soda-bottle-thick glasses and he announces the girl will be able to see fine without the "corrective lenses" (Weeks luxuriates on that phrase) sometime within the next year as long as she minds the Lord. The POV runs through the muddy field toward some unnamed person or place, and as he runs he can still hear The Rev laughing and telling folks he can "see" things sometimes before they happen. Scene jump to Weeks resting in a sketchy motel not too far from the church's weekend tent festivities. He washes down some high-blood-pressure meds with nips of vodka and he sits on the edge of his bed like a load of used, wet motel towels. There's a knock on the unlocked door and in walks a woman who's in rough shape, a tweaker or meth head. Her hair is fried from too many bleachings and thinning as a result of her recreational activities. Her pale skin is milky, translucent but for the ugly red sores. She looks like she is in her late twenties or her late forties depending on the light. She asks Weeks for help, saying her son isn't doing well, isn't quite right, and needs help, needs a man in his life to both toughen him up and maybe knock some sense into him. She mumbles about her boy not talking to her, not talking to anyone, and that he hurt another boy real bad in school. Weeks and the woman talk like they know each other, although the trick of the narration here is that she's never identified. They never call each other by name. She asks Weeks if he made good money tonight and he tells her he did okay. She laughs (an awful sound) and asks if Weeks can "see" (she stresses the word as though she's making fun of him) into tomorrow, "see" if he's going to make more than he did today. He's pleasantly buzzed and plays along without really committing to anything. He gives her a couple of nips of vodka. She offers something wrapped in foil to him, but he tells her not tonight. She asks if he needs her to be a plant in the audience tomorrow and if he does, would he mind kicking back a little of the gate money. He tells her that might work out. She asks if he's planning on sticking around for long. He tells her he might now that the church wants someone to help run a youth group focusing on at-risk preteens and teens (you might want to describe, despite his intoxication, the icky excitement in his voice at his mentioning those age groups), and if he did then they'd likely put him up in the motel or in the small church rectory. He's not all that fired up to stay in the church. Too small. Too confining. Too many other eyes. The woman says he could live with her and her son if he wanted. She says it would be good to have Weeks back around (this is important: you make sure you describe the way she says it as being false, filled with sarcasm and hate and despair). He tells her that might work out too. The woman leaves and you describe the end of the scene like she might not have ever been there, might've been some kind of apparition. The next morning the revival tent is almost full. The Rev goes through his shtick and the same POV character hangs in the back of the tent again. The woman (looking less like a corpse than she did last night, wearing her clean Sunday's best) rushes to be the first in line once Weeks invites folks to walk up to his podium. There's a real clamoring to be heard among the crowd and maybe you write this scene to be reminiscent of <u>The Cabinet of Dr. Caligari</u> (I know you love to slip in references to your favorite books and movies), and Weeks, he's Cesare and Caligari both. The woman (and you still haven't said outright that she's his half sister but you leave enough clues, or save the clues or official reveal till the end) announces that since the good Reverend Weeks returned (maybe you could play with why he returned or why he had to leave in the first place, though like I said earlier, you don't want to dig too much into his past, keep him purposefully shadowy) he has cured her leukemia, and while it'll take time for her skin to heal (she's covered her skin sores with heavy foundation makeup), Reverend Weeks promises her skin will clear up just fine too. She manages to pull off a believable performance, and as she smiles and bows her head, the crowd shouts Amen and applauds, and the POV in the back of the tent smiles and wants to believe she's cured of everything. The POV whispers, "Amen, Mom." As the line of people come up to see Weeks there's another boy who breaks through the line and runs up front and begs Weeks for help. The boy's mother and father shout after him; the father is red-faced and yelling that his son should not be listened to and is a foul liar. Weeks holds up a be-steady hand and it's enough to quiet everyone. He asks the boy (he's tall and heavy and looks older than his age, which, judging by his vocabulary, can't be more than nine or ten years) why he is there. The boy's face and neck are swollen and dark with bruises. He shifts on his feet uncomfortably and has lost what he was going to say. His voice hitches and stutters and leaks into defeated sighs that are all too familiar to the POV. Weeks asks if he's been getting picked on at school. The boy shakes his head no, slowly at first, but then fast and hard enough to make him wobble off-balance. Weeks asks if someone in his family, Mom or Dad maybe, gave him those bruises. The boy nods his head and is crying now. No one else says a word in the tent. You can hear the straw cracking under the boy's feet. Weeks, in a near whisper, asks why he'd been struck. The boy doesn't answer and he's still crying but he's working to keep from crying too loudly. Weeks is wild-eyed and in a near whisper asks again why he'd been struck. Then he outpours a litany of questions about the possible infractions and sins the boy committed (Did you do your chores? Have you been a lazy and slovenly good-for-nothing around the house? Did you talk fresh? Did you take the Lord's name in vain? Did you take money from your parents? Did you sneak into your parents' room or sister's room? Did you look up dirty pictures on the computer? And more and more . . .) until Weeks shouts DID YOU HONOR THY FATHER AND MOTHER? People in the tent are shouting Amens and Hallelujahs, and Weeks roughly shoves the boy down onto his knees and demands the boy thank his mother and father for teaching him right from wrong and to pray for forgiveness, and he goes on and on, and to our POV who is shaking and terrified in the back of the tent, it appears that The Rev is shouting to and about him. Jump to the fourth and final scene as Martin Weeks walks into his half sister's place, which is in a state of unholy neglect. This scene is from Weeks's POV. He's disgusted with the ratty apartment but not with the amount of money he made in one weekend. Her son stands in the bathroom doorway, peeking around the frame. The boy is twelve and slight of build, to Weeks's eyes, and as docile as a lamb (yeah, I know, obvious religious imagery, but you can punch it up). As she explains to the boy where Weeks comes from, Weeks interrupts and says he's an old friend of the family. The woman corrects him, saying that he's the boy's uncle, or half uncle, and he lives in their town now and is going to be staying in the apartment for a while. Weeks walks across the room and crouches down to the boy's level and says he's grateful for their hospitality and he goes on about how important it is for family to help each other out. Weeks says he can see things that haven't happened yet and he can see they're going to be great friends, thick as thieves. The boy shakes his head and his mom shouts at the kid to say something to his uncle. "Can't you even say hi to your uncle?" Weeks stands (staying crouched low hurts his knees and back) and his junkie half sister (remember: this is Weeks's POV) is still yelling at the kid. He plays peacemaker and tells her to go outside for a smoke or something because he wants to talk to his nephew man-to-man. She goes, mumbling to herself. Weeks smiles and creeps closer to the boy, who retreats into the bathroom. Weeks doesn't lie to himself about being anything more than a con man, but he knows he'll be able to get this kid to do anything and everything he wants. Inside the cramped bathroom, Weeks aims to sit on the edge of the bathtub, but there's suddenly an odd gap in time within his current sit-on-the-tub perspective. He slips into a blink or a blip or a hole, a blankness, and in that suddenly eternal moment everything is dark and Weeks is sitting on a cold tile floor. He knows this even though he can't see anything and he can't move and the air is dark and heavy, he's never felt anything so heavy, and there are voices, faraway voices of kids, and they are familiar; not familiar as in their voices are recognizable but familiar as in he can anticipate what they are saying, or what they are going to say. He can't open his eyes or lift his head or even twitch a finger and he feels the ebbing away of his physical presence. He's scared, as scared as he has ever been in his life, and then there's only one voice he hears, and it is shouting at him; shouting about the awful things he did. That break, that split in his <u>now,</u> ends as suddenly as it began and he is sitting on the bathroom floor of his half sister's apartment. Weeks missed the tub and fell on his ass. He recovers composure and says whoops, got a little light-headed, my aim isn't what it used to be, especially in the bathroom. He laughs, and the boy is leaning up against the sink with his arms crossed. Weeks is already forgetting the gap, the blankness, and the voices, and the heaviness, and his forgetting is purposeful and easy, until the one day in his future when he won't be able to forget, and he will remember, and it's in that future he will also remember this bathroom and this moment of forgetting and the moment he thought he lost and the moment that will be his forever. Weeks says to the boy, "I saw you in the back of the tent. I saw you watching. You looked a little scared of me. You look scared of me now. No need to be afraid. I promise. Hey. Do you want to know how I do it, how I 'see' things?

Yeah, I think you do. I'm going to teach you how to see. I'm going to teach you all kinds of things."

Holly had a fine walk until she rolled in something stinky and dead. The corpse was too flattened and desiccated to identify. I suggest you run her a bath.

                                                                    KB

Pee: ✓   Poop:

—11/16
12:15 to 12:35
Holly and I did not go for a walk. She did not want to leave the front yard and I do not blame her because there was a person hiding some- where in or around your property and that person was barking at us. The barks were not real. I know the difference. I mean, they were real barks but they were person-made. It wasn't the dog from across the street or that goddamned Goldendoodle. It was a person, a someone. I'm sure it was KB, yes, I know, even though I didn't see anyone. I've never been so frightened. Can you imagine? Try. Imagine walking outside of your house where for most of your waking hours you as- sume you are safe, or safe enough, and I'm sure that bubble of safety extends well beyond your front door and out into your neighborhood (but how could you possibly assume that you're safe anywhere?), and you walk out the front door and have time enough to enjoy that you're outside, and you inhale the cool, clean air of a perfect fall day, and it's the kind of moment that keeps so many of us living in the Northeast, and the sun is low but bright, and beautiful crinkly leaves are every- where, but then your dog knows something is off before you do and you listen to the split second of nothing, or the split second of noth- ing's amiss, and there's already anticipation even though that's only possible in the remembering afterward, and then there's a fucking person barking at you, and it's such an unexpected and insane sound you are reeling and you don't know what to do, and worst of all you can't see that person, which seems impossible because there are only so many places to hide in the front or backyard. Holly and I couldn't

see the barker. I'm not sure how the person managed it, but that person barked and barked, and it sounded like it came from the woods on our left, and then from above us, and most disturbing of all, from right behind us, but whenever we turned there wasn't anyone there. This really happened. I wouldn't make something like this up. We ran back in the house and the barking stopped. I called the police, but they didn't sound like they were going to do much since I didn't see anyone (I should've lied, I'm so mad at myself for not lying) and because no one was trying to get in the house. Short of doing a drive-by (which they said someone would), there wasn't much else to do at the moment. I hung up and I called Jane, but she didn't answer. I left a message and told her that yesterday I got sick of KB filling up Holly's schedule so I crossed her (or him? I still don't know) off the Holly spot for today and wrote my name down in all caps, and triple underlined with a permanent marker. And then I came here to walk Holly and got barked at by a psychopath. I told Jane that I quit. And I do quit. I have to go now. I will feel terrible leaving Holly here all alone but—I can't. I can't do this, any of this, anymore. I'm sorry. Holly did go pee before the barking started, but we didn't walk.

Elisa

Pee: ✓   Poop:

—12/14
1:00 to 1:20
I suppose this has gone on long enough. All things (good, bad, indifferent) must come to an end. And this is going to end like you expect it to, like you want it to. This ending isn't so much predictable as it is inevitable. You know the difference. I do worry the ending will not be ambiguous enough for your tastes. I do want you to be—happy isn't the right word, but satisfied? I'll even settle for placated. I'm not calling you a one-trick pony as a writer, but your agent and editor do playfully call you "Mr. Ambiguous Horror" and it's a nickname you adore even though it scares the crap out of you because you know there's no possible way to keep doing the ambiguity thing in each book ad infinitum and have it not get stale or predictable (ah, that word again). But

fine, let's play along for a little while longer, Mr. Ambiguous Horror. There's plenty of ambiguity here even though the last lines of this will be clear, as in crystal lake (none of this has anything to do with Jason Voorhees or marauding slashers in general, but I couldn't resist the reference). Don't the impracticalities and improbabilities of the logistics contained within the notes (their increasingly strange and/or unhinged and/or exhaustive subject matter, the absurd lengths of the notes themselves) imply ambiguity regarding what is real and what is fantasy? Would anyone seriously put up with actual dog-walker notes that read like these do? Unlikely, though it's only fair to point out that as of the most recent note of 11/16 you have severed—pesky word choice again—ties with Happy Dog Services and have had all the locks on your doors changed, not that that has stopped me from coming into your house each and every day since. Let's not get ahead of ourselves here, though. More ambiguity. There has to be a reason why my longest notes are the only ones with a line break in the end (you noticed that, yes?) with the last lines post-break relating solely to walking Holly. Maybe it means you imagined the entirety of the notes about literature, genre, your books, etc. that came before the line breaks, and the little notes about your dog are the only parts that are real. The rest of the text? Maybe it represents your anxiety concerning the strangers who enter your house with permission (like dog-walking vampires), and you worry about what they are thinking and doing when they are alone inside your house, and to go full metaphor, it represents your worries about strangers being allowed to peer into your life through your writing (which is more personal than you care to admit) and via social media, on which you spend waaaaay too much time. Ambiguity aside, I think there's a lot more to your not responding in the proper way to the outrageously inappropriate notes, whether or not they are real, but I hesitate to go too armchair-psychologist on you. Then again, I have been watching you for a long time. These notes (real or not) <u>and</u> your changing the locks and leaving a wooden baseball bat (no, not a gun, never a gun; I know from your home invasion novel how you feel about guns . . .) leaning against the wall on your side of the bed and your stalking through the house at night hunting for an evil, home-invading nocturnal dog walker (last night you did two ghost laps through the house wearing only a gray Hüsker Dü T-shirt and black underwear) speaks to the meaning of all this seemingly unconnected mess, even if you're afraid to directly articulate it. Or admit it. It's not all that complicated and it's not any different than what everyone else who has ever lived fears. [[Hey, semi-quick aside and we'll even use a double bracket here to wall it off, like keeping Fortunato in his cask, as it were: Do you remember the first time you were on a panel at New York City Comic Con? Remember how nervous you were, and how mortified you became when you accidentally referred to one of the big-shot panelists by his equally big-shot brother's name? Oops, right. Yeah, that panel. It didn't go well. Which isn't why it's relevant, but I, as they say, digress. One co-panelist was an obnoxious middle-aged YA author who showed up fashionably late and you decided he was full of himself and loathsome, and you used the negative energy to fuel your argument with him when the question of "deathless prose" came up. Rock Star YA guy said you should avoid including social media, cell phones, and other now references in your work, otherwise the story will be dated when people read it years from now. Hahaha, I know, right? That fucking guy with the kind of crap he wrote assuming people would read his literary spasms (okay, I'm being a bit harsh on Rock Star YA guy, but that doesn't mean it's not an accurate assessment or forecast of his work) in the future because he didn't date and sully his stories by mentioning smartphones or the Internet or electric toothbrushes or Nerf footballs or the Electric Slide dance or Reebok air pump sneakers or cable television or movie theaters with stadium seating. I'm not sure how far back in history the technological cutoff is for universally approved deathless prose, but perhaps, to play it safe, make no mention of refrigerators, horseless buggies, paved roads, landline telephones, radios, or the telegraph, or the printing press. So yeah, he of the . . . cough . . . deathless prose. You began your response with "I couldn't disagree more with everything you said," and you said it with a half sneer and half smile. You followed up with (paraphrasing): To presume you're writing something that will go down through the ages is hubristic and folly (did you actually use those words on the panel? Now who's a little full of himself, hmm?), and more practically, it's hard enough to write something for readers who are, you know, actually breathing and buying books now without putting undue pressure on yourself to write something that will be read by people fifty years from now, assuming there will be anyone left alive in fifty years, or five, and even if our melting, flooding, smoking cinder has flealike mutant people scratching around, who's to say their Skynet overlords will allow them to read anything? (You tried to make that sound like an oh-horror-guy-is-dark joke.) You said a writer's only concerns should be serving the story. If you need to use texts or tweets or reference crowdsourcing or whatever cultural element du jour, that's fine as long as the <u>now</u> bits weren't included as mindless fluff and pop-culture references for the sake of doing so (and here you took a shot at a hugest bestest-selling book—now tentpole movie—because you were on a roll). And if you make those details integral to your story, and you do that well enough so that story has something to say, something worth listening to, something of emotional import, then the "deathless prose" thing will take care of itself. You then referenced Gibson's <u>Neuromancer</u>'s opening line and even though younger readers won't have firsthand-experienced the gray fuzz of an old TV tuned to a dead channel, the line and scene still work in context because that detail builds his world and informs the story and is a part of the story, a story that will continue to speak to its readers because it actually has something to say.]] Despite your semi-eloquent and righteous (that guy was indeed a toolbag) public statements made to the contrary on a Comic Con panel attended by fewer than forty people, you fear your death and the death of your work, you fear being forgotten, you fear there's no point to anything you're doing and have ever done and that it's all as useless as Elisa's counting holes in ceiling tiles and as sadly pathetic as Geoff's mummy costume, and ultimately you fear the blank, empty space to which Martin "The Rev" Weeks will forever be confined. I mean, seriously, why else would KB (is that really who I am? is KB a stand-in for you, Mr. Ambiguous?) go on and on about the virtues and fun of interconnecting stories and creating a literary universe, one in which you are its stars and you are its black holes and you are its god and you are its devil? Perhaps even my very initials "KB" (hmm, where have you seen those before? I will spoil you!) represent your obvious (sometimes it's okay to be obvious, there can be virtue in

heavy-handedness too, Mr. Ambiguous Horror) writerly desire (as unspoken and unconscious as it can be at times) to create something that
will outlive you and outlive you well; to create something that will
somehow fill the never-ending void at the end of this book. Listen, I
get it and I don't blame you. You are not unique in thinking this way.
And I look forward to discussing this with you in person as soon as
you are done reading this. Make sure to read it all the way to the end,
though. Quitting before the end would be cheating. You cannot simply bookmark this and put it away. I haven't decided if you'll be reading this while standing at the kitchen counter, or maybe you'll sink
into a chair, or most likely, the fight-or-flight instinct will kick in and
you'll pace the length of the first-floor hallway with this note in your
hands (and Holly will follow you, but she'll be walking carefully, ap-
prehensively, as she'll sense your mood, she'll know that you're upset
and she'll start shaking, and in that way, she'll be your familiar) and
you'll be listening to your own footfalls and the light tapping of Holly's
paws and nails, and you'll scan for other sounds from elsewhere inside your house, and you might hear other sounds and you might not,
but it won't matter if you do, because you won't be able to stop what
will happen at the end, and you'll be angry at yourself for not noticing
everything was wrong when you came into the house and not noticing
Holly's greeting was less than enthusiastic. You'll be reading this and
imagining that I'm crouched, huddled next to your bookcases, ready
to spring, a loaded trap, and I'm holding a weapon (maybe it's homemade), or worse, maybe I'm holding nothing, I have only my bare
hands, outstretched and greedy, and you'll know how vulnerable you
really are, and maybe you'll stop reading here and simply pretend to
read the rest of this to give yourself more time to think, to plan, to get
near the front door (locked; you won't get it open in time) or back
slider (locked; ibid.), but I won't let you get that far. You needn't worry
now, while you're still reading, because you still have time, the time it
will take to read this, and maybe more, though I can't really promise
anything. You know that, right? I would like to talk to you first, if time
does indeed allow, and I will get you to admit your fear of not only
death but the oblivion of everyone you've ever loved, everything you've
ever touched, everything you've ever cared about from the most trivial

to what you might consider to be your raison d'être. After initial moments of panic and terror, you'll admit you've seen me before, there in your darkened house when you're alone, and sometimes when you're not. You'll tell me on the good days you take meaning from the ephemeral and ethereal nature of everything; the universality of that ethereality. Every bit of life will meet the same fate of utter oblivion and nothingness and there's an ineffable beauty in our all being in it together, blah blah blah. I don't mean to mock you. I really don't. The sentiment is nice, really, and I'm not here to tell you that you're wrong. I'm not in the "meaning of life" business. That's not for me to decide. I understand why you would grapple with it. I can only tell you there's no such thing as immortality (not for Shakespeare, not for Tiny Tim [character or Vegas performer], not for our greatest heroes, not for our worst villains, not for you, not for anyone) and there is only physical and total void. You'll tell me you understand that. You do. Then it will be my turn for an unexpected epiphany. I'll surprise you and ask you the question of <u>why horror</u>, one you've never properly been able to answer for anyone, least of all yourself. You'll think (if time allows) and say it's because of the hope of horror and it's because of the horror of hope. You will not elaborate or explain or expand. Neither of us will be entirely sure what you mean, but we'll think you're close to a truth, and really what else can we ask for? After that exchange, we will not speak again, and you will leave your writing office, and I will follow you from a distance as I follow everyone else. We'll be apart for a time. It could be an hour, it could be fifty years. However, there will, eventually, come that final time. Without regard to my arrival being heralded as a balm or a terror, I will take you away.

And your little dog too.

FURTHER QUESTIONS FOR THE SOMNAMBULIST

He is taller than the tent pole and dressed in black and his hair is black and his eyes are black, those giant holes in his head with no end; that is to say we cannot see the bottoms of those holes that are his eyes. And those holes that are his eyes see us even from where we are standing. That his eyes see through the crowd and choose *us* is the promise of the Somnambulist. We are promised the Somnambulist will answer our questions and that he knows every secret and he knows the past and sees the future. A small man approaches the stage before we are ready. We cannot hear what is asked or what is answered, for we are too far away. We rush the stage after the terrified little man leaves. We are not afraid nor are we intimidated when standing in the shadow of the Somnambulist, even as his shadow settles over us in the outline of a giant. We will ask our questions and we will have our answers, no matter what the answers are.

We are

a woman   a man   a child

There is a sharp pain
behind my left eye
and numbness in my
extremities; when will it
stop?

What is the   When will I stop
cultural value of   being scared of
oppression?   the dark?

When will I lose
When will I feel better?   my last baby
tooth, and what
will my mouth
Is society a   taste like then?
madman?

How come the
walls are so thin
in my bedroom
that I can hear
my parents
talking, but
it sounds like
whispers, like
it's nothing but
secrets in their
Will I hear their whispers   room?
and crying, and if so,
for how long will I hear
What will we do   them?
if there is another
war?

Do all moral
concepts
collapse?

Will I be surrounded by
strangers in mask and
gloves or left alone in a
white room?

How many times
can I blink my
eyes before
the lids stop
working?

Who will lead us,
we who cannot be
led?

Will I know where I am?

Will it be you?

How will they go on
without me?

Am I strong
enough to break
through my
bedroom walls
with my hands?

Is there more
space between
our walls than I
think?

Can I please sleep
like you?

Will they be relieved?

Is it strange that when I'm alone in my room I hear noises in my walls, and when I knock the noises stop and do not return until the following night, although I suppose it's possible the noises return when I'm asleep or when I'm not there at all, and it's frustrating because if I could only figure out who or what is making the noises then I wouldn't feel the need to ask you any questions?

What will the world be like when I'm gone?

Will there be enough room for me, even when I'm getting bigger?

What happens to the small old me when I'm the big new me?

Will the old me be put in a drawer like a crayon drawing?

Will anyone remember me?

Will they still love me and tell me that they are proud of the things I do?

Why can't I describe what the noises sound like exactly as they are, not scratches or bangs or groans or creaks, though perhaps that's what gentle but consistent pressure upon a barrier sounds like?

When will the last person who remembers me die?

Will anyone notice?

If I make a hole big enough to crawl into the walls, will I be able to see them through the cracks?

Why do I then imagine a lost child navigating the space within my walls?

Will people know and say my name, but the name will have come to no longer be associated with me or any other person but will have taken on a new meaning, something else, something funny, pathetic, wondrous, something horrible?

For whom or what is the child searching?

Will they know that I am there above their heads?

Will she find it?

Are they telling the truth when I'm listening to them?

What if she gets lost in a vast network of passages? What if the space between my walls was folded and curled in and around itself, like a maze, and if unfolded or unspooled the space was equivalent to all Germany, all Europe?

What if, like my name, a photograph of my body becomes an avatar for something else?

When I look down at them sleeping or doing their secret things and keeping their secrets, why will I be afraid of them?

Will someone use my bones as instruments or tools for a purpose not yet imagined?

Is she trapped and am I her captor?

What if she were
to light lamps to
mark all the places
in the walls she'd
been?

Why will they
look different,
like strangers,
like other people
who aren't the
ones who belong
to me?

What if she
watches me for
the rest of my life,
from inside the
walls?

Why am I always
afraid?

If I ask her these
same questions,
will she answer
me?

Will someone
comtemplate those
artifacts of an identity
that has been lost
forever and speculate
upon its original
existence, its original
purpose?

When will the
lamps go out
everywhere?

If I crawl into the
wall, will I ever
be able to get out,
will I be there
forever?

Must I become?

How long do I have to
live?

How long do I
have to live?

How long do I
have to live?

"Till dawn. Tomorrow."

THE ICE TOWER

(THE CLIMBERS)

The sun doesn't go down here. It moves and dips in the sky, like it's floating along a blue river. We know it's a new morning only because of our watches.

Roger and Mike the cameraman are the first to climb the ice tower. They are supposed to be the first.

The rest of us ice climbers ring the tower's base and cheer even though some of us are envious because we're not as talented and accomplished as Roger. We think we can almost see the top of the ice tower as they start the climb. The weather and visibility are as good as they have been since we made camp. The temperature has climbed to fourteen degrees Fahrenheit, which is within the range of favorable ice-climbing conditions. Our guide, Liz, tells us the temperature is likely a record high for this sector of the Western Antarctic Ice Sheet.

We lose sight of Roger and Mike in the gray-blue sky at around two hundred feet, and then soon after, a nasty squall bullies in and we can't see our own gloved fingers in front of our faces. The temperature drops without a parachute. Neither climber answers when we attempt contact on the two-way radios. We try yelling and our desperate cries freeze and lodge painfully in our throats.

We wait for Roger and Mike to rappel down. We try to wait longer. Liz forces us to retreat to our tents. She pushes and pulls some of us away from the ice tower.

Liz tells us that because of the storm it might be days before some-one from any of the other main camps can get to us. Liz buzzes around her tent, fiddles with the two-way radio and other equipment like she doesn't know how to use it, and that's not fair but we all think this. We want her to fix everything.

We hunker in our tent, no one saying out loud what we already know. A few hours later there's a brief lull in the storm. We venture out with safety tethers and Liz finds Mike's rag doll body and his camera at the tower's base. His belay lines are wrapped and knotted around his arms and legs.

We stare at him. His lower half is buried in a snowdrift, the purest snow we've ever seen. His face looks fake, and his eyes are dark rocks, the eyes of a doll. There is no sign of Roger.

(LIZ)

A few hours before the climb, Roger was in my tent sharing my sleep-ing bag, both of us sleeping off the whiskey, or as he called it, "pre-climb courage." Roger was an impulsive jerk. He had big hands and shoulders with topography as impressive as any mountain chain.

When Roger was dead-to-the-world asleep, I drew small cartoon eyes on the toes of his crampon boots with a Sharpie. I wonder if Roger saw the eyes when he dressed for the climb, or if he didn't see them until he was up on the tower, daring to peek down at his feet and the metal spikes desperately digging into the ice. I wonder if he saw them before the squall hit. I wonder when he stopped seeing the eyes.

(THE CLIMBERS)

The storm cranks back up as we carry Mike's body to camp. We wrap him in a cocoon of tarpaulin and anchor him next to our tent. We can't go looking for Roger. We have no choice but to wait out the storm or wait for help to arrive.

We are somewhere between the American-run Amundsen-Scott South Pole Station, which is at the geographic South Pole, and the newly restarted Byrd Station of western Antarctica. The ice tower was discovered by a transport helicopter flying to Amundsen-Scott from the city-sized McMurdo Station. We were at McMurdo before coming out here. It houses more than a thousand people and even has its own ATM. We didn't sleep and partied it up for three days. Roger streaked on one of the landing strips after an Antarctic pub crawl.

Liz told us that they (they being other scientists) aren't sure how a freestanding ice tower of even a fraction of its size could form, never mind go undetected for as long as it apparently had. The scientific community was spooked. Liz thought it might have something to do with the rapidly melting ice sheet and shifting glaciers acting like ter-raforming tectonic plates on speed. She said that ice spikes grew in birdbaths and shallow water containers, and reportedly on Lake Erie, but those spikes were measured in inches, not hundreds of feet. Con-sequently, there were whispers of a hoax, of one of the twenty-five countries with a base on the frozen continent secretly manufacturing an ice tower like the recreational ones in Maine and Switzerland. But to what purpose? Who could afford the trip to the most remote place on earth for an ice climb?

The ice tower gleams white, so bright in the sun, it fuzzes and blurs out if you stare at it too long. We think it's shaped like a giant upside-down icicle. Liz said it reminded her of something else. The tower is roughly 750 feet tall, which is about half the size of the Empire State Building. The makers of Red Bull energy drink announced they would sponsor a temporary research camp at the base of the tower. When they sent a press release detailing how our merry band of half-assed King Kongs would be the first at the camp and our climbs would be filmed, many people concluded that the tower had indeed been manufactured. We played coy in interviews and let Roger speak for our group.

When we arrived at camp, the six of us shared two pyramid-shaped Scott tents, with Liz, our one-woman communications/scientist/keep-us-ice-climbers-alive Sherpa, staying alone in the smaller of the tents. We were supposed to be here for only three days. Five days tops, with emergency provisions that could last two weeks.

Roger has been stuck on the tower for two days now.

(LIZ)

I've been on the radio all night and I can't get anyone at McMurdo to commit to a time to come out here. They tell me it's not safe.

I don't know what to do, so I finally send the other climbers back to their tent. I can't take their standing and staring at me, like a silent Greek chorus. None of this is my fault. They knew the risks of attempting such an extreme climb, extreme both in terms of height and environment. They knew that it can actually be too cold to climb, as the ice will turn brittle and break off in dinner-plate-sized slabs under the tips of their handheld ice tools.

When we first arrived, the climbers stood at the tower's base; they hooted, whistled, bumped fists, and made penis jokes. Roger patted its side like the tower was a tired dog and called it the world's biggest inverted icicle. I thought the ice tower looked like one of those giant termite mounds found in the Australian outback, its structure seemingly random and ready to fall apart, but in reality, its alien design was ingenious and infinitely complex.

The climbers argued about what type of ice had formed the tower: Was it water ice or hard-packed alpine ice, or a combination? Roger was the only one who seemed concerned at all, and he said its white color meant that the ice was likely full of air and would make anchoring the ice screws tricky.

I asked him if he thought the ice tower was hollow. I meant it as a joke.

He said no, but he said it with a question mark.

(THE CLIMBERS)

Liz asks that we leave her alone for a few hours as she attempts to arrange emergency rescue and early extraction. We take one of the two-ways with us to our tent and we sit and say Roger's name and we listen. In the static, we hear things: a drone beneath the white noise, an impossible pattern that is both beyond rhythm and melody and is more about frequency, the kind we can feel inside our heads. We hear without hearing. But we are listening, learning, and we respond.

The Wall Street type, the business major who dropped out of Yale when he was a second semester senior to follow his Parkour-enthusiast boyfriend out to Portland, begins to put on his cold gear. He pauses to flex his hands, and then he puts his fingers in his ears and opens and closes his mouth. He's crying, sobbing, drooling, and clearing his throat. He tries to talk, but he doesn't make any sense. His words aren't words, and we forget what he's saying as soon as he says it.

The Vermonter shimmies into his marbled, Holstein cow snow pants. He doesn't put on his anorak and has only a thermal undershirt on his torso. He plucks his ice tool from his belt and presses his tongue against the sharpened tip of the pick hard enough to draw blood. His other hand dives inside his pants and he begins screaming.

Our youngest ice climber is a twenty-two-year-old woman. She wears an upper bridge because she'd lost a handful of her front teeth playing rugby. She lashes crampons to her bare feet, using the nylon shoelaces from her boots to remake her feet into flesh and steel talons. She chews and crunches on her bridge, spitting out pieces of ceramic teeth.

The self-taught line cook, who grew up in four different foster homes in and around Atlanta before he ran away for good at the age of fifteen, carefully wraps a belay line around his neck. He attaches each end of the line to ten-centimeter ice screws. He attempts to twist one into place on his forearm. It won't hold and the screw's cutting teeth chew a ragged hole in his skin.

(LIZ)

When we were drinking whiskey in my tent, Roger kept brushing his foot along the back of my calf. I hate other people's feet, but I let it slide. The whiskey made everything warm.

He asked me why I would spend nine out of twelve months living in Antarctic outposts instead of—and he trailed off, letting the implications of better options elsewhere hang. I considered lying, making up a story about growing up off the grid and dirt poor in Alaska with drunk and indifferent parents, and that being in the snow and cold was all I deserved. Instead I told him about how when I was a kid I'd once found a dead rabbit in a snowdrift in our backyard. How I'd taken her inside, wrapped her in a blanket, and held her against my chest to try and warm her up and save her.

I went quiet after the rabbit story. We drank more. Then I teased him about me being the only person who could keep him alive out in the middle of Antarctica.

He asked me to save him if he got stuck in a snowdrift.

I told him to stop touching my leg with his nasty foot, and then I kissed him.

(THE CLIMBERS)

We go outside and it's so cold it slows down our blood. We can't see the tower, but we know where it is. We don't need the radio to hear it. We hold hands until we bump into its base. We swing our axes blindly. The familiar vibrations go up our wrists and arms, and it feels right. The tower acquiesces to the hardened tips of our ice tools and the toothed claws of crampons. We pull ourselves up and off the surface of the frozen continent. The storm stops, or if it doesn't stop, it blinks, and we look inside the tower, and we see something moving, swarming, or flowing; water in a stream, blood in veins.

We look up and we look up and we see the tower and its perfect white ice, so bright, shining into eternity, shining into the abyss.

(LIZ)

I finally get word that two helicopters from a nearby Swiss base will attempt a rescue and extraction of our base camp sometime during the next twelve hours, as they anticipate a brief flying window in the surprise but dumbly persistent storm.

The window might already be open a crack. Weak sunlight pokes through the gray sky. I try the two-way radio but get no response from anyone in the climbers' tent. I shouldn't have left them alone for so long. I follow the safety line even though I can see fine, and shit, they're not inside their tent. Blankets, empty bottles and food wrappers, clothes, and ice-climbing equipment are strewn about as though it were a messy teenager's bedroom. I find spots of blood on the floor and walls.

I light a flare even though the sun is now full-on shining. I squint and fumble for my sunglasses in the unrelenting light. I leave the flare burning outside their tent. I hope against hope that the climbers will be waiting for me at the base of the tower, performing an ill-advised vigil for Roger. I have no idea when they left their tent, and visibility could've been poor enough that they missed the tower completely and have wandered miles from camp. I consider their self-imposed gulag a possibility, but as I get closer to the tower, I see them.

They are maybe fifty feet off the ground and they aren't moving. They are dirty black dots on the impossibly white tower. They are bugs trapped in amber. Their legs and arms have sunk into the ice, into the tower. I can see the shadows of their body parts hidden inside. The only climber with both arms free is sunk up to her waist in the ice. She's bent over backward, stretching out and away from the tower, stretching for the ground she'll never reach.

I pound on the ice with my fist and it feels soft, pliant, even sticky. There's a flicker, a shadow, a hallucination in the ice, and I spin away and shout and scream their now-forgotten names and the silence afterward buzzes in my ears and I go dizzy with vertigo. I fall to my hands and knees and there's something underneath me, under the new snow. I dig fast with both hands and unearth Roger. He's face-down, turned away. I dig out enough snow to be able to turn him over, but I'm afraid to.

So I talk to the back of his head. I tell Roger I'd found the dead rabbit a week after my father had committed suicide. He was a high school physics teacher, who by all accounts was well liked and well regarded. People at his school and in our family had said no one saw it coming, his killing himself was out of the blue. But the truth was, Mom and I had known something was wrong because he'd been going inside himself, without us. Mom and I hadn't known what to do or how to fix him. How does anybody fix anything? Dad had told me that he spent so much time alone because he liked to listen to the sounds in his head, and he'd been listening for longer and longer stretches. Of course he'd told me about the sounds in his head only because he'd wanted me to ask about them.

I kept that dead rabbit with me in my room, in my bed, for two weeks. I left my bedroom window open to help clear out the smell and the flies. I was surprised by how many flies there were, even in winter. The rabbit's fur fell off in mealy clumps, and I still kept it. Along with my pillows and bedsheets, I finally buried the rabbit out back after its head had deflated, like a week-old birthday balloon.

When I'm done telling Roger the full story—but it's not really the full story, just more of it—I hear helicopters approaching. They don't sound right. The syncopation of the propeller blades sounds off rhythm, and then so loud, like the helicopters are landing on top of me, and now I can feel it in my head and in my blood, and in my head are also these whispers and they're made of noises that are older than language, and it fills me, and I know these are the sounds my father was listening to, and these are the sounds everyone hears in their own heads eventually.

I look up and the ice tower stretches up into the blue and then out of the blue. The tower is indeed hollow. It has an inside. And inside are faces filled with flies. I look away and down. There are no eyes drawn on my feet that I can see and the ice is above my ankles and I can't move. And that's when I hear Roger ask me again if I'll save him.

THE SOCIETY OF THE MONSTERHOOD

AN EXPLANATION FOR THE READER

You do not speak the languages of our city, certainly not of our neighborhood. You don't because you don't want to. You are as purposefully deaf as you are blind and have been so for so long that no one remembers it being any different. This isn't that kind of story.

No, every story is that kind of story. I want you to know that we know. You may have difficulty understanding the actions of the Society of the Monsterhood, and those difficulties are all yours.

THEY USED TO BE THE NOT-SO-FANTASTIC FOUR

They are our neighbors. They live in the same tenement buildings stacked and leaning against each other like the empty pizza boxes all piled up in that Greek place on Norton Street. They are four of our children; three girls, one boy. Every school-day morning a little white van, a private school's crest with a Latin motto stenciled on the side in red and black, picks them up on the corner of North Prospect and Downey at 5:30 A.M. When the van picks them up, the sky is dark and metal grates are still pulled down over our storefronts like drawbridges on castles.

Look at them in their school uniforms: the girls in blue and green plaid skirts, regimented hems at the kneecaps, blue socks covering the rest of their legs, white button-down shirts, blue blazers; the boy in too-skinny khaki pants graffitied with stray pencil slashes, the same blue blazer, green tie fastidiously tied, black hair plastered to his forehead. The van drops them back at the same corner at 6:00 P.M., normally, sometimes as late as 8:00 P.M. if they are participating in extracurriculars. Two of them play sports (even if they aren't very good at them) and one of them is in the drama club, and the fourth doesn't do anything but read. They are now two months into their freshman year at their K-through-12 private school with a tuition more than many of us take home in one year. They won the life lottery back in fifth grade and go to Our Lady of the Saint Suburb Day School for free. Many of us are happy for them and support them and we are in their ears reminding them of the opportunity they're being given, to not blow it, to not let what some people (both at their school and here back home) call them, say to them, do to them to keep them from graduating and getting out of here. Some of us think that handpicking four kids and only four kids from the neighborhood is bullshit, a slap in the already battered face, a reminder of the exclusion practiced on us unwashed masses every day. Some of us take it out on those four kids. It's not fair and we're not proud of it, but it's something we have to do, are moved to do, as though there were no other way. Kids their age, and the younger ones, too, and yeah, the older teens, the dropouts, and sure, the adults who hate them for having the chance they never had, we make it hard for them. We treat them like traitors, the worst kind of enemy.

When they started seventh grade they called themselves the Not-So-Fantastic Four (one of them reads comics, typical), a lame lifeline of self-deprecation. If anything, that bogus nickname made things worse, made it sound like they thought they were separate from us, not of us, that they were better than us and they deserved their free education and by proxy, none of us deserved it but they did.

And then they changed their name this year, freshman year. Everything changed this year.

WHAT THEY TOLD US

Early September, and the four of them were starting to look not like little kids but gangly, metamorphing teenagers; and like all teens they were bigger, louder, stronger, smarter, and stupider at the same time, and more dangerous. But how dangerous can you be in that Catholic school uniform? Still, they were now old enough, and more important, big enough (size matters; attitude gets one only so far) to take out their frustrations on the younger kids who'd follow them around and taunt them (no need to recount exactly what was said; we all heard it when they said it and only some of us would try and make them stop saying it).

The four of them told those little kids (and their not-so-little insults) that they had a new name and no one was going to fuck with them anymore. Then they told those kids they had a new name because they found a monster. They said that on their first day of high school they were waiting for the van in the morning and it was late and the empty 9 bus rumbled through the square and one of them, the tall one, the one who will be even more beautiful someday, saw it hanging off the rear of the bus, curled up around the bumper. When the 9 turned the corner, that thing fell off and rolled across the street and into the side of the Brazilian market, denting the brick wall. (There is a dent in the wall, down at its base, close to where brick meets sidewalk. No one else knows why that dent is there; or no one else can prove they know why.) One of them said the thing was a like a giant sloth with arms as long as firehoses. One of them said it had spaghetti-long white hair, like some city yeti, but that wasn't quite right and didn't explain how it moved like it was made of something other than thick bones. One of them said its fur wasn't really fur and looked more like filaments, tendrils, thin tentacles that were alive and could move and pick up anything it wanted, and she said it wasn't white, either; dingy, dirty, slightly changing color to match the sidewalk. The four of them weren't scared, so they went to it, and it was lying there making noises none of them could really describe, and without saying a word to each other they helped it up, and when it stood, it was massive, taller than the market, which put it over ten feet. They weren't ever clear on whether or not they actually touched it; they said "helped it up" but didn't detail how they helped it, and they never said what touching it felt like, not from a lack of our asking. Anyway, they directed the ugly thing into that little U-shaped dead-end alley behind the market and Mr. Chef's and the Dollar Store with Dumpsters and trash bags and tied-up corrugated boxes that never get recycled and rats the size of dogs. They said they built it a nest, a home, and they visit it each morning before school to make sure it's okay and they can talk to it without having to talk and one of them always sneaks out at night, too, to make sure it's okay, keep it company, feed it. They said if anyone gives them any more shit about going to school where they go to school, they'll feed them to the monster.

They said they had a new name; they're the Society of the Monsterhood now, which is a dumb name, yeah. Drama geek came up with it. One of them said (as an afterthought, because the story was more weird than threatening at this point) the monster was big, mean, and always hungry.

K.G.: WHAT WE KNOW AND DON'T KNOW HAPPENED TO HIM

K.G. was a big fifteen-year-old and a bully's bully. He had a mustache and muscles and attitude. He went to school two, maybe three days a week. He wasn't all that coordinated, but he was strong, could take a punch and then give more than he got. The kids said his temper wasn't a temper, it was who he was. He also liked to sing to himself when he didn't think anyone was paying attention to him. He wasn't a very good singer. His dad worked third shift at the electrical plant and his mom didn't come home sometimes. K.G. didn't come home all the time, either, which was why when he went missing, some of us thought it wasn't a big deal for the first day.

We know that he called bullshit on the Society's monster story when his little brother came home crying with it, or a version of it. None of us really believed the Society's story and we ignored it. If we didn't ignore it, it was more like we were waiting to see what the repercussions of the story and the new group name would be. K.G. was such a repercussion. The morning after the unveiling of the Society, K.G. didn't go to school and he sat at the corner all afternoon and into the early evening, waiting for the school van to drop the Society off, which it did eventually.

K.G. didn't even wait for them to get off the van. He started yelling and threatening and he punched the van in its side before it pulled out into traffic. He dented a panel, swear to God. There is a dent in the panel and it looks like the dent in a soda can and the dent in the

Brazilian market. We don't know if there's some sort of coincidence or connection there, like there's a special power to the Society's story, like the act of telling it makes things fit, but afterward, we always talked about how K.G. denting the van first like this was where it really started, that the dent was where the monster came from. The van limped away and the rest of us were either laughing or shaking our heads as K.G. yelled at the Society some more and knocked book bags off their shoulders and kicked their feet into each other as they tried to ignore him and walk away, and then he had his thick arm around the boy (who had gotten bigger, but not K.G. big, not even close), squeezing him tight, sneaking in quick gut punches and one oops-my-fault-didn't-mean-it-but-I-did-mean-it head butt. That abuse, it all happened in the short trip from the corner past the dented market to the alley. They stopped at the alley, stood there like acolytes, and stared into it. We don't know if K.G. saw anything. He didn't say. The Society told him to meet them there, same spot, later that night. They told him to come alone. Maybe because he saw it, saw something, sensed something, or maybe it was such a weird unexpected request that sounded like a threat (he had to be thinking, *Do the four of them think they can jump me in the alley and take me?*) that he must not have known what to do or say right then because K.G. only said, "All right," and he let them walk away while he still stood there in front of the alley and not in it.

Some of us saw K.G. walk home after that and some of us saw him milling around the streets. Some of us saw him with friends getting a burrito at Roseanne's Taqueria and some of us saw him by himself stalking the corner at the Brazilian market that night. I saw him feeling that dent in the wall. I did. No one saw him go into the alley. No one saw him come out. No one from our neighborhood has seen him since. Sure, there are some of us who say that he got in trouble and couldn't get out or that he ran away because so many run away or go missing (monsters or no monsters). Some of us say he's living in another part of the city with his cousins. There's almost anything that could've happened to him.

This is what we know: No one has seen him. No one can prove that they've seen him or knows where he is.

WHAT THEY SAID HAPPENED TO K.G.

The Society said they didn't do anything. They only met him in the alley that night and watched him with the monster. They said that K.G. walked over to the monster of his own accord (their own words) and he kept saying, "What is it?" and first he got close but not too close, he didn't want to touch it, make contact. If he wasn't full-on afraid, to his credit, he had the proper sense of awe. Then he started acting tough, saying it was nothing but a sick dog, or a couple of sick dogs, and he pushed all the kids away from him. The drama geek bounced off the back wall of Mr. Chef and she later showed us a scab on the back of her head from the bouncing. The Society said it was all over once he did that and there was nothing they could do to protect him, save him. There was no turning back. They said he'd had his chance. The monster filled the alley and grabbed K.G. with two monster hands at the end of two monster arms and it pulled him into its mouth. Its mouth was open wider than a freeway and took up more than half its body, its whole body, it became all mouth. And teeth. There were teeth, they said. Big jagged triangles that dripped saliva and digestive juices. They told everyone that the monster ate K.G., and that the eating wasn't clean, wasn't a sit-down restaurant eating. It was messy. It tore him apart, literally. Biting and pulling him into twitching, quivering pieces. They said it was the worst thing you could ever see. The Society said they were forced to read *Beowulf* at school and what happened to K.G. was way worse than what Grendel ever did. They said they named their monster Grendel, too, and the alley was now Grendel's Den (too-smart-for-their-own-good kids always naming everything, right?). The Society said they don't want to see it do what it did to K.G. ever again, so please do not pick on us anymore.

WHAT WE FOUND

Nothing.

After K.G. was missing for a fourth day, a whole bunch of us went into the alley and couldn't find anything other than what was supposed to be in an alley. No evidence of a nest, never mind a Grendel's Den. No signs of a great struggle. Certainly no blood or spit-up bones and clothes and sneakers, no ooze or ick that would be expected leave-behinds from a ravenous monster. And no monster. It was an alley damp with garbage and stink, and it rumbled and echoed with the buses, trucks, and cars that needed new mufflers. Just an alley, right? But it wasn't just an alley. Something had happened there. We could sense it. There was the unease of the aftermath, aftereffects, afterimages of violence. It's like a presence and the lack of a presence at the same time; the feeling you get when you stare at a broken window. We had that feeling and that's all we had, and we argued about it and then we got angry because, come on now, the monster was bullshit.

We went to the Society's apartments and we banged on their doors. We demanded they address us, answer our questions. We confronted them with all the nothing we found (including K.G. in that nothing. Where was he? Where did he go?).

Each one of the Society, with their solemn parents standing behind them, eyeing us, telling us that K.G. deserved what he got and if we got it, too, well, then, we deserved it (and maybe they were right about some of us, but fuck them for saying it). They told us the story of K.G. and the monster again, and ended the story with "Leave us alone. Or else." They all said the same thing, like they were giving out a practiced statement.

They didn't really say the *or else* part out loud, but it was there if you were listening. We heard it. All four times.

THERE ARE MANY MORE WHO WENT MISSING

Every school night after we confronted the Society there was someone else there at the corner to meet them when the van dropped them off. It became the new normal, which is to say it was like a ritual; it was something that just happened and we were supposed to accept, deal with, like everything else shitty everyone is supposed to accept, deal with, and to our immense shame we followed the unspoken rules. But don't think you are any different. You would simply follow the rules, too.

The van and the Society weren't overrun by a wave of angry and righteous humanity. There'd be one kid, barely taller than a fire hydrant, or one teen who was confused about everything, confused about why things were the way they were, or one adult who'd given up on trying to figure out why things were the way they were. There'd be a *whoever* there every night and whoever would punch the van in the same spot K.G. punched the van and then whoever would be led over to the alley, the empty alley. (We'd checked that alley, remember? Empty. And we would check it again and it would still be empty the next day after another whoever would go missing.) And then at night, again inexplicably following the inexplicable rules, whoever would come back and go into that alley with the Society and whoever would disappear.

It's late October now and I want to make some comparison to fallen leaves, because it's autumn, but comparing our missing persons to leaves is wrong, so wrong that you almost don't notice how wrong it is.

Anyway, in the early evening, we would also go back to the Society's apartments. (Our little group was growing larger as the number of people, mostly kids, who went missing also grew larger.) We would knock on their doors like we did for K.G. We wouldn't expect answers or satisfactory conclusions, and our demands for action were more feckless and desperate. The Society wouldn't lose patience with us; they would repeat the same story each night and tell us to leave them alone.

YOU AND I GO INTO THE ALLEY AND THEN LEAVE IT
The youngest kid yet is there, sitting on the corner. He can't be more than eight or nine. He sits on the curb, hands on knees, rolling a glass bottle under his feet. I don't know his name. I ask him what it is when I walk by and he doesn't answer me. I ask where his parents are or his grandparents, a grandmother? Then I ask why he isn't in school and he doesn't answer me. I walk back up and sit on the front stairs of my building, only a few doors down from the corner. I watch the kid watching for the van. I imagine the monster, if there is one (how can there be one? how can there not be one?), wouldn't have to open its mouth all that much to eat him. I don't know about you and everyone else, but I can't abide this anymore. Something has to change. We have to change it.

The van rolls in. The kid doesn't move from the curb and makes the van stick out into the street. Cabs and cars beep at it lazily as they swerve by. The Society gets out of the van. They look older. In two months how did they get so much older? They're still just kids, we need to remind ourselves. The other kid, the little one, sitting on the corner, he stands up and throws that glass bottle off the side of the van. The bottle explodes into glittering shards. It's almost beautiful. The van doesn't stop and drunkenly waddles off on its christened voyage. I stay on my stairs, on my stoop, and I don't do anything. Not yet. It's too early. I can see what I need to see from here, for now. The Society doesn't say anything to the kid and the kid doesn't say anything to them and together they walk over to the mouth of the alley. It's an obvious mouth, isn't it? They stand and stare and nothing special seems to happen, not that I can see. Time doesn't slow down, the city doesn't stop doing its city thing.

The Society walks away first, like they always do, but they'll come back. The kid stays there. He sits down right on the sidewalk, a period placed in the middle of a sentence. When we walk by (because we have things to do, city being city, like I said) he doesn't move and we have to go around him. I walk by him three times and each time I pass I tell him to go home, to forget about it, go eat dinner. He doesn't do anything. The kid is so small and thin, hands and feet like a puppy's. I get him one of those sports drinks and a protein bar. Not much of a dinner, but it's better than nothing. To my surprise, the kid takes it from me and drinks and eats. He tells me in his hardest voice (still little, still small, and it breaks our already broken hearts) he's K.G.'s brother (we should've known that). He tells me to go back to my stoop. I tell him that I'll be back later.

I'm watching him and watching for the Society as the streetlamps flicker on and the temperature drops, and it drops fast now as the sun flees behind the building tops. Hours go by and I keep watch. I don't get distracted. The rest of us walk by the kid and the alley like nothing is going to happen there, like we're not supposed to look.

Later The Society of the Monsterhood shows up, and they show up one at a time, each from a different direction. The kid doesn't get up off the sidewalk until the four of them are there.

I yell at them. That's all I have to do to stop it, right? Dumb-ass that I am, hoping it's that easy to stop whatever it is that's going to happen. The Society ignores my rants from the stoop and walks into the alley first, one at a time, single file, a progression. I'm off my stairs and running (I can't run that fast, not anymore, and it's less a run and more a fast limp), and I need to get there to stop the kid from going into the alley. He's too young (would him being two years older, five, ten, make a difference?). He's too everything. This isn't right. We've all had enough of the monster, and yeah, we all believe there is a monster, we always did.

The city is still the city. It doesn't stop for this or for us, it never has and never will. I'm not quite sure how I manage to do it, but I must be faster than I think because I get to the alley before K.G.'s brother goes in. I grab his shirt, the back of his collar, and he yells and hits my arms. He squirms out of my grasp but has to go backward, away from the alley, to do so. I'm not fast or strong or tough, or that kind of tough, anymore, but I'm big enough to block the entry to the alley. K.G.'s brother is full-on crying now and he tries to scoot by me, to scramble under my legs, but I stop him. He yells at me. I tell him in a quiet voice to go home. He doesn't give, and he's wearing me down. I'm breathing hard enough that there's a stitch, a little knife in my chest. He rams into my stomach, shoulder first, but I push back, harder than I should, and he goes flying backward and lands on his butt on the sidewalk. I say, "Please." Maybe the please does it. Or maybe he just gives up. I don't know. I don't exactly see him go away because I take the opportunity with him stunned to turn and run into the alley ahead of him. Only one of us can go in, right? That's the rule.

And it's still just an alley. That's it. Garbage cans and Dumpsters and bins spray-painted all different colors. Black skeletons of fire escapes dripping from the back walls. There's no monster.

The Society of the Monsterhood stands up against the back of the Brazilian Market. If they're surprised to see me come in and not the little kid, they don't say it or show it. The Society holds a chair leg, a piece of rebar, a folded-in-half NO PARKING sign, a metal rod that might've had a bike seat on its end once. They stare at me. They stare at me and hold those things like weapons.

I yell at them, ask them what the hell they think they're doing, ready to, what, beat down that little kid out there who doesn't know any better, and now me, instead? They don't react. I lose it and I'm yelling all the terrible and unfair things that have been said to them by some of us and I yell the stuff that I know they've been hearing at their rich school, too; I make sure to say those things, to say everything. And then I hear it behind me, coming up from underneath the garbage bags, growing from out of nothing. It knocks over the barrels and even flips one of the Dumpsters and black, garbage-smelling Dumpster water rushes over the tops of my sneakers. It's bigger than I am, so much bigger, and it's humanoid for an instant and then it's not, and how it moves, like a movie with frames missing, and it's kind of white, then it's dark, and has two arms, then more, then none, and it grows and shrinks, expands, retracts, and it's coming toward me. I turn away and the Society is walking toward me, too, and I'm shaking and my legs won't work anymore, so I bend down, a dead-battery robot, and one knee crash-lands on the dampened alley floor. The Society raises their weapons over their heads and over my head for their mightiest swings and smashes but they sail right by me and attack the monster, wildly swinging their weapons. I scuttle away and don't get too far, sitting on my butt like that little kid was, and I watch. At first I'm thinking I got through to the Society, showed them how wrong this all is; yes, I got through to them and now this will be the end. But as I watch them hit the thing, bashing it like a piñata, and opening holes in it, and there is blood, and then they lose their weapons but they beat it with their bare hands and they snap its arms and legs over their knees and stab and pry with their fingers and tear open deep gashes in its hide, in its skin, and the sounds the monster makes, so awful, I can hear it without my ears. I know that this isn't happening because of what I said or did; this is what happens every time they take someone into the alley and to the monster. They do this every time.

I'm crying and I can't help it because they won't stop and the monster looks like a toy with everything twisted and warped into unnatural directions, and it twitches, painfully trying to correct itself, and it's one of the worst things I've ever seen. The beating goes on for hours, but they don't kill it. I can still hear it and see it breathing.

The Society does stop, finally. They stop. And they stumble out of the alley without saying anything to me or to each other. The monster is still there, smaller than it was before, or maybe it's always been that size and what I remembered from before is a trick, you know? I'm already not sure what I saw earlier or even what I'm seeing now. But what I do know is that I'm going to disappear from this neighborhood, too. I'm going to get up and walk down to the Downey Street Metro stop and get on the train and take it to somewhere else and I'll never come back. How can I come back here after all we did and didn't do, and then seeing this? How can any of us? This isn't to say I know where the rest of us went when we disappeared, because I don't. We just go.

It's cold out but I'm not cold. I stand up and the stitch in my chest is gone and my legs work again. Maybe I won't take the Metro and I'll walk. And then I get this idea. It's the best idea that I've ever had: I'm going to take the monster with me. I am. It's that simple. I can save everyone else in the neighborhood from this continuing madness. I can save us and you and take away this poor, terrible thing.

I go over to the monster and I'm not sure how to pick it up, how to get my arms around it and its ripped and rent pelt, broken and bent corners, holes leaking blood and fluids, mouth somewhere leaking pitiful cries. Its fur feels mealy, like the hairs (is it hair? something else entirely?) will slough off at my touch, but it doesn't. It stays together. I feel it straining to stay together for me and it allows me to compact it gently, a collection of untied, loose sticks. I sling some of it over my shoulder and hold the rest of it to my chest with both arms. I try not to gag at its smell and then one step, two steps, and I'm walking out of the alley.

Concentrating on walking away, going away, disappearing, and as I'm walking out of my neighborhood and into the next and then the next and then the next, my biggest fear is not that the monster will heal and subsequently attack me. No, my biggest fear is that my best-idea-ever isn't so best, you know?

What if all those who went missing before me are walking around in their somewhere-elses carrying their own busted-up monsters, too?

HER RED RIGHT HAND

The house in which they now lived was quite small, a one-level cabin with two bedrooms separated by a thin hallway adjacent to a teacup kitchen. The one bathroom was a dot to an *i*. The walls were wooden, and despite the surprising number of windows, it was always dark inside.

The house in which they now lived was quite far away from where they'd used to live and far away from Gemma's friends. It was far away from new neighbors and from Gemma's new school. In the fall, she would have a twenty-five-minute walk to the bus stop and a twenty-minute ride to school. In the winter, when the ground sulked beneath a layer of snow and ice, the walk and ride would be longer.

The house in which they now lived had a large yard of lazy yellow grass and weeds. The property was surrounded by acres of woods. The woods had tired trees that were always bent and gave up their leaves, needles, and secrets too easily. The trees could not be trusted.

Gemma's father had found the cabin, this place, because at the edge of the property, at the wooded line, was the Trundell Well.

The well was hundreds of years old. Its wall was a ring of stone and crumbling mortar, jutting three feet above the ground with an opening that had a circumference wide enough to fit Daniel Webster and the devil. The wooden canopy was the well's crooked hat, with shingles as loose and wiggly as baby teeth. There was no pump for water, only a windlass and a wooden bucket on a rope that had gone black.

A priest named Reginald Trundell, founder of, so he claimed, the northernmost English-speaking Catholic parish in New Hampshire, had blessed the well 130 years earlier. He was a squirrelly-looking man. Short and curved, he had large, round brown eyes, a tight mouth, and big teeth that were browner than his eyes. He consumed rashers of bacon, whiskey, and British folklore in equally gluttonous quantities. The proud Anglophile became obsessed with tales of sacred springs and holy wells that dotted the British countryside. Alarmingly to Father Trundell, the wells that had not been christened remained pagan and subject to goblin or demon infestation. The English called the well devil *Puck*, and the Welsh *Pwka*. Father Trundell believed denying the existence of the devil was to deny the existence of God. He would help protect the souls of his parishioners by blessing all the local New Hampshire wells he could find. He managed to bless one. In 1887, he died of a heart attack at the age of thirty-seven after a heroic two-day/two-night bender celebrating the completion of his three-hour-long ritual christening of what has been since dubbed the Trundell Well.

If we're being honest, despite an impressive and fiercely protected local reputation as a healing well, the Trundell Well hasn't had a successful historical run in terms of numbers of locals healed, either physically or spiritually. In actuality, the Trundell Well has been a blight to all.

Gemma's mother suffered from cystic fibrosis. Her chronic lung infections progressed to a stage beyond conventional medical help. Instead of moving Mom into hospice care, they all moved to the cabin at the beginning of summer. Gemma was ten years old.

In the mornings, Gemma went to swimming lessons at a local pond. She didn't want to go, but her father insisted, saying she would make new friends, which didn't happen, as most of the other kids in her class were at least two years younger than her. Gemma liked to swim, but she didn't like the pond, as its mucky bottom oozed between her toes and the dark water was cold and had a coppery smell.

Upon returning home from the lessons, she followed her dad through their yard and to the edge of the woods and the Trundell Well. The windlass squealed rhythmically as the bucket descended into the darkness but was silent upon the bucket's return. Her dad wasn't an old man, but he had begun to pass into some unidentifiable age defined by hardening eyes, pallid skin, downturned mouth, and receding hairline. Prior to Mom's illness Dad was a kind, warm man. He used to fill recycled mustard squeeze bottles with pancake batter and then create all manner of letters and shapes on the skillet. He'd ask, "Ever eat a Q, Gemma? It's exquisite, of course. Ever wanted to nosh on a monkey's paw? Well, give it a go anyway." He used to sing songs with the lyrics hilariously improvised . He used to perform sock puppet shows, give endless piggyback rides, and brag about the utterly fabulous dust bunny collection he kept under his bed. He was never a particularly religious man, but he'd become a desperate one. In the year-plus since Mom's health had deteriorated, Dad descended into the fortress of himself, and like a bucket dropped without its tether into the deepest well, he had become unreachable.

Dad filled a single glass with water directly from the well bucket. The water was cold, but not clear, and, like the pond, smelled coppery. There was a mineral tint, and unidentifiable bits floated like dust in a sunbeam. Her father soon tired of Gemma's complaints about the look of the water (it wasn't for *her* to drink, now was it?) and stopped using a clear glass. Gemma dutifully brought the well water to Mom, who sometimes drank without complaint, and sometimes she didn't drink any of it and had Gemma pour it out the bedroom window.

Gemma spent the warm afternoon hours before dinner camped out on the floor of her parents' bedroom. Her sketch pad was half her size. She drew pictures of Mom with a charcoal pencil, rubbing and blending shadows with a paper towel or sometimes her finger and thumb. The lines were rough and thick. The shapes she created bordered on abstract, but her mother was undeniably there in the drawings. Gemma's fingers, palms, the sides of her wrists and forearms were black with stubborn charcoal dust that did not remain on the paper.

That terrible summer leaked away like all summers must, and

her sketch pad filled with pictures of her mother lying in bed as encroaching late-afternoon shadows clouded the room. Within the progression of drawings, her mother deteriorated and shrank into a valley between the mountainous bedcovers. Gemma showed her mother each drawing when finished, even waking her when it was necessary.

Her mother coughed, and sometimes the coughing lasted until the walls and floorboards shook. Even in the depths of illness, her mother looked like Gemma: dark, almost black hair, forehead as wide as a wheat field, pale skin that passed into shades of red and pink at the slightest temperature or mood change.

Mom said, "It's lovely. My daughter is so talented." She said that every time until she couldn't say anything at all.

In the last picture Gemma drew of her mother, she had a red right hand.

When Mom had been healthier (never fully healthy, at least not in Gemma's memory), they played games of Monopoly that would last months because they gave each other breaks on rent, and she took Gemma to the movies on weekday afternoons so they were the only ones in the theater, and she took her to the library and told Gemma she could bring home a book if it fit her theme of the day (the cover was blue; either the word *grass* or *time* had to be in the title; length between 136 and 147 pages; an author with initials M.L. or L.M.; and so on), and she would play ineffectual soccer goalie in the backyard and always let the winning shot in, and she taught Gemma to braid her own hair and how to make pizza and, most important to Gemma, how to draw, or as Mom described it: how to build with lines, shapes, and shadows.

After the wake and the funeral, impossible days of constant despair and tears, Gemma became angry. Her anger was a decision, one she spoke out loud: "Today and all day, I will be mad." She had an idea in her mind, like a grasshopper cupped in her hands, that destroying the well was a solution to the inexplicable set of problems life without Mom had become.

Relatives and assorted family friends were long gone. Dad was alone in his bedroom with a bottle of whiskey, the door shut and latched. Gemma snuck out of the house and to the small, dilapidated toolshed, which was as gray and bent as a mushroom. She plucked a rusty-headed hammer from its cobwebbed spot on the wall and stormed across the almost knee-high grass toward the Trundell Well. She would smash the canopy first, splintering the wood until it collapsed, sending the bucket tumbling to the water, never to return. She would chip away at the mortar and force stones down the well's gullet until there were no more splashes, until it was choked dry.

The sun already had begun its descent behind the trees and the well was an outline in shadow. It occurred to Gemma that she could put the hammer back in the shed, retrieve her sketch pad, and draw the well as it was now because it looked like she felt. However, she was determined to hold on to her anger. As she got closer, there appeared to be the silhouette of a small child sitting on the stone wall. The child hugged its knees to its chest and rocked side to side, bumping the well bucket with an elbow and a hip, which made the windlass squeak and complain.

Gemma was afraid; the child might lose its balance and fall into the well, or maybe it wasn't a child at all. She thought that its not being a child was somehow more likely. The more watching she did, the more the figure became a *not-child*. She tightened her grip on the hammer and called out, "Hello?"

The figure clucked its tongue and leaned away from the well, tottering and then falling toward Gemma. As it fell, it speedily unraveled, spooling over the well's side. Its body elongated and thin, whiplike arms and legs shot out to secure hand- and footholds in the mortar cracks. It curled and scrabbled along the exterior, tracing the wall, ringing it twice. It laughed, high-pitched and a fraction of an octave below a bird's call. It laughed with such abandon and glee, Gemma wanted to laugh, too, and the edges of her mouth quivered and the corners of her eyes stung with tears.

Without warning, it left the well and scrambled through the dry grass toward Gemma. The familiar coppery and fetid smell of well water was heavy in the humid air. Gemma raised the hammer with a shaking hand and she did not run. She held her ground.

Once it was within arm's reach, it stood, slowly straightening its spine, as if it wasn't used to or didn't enjoy standing upright. At its full height it was as tall as her father. Its skin was the color of dried dead moss, the darkest of greens, and then even darker. Its arms and legs were knobby tree roots. Its face and features were an amphibian blur, with glimpses of the wide, bottomless lakes of its eyes.

It opened its cruel mouth, expelled warm swampy breath, and shouted "Gemma!" in her father's voice. It was not an imitation; it was Dad's voice, his angry voice, deep and throaty. Dad didn't use that voice very often, but when he did, it would flip her power button and shut her down.

The well goblin continued to talk in Dad's angry voice, saying, "Things are going to have to change around here."

Gemma looked to see if Dad was standing behind her, and if so, was he angry about her taking the hammer without asking? He wasn't there.

The goblin said that Gemma was so lazy, wasting time drawing her stupid pictures, so fucking lazy she didn't get the glasses of well water to Mom quick enough, or so clumsy she'd spill half of it, and then she was always waking up and bothering Mom, so goddamn whiny and needy and not letting Mom get the rest she needed.

The goblin still sounded like angry-Dad, but it wasn't angry. That laugh was there, a sea beneath the waves. Gemma heard the goblin smiling when it said it was Gemma's fault Mom died when she did. Mom could still be alive. Gemma could've saved her, but she hadn't.

Gemma was in bed, tented under her bedcover with a flashlight, her charcoal pencil, a rubber-banded clutch of tired crayons, and her sketch pad. Her door was locked and she'd moved the spidery wooden chair in front of it. Her drunk father had banged on her door earlier, tripping through her name and slurred threats. He was still out there, raging through the cabin, and was now in the kitchen, throwing dishes into the sink. He yelled, "Things are going to have to change around here!" And then he yelled some more.

Gemma tried to ignore him. She stared at the last picture in her sketch pad, the one of Mom in bed and holding up the palm of her red right hand. Gemma touched the hand and felt the wax of red crayon on the tips of her fingers.

She closed the sketch pad and flipped it over so when she reopened it, the glorious blank backsides of her old drawings faced up. She furiously sketched the well and the goblin with jagged lines and chaotic crooked angles. She wrote down all the things the goblin said to her, the letters made of slashes and trapped in a large, billowing dialogue bubble. Then, above the well and the goblin, she drew a disembodied red right hand.

It started out as Mom's hand, but she added to it. Mom's hand became the kernel, the soul and seed, to a larger hand. That hand became a large fist, made of brick, the knuckles thick and round, the size of dinner plates. This hand hovered over the goblin like the sword of Damocles. It was a promise.

Gemma returned to the well the next day and every day after that. She brought the hammer with her each time. If the goblin hadn't been there she was going to smash and seal up the well for good. But the goblin was always there, sitting on the ledge, a cruel impostor Humpty Dumpty.

It continued to speak with her father's voice, and how extra-cruel it sounded echoing from that great and horrible mouth. It continued to blame her for Mom's death. The goblin said it was her fault so often, she began to believe it was true. Maybe if she'd gotten the well water to Mom quicker, maybe if she'd let her rest more, maybe the charcoal dust from all those drawings got into her lungs and had taken root and further poisoned them, maybe if she'd gotten her father to come to the room, maybe, maybe, maybe . . .

In the evenings, when her father was drunk and threatening to make her late for school in the morning, he said terrible things, too, and it was almost impossible to not believe him.

The children at her new school whispered that she was *the girl without a mom*. They were not actively cruel, but they kept their distance, safe and cold. They spoke to Gemma only when she spoke to them. Soon she didn't do any speaking and her classmates' indifference was as vast and complete as a desert.

Gemma was in her bedroom, door locked, hidden under the bedcovers with her sketch pad on her folded legs. This was her only safe space and the only time it was safe to return to herself, as though returning from a long, arduous voyage. On the backside of another drawing of her mother, she again sketched the well and the goblin in one of its fits of mocking laughter and she transcribed what it had said to her. She added the talisman of her mother's hand, which again became this other's hand, a red right hand of doom.

Each night, on the backside of another sketch of Mom, she redrew the well, the goblin, and the red right hand. One night she attached the great fist to a similarly proportioned, cylindrical forearm, and in the next drawing, the fist/forearm was connected to an elbow and a boulder-sized bicep. In each successive sketch, she added more. She affixed the arm to a wide chest. The chest was then stanchioned on sinewy legs, and curling out from behind the legs was a tail. The tail made her giggle. His normal-sized left hand and arm made her stop giggling, and she wondered if he would be strong enough. He had to be. Then came the curious overcoat. The drabness of color and material made Gemma smirk; she was either proud of herself, of her artistic invention, her discovery, or pleased with the hero on the page because he chose that coat, because the coat told her who he was and who he would be, and she couldn't help but think the coat was proof that he was strong, funny, mischievous, and he would lend her Monopoly rent money if Gemma needed it.

On the night she drew his head, she spent hours getting the oblong, slightly bent rectangle right, and the square chin that jutted off the page, and the bushy sideburns (her father wore the same sideburns in photos from before Gemma was born), and his yellow eyes, those piercing spotlights shining out from all that red, and the round bases of broken horns that looked like goggles resting on his forehead. She wondered if the broken horns hurt, if they ever healed.

The next day was Saturday. It was a gray, cold day, the kind typical to northern New Hampshire once the calendar turned traitor, the kind made for sweaters, blankets, and shutters on drafty windows.

Dad made a surly appearance at breakfast, which was more like lunch if the kitchen clock could be believed. He muttered to himself, slammed drawers and shelves, content with inanimate enemies and combatants, and made himself two slices of burnt toast. He stood at the sink, bent and slumped, and he nibbled on the dry toast, his back turned to Gemma.

Gemma had already eaten a bowl of instant oatmeal. She wasn't hungry but asked, "Dad, can you make me pancakes?"

He slowly straightened his spine, like he wasn't used to or no longer enjoyed standing upright anymore. Or maybe it was too painful to unbend, to unslump. He turned and faced Gemma. She expected a furrow and snarl. His eyes were wide and his mouth formed an O. She expected words sharpened into razors, but there were none. Gemma couldn't tell if he was surprised that she was there or surprised at her question, or surprised at himself, or at something else entirely.

The cloud of some memory passed over his face and he said in a smaller voice, "Not now, sorry." He grabbed a bottle half filled with amber liquid off the counter and disappeared into his bedroom. She imagined the bottle filled with the ineffectual and coppery-smelling well water.

Gemma spent the day tweaking her most recent drawing, and also thinking about what her hero would say to the goblin. She left space on the page for him to say something, something important.

She waited until dusk to go out to the well.

Instead of the hammer, she brought her sketch pad and her pencil. She felt stronger this way. Not necessarily safer or more protected, but stronger. The pencil was in her front shirt pocket and she held the sketch pad behind her back.

The goblin was there muttering to himself and idly swiping at the bucket, and for a moment, she pitied the creature. Upon seeing her arrival, the goblin swelled with horribleness and did not hesitate to laugh at her. He bounded off the well, prancing like a dog excited that his family had returned home. Gemma and the goblin went through their now ritualized meet and greet. They stood face-to-face. The coppery smell made her gag; she would never be used to it and she would never forget it.

The goblin started in with what a lazy good-for-nothing girl she was and her mother would be so disappointed in her, in who she was becoming, and of course her mother wasn't around anymore, was she, and whose fault was that?

Gemma had planned on—she didn't remember what she'd planned. Why would bringing her sketch pad do anything? How could she have believed that it would've made any difference? This was her new life now. Rather than growing stronger, bigger, older, Gemma would instead be chipped away, eventually eroded into nothingness by an unrelenting tide of terrible words.

He said, "What's behind your back? Come on. You brought it out here. Show me."

Gemma showed him. She held out the sketch pad in front of her chest like a shield. But it wasn't a shield. It deflected nothing.

He laughed and said, "What a waste of time. You wasted all those hours in that room with her drawing when you could've talked to her, helped her, stopped her—"

Gemma flipped the unadorned cardboard back cover over the sketch pad's spiral wire spine and revealed the last drawing of her mother, the one with her red right hand extended.

The goblin stopped talking. He blinked hard once, twice, and a third time. His mouth became an O.

Gemma carefully turned the page over to reveal the most recent picture, the one she had drawn last night and had worked on all day: the goblin and the completed hero. She stepped forward, held it out closer to the goblin so he could see it and know he should be afraid.

The goblin woke from a fugue, returned to his miserable self, and cackled and snorted and guffawed and made all manner of noises and subnoises.

Gemma fought the urge to collapse to the ground and melt into the grass and dirt. With a shaking hand she pulled the charcoal pencil from her shirt pocket. She drew a large dialogue bubble coming from the hero's mouth in angry, righteous arcs. But she didn't know what he would say, what he must say, until he said it.

What the hero said was "Hey, kid, that's pretty damn good."

The goblin laughed harder, drunkenly swaying on his feet, stumbling, zigging and zagging aimlessly.

Gemma said, "Thanks."

The hero stood behind her, looking over her shoulder at the picture. "Yeah, I mean, my legs are kind of too skinny."

"But they are a little skinny. Not like that hand."

"Jeez, not that skinny. But, fine, yeah. Hey, great job with my right hand." He flexed it somewhere behind her. She heard it. "It's perfect."

Gemma said, "I know."

"How'd you know I was coming?"

Gemma said, "I didn't. How did you know to come here?"

"I don't know. I just did."

Gemma looked down and the charcoal pencil was in her hand, her fingertips black, and the words they'd said to each other were there on the paper.

The hero pushed the sleeves of his overcoat up over both of his elbows. He said, "Excuse me, kid. He and me need to make acquaintances," and walked toward the goblin.

Gemma sat cross-legged in the cold, damp grass. The sketch pad was out of blank paper. She sectioned off the inside of the cardboard back cover into nine rectangles. And she drew and drew and drew.

The goblin leapt onto Hellboy's back, wrapped its boa-like arms around his head, covering his eyes, and then it bit his shoulder.

"Son of a . . ."

Blood ran hot down his chest and back. Hellboy reached behind him but the goblin was too high up and too slippery.

"Screw it."

Hellboy ran blindly away from the house and Gemma, intending to smash himself into a tree, hopefully goblin-side first.

The goblin clung on and chomped and chattered terrible nothings into Hellboy's ear, telling him how Gemma hadn't done anything to help her own mother when she did it and instead of getting her dad or calling 911 she sat there and did nothing until later when she drew a goddamn picture—and then the goblin bit off the tip of Hellboy's ear.

"Ow! You little . . ."

Hellboy punched the goblin and, by proxy, the side of his own head.

The goblin slackened its grip enough for Hellboy to pull its arms from over his eyes.

Hellboy expected to see a tree, but instead there was the Trundell Well wall about to take him out at the knees.

"Oh, right."

Hellboy busted through the well wall and pitched forward. He and the goblin tumbled down into the mouth of the well.

They grappled and bounced off the walls, falling in the dark, falling *into* the dark.

Hellboy's yellow eyes glowed.

He finally got a grip on the goblin with his left hand that was strong enough after all, and he hit the goblin repeatedly with his right hand of doom.

And they fell.

And they fell in silence, and they fell for a really long time, passing into more darkness, passing into the greatest depths of darkness.

And they fell until they were unreachable.

And they fell until they splashed into water so cold it must've leaked into the well from a hole in the bottom of the deepest sea.

Gemma filled eight of the gridded rectangles so there was only one blank rectangle left on the cardboard cover. Gemma wasn't sure what to draw.

Her father had come outside into the backyard. He started yelling, asking what she was doing out there by herself in the dark. He had yet to see the smashed well, or if he did, he didn't comment on it.

Gemma said, "Nothing. Just out here drawing. Dad, can I show them to you? Please? You don't have to look at the old ones of Mom, just the new ones."

He was a silhouette, a ghost, a shape, a hole; maybe he wasn't really there. Then he tilted his head and he said, "I will. But come inside with me first."

Gemma squinted in the harsh light of the living room. Dad sat down on the couch, blinking and wiping his eyes. He wiped his hands on his jeans, then folded his hands together, fingers entwined, and he unfolded them, turned them to rocklike fists and put them in his pockets. He said in his smallest voice, "Okay, show me."

Gemma was careful to show him only the progression of pictures of the well and the goblin and eventually the hero, and not the portraits of Mom on her deathbed.

On the first viewing of the goblin drawings Dad sobbed into the back of his hand, and he said he was sorry over and over, and he asked if she could she ever forgive him.

On the second viewing, he said the drawings were amazing and she was so talented and gifted.

On the third viewing, Dad flipped through the pages and flipped them so quickly the emergence of the red right hand and then the hero, piece by piece until he was whole, appeared animated, as if he were alive.

Hellboy, soaked to the bone, sat atop the ruins and rubble of the collapsed Trundell Well.

The night sky had cleared and the half-moon emitted enough light that he could study a drawing that featured a red right hand. A hand that wasn't his.

"Jeez . . ."

Like the other drawings, it was good. No, it was great.

His heart broke because it was so great.

It was great because the whole story was there.

It had always been there.

Gemma walked into Mom's bedroom with another cup of water from the well. This cup was the biggest yet. The doctor who'd come to the cabin the day before had said that Mom had only weeks, maybe days left. Dad had refused to listen and had promised Gemma and Mom that the well water was helping and would help. Mom was half propped up on her stack of pillows and in the midst of a coughing fit. The wet, choking sounds were impossibly loud and coarse. Gemma waited for it to pass, thinking it might not pass this time. Gemma shakily held out the cup of water. Mom held up her right hand, like a stop sign. The red was so bright and shocking and wet. It dripped and ran and stained. Had she coughed up that much blood, that much of her insides? Gemma dropped the cup of water and it spilled everywhere and that damn coppery smell filled the room. She started yelling for Dad, and Mom interrupted her. Mom stopped her. She said, "Gemma, don't. Please." Her hand was still held up, a red setting sun. There was a deep gash parting the skin and muscle of Mom's wrist, a pond of blood in the bedcovers, and a paring knife from the kitchen clutched in her left hand. Mom said, "Don't, please." Her eyes were clear, full of sadness and pain and love. She said, "Stay with me. Stay with me until I fall asleep. And hold my hand." Mom let go of the knife. Gemma did as Mom asked.

Hellboy looked at the moon.

It was the same color as his eyes.

He gently pressed that fearsome hand of doom over the drawing of her red right hand.

He felt the wax of red crayon under his fingers.

Gemma is in her bedroom, tented under the covers and with a flashlight. She has two sketch pads with her, her old one and a brand-new one in which the blank pages glow deliciously clean and white.

Her bedroom door is open. Dad is in the kitchen cooking. Earlier, the two of them decided to have breakfast for dinner. Butter hisses on the skillet and Gemma smells the pancake batter even from under her bedcovers.

Gemma swaps old sketch pad for new on her lap. She turns the old one over to look at the inside of the back cardboard cover. The last rectangle, the one in the lower right corner, is the last panel of the story.

The hero is perched atop the rubble of the destroyed well. He has a sketch pad on his lap. His head is turned up to the moon. His right hand covers the drawing.

Gemma writes a capital *G*, her signature, there on that last panel, hiding it down by the grass on a fallen stone.

For Mike Mignola

IT'S AGAINST THE LAW TO FEED THE DUCKS

SATURDAY

Ninety-plus degrees, hours of relentless getaway traffic on the interstate, then the bumps and curves of Rural Route 25 as late afternoon melts into early evening, and it's the fourth time Danny asks the question.

"Daddy, are you lost again?"

Tom says, "I know where we're going, buddy. Trust me. We're almost there."

Dotted lines and bleached pavement give way to a dirt path that roughly invades the woods. Danny watches his infant sister, Beth, sleep, all tucked into herself and looking like a new punctuation mark. Danny strains against his twisted shoulder harness. He needs to go pee but he holds it, remembering how Daddy didn't say any mad words but sighed and breathed all heavy the last time he asked to stop for a pee break.

Danny says, "Mommy, pretend you didn't know I was going to be five in September."

Ellen holds a finger to her chin and looks at the car's ceiling for answers. "Are you going to be ten years old tomorrow?"

"No. I will be five in September."

"Oh, wow. I didn't know that, honey."

Tom and Ellen slip into a quick and just-the-facts discussion about what to do for dinner and whether or not they think Beth will sleep through the night. Danny learns more about his parents through these conversations, the ones they don't think he's listening to.

It's dark enough for headlights. Danny counts the blue bug zappers as their car chugs along the dirt road. He gets to four.

"Daddy, what kinds of animals live in these woods?"

"The usual. Raccoons, squirrels, birds."

"No, tell me *dangerous* animals."

"Coyotes, maybe bears."

Their car somehow finds the rented cottage and its gravel driveway between two rows of giant trees. Beth wakes screaming. Danny stays in the car while his parents unpack. He's afraid of the bears. They don't celebrate getting to the cottage like they were supposed to.

SUNDAY

They need a piece of magic yellow paper to go to Lake Winnipesaukee. Danny likes to say the name of the lake inside his head. The beach is only a mile from their cottage, and when they get there, Danny puts the magic paper on the dashboard. He hopes the sun doesn't melt it or turn it funny colors.

Danny runs ahead. He's all arms and legs, a marionette with tangled strings, just like Daddy. He claims a shady spot beneath a tree. He doesn't know what kind of tree. Ellen and Beth come next. Beth can only say "Daddy" and likes to give head butts. Tom is last, carrying the towels and shovels and pails and squirt guns and food. Danny watches his parents set everything up. They know how to unfold things and they know where everything goes without having to ask questions, without having to talk to each other.

Danny likes that his parents look younger than everybody else's parents, even if they are old. Danny has a round face and big rubber ball cheeks, just like Mommy. Ellen has a T-shirt and shorts pulled over her bathing suit. She won't take them off, even when she goes into the water. She says, "You need sunscreen before you go anywhere, little boy."

Danny closes his eyes as she rubs it all in and everywhere. He's had to wear it all summer long but he doesn't understand what *sunscreen* really means. *Sunscreen* sounds like something that should be built onto their little vacation cottage.

Danny is disappointed with the magic beach because there are too many other people using it. They all get in his way when he runs on the sand, pretending to be Speed Boy. And the older kids are scary in the water. They thrash around like sharks.

Lunchtime. Danny sits at the picnic table next to their tree, eating and looking out over Winnipesaukee. The White Mountains surround the bowl of the lake, and in the lake there are swimmers, boats, buoys, and a raft. Danny wants to go with Daddy to the raft, but only when the scary older kids are gone. Danny says Winnipesaukee, that magical word, into his peanut butter and jelly sandwich. It tastes good.

A family of ducks comes out of the water. They must be afraid of the older kids, too. They walk underneath his picnic table.

Ellen says, "Ducks!" picks up Beth, and points her at the ducks. Beth's bucket hat is over her eyes.

Tom sits down next to Danny and throws a few scraps of bread on the sand. Danny does the same, taking pieces from his sandwich, mostly crust, but not chunks with a lot of peanut butter. He eats those. The ducks get mostly jelly chunks, and they swallow everything.

Tom stops throwing bread and says, "Whoops. Sorry, pal. It's against the law to feed the ducks."

He doesn't know if Daddy is joking. Danny likes to laugh at his jokes. Jokes are powerful magic words because they make you laugh. But when he's not sure if it's a joke or not, Danny thinks life is too full of magic words.

He laughs a little and says, "Good one, Daddy." Danny is pleased with his answer, even if it's wrong.

"No, really, it says so on that sign." Tom points to a white sign with red letters nailed into their tree. Danny can't read yet. He knows his letters but not how they fit together.

Ellen says, "That's weird. A state law against feeding the ducks?"

Danny knows it's not a joke. It is a law. The word *law* is scary, like the older kids in the water.

Danny says, "Mommy, pretend you didn't know it was against the law to feed the ducks."

"Okay. So, I can go order a pizza and some hot dogs for the ducks, right?"

"No. You can't feed the ducks. It's against the law."

Danny eats the rest of his sandwich, swinging his feet beneath the picnic table bench. The scary older kids come out of the water and chase the ducks, even the babies. Danny wants to know why it's not against the law to chase the ducks, but he doesn't ask.

Their cottage has two bedrooms, but they sleep in the same bedroom because of the bears. Danny sleeps in the tallest bed. There's a ceiling fan above him, and after Daddy tells a story about Spider-Man and dinosaurs, he has to duck to keep from getting a haircut. That's Danny's joke.

Beth is asleep in her playpen. Everyone has to be quiet because of her.

Danny is tired after a full day at the beach. His favorite part was holding on to Daddy's neck while they swam out to the raft.

Danny wakes up when his parents creep into the bedroom. He is happy they are keeping their promise. He falls back to sleep listening to them fill up the small bed by the door. He knows his parents would rather sleep in the other bedroom by themselves, but he doesn't know why.

Danny wakes again. It's that middle-of-the-night time his parents always talk about. He hears noises but gets the sense he's waking at the end of the noises. The noises are outside the cottage, echoing in the mountains. He hears thunder and lightning or a plane or a bunch of planes or a bunch of thunder and lightning (he is still convinced you can hear both thunder and lightning) or he hears a bear's roar or a bunch of bears' roars or he hears the cottage's toilet, which has the world's loudest superflush according to Daddy, or he hears a bomb or a bunch of bombs. Bombs are something he has only seen and heard in Spider-Man cartoons. Whatever the noises are, they are very far away and he has no magic words that will send his ears out that far. Danny falls back to sleep even though he doesn't want to.

MONDAY

The beach lot is only half full. Ellen says, "Where is everybody?"

Tom says, "I don't know. Mondays are kind of funny days. Right, pal?"

Danny nods and clutches the magic yellow paper and doesn't care where everybody is because maybe this means Daddy and he can spend more time out on the raft.

They get the same spot they had yesterday, next to the tree with its against-the-law sign. They dump their stuff and boldly spread it out. Beth and Ellen sit at the shore. Beth tries to eat sand and knocks her head into Ellen's. Tom sits in the shade and reads a book. Danny takes advantage of the increased running room on the beach and turns into Speed Boy.

By lunch, the beach population thins. No more young families around. There are some really old people with tree-bark skin and a few older kids around, but they are less scary because they look like they don't know what to do. The lake is empty of boats and Jet Skis. The ducks are still there, swimming and safe from renegade feeders.

Tom swims to the raft with Danny's arms wrapped tight around his neck. Somewhere in the middle of the lake, Tom says, "Stop kicking me!" Danny knows not to say I was trying to help you swim. Danny climbs up the raft ladder first, runs to the middle, then slips, feet shooting out from beneath him, and he falls on a mat that feels like moss. Tom yells, "Don't run, be careful, watch what you're doing." Danny doesn't hear the words, only what's in his voice. They sit on the raft's edge, dangling their legs and feet into the water. Daddy's long legs go deeper.

Tom takes a breath, the one that signals the end of something, and says, "It is kind of strange that hardly anybody is here." He pats Danny's head, so everything is okay.

Danny nods. Commiserating, supporting, happy, and grateful to be back in Daddy's good graces. He's also in his head, making up a face and body for a stranger named Hardly Anybody. He can't decide if he should make Hardly Anybody magical or not.

They wave at Mommy and Beth at the shore. Ellen's wave is tired, like a sleeping bird. Ellen wears the same shirt and shorts over her bathing suit. Danny wonders how long it takes for his wave to make it across the water.

They leave the beach early. On the short drive back, Tom makes up a silly song that rhymes *mountain peaks* with *butt cheeks,* and it's these Daddy moments that make Danny love him so hard, he's afraid he'll break something.

Back at the cottage. Beth is asleep and Ellen dumps her in the play-pen. Danny sits at the kitchen table and eats grapes because he was told to. Tom goes into the living room and turns on the TV. Danny listens to the voices but doesn't hear what they say. But he hears Tom say a bad word, real quick, like he is surprised.

"Ellen?" Tom jogs into the kitchen. "Where's Mommy?" He doesn't wait for Danny's answer. Ellen comes out of the bathroom holding her mostly dry bathing suit and wearing a different set of T-shirt and shorts. Tom grabs her arm, whispers something, and then pulls her into the living room, to the TV.

"Hey, where did everybody go?" Danny says it like a joke, but there's no punch line coming. He leaves his grapes, which he didn't want to eat anyway, and tiptoes into the living room.

His parents are huddled close to the TV, too close. If Danny was ever that close they'd tell him to move back. They're both on their knees, Ellen with a hand over her mouth, holding something in, or maybe keeping something out. The TV volume is low and letters and words scroll by on the top and bottom of the screen and in the middle there's a man in a tie and he is talking. He looks serious. That's all Danny sees before Tom sees him.

"Come with me, bud."

Daddy picks him up and plops him down in a small sunroom at the front of the cottage.

Tom says, "Mommy and Daddy need to watch a grown-up show for a little while."

"So I can't see it?"

"Right."

"How come?"

Tom is crouched low, face-to-face with Danny. Danny stares at the scraggly hairs of his mustache and beard. "Because I said it's only for grown-ups."

"Is it about feeding the ducks? Is it scary?"

Daddy doesn't answer that. "We'll come get you in a few minutes. Okay, bud?" He stands, walks out, and starts to close the sliding glass doors.

"Wait! Let me say something to Mommy first."

Tom gives that sigh of his, loud enough for Ellen to give him that look of hers. They always share like this. Danny stays in the sunroom, pokes his head between the glass doors. Ellen is to his left, sitting in front of the TV, same position, same hand over her mouth. "Mommy, pretend you didn't know that I could see through these doors."

Mommy works to put her eyes on her son. "So, you won't be able to see anything in here when we shut the doors?"

"No, I can see through them."

TUESDAY

It's raining. They don't go to the beach. Danny is in the sunroom watching Beth. His parents are in the living room watching more grown-up TV. Beth pulls on Danny's shirt and tries to walk, but she falls next to the couch and cries. Ellen comes in, picks up Beth, and sits down next to Danny.

He says, "This is boring."

"I know, sweetie. Maybe we'll go out soon."

Danny looks out the front windows and watches the rain fall on the front lawn and the dirt road. Beth crawls away from Ellen and toward the glass doors. She bangs on the glass with meaty little hands.

Danny says, "Mommy, pretend you didn't know we were in a spaceship."

There's a pause. Beth bangs her head on the glass. Ellen says, "So, we're all sitting here in a cottage room, right?"

"No. This is a spaceship with glass doors."

Beth bangs on the glass harder and yells in rhythm.

Ellen says, "If we're in a ship, what about Daddy?"

"We'll come back for him later."

"Good idea."

Ellen and Beth stay at the cottage. Tom and Danny are in the car, but they don't listen to the radio and Daddy isn't singing silly songs. Danny holds the magic yellow paper even though he knows they're going to the supermarket, not the beach.

They have to travel to the center of Moultonborough. Another long and obviously magical word that he'll say inside his head. There isn't much traffic. The supermarket's superlot has more carts than cars.

Inside, the music is boring and has no words. Danny hangs off the side of their cart like a fireman. He waves and salutes to other shoppers as they wind their way around the stacks, but nobody waves back. Nobody looks at one another over their overflowing carts.

The line isn't long, even though there are only three registers open. Tom tries to pay with a credit card. Danny is proud he knows what a credit card is.

"I'm sorry, sir, but the system is down. No credit cards. Cash or check." The girl working the register is young, but like the older kids. She has dark circles under her eyes.

Danny points and says, "Excuse me, you should go to bed early tonight."

Tom has a green piece of paper and is writing something down on it. He gives it to the register girl.

She says, "I'll try," and offers a smile. A smile that isn't happy.

In the parking lot, Danny says, "Go fast."

Tom says, "Hey, Danny."

Danny's whole body tenses up. He doesn't know what he did wrong. "What?"

"I love you. You know that, right?"

Danny swings on those marionette arms and looks everywhere at once. "Yeah."

Then Tom smiles and obeys and runs with the full cart. Danny melts and laughs, stretching out and throwing his head back, closing his eyes in the brightening haze. There are no other cars between the cart and their car.

WEDNESDAY

They spend the day in the cottage. More sunroom. More grown-up TV. When Tom and Ellen finally shut off the TV they talk about going out just to go out somewhere, anywhere but the TV room and sunroom, and maybe find an early dinner. Danny says, "Moultonborough." They talk about how much gas is in the car. Danny says, "Winnipesaukee." They try to use their cell phones but the upper corners of the screens say *no service*. Danny says, "Pretend you didn't know I say magic words." They talk about how much cash they have. Everybody in the car. Tom tells Danny it's his job to keep Beth awake. There are no other vehicles on the dirt road and more than half of the cottages they pass are dark. Beth is falling asleep, so Danny sings loud silly songs and pokes her chin and cheeks. They pass empty gravel driveways and the blue bug zappers aren't on. Beth cries. Danny is trying not to think about the bears in the woods. Ellen asks Danny to stop touching his sister's face and then says it's okay if Beth falls asleep. They don't have to look left or right when pulling out of the dirt road. Danny still works at the keep-Beth-awake job Daddy gave him and there's something inside him that wants to hear her cry and he touches her face again. They're into the center of Moultonborough and there's less traffic than there was yesterday. Beth cries and Ellen is stern but not yelling. She never yells telling Danny to stop touching Beth's face. Maybe the bears are why there aren't as many people around. Beth is asleep. There's a smattering of parked cars in the downtown area, but they don't look parked; they look abandoned. Danny gently pats Beth's foot and sees Daddy watching him in the rearview mirror. The antiques stores, gift shops, and hamburger huts are dark and have red signs on their doors and red always means either stopped or closed or something bad. Tom yells did you hear your mother keep your hands off your sister! They pass a row of empty family restaurants. Ellen says Tom like his name is sharp like it hurts and she says I only asked him to stop touching her face I don't want him to be freaked out by his sister he's being nice now why are you yelling when he was doing what you asked him to do you have to be consistent with him and she is stern and she is not yelling. They pull into a lot that has one truck another empty restaurant this one with a moose on the roof and they stop. Then Tom is loud again this time with some hard all rights and then I hear you I get it okay I heard you the first time. Tom gets out of the car and slams the door and an older man with white hair that could mean he's magic and a white apron walks out the restaurant's front door. Danny waves. The older man waves them inside. Ellen gets out of the car and whispers but it's not a soft whisper not at all it's through teeth and it has teeth she says don't you dare yell at me in front of the kids. Beth wakes up and points and chews on her rabbit. They go inside. The older man says they are lucky he was cooking up the last of his nonfrozen food so it wouldn't go to waste and it was on the house. Danny thinks about the moose on the house. They walk by the bar and there's a woman sitting on a stool staring up at a big-screen TV. Tom asks if they could shut that off because of the kids. The old man nods and uses a big remote control. Danny doesn't see anything again. The old man serves some BBQ chicken and ribs and fries and then leaves them alone. The lights are on and nobody says anything important in the empty restaurant.

On the way back to the cottage they see a lonely mansion built into the side of a mountain. Looking dollhouse-sized, its white walls and red roof surrounded by the green trees stand out like a star even in the twilight.

Danny says, "What is that?"

Tom says, "That's called the Castle in the Clouds."

"Can we go see it?"

"Maybe. Maybe we'll even go and live there. Would you like that?"

Danny says, "Yes," but then he thinks the castle is too alone, cloaked in a mountain forest, but too open, anyone can see it from this road. He doesn't know what's worse, being alone alone or watched alone. Danny doesn't change his answer.

It's past Danny's bedtime but his parents aren't ready to put him to bed.

Ellen is on the couch reading a magazine that has a tall, blond, skinny woman on the cover. Tom sits in front of the TV, flipping channels. There's nothing but static. The TV is like their cell phones now.

Tom says, "Well, at least they've stopped showing commercials for the *War of the Worlds* remake."

Danny wants to laugh because he knows it's what Daddy wants. But he doesn't because Mommy isn't. Danny has a good idea what *war* means even though no one has ever explained it to him. Tom shuts off the TV.

There are pictures of other people all over the cottage. Now that Danny is allowed back in the TV room, he's looking at each one. Strangers with familiar smiles and beach poses. He looks at the frames too. They have designs and letters and words. Maybe magic words. Danny picks up one picture of a little girl and boy hugging and sitting on a big rock. He doesn't care about those kids. He wants to know what all the letters etched onto the wooden frame say. Those letters wrap all the way around the photo.

"Read this please, Daddy."

"'Children are the magic dreamers that we all once were.'"

"Mommy, pretend you didn't know I was a magic dreamer."

"So, you dream about boring, nonmagical stuff, right?"

"No. I'm a magic dreamer. Are you a magic dreamer?"

Ellen sleeps with Beth in the small bed next to the bedroom door, Danny sleeps in his Princess-and-the-Pea tall bed. Tom sleeps in the other bedroom. Alone alone.

THURSDAY

A perfect summer day. The corner Gas 'N Save is open. The pumps still work. Tom fills up the car's tank and five red two-gallon containers he took from inside the market. Danny is inside, running around the stacks. No one tells him to stop. He climbs onto an empty shelf next to some bread, though there isn't much bread left, and he lies down, breathing heavy from all the running.

Tom makes multiple trips from the market to the car. On the last trip, he plucks Danny off the shelf. He says, "Hmm, this melon doesn't look too ripe." Danny giggles and squirms in Daddy's arms. "But I'll take it anyway."

The older woman behind the counter is smoking a cigarette and has a face with extra skin. She looks like the girl from the supermarket but one thousand years older. Tom extends a fistful of money and asks, "Is this enough?"

She says, "Yes," without counting it. Danny thinks she is lying and that she wants them gone like everyone else.

Tom buckles Danny into his seat. Danny says, "What would you do if you were a giant?"

"A giant? Well, I'd use a mountain as my pillow and the trees as a mattress."

Danny thinks about a Giant Daddy lying on a mountain, crushing all the trees and bears and other animals and the Castle in the Clouds with his back and arms, and his legs would be long enough to crush Moultonborough and the other towns, too, maybe his feet would dangle into Winnipesaukee and cause huge waves, drown the poor ducks, flood everything.

Danny says, "That would hurt."

At night the electricity goes out, but it's okay because they have two lanterns and lots of candles. They sit in the backyard around a football-shaped charcoal grill eating hot dogs and holding sticks with marshmallows skewered on the tips. The smoke keeps the bugs away. They sing loud to keep the bears away. Danny sits on Mommy's lap and tells stories about magic and the adventures of Speed Boy and Giant Daddy.

Then Tom carries him to bed and Ellen carries a candle. They kiss him good night. Danny closes his eyes. He almost knows why they are still here when everyone else is disappearing, but he can't quite get there, can't reach it, like the night he tried to send his ears out to the noises.

Danny tries to send his ears out again and this time he hears his parents in the hallway. They speak with one voice. He hears words that he doesn't understand. They might be arguing and they might be laughing and they might be crying but it doesn't matter, because Danny knows tonight was the best night of their vacation.

FRIDAY

Danny wakes up before anyone else and goes into the sunroom. There's morning mist and a bear on the front lawn. The bear is black and bigger than Danny's world, although that world seems to be shrinking. Danny thinks bears, even the dumb-looking teddy bears, always know more about what's going on than the other animals, which is part of what scares Danny. He's scared now but he wants a better view so he opens the front door and stands on the elevated stoop, his hand on the door, ready to dash back inside if necessary. The bear runs away at the sound of the door and it disappears. Danny hears it crashing through some brush, but then everything goes quiet. Why would a bear be afraid of him?

Now that it's gone, Danny steps outside, the wet grass soaking his feet. He says, "Hey, come back." He wants to ask the bear, where are all the people? The bear must know the answer.

Danny and Ellen sit out back, playing Go Fish at the picnic table. Tom went shopping for supplies, a phrase he used before leaving by himself. He's been gone most of the morning.

Danny loses again but Ellen calls him the winner.

Danny says, "Mommy, pretend you didn't know it was a beautiful day."

Ellen shuffles the cards. "So it's really rainy and cold out, right?"

"No. There're no clouds. And the sun is out and super hot. It's a beautiful day."

They play more card games. They play with Beth. She's almost ready to walk by herself, but she still falls, and after she falls, she rips out fistfuls of grass and stuffs it in her mouth. They eat lunch. They nap.

Tom comes home after the naps. Supplies fill the car, including a mini-trailer hitched to the back. Tom gets out of the car and gives everyone an enthusiastic kiss and puts Danny on his shoulders. Ellen shrinks as he goes up.

Ellen says, "Did you see anybody?"

Tom whispers an answer that Danny can't hear because he's above Daddy's head.

Ellen says, "What you got there in the trailer?"

"A generator."

"Really? You know how to set one of those up?"

"Yup."

Danny comes back down.

"Where'd you learn how to do that?"

"I just know, okay?"

Ellen goes back to the picnic table with Beth, Tom to the trailer and the generator. There are no more enthusiastic kisses.

Danny watches Tom setting up the generator. He says, "Daddy, pretend you didn't know this was a beautiful day."

"It's not a beautiful day."

"No, it is! There're no clouds. And the sun is out and super hot. It's a beautiful day, Daddy. I just know, okay?"

SATURDAY

They leave the car at the cottage and walk the mile to the beach. They don't carry much beach stuff. Beth is asleep in the stroller. Danny has on his swimming trunks, but his parents are wearing shorts and T-shirts. The trip to the beach is for him. His parents don't know it, but Danny has the yellow magic paper folded up in his pocket.

Danny asks, "Is today supposed to be the last day of vacation?"

Ellen says, "I think we're going to stay here a little while longer."

Tom says, "Maybe a long while longer."

Ellen says, "Is that okay?"

"Sure."

Tom says, "Maybe we'll go check out that Castle in the Clouds to-morrow."

Danny almost tells them about the bear. Instead he says, "Mommy, pretend you didn't know we were still on vacation."

They pass empty driveways of empty cottages. Danny, for the first time, is really starting to feel uneasy about the people being gone. It's like when he thinks about why and how he got here and how are his parents his parents and how is his sister his sister, because if he thinks too much about any of that he probably won't like the answers.

The beach lot is empty. They stake out their regular spot next to the tree and its duck sign. There are ducks on the shore scratching the sand and dipping their bills in the water. It's another beautiful day.

Tom says, "I don't get it. I thought this is where everyone would want to be."

Ellen finishes for him. "Especially now."

The ducks waddle over. They don't know the law. Tom pulls out a bag of Cheerios, Beth's snack, and tosses a few on the sand. The ducks converge and are greedy.

Ellen pushes the stroller deeper into the shade away from the ducks and says, "Are you sure we can spare those, Mr. Keeper-of-the-Supplies?" It walks like a joke and talks like a joke, but it isn't a joke.

Danny says, "Daddy! Don't you remember the sign? It's against the law to feed the ducks." Danny looks around, making sure the people who aren't there still aren't there.

"It's okay now, buddy. I don't think anyone will care anymore. Here, kiddo."

He takes the Cheerio bag from Daddy. Daddy pats his head. Danny digs a hand deep into the bag, pulls it out, and throws Cheerios onto the sand. The ducks flinch and scatter toward the water, but they come back and feed.

THE THIRTEENTH TEMPLE

To state the obvious, you look different. It's no surprise twenty years later you're no longer the precocious eight-year-old we all watched and rewatched in your six episodes of *The Possession,* the refurbished, extended twentieth-anniversary edition now streaming. Still, it's shocking to see what you look like now as an adult. When the tell-all was announced only three weeks before the book could be purchased, we pored over the publicity shots of the adult you: *Your super dark hair! No curls! And, gasp, you are not wearing glasses!* Some of us have had a difficult time with the no-glasses thing. We read your horror blogs and columns and we discussed and dissected your pseudonym, Karen Brissette, and what it means and how you've changed and who you've become.

The new images won't erase the old, Merry. They never will. You have to know that.

This morning I waited in line for ten hours to be one of the first into Hall C for your Q&A. The stage was huge and too far away from our seats, so none of it seemed real. Could you even see any of us? Being on a stage is still a filter between you and your audience, between you and reality. That not-real vibe wasn't helped by you and the *Entertainment Weekly* reporter (he of the big white teeth and handsome hair) being projected onto the jumbotron. I tried not to watch but it was distracting and insulting, frankly, like we could understand or consume your message only if you were on another fucking screen. I was so disappointed in the setup and it's part of the reason why I'm in your hotel room now.

Many people have ascribed scurrilous motives for publishing a book that is ostensibly about the exploitation of your sister (including, obviously, the attempted exorcism) and the particulars of your unwitting role in the gruesome death of your family, and then making these glad-handing promotional appearances, but I'm not one of them. I trust your judgment and I truly care about you, Merry, and simply want to know more about you.

I thought it a savvy move on your part to begin the interview by announcing you'd donated your Comic Con appearance fee to the National Alliance on Mental Illness. We were yours pre-announcement and then we were *really* yours, not solely because of the generous gesture, but because you were so visibly uncomfortable and ill at ease. I don't know if you're aware, but when you mumbled through saying that the donation would be in your sister's name, you literally squirmed in your chair, shifting your sitting position, folding and unfolding your legs. In that moment you were our Merry again.

Is that weird of me to say? Well, I know it's weird of me to say, but how does hearing it make you feel?

You don't answer me. We're not in Hall C now and we're standing across the hotel room from each other. Your twenty-third-floor suite overlooks the San Diego harbor and the recently built interlocking levees that attempt to protect the Gaslamp district from flooding. The air-conditioning in your room is on full blast. When I first broke into your suite I turned the thermostat down as low as it could go and—now this was smart of me, admit it—I opened the curtains to let in all that warm San Diego sunshine to keep that AC running and running loudly on the off chance we needed the ambient noise to help keep our private meeting from being interrupted by nosy neighbors. Am I making any sense?

"How did you get into my room?"

I hold up a black key card. Universal key. I made it special for Comic Con. Fifty bucks worth of hardware/software and one ten-minute YouTube tutorial. Finding out what room you were staying in was the hard part.

You uncross your arms, which jangles the guest/speaker laminate pass hanging off your neck on a lanyard you've festooned with horror-movie and comics pins. Your plain white T-shirt has Sharpie signatures on the sleeves. I am not going to ask who you allowed to sign your shirt.

You glance at the closed hotel room door a few feet behind you. If you go for it I won't stop you, but I don't tell you that.

The rest of your Hall C interview was fine. Though the venue wasn't ideal, it was nice to see you in person, to watch how much you gesticulated with your hands, and it was even better hearing your voice, your new voice, and being able to add this new voice to the old story. But there was something missing. I don't know what it was, but that's why I'm here.

You say, "If you don't know, I'm sure I don't. I'm not going to be able to help you—what's your name?"

"Call me M."

"Seriously?"

I talk more about the interview and how you didn't tell us anything we didn't already know. I'm sorry, but it's true. The interviewer's questions were softballs. Pure surface. Nothing deep. Nothing profound or difficult. As one of your biggest fans, I'm all for hagiography, but I'd come all this way to see you and I wanted him to ask you difficult questions, Merry. Were his questions preapproved by you, or your people? With all that's happened since the release of the book, do you have people now?

You say, "I don't have people. That's not my style. I pride myself on being self-sufficient. Being such a self-professed fan, you should know that. I gotta say, I'm not sure what you're a fan of, M. Maybe I'm being hypocritical—I'm not sure that's the right word—with my doing conventions now, but when you really think about it, I haven't done anything other than live through what I've lived through. Not sure what there is for you to root for, you know?"

Your biographer Rachel Neville hasn't been appearing much in public, only two readings/signings on the East Coast. I attended both. She said that you were wonderful to work with. She was careful to say that repeatedly and at both stops. I think that means something.

You laugh and shake your head. You're shorter and thinner than I am, but you don't seem the least bit cowed by my unexpected physical presence. You're not afraid of me at all. You don't need to be afraid of me, of course, but I thought you might be. Now you stand with your hands on your hips, a superhero pose, and you smirk and stare at me, and you blink in regular, no-panic-here intervals. Are you amused, annoyed, impatient? Are you already disappointed with me? Is that right?

I say what I ultimately want to know is how exactly did you live through all this?

"That's the question, right? The one we all have to ask ourselves. At the risk of sounding like a shill, it's all in the book, M. Leave me your address and I'll have the publisher send you a signed copy. First edition."

You are definitely amused. I wasn't expecting this reaction from you. I shiver as the AC chills my bare forearms.

I tell you I had the opportunity to ask Rachel about your relationship, if it's one that you continue to have. I pause and I can tell you want to know what Rachel said. If I spend the next two thousand days in jail, this moment will have been worth it.

I tell you Rachel said she thinks of you as a combination of a fiercely and sadly independent daughter and a dear friend one might hear from only once every ten years. She gave the same answer about your relationship at both venues at which I saw her speak. The second time, I told Rachel you would've used the term *Brundlefly* instead of *combination*. Rachel smiled politely, but it was clear she didn't get the reference.

"I get it. And I like it. Rachel is a sweet person and she got most of the story right, I think. As close as anyone could get."

When was the last time you talked to each other?

"I am not going to answer any more of your questions, M. I've been quite patient so far, but I'm not going to be for much longer."

I was disappointed you didn't take any questions from the audience. Perhaps if you had, I wouldn't be here now.

"Are you lying to me about being there today, M.? That's very un-fanlike of you. I took questions from the audience for the last fifteen minutes—"

Those presubmitted-on-cards questions don't count. They were obviously handpicked and you didn't have to look anyone in the eye, even from that dark distance between us and the stage. You didn't have to look at anyone.

"That's bullshit, M. I don't owe you or anyone else anything." You reach into your back pocket and pull out what appears to be a palm-sized aerosol canister and you flip off the red cap with your thumb and you point the thing at me, arm extended.

I hold up my hands. This is going all wrong. I admit I wanted you to be off-balance, on edge, only because I was hoping you'd be more likely to tell me something real, something you haven't told anyone else, even Rachel.

I continue to beg and plead and I know I'm not making any sense, not that there's any sense to be made. How can I explain to you how it is your story simultaneously fills me up and empties me out? How do I explain how you make me feel? It's as impossible a task as lifting the ocean over my head. I'm not explaining anything very well. I think I hoped you would understand me, understand who I am and what I need simply by looking at me, by seeing me. I keep talking and instead of begging I start telling you about who I am, where I'm from. I tell you little facts like my left kneecap is lumpier than my right and how many pillows I use when I sleep, which is ridiculous, I know, but I want you to know things no one else knows about me to show I'm willing to share and to get you to share more with me, something, anything, and then at some point I stop talking and I'm hyperventilating and I'm crying without crying.

You sit on your bed, recap the aerosol, and say, "Okay, okay. Hey, if you calm down, and stay calm, you can have one of my sister's and my stories, M."

THE FIRST TEMPLE

All three planks of wood are the same size and weight. Mom cradles hers as though it's a sleeping child. Dad carries his plank balanced on his left shoulder so the length of it trails behind him like a dumb, dangerous tail. Merry drags her plank. It's as tall as she is. Merry makes this-is-sooo-heavy sounds and grumbles about the splinters she's getting in her fingers and palms. She hates splinters. No one likes splinters, of course, but even her older sister, Marjorie, has to agree that Merry might hate them more than anyone else alive. Merry doesn't let anyone pluck or dig them out. She cries, kicks, and screams (often doing so before tweezers or a sewing needle even makes bodily contact) until the would-be splinter-remover gives up and then her sister says something mocking like "Fine, let it sink inside you, into the oblivion of your skin." Her desperate parents once snuck into Merry's bedroom and tried worrying out a nasty spike of wood lodged in the sole of her foot while she was asleep.

The village square isn't a square and is instead a circle, which is a joke they are all in on. Nothing grows inside the circle and its soil is a rusty, organic shade of red that isn't quite red. The other villagers stand at the perimeter of the circle, waiting for the three Barretts. No one talks. Merry waves a small finger at her friend Ken, but he doesn't wave back. She's mad at him now and hopes he gets a nasty splinter later.

The Barretts enter the circle. Merry walks backward and makes a snake's path in the red soil with her dragged plank. She wonders if she'll be able to follow the path back to her house and then how long before the path is erased.

The circle's center is not marked but is easily found, or determined. Dad throws his plank to the ground, kicking up a dust cloud that settles and disappears quickly. He apologizes, and Merry isn't sure to whom he's apologizing.

Mom admonishes Merry to come closer and pay attention to what she is doing. The villagers are watching and Merry feels like she's shrinking and shriveling up. She wishes she could hide. Mom holds the plank upright, its base rooted to the ground. Dad and Merry do the same with their planks and become the other two vertices of the family triangle. Dad opens his mouth as though he's going to say something but doesn't. Merry wonders if he was supposed to speak. Maybe he forgets the words. Maybe he's ruined everything.

Merry doesn't know where her parents got the wood. She doesn't think they got the planks from a neighbor or from the market. She worries her parents took boards out of the walls or from the ceiling or the floors or from some other really important area that needs those wooden planks to help keep their house from falling down.

On an unseen and unheard cue, the Barretts tilt the planks toward each other until all three intersect at their top ends. The Barretts let go and the planks form a free-standing tripod frame, the bare bones of a crude pyramid. Merry wants to sit inside and pretend this is meant for her to stay in forever.

Mom and Dad announce in unison, "This is the first temple."

Merry remembers she was supposed to say the same thing. The villagers judge her silence, *tsk-tsk*ing their disapproval. She hopes she isn't going to be in trouble later.

Everyone is still for a long time. Maybe the ceremony is over but no one realizes it.

Mom lashes out with a foot and sweeps away one plank. Dad makes a noise Merry never wants to hear again. All three planks fall to the ground.

Mom and Dad each take one of Merry's hands and they walk out of the circle. Merry drags her feet, wanting to create more snake paths to confuse anyone who might try to follow, but she can't do that and keep up with her parents.

The villagers slowly enter the circle and commune at the small pile of rubble. They begin discussions that will continue until dark, discussions that will not be of any concern of the Barrett family. At least not yet.

As soon as she gets home, Merry runs upstairs to Marjorie's bedroom and tells her all about the ceremony. Marjorie isn't well and had to stay home, stuck in bed, huddled under the covers.

THE SECOND TEMPLE

School is canceled today. No one tells Merry why, but she assumes it's because the temple ceremonies are continuing. If they'd left the first temple standing, it would've ended there. But because the first temple collapsed, thanks to Mom, the ceremonies must and will continue.

Merry doesn't know when or why or how it'll eventually end. Her parents refuse to answer her.

Merry sits at the edge of the circle and sculpts mounds in the dirt. She wipes her hands on her jeans, turning the denim rusty. A gaggle of villagers including Ken are working on the second temple. They argue about how it's all going to fit together and they ignore Merry when she tries to get their attention.

This temple is to be comprised of the original three planks supplied by the Barretts, plus three new ones, and a collection of oddly shaped wooden scraps and blocks.

Merry wants to pluck fist-sized rocks out of the nearby road and knock down the temple with them after the villagers are finished. Why shouldn't she be the one to knock it down instead of Ken or a random person she barely knows?

The second temple is ill conceived and shaky, missing the simple elegance of the first. Merry would not sit inside this one. She cannot trust that it wouldn't fall on her head.

THE THIRD TEMPLE

Marjorie's bedroom is dark, but not night-dark. The shade is down and the curtains are drawn. The nightstand lamp is on, the one with the red lampshade and the silly golden tassels. After running her fingers through the tassels (she can't help herself), Merry climbs onto the foot of Marjorie's bed and sits with her legs pretzeled so it'll take some time before she can untangle herself.

Merry adjusts her glasses and tells Marjorie that Ken said she can't watch them build the temples anymore. That she, or anyone from her family, watching from the edge of the circle, or anywhere else, is against the rules, the most important of all village rules. Merry tells Marjorie that when Ken was talking he looked like regular, nice Ken. She means he looked like he always looks, which really makes her mad that he would tell her she couldn't do what she wanted to do and then not look sorry or sad.

The rest of the villagers looked at Merry funny, though. Like they were afraid that what Ken said was going to hurt her. Or—maybe!—

they were afraid Merry would hurt them with what she would do or say next.

Merry tells Marjorie the third temple was still small, but it had one complete, solid wall no one could see through.

Merry tells Marjorie she ran away after Ken yelled at her and she didn't get to see the temple come down. Merry doesn't tell Marjorie the worst of it; Ken sounded like Dad did when he was angry.

THE FOURTH TEMPLE

The temple is a single story, but the walls reach well above the villagers' heads. The planks and boards are different colors, different shades; some have been slathered in enough shellac to make them shine, some have been painted, some have been left alone and bare their cracks and scars. If Merry squints her eyes, the temple's colors, exposed knots, and competing wood grains haze and morph into and out of patterns, and she sees a face with well-deep eyes, then a one-horned dragon, and then something unidentifiable that makes everything go quiet in her head.

Merry leaves her hiding spot, creeping out from behind the market's garbage and rain-catch barrels. The villagers don't see her until she puts both feet inside the circle. She smirks, and she imagines her smirk is as loud as a clap. There are more villagers here today than the day before and they chase her away, brandishing the planks and two-by-fours they have yet to place within the fourth temple.

Merry runs and screams she is sorry and promises she won't try to watch them again.

She isn't sorry she was able to scoop up a handful of the circle's red soil before getting chased off. She cups her prize against her chest, and once she's home, she goes directly to her sister's room.

Marjorie remains in bed, facing away from the door. The room is still dark but for the lamp.

Merry puts the soil inside a plain white coffee mug on the night-stand. She doesn't dust or wipe her hands. She likes how the dry, claylike soil fills the cracks between her fingers and the lines on her palms.

THE FIFTH TEMPLE

The Barretts sit at the kitchen table for dinner.

Dad prays silently to himself. Merry imagines the prayers transform him into a hunched stone gargoyle and that is why the wooden chair creaks and groans under his weight.

Mom smokes a cigarette. She's turned her chair so that it faces away from the table, as though she can't bring herself to look at her family. With her pointed chin held up, aimed toward the ceiling, she blows smoke above them all.

Merry swirls the greens, the last of the season's raspberries, and lumpy chunks of dark-meat turkey around her plate. She doesn't like dark-meat turkey, but she intuitively reads the mood of the room and knows this is not the time to complain about it. She drinks her now-warm milk, giving herself a sloppy white mustache.

The fourth seat at the table is empty. Merry will take a plate up to Marjorie afterward if Mom will let her. She will ask Mom because Dad would say no. He wouldn't want her carrying a plate up the stairs because she might fall, spill, make a mess.

Merry asks, "Did anyone go see the fifth temple today?" She doesn't think her parents know she went to the village circle yesterday and the day before. If they knew she was sneaking out or if Ken told on her, they would've yelled at her already. And now that she has asked about seeing the new temple, she's mad at herself because they're going to tell her they didn't see it and then explain why no one in their family is allowed to see the new temples, which means Merry can't use the I-didn't-know-I-couldn't-go excuse if she gets caught sneaking out tomorrow or the next day.

Mom surprises Merry and says, "I did." She blows out more smoke.

Dad says, "Sarah? We aren't supposed to—"

Mom stubs out her cigarette and faces Merry. "It looked like a child's drawing. And not a good one, like yours," she adds before Merry can protest.

Dad covers his eyes with his dirty hands, hands that could be covered in red soil, but Merry can't be sure in the dim light.

Mom says, "They'd started on a second floor before it fell, and it—it was crooked and ugly and stupid and pathetic looking. It was horrible. It was a nightmare."

Merry is unexpectedly upset by this. She leaves the kitchen and hides under the dining room table they never use for dining.

Mom and Dad finish eating and clean up without saying anything. When Dad walks by the table Merry sees only his feet. The stairs groan and creak under his weight like the kitchen chair did. By the sounds of it, he's walking slowly, carefully. Merry hopes he's taking a plate up to Marjorie.

THE SIXTH TEMPLE

Merry says, "I'm bored."

Mom says, "Well, you can draw, work on one of the jigsaw puzzles, read a book, make up one of your stories—"

"I want someone to play with me."

"I know and I'm sorry, but Dad and I are going to be busy today."

Mom doesn't look busy. She's sitting at the table with her legs crossed, nursing a glass of tomato juice and smoking a cigarette.

"Everyone says they're busy."

"That's because everyone is busy, Merry."

Merry asks, "Are they building a new temple today? Even in the rain?"

"Yes. They have to."

"Why?"

Mom says, "Because we asked them to. We started it."

Merry wants to say *I did not start this*. "They can stop if they want to, if they really, really want to."

Merry leaves the kitchen and her half-eaten oatmeal and goes into the front room. She sits in the window seat and watches the rain. It rains all day long. The raindrops are fat and white. It's the kind of rain that makes angry little rivers that scar the village's roads and paths.

Building anything in such a torrential downpour must be near impossible. Merry imagines the tower as dark and misshapen as a lump of moldy bread. The villagers are not proud of their work and they do not want to continue; they want to quit. She wants them all to quit.

Merry imagines the red soil in the circle turning into a bog. The sixth temple doesn't collapse or come tumbling down. It sinks. The villagers sink, too. The scary part is that the villagers don't struggle or call out for help. They stand as still as the wooden planks and as useless as a temple that is meant to stand for only a few moments. They disappear without so much as a ripple.

When the rain stops, the soil will harden again. There will be no sign, no evidence of where they all went. And someday the skeleton of their village—buildings and houses and roads and walkways and carefully plotted property lines—will disappear, too.

THE SEVENTH TEMPLE

After Mom washes Marjorie, she locks herself in the bathroom. Merry has an ear pressed against Marjorie's bedroom wall and she hears the low drone of Mom talking to herself. Yesterday Mom was crying and Dad knocked softly on the bathroom door, but she didn't let Dad in. The day before yesterday she let him in.

Marjorie's room still smells terrible despite the new clothes and new sheets. Merry covers her nose and mouth with her shirt collar. She feels bad for doing so. It's not Marjorie's fault, but it smells like she's had a week's worth of accidents that haven't been cleaned. Also, somehow, her room smells sickly sweet like when Ms. Carmilla makes licorice at the market. There are flies in the room even though they have been careful.

Merry hums a song to herself as she opens the curtains and lifts the shade. The sunlight pours in, takes its vengeance on the dark, hidden room. She stands on Marjorie's bed, careful not to disturb her sister. She steps off the mattress and onto the windowsill. The windowpanes are smudged and milky, and need to be cleaned. When Merry goes up on her tiptoes she can see the top of the seventh temple. At first she thinks she sees a spire or a flagpole, but she looks harder and spies three tented wooden planks in the same formation as the first temple. If she can see this from Marjorie's bedroom, it means the seventh temple has a roof and it has two floors below that roof, maybe even three.

Her breath fogs up the glass. She loses balance, pitches forward, and knocks into the window. Afraid she'll fall through the glass and be cut to ribbons (something her dad would say), and smash herself open on the ground like a pumpkin, Merry jumps backward off the windowsill and onto the bed, jostling her sister and dispersing a small cloud of flies.

Merry tells Marjorie she thinks the temples are getting too big.

THE EIGHTH TEMPLE

Merry spends her morning in the backyard collecting stones and stacking them into cairns, making temples of her own. She knocks over the first few with a swipe of her hand but then decides she doesn't want to be like everyone else in the village. She's doesn't knock her temples over purposefully and is careful as she builds them taller and more complex. They collapse anyway.

Merry spends her afternoon with an old jigsaw puzzle. She's good at puzzles even though she doesn't enjoy them. Finding the pieces that fit together is an inevitable and joyless process of elimination. After completing the puzzle, she breaks it up into six rectangular sections that she flips over. She reconnects the sections of the upside-down puzzle with the gray cardboard backs facing up. On the underside of the puzzle she draws a forest and a woolly Bigfoot peering out from behind the trees. Bigfoot has yellow eyes and one long snaggletooth poking out from between the lips of her closed mouth. Merry plans to take the puzzle apart when she's done and if there's nothing else for her to do tomorrow, piece it back together with the Bigfoot side facing up.

Dad bullies into the house through the front door. He's all grunts and snorts, banging around in the front foyer, clomping his boots on the doormat, then kicking them off. He smells of sap, sweat, and dirt.

He says, "Hi there, monkey."

"Hi."

He lumbers into the dining room, walking heavily, broadcasting his physicality as only her dad can. He does this when he has a secret he won't share, but he wants you to know he's keeping it, which seems like a cheat. That sap-soil-sweat smell grows stronger and makes her sad he didn't take her with him.

He asks, "Did Mom say it was okay for you to draw on her favorite puzzle like that?"

"It's only the backs. No one looks at the backs."

"Can't argue with that. Where's Mom?"

"Upstairs with Marjorie. Where were you?"

"Out." He flexes his hands, opening and closing them into fists, and he bends his arms at the elbows and then turns in place, making a show of looking around the room. It's impossible for him to stop moving.

"What were you doing?"

"Things." He smiles like he's playing a game. It's not a fair game if only one of them gets to play.

Merry takes apart the puzzle even though she's not done or satisfied with her drawing.

"Why do you need Mom?"

"There was an accident—"

"The eighth temple?"

"Yes. I'm afraid there was."

"Tell me."

Dad scratches his head, a pantomime of thought. "Don't tell your mother I told you."

"I won't." Merry doesn't know it now, but she will tell later as Mom tucks her in bed. She'll tell Mom every detail she can remember and embellish others she doesn't. She won't know why she's doing it.

Dad says, "They hadn't quite finished yet and the temple collapsed. Someone was inside, and she died."

"Who?"

"I don't know. I haven't heard yet. They wouldn't tell me."

"No one knocked it over on purpose?"

"Not this time. It was an accident."

"Does this temple count?"

"Yes, it counts even more with the accident, I'm afraid."

"Where were you?"

"Never you mind. I was out." Dad finally stops moving and shaking and Merry thinks he might fall down, too, and maybe fall on top of her. "It's very sad and it means they have to keep going. They have to build even more temples now."

Merry says, "I know," even though she doesn't.

THE NINTH TEMPLE

Dad is in the basement and Mom is upstairs with Marjorie, so Merry sneaks out the front door and runs to Ken's house. He lives only 473 steps away. He told her the fun part is that the distance between their houses will shrink as she gets older. She asked how that was possible. He said that as Merry gets older she'll be getting bigger, too, and her legs will be longer so it will take her fewer steps to get to his house.

It has been weeks since she's been by his house, yet it still takes her the same amount of steps. The whole way there she imagines growing bigger and bigger until she is a giant needing only six steps to get there and she's so big she can pry up the roof off his house if she wants.

Merry knocks and no one answers. She pounds on the yellow door with her open hand until her palm is red and throbbing. Ken is not home. He is probably at the circle and working on the ninth temple. If Marjorie had been here, she would tell Merry to crawl through a window and hide someplace dark and out of the way until he comes home.

Merry takes the folded-up note out of her pocket. It reads: I wish you would come visit me like you used to. She slides it under his door and pushes it inside as far as it will go. She drops down to look under the door, but she can't see inside. Suddenly nervous the door will open, she scrambles down the front stairs and runs until she's thirty-three (her lucky number) steps away from his house. She wishes she could go back, get the note, and tear it up.

On the walk home the ninth temple is visible to her left. It's taller than the grove of apple trees in the back of the market. It must be four stories high now, though the fourth story looks like a scribble made out of wood.

THE TENTH TEMPLE

The Barretts sit at the kitchen table for dinner.

Dad's prayer isn't silent. He says it out loud and he talks fast, but not like he's talking to someone who is actually listening. The words overlap and have no space in which to live. Merry imagines the prayer isn't made of separate, distinct words but consists of one long, terrible word. The longest, most terrible, and loneliest word.

Mom ignores him and she eats her chicken, potatoes, and corn. She drinks her wine, her glass now a quarter full. Merry doesn't think the wine looks red. It looks black.

Merry is unhappy with her meal. They don't have any butter left to make the potatoes taste the way she likes. The market has been closed since the third temple. They are out of milk, too. She sticks her tongue in her glass of water and leaves it there. Neither Mom nor Dad tells her to stop fooling around.

The fourth seat at the kitchen table is empty. Her parents stopped taking a plate up to Marjorie's room after the sixth temple, which doesn't make sense to Merry. Merry still might ask to take a plate up to Marjorie afterward, even if it's only an empty one with pretend food.

Merry asks, "Did anyone see the tenth temple today?"

Dad continues his long, terrible, lonely word. His voice grows hoarse, guttural; the word is stealing his voice.

Mom drinks the rest of her wine in three large gulps. She holds the back of her hand against her mouth, blinks hard, and holds her eyes closed long enough that Merry is afraid Mom might be stuck in this pose forever.

Mom says, "It's crooked and ugly and stupid and pathetic looking. It's horrible. It's a nightmare. It's the worst one yet."

Merry asks, "Can I be the one to knock it down? Maybe if I break the stupid rules they won't build any more of them."

"We never should've built the first one. It's all our fault."

Merry thinks about the day Mom and Dad told her she had to help carry a wooden plank to the circle. The funny thing is, she doesn't remember much else about that day. She remembers dragging the plank, the completion of the first temple, Mom's knocking it down, and the noise Dad made when it fell. That noise represents how she feels when she thinks about that day.

Merry says, "It's not my fault. Why is it my fault, too? I didn't do anything. I only did what you told me to do."

THE ELEVENTH TEMPLE

I can see the eleventh temple from your window easily now. I don't have to stand on the windowsill.

I even have to look up way above our house to see the top.

They made it too skinny, like an old man's leg. That's what Mom says.

It's more like a beat-up dragon tail sticking straight in the air. The wooden pieces that fit but don't exactly fit are the dragon's scales.

Whoa! A couple of planks fell off. I think they were planks—I mean, we're too far away to see for sure. It's hard to tell. Whatever fell, it went spinning and flipping down.

I know it stinks in here, but I can hear the villagers on the highest floors talking if I leave the window open, so I'm going to close it. Okay?

Can you hear them, Marjorie?

I don't like how it sounds like they're in your room with us. It's creepy.

I can let you borrow some of my stuffed animals and you can put them on the windowsill. Maybe they'll block out the sound.

No note back from Ken yet. In the mornings I look for one on the foyer floor and the front steps.

I heard Mom and Dad whispering in the bathroom before I came in here.

They said six people have died inside the temples. Two died in the tenth.

I didn't hear any names.

I don't know if Ken is one of them.

I don't get why they don't stop making temples when people are dying.

I wish they would stop.

I wish you would talk to me.

I wish you would tell me another story.

I wish you would tell me what to do, like you used to.

THE TWELFTH TEMPLE

A crashing, all-encompassing boom wakes Merry and shakes the entire house. Merry ducks under the bedcovers and yells for Mom until the growling, end-of-everything roar is a fading echo and the bedposts finish rattling their SOS signals against her bedroom wall.

Mom bursts through the half-open door and her billowy, amorphous dark shape rushes to Merry's bedside.

"Shhh, you're okay, Merry. Everything's okay."

That's not true. Merry knows this. Why does Mom say such an obvious lie? The lie doesn't make anything better. Nothing has been okay for a very long time.

Merry can't stop crying and her breaths are quick and shallow, not enough to fill her with the air she needs. She tries to calm down so she can ask questions and tell Mom about hearing the end of everything.

Mom sits on the bed and Merry crawls into her lap. Mom vines her arms around Merry. They rock back and forth, gently swaying together. Merry worries about another boom coming and knocking them off the bed and through the floor and into a greedy, fissured earth.

A dusty, cool breeze passes through the bedroom curtains. Mom says, "Shh, listen, that was the twelfth temple coming down. That's all. We're safe. Our house is fine. We're okay. I know it was loud and scary, but the temple was supposed to come down. It had to come down and they have to start over one more time. They have to add a little more."

Merry closes her eyes and listens to the rush of blood in her ears and to her fluttering, triple-timed heartbeat. She works up the courage to ask if they can move from this village, go somewhere far away, somewhere the rest of them would never be able to see from the top of any temple.

Mom says, "They're starting the last temple tomorrow. I promise it'll be the last one."

Mom is crying now.

Merry covers her ears.

THE THIRTEENTH TEMPLE

The villagers take more than two days to build the thirteenth temple. Merry thinks the extra time must be against the rules, but she doesn't dare say so.

On the third morning after the midnight collapse of the twelfth temple, Dad wakes Merry and tells her they are going back to the circle and Marjorie is coming with them. He wears an ill-fitting black suit; the cuffs and collar are frayed. Merry imagines tugging on a loose thread and unraveling it all.

He says, "Mom is in Marjorie's room washing her up, dressing her, helping her to get ready. I need to help Mom, too, so wait for us downstairs."

Merry says, "Can I stay home instead?"

"No."

"Can I go to Ken's house?"

"I'm sorry, no."

"I don't want to go back to the circle today. I don't want to see the thirteenth temple."

"We have to."

"Why?"

"We're doing this for your sister. Don't you want to do this special thing for your sister? Don't you love her, Merry? She would do this for you." Dad's voice is angry-loud but he doesn't look at her, can't look at her. Merry thinks he's only pretending to be angry-loud.

Merry climbs out of bed and takes her glasses off the cluttered dresser. The lenses are dusty. She does not clean them.

Dad holds out a hand and says, "Come here for a sec, sweetie."

Merry ignores him, walks out of her room, and goes downstairs. She walks slowly, placing both feet on one stair before moving down to the next, giving Dad a chance to take back everything he said.

Mom leaves Marjorie's room and quickly catches up to Merry, resting her hands on her daughter's shoulders as they walk the final steps to the foyer together. Mom wears a black dress Merry has never seen before. It's asymmetrical, the right sleeve longer than the left. It's also too long and pools around Mom's feet so that she appears to be sprouting out of a hole in the floor.

Merry leans her head against Mom's hip. Mom rubs Merry's back.

Dad isn't too far behind and he carries Marjorie down the stairs. She is wrapped in a white sheet, the whitest sheet, as white as birthday cake icing. Merry wonders if Marjorie is comfortable, if her arms are loose, folded, or pinned against her sides.

No one asks Marjorie if she's okay. No one offers to help Dad carry her. He doesn't ask for help, either. Merry holds the front door open for her parents.

The Barretts silently walk to the village square, which isn't a square, as everyone knows. The smell from Marjorie's bedroom follows them. Merry keeps her head down and concentrates on her feet crunching through fallen leaves littering the walking paths. She doesn't want to catch glimpses of the thirteenth temple until she's where she can see the entire structure at once. She hums a song to herself. It's one that Marjorie used to hum. No words, only the melancholy, addictive melody.

The walk seems longer, but perhaps it's because Merry forgets to count her steps. When they do finally arrive, the villagers mass around the edge of the circle. Every family she knows and the ones she doesn't know are there. She didn't realize there were so many people living in the village. The realization is unnerving, the exposure of an open secret. There are seven other families carrying a loved one in a wrapped sheet. She does not see Ken and assumes he left the village. She will never forgive him for leaving her behind.

Merry hears the thirteenth temple creaking and settling before she lifts her head to look at it. The base of the thirteenth temple claims more than half the area of the circle. The base is neither fully round nor geometric in footprint. At first glance it looks like a haphazard woodpile, but as she stares, its impenetrable design yields a pattern, a mindful madness as to why one piece of wood is stacked atop another. The impossible structure—one with more angles and arcs than a denuded tree in winter—loosens an insect-buzz in Merry's head.

Mom says, "Hold my hand."

Merry would rather hold Marjorie's hand, but she does as is asked.

A small, arched opening appears within the temple's base when they are a few steps from it. Merry is too flustered to know if the arch was hidden by optical illusion or if the wood parted like gilded pages in an old book, opening and exposing the entrance only as they approached.

Merry does not want to go inside, would rather do anything else in the world than go inside the temple. As though Dad can hear her thoughts, he says, "You're doing this for your sister, remember."

Without ceremony they enter the structure. Inside the air is cooler, but not still. Whorls of air push, prod, and whistle through gaps and openings in the walls. There are lamps with lit candles hanging at varying, random heights. The candlelight flickers as though the small flames know they are not up to the task before them.

There are darkened hallways to the left and right of the entrance. Straight ahead is the maw of a spiral staircase. The stairs are layered like the stacked keyboards and foot pedals of the village church's great organ. Merry pauses at the mouth of the staircase; the spaces between the stairs are empty and she worries her legs could slip through. She blinks up at the dizzying spiral overhead.

"When do we stop climbing?"

Dad says, "We'll know."

They climb up. The temple sways and groans in the wind. Merry clutches one sweaty hand around Mom's hand and she slides her other hand along the chunky, uneven walls, wincing as sharp, determined splinters bite into her fingers.

Dad's breathing is heavy and ragged. He sweats through his suit jacket. He now has Marjorie slung over his shoulder, carrying her like he carried the plank of wood all those temples ago. Merry hopes he doesn't drop her sister.

The turns in the staircase are getting tighter and smaller. The walls constrict and close in. They are not yet at the top when Mom says, "Here," and urges Merry onto a landing coated with sawdust. The landing funnels the Barretts into a hallway. The hallway slopes down and the grade steepens dangerously before leveling off, leading them to a long wall with a closed door in its center.

Mom pushes the door, which swings open easily and silently. The room is a conventional box shape, and if not for the lack of flooring and wallpaper, could be a bedroom in their home. The wall to the entrance's right is comprised of green-colored boards. She wonders where all the wood comes from and how much the villagers sacrificed of their own homes to construct the temple. Unlike the stairs and hallway, there are no lamps or candles hanging from the walls. The only light comes from a square-shaped window. Across from the door, the window is slightly larger than a boat's portal, big enough for Merry to crawl through but not big enough for Mom or Dad.

Merry lets go of Mom's hand. As Merry walks across the room the floorboards are soft and sag beneath her weight. She holds her arms out for balance. The window has no glass. She sticks her arm outside, testing the air. Her arm returns unscathed. Gripping the rough windowsill, Merry sticks her head through and peers out and down.

The forest surrounding the village goes on and on, as far as she can see. Beyond the village there doesn't appear to be anything but the forest. This is both exciting and frightening, and she imagines running away to live under the leafy canopy by herself. She would eat fruit and plants and honey, and maybe she would find ways to send her family and Ken messages, and maybe she would not.

Merry looks straight down, and she is so high above the villagers, she cannot make out their individual faces. They are on the move, though. They are no longer standing at the edges of the circle. They crowd the base of the temple, near the entrance. Each family carrying a person wrapped in a sheet is lined up to enter the temple and one by one they disappear from view. Voices and footfalls rise up from below and violent tremors vibrate through the floors and walls.

"Mom, Dad, are they all coming in here, too? I don't think they should. Is it safe? Why are we here? You never told me why—"

Merry turns away from the window and she is alone in the room with Marjorie, who is propped in a sitting position against the one green wall. Marjorie's bare, swollen left foot is uncovered and is the same color as the wall. The sheet isn't wrapped around her like a cocoon anymore, but draped over her. It would not take much effort, nothing more than a flick of the wrist, to pull the sheet away. The room's only door is closed.

Merry lets loose a whimper, staggers across the quicksand floor, and yanks furiously on the doorknob. The door is locked. She pounds and kicks and yells for her parents, but no one answers her. She faintly hears the echo of Mom's crying and Dad's saying it'll be okay. Other voices drown out her parents, and there is more crying, too. Then, as the temple hitches and spasms under Merry's feet, there are wailing screams and the crack and pop of failing wood.

Merry sinks to the floor, her hands still wrapped around the door-knob. The temple quakes, undulates, and bends into cartoon shapes, a parody of tensile strength and form. And in the final, irrevocable moment, at the precipice of the structure's failing balance and integrity, Merry cannot tell if the collapsing temple or Marjorie herself is pulling away her white sheet.

You tell the two large members of hotel security about my key card. You tell them not to hurt me as they grab my arms and pull me away from the window and the air-conditioning unit. Their hands are warm on my bare forearms. It's an odd sensation being moved against your will. My toes barely touch the floor.

During the telling of the story I never saw one of your hands disappear into a pocket or behind your back. When did you call or text them? Is that black band around your wrist a smart watch? Do you have an app that directly connects to security? It would make sense for someone like you to have such an app to protect yourself against people like me. I'm not really like that, though. I hope you know that.

The hotel manager (with his nasal voice) seems a bit of a weasel as he begs for your forgiveness and tells you nothing like this has ever happened in his hotel before, and he sputters through explaining how I might've ended up in your room.

You nod your head and you say, "Fine," impatiently, as though you wish security were removing him from your room instead of me.

I never once interrupted your story, Merry. If you remember nothing else about me, remember that.

I'm almost to the door and I don't want to leave, not yet. I go boneless and drop my weight to the floor. This move surprises the guards and I fall to my knees and wedge my legs within the door frame.

I tell you that I will go. I promise I will go and I will never bother you again.

The men are shouting, but I know you can hear me.

I want to know if the thirteenth temple is as tall as this hotel and I want to know what you do when you're all alone in your temple.

What will you do after you check into a new room, one just like this one?

What will you do after security and the manager leave?

When you are alone, is Marjorie always there with you?

Will you pull off her sheet?

Security pries me free from the doorway and as I drift away from your room, from you, Merry, you step into the doorway and you look at me. You look at me and you don't let me go. You look at me and you look into me. I feel it. I can feel you there, Merry.

You close the door and you say something that means more than even the story you shared with me.

I'm not imagining this, Merry, I am not.

From behind the door you say, "Good-bye, M."

NOTES

Below are odds, ends, anecdotes, and rants about/relating to most of the stories. Not every story gets a note. You'll be pleasantly surprised by the ones that do not get a note. Or you'll be annoyed.

And apparently I like the name Tommy/Tom and the adjective *squirrelly*, both of which make multiple appearances in the collection.

Growing Things: In 2008 this story started as a simple what-if or, more accurately, a WTF moment. I was walking my dog around the neighborhood early one spring, and along the shoulder of a dirt road stretch grew neat rows of weeds. I assume they were weeds as I am not a horticulturalist. These growing things looked like the stalks of mini-trees or possibly bamboo shoots. Not that I knew/know what bamboo shoots look like in the wild.

Anyway, the weeds grew from their inches-tall sproutlings (I ask any horticulturalists reading this, is that a word? It is now!) to taller than me in a matter of days. I am tall and these things grew taller. What kind of plants grew as quickly as that? I remembered my good friend Walter, a transplanted New Englander with a Boston accent thicker than clam chowder, telling me about his move to North Carolina and his ensuing and frightening (to me) battle with the unchecked, crazy growth of bamboo in his yard. If he didn't dig out the whole bamboo plant, roots and all, he claimed the stalks would grow one foot per day. The bamboo was strong, too, and sharp enough for a person to be impaled on its spikes. He was probably exaggerating, or maybe in my memory I added the gruesome impaled-on bit, but I could now believe Walter (Waltah!) after seeing these weeds take over the shoulder of a dirt road so quickly and completely. Thus the seed (sorry, I know, I know!) of "Growing Things" was there for me to, um, water. Sigh. (The "story notes" section is off to a thrilling start . . .)

The first iteration of this story appeared in my 2010 collection of apocalyptic short stories, *In the Mean Time*. I had no idea that five years later I would go back to the growing things and to the two sisters and their family with a terrible secret, and make the story a big part of *A Head Full of Ghosts*.

Swim Wants to Know If It's as Bad as Swim Thinks: I love giant monsters. Well, in theory. I'm sure I wouldn't like them if they were around smashing, stomping, and eating all the stuff. Let me rephrase: I love giant monster stories. I like to think I have a giant monster novel in me somewhere.

The first horror/monster movies I watched were Godzilla/Kaiju movies. A local Boston UHF (I'm that old) channel featured those movies during their Saturday afternoon *Creature Double Feature* program. The first movie would almost always star a giant monster (Godzilla, Rodan, Gamera, Reptilicus, The—somewhat—Amazing Colossal Man, Killer Shrews, Giant Leeches) and the second movie would be a non-giant-monster horror movie and scare the crap out of me and give me nightmares.

The new, being-built home in the story is now my current house. No giant monster attacks yet.

The Getaway: Once upon a time I was introduced to the world as a crime writer with my 2009 novel *The Little Sleep* and its 2010 follow-up *No Sleep Till Wonderland*. I always felt a little like an impostor as a "crime writer." All the short stories I'd written to that point were horror stories (and that included a couple of attempts at horror novels that failed miserably). I wrote *TLS* because I had an idea that wouldn't let go. I enjoy reading crime, but I had no designs on being a crime writer. At the risk of sounding glib, I wanted to be a writer.

I wanted to be a writer who wrote whatever the story needed to be. I wanted to be a writer who wrote horror, too.

Ellen Datlow swooped in to invite me to write a horror/crime story for her *Supernatural Noir* anthology (2011). "The Getaway" makes use of the hard-boiled style I'd used with the two Mark Genevich novels. Getting to mix the horror elements into the story felt a little bit like coming home.

Nineteen Snapshots of Dennisport: One more crime/horror hybrid here. David Ulin asked me to write a story for *Cape Cod Noir* (2011), which became part of the wonderful Akashic Noir series of books. I didn't grow up on the Cape, but my family and I vacationed there a few summers when I was a teen. The setting and bones of the story are constructed from the many fun memories of those summers.

Before writing the story I actually drove down to the old place we had rented all those years ago to make sure I had the geography right. And yeah, seeing Cronenberg's *The Fly* in a small, salty Cape theater messed me up something good.

Big thanks (even though he is taller than I am . . .) goes to friend and writer Seth Lindberg, whose devastating zombie apocalypse story "Twenty-Three Snapshots of San Francisco" inspired the photo-framing narrative of this story.

Where We All Will Be: When my son was in fourth grade he was suddenly not able to complete any of his classwork in the allotted time. He went through a round of academic testing that was both anxiety inducing (in me, his dad) and illuminating. I'll never forget one test in which my son was given a schematic (lines, shapes, and angles) and asked to copy it using only pencil and paper. The result didn't look all that much like the original, which wasn't shocking to me as he was only in fourth grade and he didn't have the neatest handwriting. The proctor took the schematic away and my son worked on something else for approximately fifteen minutes. Once that was completed, she asked him to draw the original schematic from memory. Not only was he able to draw the gist of it from memory (which I would've never been able to do), his schematic was nearly a carbon copy of the original. He was asked to draw the schematic again after another fifteen minutes had elapsed and again it was near perfect. He retained all the information, but he needed some extra time to process and organize the data before he could replicate it. I was gobsmacked. As a parent and an educator, I have to say no test or demonstration before or since has so impacted my empathy and understanding in regard to different learning styles.

The Teacher: I've been a teacher for the entirety of my professional life. I didn't start messing around with writing until I started teaching.

In some ways, my being a teacher doesn't make sense. When I was a student I did well academically but I did not do well at all socially. I was awkward, not very popular, and often picked on. In particular, I remember the years between sixth and tenth grades as a miserable, pride-swallowing survival trial. I was physically immature for much longer than most, and my scoliosis didn't help either (to wit, I was five foot six when I was sixteen, six feet and 140 pounds when I graduated from high school, and I'm six foot four and 205 pounds currently).

Why would someone who didn't like being at school end up teaching? I don't want to get self-analytic, so I'm going to shrug my shoulders and say, um, I don't know. But I do enjoy teaching very much, and other than writing, I can't see myself doing anything else.

So. Yeah. This story represents some of my anxieties as they relate to school (both as being a student and a teacher) and how any of us get through those adolescent years and into our scary futures.

Notes for "The Barn in the Wild": This story first appeared in the anthology *The Children of Old Leech*, stories written in tribute to the influential work of my good friend Laird Barron. It was a lot of fun getting to play in his sandbox. If you aren't reading Laird's work, well then, *shakes long finger in your direction*.

Old Leech and *The Black Guide* are both direct references to Laird's work. For years, Laird, John Langan, and I talked about writing stories in which a mysterious black guide might appear, even if it was only a fleeting appearance. I'm glad I was finally able to include the little book in a story.

I wrote the story out in longhand. I never do that. I write all my stories on a computer. I keep idea notebooks around to jot down ideas and draw doodles and procrastinate, but when it comes to the actual writing part, it's me typing. I wish I could write more stories longhand, as that travels better, but I can't. This story was different, though. I wanted to give it an authentic found-journal vibe. I hoped writing it out in a journal would do just that.

I was pleased with the result, but transcribing it as a typed story proved trickier than I anticipated. It was natural/easy adding the notes in the margins of the handwritten journal, and those notes became the less natural/easy footnotes. But who doesn't love them a healthy dose of footnotes!

_____: Five bucks if you can pronounce the title . . .

I spent five or six summers at my town's local pond, watching my two kids go through their three-week-long swimming lesson classes. I miss those days, of course, but I don't miss the invading-army-storm-the-beach level of daily preparation. Towels, sunscreen, lunches, snacks, drinks, chairs, blankets, shoes, hats, book(s) (for me), money, beach passes, and stressing out about getting there in time for the lesson, and more important, to find myself a spot in the shade. I know, I sound like a lot of fun, right? I would go in the water and do the dad thing of throwing kids into the air so they can splash down, and that was never a smart thing to do given the spinal fusion (remember my mention of scoliosis in the story note for "The Teacher"?) I had years ago. And then after the mandated fun and the lessons and lunch was the cleanup and getting kids to change out of their wet bathing suits when they wanted to stay and they got sand everywhere, and I hate sand everywhere. And yeah, I'm a lot of fun at the beach.

Anyway, I wrote this story about the pond beach.

It Won't Go Away: I have attended and participated in many readings hosted by my friends at Lovecraft Arts & Sciences (bookstore and curio/oddities shop in Providence's Arcade Mall). If you're ever in that wonderful city, you should check it out. The readings are always fun and enthusiastically attended, with readers and writers getting an informal chance to talk and hang out. I look forward to these events and always leave them energized, my writing batteries fully recharged. Honestly, LA&S is one of my cherished happy places.

So, yeah, why did I write this?

After reading Steven Millhauser's "The Knife Thrower," I thought about writing a story where a mysterious writer comes to town for a reading and does something over-the-top weird. I had a few ideas but nothing that stuck, so I filed the maybe-story away for a bit. Then one sunny afternoon at the Arcade, I happened to be sitting in the audience after having read my story (or maybe I was up next to read) and a flittering thought about the writer-doing-a-reading story occurred again: What would happen if the writer shot himself during a reading? Icky and morbid, yes, but that's kind of what I do.

Notes from the Dog Walkers: Not to say it was easy to write this novella (because it was not easy), but it was a lot of fun. I enjoyed giving myself permission to follow the logic through lines and rabbit holes and indulgences the dog walkers presented. I do want to say KB is not my raging id, or not solely my raging id. The bio and descriptions and class anxieties of the nameless author stand-in for me within the story are full of half-truths and exaggerations, of course. That said, I was going to work in the closing of the Parker Brothers (or Barter Brothers, as it was named in *A Head Full of Ghosts*) factory into this story, but it didn't quite fit. Which is okay, as I've already referenced the plant's closing in more than a few of my other stories/ books. But while we're here, let's go down one more rabbit hole.

My father worked for Parker Brothers for twenty-five years. The manufacturing plant was in downtown Salem, Massachusetts, across the street from an old prison (no longer there), and only a handful of blocks away from the Hawthorne Hotel and the Salem Witch Museum. Starting at age sixteen, I worked summer jobs at the factory. My main gigs were unloading trucks (when I was older I was allowed to use power handcarts and even an old forklift . . . don't tell OSHA) and being a "material handler" (supplier of game pieces for the assembly lines). There were other odd jobs along the way, including a two-week stretch where I beta-tested an ill-fated Nintendo game called Drac's

Night Out. The game was never released, but you can find it—like everything else—on the Internet and even play it now if you'd like.

I really enjoyed working there. Everyone knew everyone, and everyone knew and loved my father. Granted, the glow of nostalgia is deceptive, but the vibe of that place really was family-esque.

In the summer of 1991 (I was going to be a junior in college) there were rumblings of Hasbro's potentially purchasing Parker Brothers. People were nervous, the kind of nervous that became a collective storm cloud. I overheard people talking about it in the lunchroom; there was uncertainty, but there was also hope and resolve: *hey, we've been through company sales and takeovers before, but we'll get through it.* Late one morning, with no warning, every employee of the factory was called down to the lunchroom. The executives in suits were at the front of the room. My father was not one of those suits; he was in charge of the mailroom. I don't remember seeing him at the company-wide meeting. I only remember the big crowd in that lunchroom. There might have been a podium and a microphone, but I can't be sure. Maybe that's an embellishment to the memory, one that makes it somehow feel worse. Without ceremony, someone walked up to the mic and announced that Hasbro had purchased Parker Brothers and the Salem factory would be closed by November 1. All three hundred employees were to be out of a job. My father was the only one who managed to hang on for a few more years, getting transferred over to the mailroom of the corporate offices in Beverly that were now run by Hasbro, but he, too, eventually got the heave-ho and his thanks-for-twenty-five-years severance check.

The twenty-year-old me who willfully knew nothing about business stood numb in that cafeteria. People around me gasped and shouted "No!" and there were a few screams, and there were tears, too. I couldn't understand how/why I (who was nothing but lousy summer help) was hearing about the factory closing at the same exact moment as my dad and other employees who had spent the bulk of their lives working there.

That twenty-year-old has since spent a solid chunk of his life writing about that moment and the ripples of its aftermath; sometimes obliquely, sometimes not so much.

Further Questions for the Somnambulist: In "Notes from the Dog Walkers," when KB wrote "the author (subconsciously feeling unencumbered by the demands of the marketplace) dares to be a bit more obtuse and experimental (with her short fiction) than she would in a novel," she might've been writing about "Further Questions for the Somnambulist." This odd little story could rightly be described as *The Cabinet of Dr. Caligari* fan fiction. If you haven't seen the silent movie, you should do so. Everyone has a little German Expressionism in them somewhere.

Also, I'm intrigued by the idea of writers using the presentation of text and blank page space to augment the story's atmosphere or mood. Mark Danielewski's *House of Leaves*, Jennifer Egan's *A Visit from the Goon Squad*, and Dan Chaon's *Ill Will* are examples of novels that use their space and antispace brilliantly. I figured I'd try it out on a much smaller scale.

The Ice Tower: Perhaps it's because I'm a lifelong New Englander who complains about the snow and cold with the best of them, but I'm a sucker for winter/ice horror. I dub thee a subgenre if someone hasn't done so already. John Carpenter's *The Thing* is one of my favorite movies and the winter/ice horror exemplar. Other favorites include *Let the Right One In* (film and novel by John Ajvide Lindqvist), Bracken MacLeod's *Stranded*, Michelle Paver's *Dark Matter*, Clare Dudman's *One Day the Ice Will Reveal All Its Dead* (not a horror novel, but one with a horror attitude, if that makes sense), Mat Johnson's *Pym*, and the Finnish horror film *Sauna*. "The Ice Tower" is my little crack at the subgenre.

Her Red Right Hand: Friend and writing superhero Christopher Golden approached me in late spring of 2016 with an invitation to write a short story featuring Mike Mignola's Hellboy character. I enthusiastically told him I would, without knowing how in the heck I was going to write a Hellboy story. Fast-forward through the summer, a summer in which I had to prepare to teach AP BC Calculus (essentially, a high school class that represents the first two semesters of college calculus), so I was kind of stressed about that. And the short of it was September and back to school was around the corner and I hadn't started my Hellboy story yet. Every September is a freak-out time for me, where I get overwhelmed at all the work ahead of me (both schoolwork and writing projects to come). Even though I know I do this, I can't stop the freak-out and only hope to manage it to some degree. Anyway, with BC Calc looming, I had a particularly messy freak-out and I went to Chris and asked if I could back out of writing the story. I think he could tell I needed him to gently say, "Just write the damn story," because that's essentially what he did. It was what I needed, and writing "Her Red Right Hand" was ultimately one of the most rewarding experiences in my career.

I found my way into the story by focusing on the pathos and melancholy that Mignola magically evokes with his wisecrackin' Hellboy, often without a lick of text.

It's Against the Law to Feed the Ducks: My novel *The Cabin at the End of the World* isn't the first time I've turned one of my family vacation spots into a horror show. To quote Lisa: "You're going to ruin vacation spot X for us? Again?"

The bones of this story came right out of one of our vacations near Lake Winnipesaukee. I used the exact location as was, or as is. We rented a small cottage from a coworker of Lisa's. The cottage and association beach are as described in the story; so, too, the beach pass and the raft and, of course, the beach sign the story takes its title from.

I wrote "Ducks" when I was still a relatively new parent (my kids were five and one), full of kid-love and wonder, yes, but also full of anxiety and fear. So many of the stories I wrote from 2004 to 2010 were preoccupied with that parental fear, which expressed itself as apocalyptic fiction more often than not.

The story started with a simple premise: some mysterious apocalyptic event happens while a young family is on vacation. It was never important to me what exactly the event was and I thought (and still do think) that knowing what the event was would be too much weight on the quiet, personal story. Although there are some hints in the story as to what the event *could be* if you want to play that game. . . .

This story is the oldest in the collection, and I think one of my earliest successes with messing around with ambiguity in a way that did more for the story than simply represent a little twist or tweak. The ambiguity was central to the tone, feel, and vibe. There isn't a lot you could point to in the story and say, oh yeah, that part right there, that's why this is a horror story, yet I think this story is one of my most horrifying.

The Thirteenth Temple: This story has been rolling around in my head for years. For one reason or another its status remained *the story I'm definitely going to write someday.*

I'm not one of those lucky writers floating in their luxury pool of story ideas. You know the ones: they go to all the parties, dress nicely, smell appropriate, and say things like, "Oh, I'll never run out of stories. In fact, my only worry is that I'll never have the time to write all the stories I already have mapped out in my head." Bite me, lucky writer. Bite me.

I don't have a list of stories waiting around for me to write them. As of the writing of this story note, I have maybe one short story I'd like to write and a novel idea I might write (I haven't decided if the current novel idea is going to be the next novel. Now I'm making myself nervous . . .), and notebooks full of quirky phrases, what-ifs, and failed story sketches/plot plans that for one reason or another I decided not to write. I keep those around, semi-alive in my notebooks, for emergencies and maybe to use for spare parts.

Anyway, I'm saying that having a story hanging around for so long in my head before writing it is unusual. I waited to write it because I knew "The Thirteenth Temple" would be the last story of this collection and I wanted to write it last, only after the rest of the book was set.

It was a little intimidating, to be honest, to finally sit down and write the thing after all the time it'd been floating (marinating?) in my inner ether. (That sounds kind of icky.) And even more intimidating, initially, to have Merry back for a brief stay. And even *more* intimidating to find out what it was Merry was going to say and how she would say it. I mean, I knew some of what the story was going to be, but I didn't know everything. I never do.

I'd never write a sequel novel to *A Head Full of Ghosts,* but I liked that there could be one more, short Merry/Marjorie story to tell. Beyond the connection to that novel, I hope "The Thirteenth Temple" is a fitting end to the collection with its two desperate-in-their-own-ways characters attempting to make a connection via an ineffable story.

Some fears can be explored only by story. Some emotions can be communicated only by story. Some truths can be revealed only by story. That's the unique experience I crave as a reader and I strive for as a writer. I'm terrible at remembering plot and character specifics (even of my own work if enough time has passed . . . proof? How many times am I going to keep using the name Tommy? Heck, the older brother in "Our Town's Monster" was originally named Tommy, but I changed him to Teddy for the collection because there are too many Tommys), but if the story is successful, what I do remember and will never forget is what and how that story makes me feel. And the only proper way for me to then describe that experience is to point at the book: that story *is* how I felt and how I was made to feel.

ACKNOWLEDGMENTS

Thank you first and foremost to family and friends who allow me to do what I do. Thank you to all the editors who helped shape these stories. Thank you to Jennifer Brehl, Camille Collins, Nate Lanman, Katherine Turro, and everyone at William Morrow; to Gary Budden, Lydia Gittins, Natalie Laverick, and everyone at (Team) Titan Books; to Stephen Barbara and InkWell; to Steve Fisher and APA; to so many of the first readers of these stories, including Nadia Bulkin, John Langan, and Stephen Graham Jones. And thank you (yes, you) for reading.

CREDITS

The following stories have appeared elsewhere and are reprinted here with permission.

"Growing Things": *In the Mean Time*, Chizine Publications, 2010.

"Swim Wants to Know If It's as Bad as Swim Thinks": *Bourbon Penn*, Issue 8, 2013; also *Year's Best Weird*, vol. 1, 2014.

"Something About Birds": *Black Feathers* (anthology), Ellen Datlow, ed., Pegasus Books, 2017.

"The Getaway": *Supernatural Noir* (anthology), Ellen Datlow, ed., Dark Horse, 2011.

"Nineteen Snapshots of Dennisport": *Cape Cod Noir* (anthology), David Ulin, ed., Akashic, 2011.

"Where We All Will Be": *Grimscribe's Puppets* (anthology), Joseph Pulver, ed., Miskatonic River Press, 2013.

"The Teacher": *Chizine*, 2007; also appeared in *In the Mean Time*; Bram Stoker Award nominee.

"Notes for 'The Barn in the Wild'": *Children of Old Leech* (anthology), Ross Lockhart and Justin Steele, eds., Word Horde, 2014; reprinted in *Wilde Stories 2015: The Year's Best Gay Speculative Fiction*, Steve Berman, ed., Lethe Press, 2015.

"_____": *Letters to Lovecraft* (anthology), Jesse Bullington, ed., Stone Skin Press, 2014.

"Our Town's Monster": *Chizine*, 2010.

"A Haunted House Is a Wheel upon Which Some Are Broken": *Gutted: Beautiful Horror Stories* (anthology), Doug Murano and D. Alexander Ward, eds., 2016.

"It Won't Go Away": *Dark Discoveries* (magazine), issue 37, 2016.

"Further Questions for the Somnambulist": *The Madness of Dr. Caligari* (anthology), Joseph Pulver, ed., Fedogan and Bremer Publishing, 2016.

"The Ice Tower": *The Burning Maiden,* vol. 2 (anthology), Greg Kishbaugh, ed., Evileye Books, 2015.

"The Society of the Monsterhood": *Dark Cities* (anthology), Christopher Golden, ed., Titan Books, 2017.

"Her Red Right Hand": *Hellboy: An Assortment of Horrors* (anthology), Christopher Golden, ed., Dark Horse, 2017.

"It's Against the Law to Feed the Ducks": *Fantasy Magazine,* issue 2, 2004; also appeared in *In the Mean Time.*

P.S.

Insights,
Interviews
& More . . .

About the author

Read on

Meet Paul Tremblay

Allan Amato

PAUL TREMBLAY has won the Bram Stoker, British Fantasy, and Massachusetts Book Awards and is the author of *The Cabin at the End of the World*, *Disappearance at Devil's Rock*, *A Head Full of Ghosts*, and the crime novels *The Little Sleep* and *No Sleep Till Wonderland*. He is currently a member of the board of directors of the Shirley Jackson Awards, and his essays and short fiction have appeared in the *Los Angeles Times*, *Entertainment Weekly* online, and numerous year's-best anthologies. He has a master's degree in mathematics and lives outside Boston with his family. ᴄ

Paul Tremblay
Recommends . . .

For the first half of my writing life, I wrote—almost exclusively—short stories. My early attempts were not very good (to be kind), but I kept stubbornly writing the next story as well as reading all the collections I could get my hands on.

What I discovered, regardless of genre, was that my favorite short stories were the ones that created an eternity within a few scenes, or even within a single moment.

The list (and it's long, sorry-not-sorry) is alphabetized by author. I've included more than one title for some authors because they told me I could. Who are they? Wouldn't you like to know . . .

Despite the length of the list, this is by no means meant to be exhaustive. There's a mix of older and newer collections, and I do hope you'll be inspired to explore many of these titles.

Of course, pay no mind to what that pesky dog walker, KB, says about collections.

- **Nathan Ballingrud:** *North American Lake Monsters: Stories*; *Wounds: Six Stories from the Border of Hell*

The stories in his first collection are Southern Gothic–inflected, Raymond ▶

Carver bits of working-class nightmare/horror. His second collection mixes pulp and Clive Barker grandeur. Both books are must-reads. I adore and have taught his story "Wild Acre" in workshops.

- **Clive Barker:** *Books of Blood* **(all volumes)**

No author has made me feel as fundamentally *unsafe* when reading their work as Clive Barker has. On the short list of my all-time favorite stories, "In the Hills, the Cities" is a jaw-dropping feat of vision, imagination, and storytelling.

- **Laird Barron:** *The Imago Sequence and Other Stories*; *Occultation and Other Stories*; *Swift to Chase*

No one mixes cosmic horror, noir, pulp, and literary fiction in quite the way Laird does. His fingerprints are all over the boom/renaissance of horror fiction in the twenty-first century. I defy you to read "Hallucigenia" or "The Broadsword" and not be totally frightened to your core.

- **Aimee Bender:** *The Girl in the Flammable Skirt*

Full of vivid yet humane fever dreams, Bender's stories are typically wild yet also subtle in their approach to our daily absurdities. The title story is a showstopper.

- **Nadia Bulkin: *She Said Destroy: Stories***

A heady, unerringly intelligent collection of sociopolitical horror stories, so of our time as to be prescient of what's to come. After first reading "Intertropical Convergence Zone," I decided that I would read everything she wrote.

- **Emily Carroll: *Through the Woods***

A graphic novel collection (Huh? Yeah, just go with that as a description) of five short stories with some referring to or connecting with one another. Carroll magnificently balances modern storytelling with a classic ghost-story feel. Her characters exist in their own world, a shadow reflection of ours, and as disturbed as I am by it, I want to climb down into the pages and walk around.

- **Stuart Dybek: *I Sailed with Magellan***

A simmering, harrowing, and often beautiful collection of interconnected stories set in Chicago's South Side. ▶

- **Mariana Enríquez:** *Things We Lost in the Fire: Stories*

  My favorite collection of the twenty-first century. Mixing literary fiction, sociopolitics, and horror, every story is different in approach and tone, yet the unity of effect is what continues to linger. "The Dirty Kid" is a brutal and perfect opening salvo.

- **Brian Evenson:** *A Collapse of Horse; Song for the Unraveling of the World*

  Brian's short jolts of surrealism, ontology, and existential dread are as playful as they are bizarre and disturbing.

- **Jeffrey Ford:** *A Natural History of Hell: Stories*

  Like many, if not most, of the writers included in this list, Jeff is a writer that cannot be pigeonholed into a single genre. His fierce intelligence, mischievous sense of humor, and dark heart shine through in everything he writes. How could I not give a mention to his story "The Blameless," which features suburban exorcism parties?

- **Karen Joy Fowler:** *The Pelican Bar*

  Karen writes expertly in multiple genres and her work is almost always heartbreaking, the kind that leaves a permanent mark. The title story is as dark and devastating as it gets.

- **Elizabeth Hand:** *Errantry: Strange Stories*

  Liz is one of my favorite contemporary writers: from horror to noir punk polemics to historical fiction, there's nothing she can't write and write exceedingly well. "Near Zennor" aches with a unique blend of dread and melancholy.

- **Amy Hempel:** *Tumble Home: A Novella and Short Stories*

  These quiet (until they're not) stories are loaded with secrets and insights. Heartbreaking and hopeful, and written with a measured yet mesmerizing style.

- **Joe Hill:** *20th Century Ghosts*

  Joe's first book is a stunner, full of energy, wit, and his trademark compassion (as in "Pop Art"). That's not to say some of the stories don't ▶

have bite, though, like "Best New Horror," which remains one of my favorite stories written about the horror writer and fan community.

- **Shirley Jackson:** *The Lottery and Other Stories*

Where would we be without Shirley Jackson? There's an off-ness to her work that can only be described as Jacksonesque, or Jacksonian? Nah, "-esque" sounds more literary. Anyway, I dare you to reread "The Lottery" and not find something new to glean from the classic. My favorite story of hers, though, is "The Intoxicated." A high school–age girl is confronted in the kitchen by one of the adult male revelers at a party her parents are hosting. The story is their conversation. It's only about ten pages long, but so much is said and unsaid. Funny, threatening, and gloriously righteous in a way all outsiders can recognize.

- **Stephen Graham Jones:** *The Ones That Got Away; After the People Lights Have Gone Off*

Stephen never pulls any punches, never flinches. Hell, he doesn't blink. And he makes you feel it all. I still have one scene stuck in my head from "Raphael" and it will never go away,

and you'll exclaim in both delight
(at the realization) and despair at the
revelation in "Father, Son, Holy Rabbit."

- **Stephen King**: *Night Shift; Skeleton
Crew; Nightmares & Dreamscapes*

As much as I love and have been
inspired by his novels (reading *The
Stand* shortly after reading a Joyce
Carol Oates short story were what
turned this mathematics major into
a reader for life), I find myself returning
more and more to his short fiction.
There are too many favorites to pick
just one, so I'll mention two that don't
get mentioned as often as others:
"The Reach," about a ninety-five-year-
old woman attempting to cross "the
reach" to the mainland for the first
time in her life; "Umney's Last Case,"
a wonderfully imaginative and affecting
Raymond Chandler riff.

- **John Langan**: *The Wide,
Carnivorous Sky and Other
Monstrous Geographies; Sefira
and Other Betrayals*

Perhaps you can tell by the lengths
of the titles (sorry, John), but his short
fiction isn't all that short. His novelettes
and novellas are always inventive
(the genius "How the Day Runs
Down"; think *Our Town* with ▶

zombies); packed with wit, intelligence, and integrity of vision; and creepy as hell.

• **Livia Llewellyn:** *Engines of Desire: Tales of Love & Other Horror; Furnace*

Livia's weird/horror/erotic stories are as disturbing as they are exquisitely and grotesquely beautiful. Another stellar writer with an integrity of vision. "The Last, Clean Bright Summer" is a coming-of-age story that's unlike any you've previously read.

• **Kelly Link:** *Magic for Beginners*

Kelly's stories are modern, messed-up, fully fanged fairy tales. Her "Some Zombie Contingency Plans" is one of the best stories about zombies without there actually (maybe) being a zombie in it.

• **Joyce Carol Oates:** *High Lonesome: New and Selected Stories 1966–2006; Haunted: Tales of the Grotesque*

Reading Joyce Carol Oates's "Where Are You Going, Where Have You Been?" as a twenty-one-year-old mathematics major, weeks away from college graduation, was a eureka moment for me. I remember thinking, "I didn't

know people wrote things like *this*."
It's not an exaggeration to say that
story about the terrifyingly charming
Arnold Friend trying to sweet-talk
young Connie into his car changed my
life, turning me into a lifelong reader.

- **Yoko Ogawa: *Revenge***

  Her book of three novellas, *The
  Diving Pool*, was my introduction to
  her work. *Revenge* made me a fan
  for life: eleven tales of revenge that
  interconnect, forming a larger puzzle
  box. Obsession and violence abound,
  so, too, world-weary, broken, and
  familiar characters. "Afternoon at
  the Bakery" is my favorite.

- **Helen Oyeyemi: *What Is Not Yours
  Is Not Yours***

  A surreal, strange, and spellbinding
  collection of stories connected by locks
  and keys. Helen's prose is always a joy,
  as are the mysteries of her characters'
  hearts and lives.

- **Karen Russell: *Vampires in the
  Lemon Grove; Orange World and
  Other Stories***

  Karen writes stories in whatever genre
  she wants (a life goal of mine). "The
  Tornado Auction" and its tornado ▶

grower/farmer is as moving as it is audacious.

- **George Saunders:** *Pastoralia; CivilWarLand in Bad Decline*

I enjoy his later collections as well, but these two earlier ones, which might be a little scruffier by comparison but perhaps even more effective, strike a Vonnegut chord that continues to, um, vibrate now? Work with me, people.

- **Priya Sharma:** *All the Fabulous Beasts*

Priya's stories mix the fantastic and the ineffable ominousness (that's a word, right?) of *weird* fiction while also making us care deeply about what happens to her characters.

- **Jim Shepard:** *Love and Hydrogen: New and Selected Stories*

Shepard manages to pack a novel's worth of research into his stories while somehow still letting the stories live their human lives. My favorite stories include "The Creature from the Black Lagoon" (told from the POV of the creature) and "Mars Attacks."

- **Peter Straub:** *Interior Darkness*

Another writer who I consider to be formative to my own writing, and this collection is a career retrospective with Peter curating his favorite works of short fiction spanning four decades. "Mr. Clubb and Mr. Cuff" is *Bartleby the Scrivener* mixed with a diabolical revenge story. You feel that story's heart beating as your own when reading it.

- **Shaun Tan:** *Tales from Outer Suburbia*

The second graphic novel collection of stories (So, it's not really a novel then; do I call it illustrated stories? Whatever. It's a collection.) on this list. The dark yet whimsical short tales achieve bigger stories without having to resort to using very many words at all.

- **Jeffrey Thomas:** *Punktown*

The collection (far in the future stories set on a distant planet) was first published in 2000 and, in many ways, the stories still feel as revolutionary to me now as they did then. His mashing together of Lovecraftian horrors, noir, and P.K. Dick–style science fiction works because of the empathy extended toward his flawed, working-class characters. ∽

Discover great authors, exclusive offers, and more at hc.com.